The Mermaids of Chenonceaux and 828 Other Stories

by Phyllis Méras

The Mermaids of Chenonceaux

and 828 Other Stories

An Anecdotal Guide to Europe

CONGDON & WEED, INC.

New York

Library of Congress Cataloging in Publication Data
Main entry under title:
The Mermaids of Chenonceaux and 828 other stories.
Includes index.
1. Europe—Description and travel—1971- —Guide-
books. 2. Europe—History—Anecdotes, facetiae, satire,
etc. I. Méras, Phyllis. II. Title: Mermaids of Chenonceaux
and eight hundred twenty-eight other stories.
D909.M47 1982   914′.04558   81-22135
ISBN 0-86553-038-6   AACR2
ISBN 0-312-92525-5 (St. Martin's Press)

Published by Congdon & Weed, Inc.
298 Fifth Avenue, New York, N.Y. 10001

Distributed by St. Martin's Press
175 Fifth Avenue, New York, N.Y. 10010

Published simultaneously in Canada by Thomas Nelson & Sons Limited
81 Curlew Drive, Don Mills, Ontario M3A 2R1

*For Paul and Alice Langellier-Bellevue
and in memory of
Donald A. Roberts*

Contents

Author's Note

Perhaps the most stirring aspect of a place we visit is the sense of lives led. The guidebooks tell us how many meters long the nave of the cathedral is, or when the tower was built, but what we remember and carry away with us are the little stories, lovingly told by a caretaker or an innkeeper, about the people who played out life's dramas in these places. Stories are important. They are the stuff of history, and they organize it for us. In the most memorable way they tell us what happened on whatever spot we happen to set foot, enhancing both our journey and our understanding.

Because of its antiquity, virtually every inch of Europe is rich in such tales. The traveler to Hamburg, if told, will never forget that the composer Johannes Brahms, when he was only ten years old, had to play the piano in one of the city's notorious brothels to help support his impoverished family—or that the crown atop the church steeple is said to have been made from pirate gold. What an intriguing, indelible detail—that Sigmund Freud's wife unfailingly left a squirt of toothpaste on the great psychoanalyst's brush in the bathroom of their Vienna apartment.

For the last twenty years, I have been an inveterate and supremely curious traveler, less interested in how much the trip might cost and the quality of my accommodations than in the stories behind the sites that I was seeing. I have twice lived in Europe. I have been a travel editor on major newspapers for a total of more than a dozen years. Always I have studied the small print in the guides to cathedral crypts (how full they are of anecdotal fare!). I have listened with rapt attention to the tales of tour guides, even when their tales were obviously apocryphal—for even in apocryphal tales, I have learned, there is always a kind of truth. And in this book of anecdotes, I have collected my favorites from among the thousands of tales—literary, historical, musical, tales from art and from legend—that are concerned with people as related to well-known places.

This is not a guidebook in any ordinary sense. It is not topographical. The Château of Chillon merits an entry here, not because it is a castle, not because of its exquisite situation on one of Switzerland's loveliest lakes, but because, in the sixteenth century, François Bonivard, chained in its dungeon, wore a path in the cold floor, and the English poet Byron, hearing of it, wrote a poem about the ordeal.

Of course, because of the endless source of material, this is a selective collection. The countries with which it deals are the major countries of western Europe, and the countries that I know best. Much of the material presented here was garnered on my own visits abroad, but some was also researched from histories, biographies and travel guides.

To make entries easy to find, they are listed alphabetically by country; then by city or town, then by specific site. Place names are generally given in the spelling of the country where a site lies, except in cases where the site is better known to English-speaking readers by its English name, i.e., Vienna not Wien; Helsinki not Helsingfors. But to facilitate the finding of particular buildings, they are more often given the name they bear where they actually are, i.e., in Berlin, the reference would be to the Reichstag rather than to a translation of it as Parliament.

Cruising the Rhine River in Germany once I heard the outlandish story —or so I thought at the time—that it was the Rhine, the queen of European rivers, that Emmanuel Leutze had painted in "Washington Crossing the Delaware," not the Delaware, and that his models for the oarsmen ferrying George Washington were not Americans but townspeople of Leutze's native Düsseldorf.

When I see Italy's Gulf of Spezia, it is not the blue-green waters alone I see. It is the body of the drowned poet, Percy Bysshe Shelley, being washed ashore.

Such anecdotes have given great dimension to my travels. May they also to yours.

Acknowledgments

I am grateful to many for their aid in the preparation of this book—in particular to John Baldo, Audrey Foote, Andrew Giarelli, Barbara Hess, H. Constance Hill, Nina Budde Scott, Henny Wenkart and Nell Wright for research; to Nancy Luedeman for secretarial work; to Peg Cameron, Richard Freedman, Cynthia Meisner and Carol Siegel for copy editing and fact-checking.

Also contributing from their special fields of knowledge were Edmund Antrobus, Harry Best, Stanley Burnshaw, William A. Caldwell, Elsa de Brun, Patric Farrell, Niels Gabel-Jorgensen, Thomas R. Goethals, Len and Chantal Haas, Albert and Frances Hackett, Walter P. Houghton, Garson Kanin, T. Edward Karlsson, Henrik Krogius, Nino Lo Bello, Ivo Meisner, Donal MacPhee, Dan and Ellen Olivier, John, Carole and Ursula Parry, Seymour Pearlman, Lars Rasmussen, Ruth Cooke Roberts, William and Kelly Roos, Hildegarde Ruof, Henry and Peggy Scott, Robert Selby, Donald R. Shanor, Sayre Sheldon, Ursula Sturzenegger, Harold L. Tinker, Robert W. Tolf, John E. Wallace, Angela Watson, Nancy Convery Young, the late Charles H. Spilman and the late Milton Weissberg.

Aiding in the verification of details were Elisabeth Brandl and Gerhard Marcus of the Austrian Tourist Commission, Ann Neville of the Belgian National Tourist Office, Nils Flo of the Danish Tourist Board and Niels-Pieter Albertsen of the Danish Consulate, Pat Patricoff of the Finnish Tourist Board and Eero Korpivaara of the Finnish Consulate, George Hern and Nora Brossard of the French Government Tourist Office and Robin Massee of the French Information Service, Petra Lokez and Hedy Wuerz of the German National Tourist Office and Peter Flory of the German Information Service, the Greek National Tourist Organization, Amelia Medwied of the Italian Government Travel Office, Marjolyn Conrad and Jean van Zuiden of the Netherlands National Tourist Office, Bjorg Waage of the Norwegian Information Service, Charles Ocheltree of the Spanish National Tourist Office, Ed Conradssen of the Swedish Tourist Board and Eli Weisman of the Swedish Information Service.

My thanks also to Erika Faisst and Reto von Tscharner of the Swiss National Tourist Office, Marianne Crosby, Evelyn Heyward and Antonio Madeira of Heyward Associates, and Ray Chambers of SAS.

For their patience while the book was in progress, I am indebted to Bridget L. Cooke, Ruth N. Gottlieb, John and Bonnie Méras and Frances Tenenbaum, and to Deborah Christiansen, Douglas Fellow, Charles Hauser and Jack Major of the Providence *Journal*, and Joyce Dauley, Mary Jane Ertman and Anne Morgan of Wellesley College, as well as to my husband, Thomas Cocroft, and above all to my editor, Thomas B. Congdon Jr.

For miscellaneous tasks, thanks are due to John Brannon Albright, Florence Brown, Jacques Case, George and Lena Costa, Andy Dickerman, Marie Flodin, Sam and Marian Halperin, Robert Leddy, Mary McGovern, Chèle Méras, Don Page, Drusilla Parks, Winifred Redman, Yvonne Roberts, Jean Rossi, Robert Sanborn and Marianna Winslow.

Research facilities were provided by the Boston Public Library, Kathy Norton and Dorothy McGinniss of the Chilmark (Mass.) Public Library, Florence Hindle and Norma Colman of the Providence (R.I.) Public Library, the Vineyard Haven (Mass.) Public Library, Nancy Whiting of the West Tisbury (Mass.) Public Library, the Swedish Book Nook and the Complete Traveller in New York City and Book Den East in Oak Bluffs, Mass.

The Mermaids
of Chenonceaux
—— and 828
Other Stories

Austria

AGGSTEIN ✦✿✦ ─────────

Castle Ruins

Infamous for his hospitality was Jorg Scheck von Wald, the owner of this castle in the fifteenth century. Until he gained renown, his unsuspecting guests would be invited to admire the roses in his garden, and once they were there he would gleefully hurl them to their deaths on the rocks below.

ALTAUSSEE

Salt Mines

No one knows who it was who saved the rich cache of paintings hidden here by the Nazis in World War II from demolition. When the defeat of Germany seemed inevitable, messages were sent here advising that the art work Hitler had ordered hidden should be blown up, and explosives were provided for the purpose.

But that wasn't what happened. Instead, the dynamite was used to seal off the chambers full of art so that no one, Nazis or otherwise, could reach them. When the SS commander charged with the demolition operation heard what had been done, he ordered the Austrians believed responsible shot. But his order came too late. Rescuers of the Austrians—and of the art for which they were ready to give their lives—were approaching.

BAD AUSSEE

Former Post Office (37 Meranplatz)

It was the most gossiped about romance of its day—the love of Archduke John, brother of the emperor Francis II, for Anna Plochl, the daughter of the Bad Aussee postmaster. They met on the banks of the Grundisee here in 1816, and the prince fell head over heels in love. No matter that marrying a commoner would mean that he could never again live in the royal palace! No matter anything! He would marry Anna, and three years later they met again and he proposed. A year after that they exchanged locks of hair—a sign that, in their eyes at least, they were truly affianced. But there was always the emperor to contend with. It took John—his great love notwithstanding—three more years to gather together the courage to ask his brother for his permission. The emperor refused. A heartsick John returned to tell Anna.

But that was hardly the end of it. John continued to proffer his suit, and to try to win over his brother. And finally, in 1828, when Francis realized John would not marry at all unless he married Anna, the emperor relented. After a wait of thirteen years, the pair was discreetly married in John's hunting lodge at Brandhof. To Anna's delight, their firstborn son showed his royal heritage by having the heavy-hanging Hapsburg lip of his father.

BAD ISCHL

A famous story proudly told here to prove that the emperor Francis Joseph I was a simple man, recounts how a peasant in his cart passed three hunters one day and asked if they would like a ride. The hunters responded eagerly in the affirmative. As they went along, the peasant sought to chat and asked one of his passengers who he was. "The king of Saxony," was the reply. The peasant nodded understandingly and asked the next man his identity. "The king of Bavaria," said the second passenger. "And you?" he reportedly said to the third, "I suppose *you* are the emperor of Austria." Francis Joseph simply nodded.

DÜRNSTEIN

Fortress Ruins

High in a tower of this fortress, Richard the Lion-Hearted of England was held captive from 1192 to 1193 by Duke Leopold the Virtuous—and might have languished here forever had not his friend the troubadour Blondel come searching for him.

Those were the days of the Third Crusade, and both Richard and Leopold had embarked and fought valiantly on it. At Acre in the Holy Land, it is said, Leopold captured a Moslem fort and raised his Austrian banner above it. Arriving at the same fort later, Richard—so the story goes—had taken down the Austrian banner and flown his own in its stead. Richard had dreams of conquering Jerusalem, but failed in them and started back for England. Leopold, furious, had already returned home.

As Richard made his way toward England, a fierce storm arose, wrecking his vessel. With no boat, Richard had no choice but to cross his rival's territory. It was no time at all before he learned he was not welcome there. Nevertheless, for several days, all went well. Richard and his party traveled by night and through the woods, drinking from streams, eating largely what they could pick or hunt, for they were fearful of being recognized by asking for food or drink. Finally, though, in the village of Erdberg near Vienna, Richard saw a roast being carried across a courtyard. Too hungry by then to take any more than minimal precautions, he asked if he might have some scraps if he would turn the spit. The cook agreed.

Pulling his hood closer over his face, Richard worked efficiently at his task, but suddenly fat from the meat made the fire flare and in its brighter light the cook looked at the spit-turner. The cook, too, had been on the Third Crusade. There was no doubt about it. It was the English king who was turning the spit in the courtyard.

By then, Richard's wrecked vessel had been found, and it was known all over Leopold's territory that the duke had put a bounty on the Englishman's head. The cook hesitated briefly, but only briefly. He had a sick wife and several children to support. He needed the bounty.

"You are too good for this work, Your Majesty," he whispered to the king. "Surrender. I know you."

So Richard was arrested and held here while all England searched for him. It was known he was a captive. A ransom had been put on his head, but where he was remained a mystery. All over Germany and Austria his loyal friend Blondel went, seeking him at every castle. At each of them Blondel would sing his master's favorite song at nightfall and hope to hear a refrain sung in return. At last, here at Dürnstein, to his great joy, he heard the king's voice join him from the tower. The two talked until morning. Then the singer left for England to raise the ransom for Richard's freedom.

GRAZ

Schlossberg (Castle)

Graz almost lost the beloved bell tower of this castle in 1809. An angry Napoleon had already blown up most of this fortification and the word was that this tower, too, was doomed. The town fathers begged him not to wreak more destruction, but he would not be moved—until the town proposed that they would *pay* him for their tower. Then—apparently greedier for money than for reprisal—Napoleon agreed to be bought off.

HEILIGENSTADT

Probusgasse 6

A deeply depressed Ludwig van Beethoven spent the summer of 1802 in this little cottage trying desperately to cope with his increasing deafness. Here he wrote his Testament of Heiligenstadt, to let it be known that he was not "morose, crabbed or misanthropical" but simply could not hear.

INNSBRUCK

Berg Isel

The staunch Tyrolean innkeeper-patriot Andreas Hofer was beside himself that spring of 1809. Napoleon had won the Battle of Austerlitz against Austria, and in the peace settlement Bavaria became the ruler of these Tyrolean mountains and valleys. For 400 years, these had been Austrian lands. How, now, could they become Bavarian? Hofer would not hear of it. And so he gathered about him others who would not hear of it either—simple peasants, but powerful when armed with scythes and axes and a handful of shotguns.

Walking the mountains and valleys, speaking from the balcony of the Goldener Adler here (*see* Innsbruck, Goldener Adler), he roused a force of 15,000 men to fight the oppressor. The signal for the start of combat was to be a blaze of fires on mountaintops. And on the night of April 10, 1809, the Tyrolean sky was red with flames. The next day, Hofer's fighting peasants descended from the mountains to the valley to do combat with the Bavarians and their French friends.

It was on this hilltop that the enemy had their principal point of defense, and it was here that—three times—the gallant peasant band battled the well-armed French and Bavarian armies. Incredibly, in their very first attack the peasants captured the Bavarian stronghold.

There were more battles required, however, to wrest the Tyrol from the grip of Bavaria, and to convince the dispirited Austrian government, as well, that the Tyroleans were fighters worth standing behind. Finally, the government was convinced—briefly, at least—and made Hofer the governor of the Tyrol. But his joy and that of his fellow peasants was short-lived. Within three months, nervous Austria had agreed that the Tyrol should go to Bavaria. So Hofer and his wife and son were forced to flee from the city to the mountains. And it was on a snowy winter's day in early 1810 that a turncoat, Franz Raffl—eager for the money that had been put on Hofer's head—betrayed his whereabouts to the French.

Hofer was taken in chains to Mantua in Italy, on January 28, tried, and sentenced to death. Despite pleas to Napoleon, then about to marry Princess Marie Louise of Austria (*see* Vienna, Augustinerkirche), he was executed by a firing squad, proudly refusing to have his eyes covered as the execution was about to take place—simply advising the men who were shooting at him to fire straight.

Goldenes Dachl (Golden Roof) (Henzog-Friedrich-Strasse Platz)

Legend has it that this roof, consisting of 3,450 gilded copper tiles, was built for a fifteenth-century duke believed to be poverty-stricken. Indeed, his nickname was "Duke Frederick Empty-Pockets." His feelings hurt by his nickname, to prove that he was *not* poor he had a heavy gilt roof put on his house.

Hofkirche: MAXIMILIAN'S MAUSOLEUM

Among the artists lured here to Innsbruck to work on the construction of this monumental tomb for Maximilian I was the gay-blade sculptor Gilg Sesselschreiber of Munich, notable for his designs but also for his fondness for wine, women, and song. All of these abounded here in the sixteenth century, and it was not long before the talented sculptor was spending as much time carousing as designing statues.

In 1500, the emperor had made up his mind he wanted a mausoleum here, but it took eleven years before the first bronze statue for it was cast. Maximilian was fifty-one by then, and although in good health, he longed to have his artists and artisans get on with the work. By 1516, the tomb's effigies were *still* scarcely under way, and he had had enough of Sesselschreiber's excesses and excuses. Maximilian clapped him into prison for three months to teach him to mend his ways, then dispatched him to a remote village to ponder his iniquities. Apparently the punishment worked, for at last eighteen of the Sesselschreiber statues were turned out. But by then it was too late. Maximilian was dead and his mausoleum still incomplete. Indeed, he had been dead and buried sixty-three years at his birthplace of Wiener Neustadt before this tomb he had so longed for, never saw, and never lay in, was completed.

Hotel Goldener Adler

Ever since 1573—when the owner of this inn managed without a murmur (and for a remarkably low fee) to put up crowned heads of state and an army of 400 men, and to provide shelter and fodder for 600 horses during a gala given by the archduke Ferdinand II and his wife Philippine Welser—this has been a popular hostelry with royalty and the renowned (*see* Innsbruck, Berg Isel). Metternich and Napoleon, the poet Heinrich Heine, the violinist Niccolò Paganini, and the poet Goethe have been among its guests. One hot summer night in 1777 a pleasant fellow who identified himself as Count von Falkenstein asked for lodging here as he returned from a journey to France. It turned out that he was the emperor Joseph II himself, who liked to travel incognito, and had, like any affectionate brother, gone to see how his sister living abroad was faring—except that his sister was Marie Antoinette who, three years earlier, had become the queen of France.

Triumphpforte (Triumphal Arch)

For months, the empress Maria Theresa and her husband, Francis I, had been looking forward to the marriage of their son, Leopold, to the Infanta Maria Ludovica of Spain. As for the bridegroom himself, he was so impatient he went off to the Brenner Pass after his affianced to make sure she arrived here safely. But he grew overtired on the journey and caught cold. Though he made it through the ceremony, immediately afterward he had to be carried to bed, and for several days, ill with pleurisy, he fought for his life.

While he did, the court that had assembled here waited patiently and hopefully to continue with the marriage festivities. Finally, the prince was out of danger, and the round of balls and theatrical performances began. Though Leopold himself wasn't always up to attending, his father and mother outdid themselves in trying to make the celebration charming— dancing tirelessly, smiling their greetings to guests, applauding the theatricals.

Whether he caught his son's cold, wore himself out with partying, or simply died of a heart attack, no one knows, but one evening in 1765 Francis I said he would lie down for a while before supper. He died on his way to bed.

Two years later, a still brokenhearted Maria Theresa had this arch built to commemorate both the joyous event of her son's marriage and the tragedy of her husband's death. His philandering notwithstanding (*see* Vienna, Kapuzinerkirche), Maria Theresa always had adored her husband.

KITZBÜHEL

Schwarzsee

It is said that a great pine forest once stood where this lake is now. Two farmers of the neighborhood claimed the forest, and for years were engaged in lawsuits over its possession. Finally one proved conclusively that it had belonged to his ancestors. On the day he lost the case, the other farmer uttered a terrible curse: "Devil take this damned forest and turn it to water!"

The very next night water gushed up from the forest floor, drowning the forest and the farm with all its inhabitants. And on a clear day, natives insist, you can just make out the tops of the pines under these dark waters.

KLOSTERNEUBERG

Stift Klosterneuburg (Klosterneuburg Abbey)

A grateful Leopold III of Babenberg built this abbey, which was consecrated early in the twelfth century, when he learned that his wife had not deceived him.

As a wedding gift, he had presented his pretty bride, Agnes, with a veil she had promised to treasure always. But one day not long after their wedding, it was gone. When a jealous Leopold asked what had become of it, Agnes tried to explain that the wind had blown it from her head, but Leopold would not believe her. She had either misplaced it because she did not care for him or given it away to some other man as a token of her affection, Leopold insisted. And for seven years their marriage was blighted by Leopold's suspicion. Then one day, hunting near this site, he spied a touch of white in a treetop. To his amazement and chagrin, it turned out to be the remnants of Agnes's missing veil. A contrite Leopold galloped home to humbly ask his wife's forgiveness for ever having doubted her word. And seeking to make amends—to her and to God—he had this abbey built.

LINZ

There are those who say that walking along the Danube here where he went to school, and in Vienna, where he sold postcards along the riverbank, Adolf Hitler first began to dream of an empire greater than the Hapsburgs'.

MARIAZELL

Gnadenkirche (Basilica)

A frequent worshipper here in 1679 when the Viennese were dying of the plague was the emperor Leopold I, who had fled here from the capital, both for safety's sake and to pray in this holiest of holy places for relief for his people. And when, at last, the deaths began to diminish (thanks, he trusted, to his prayers), and he returned to Vienna, he built the Pestsäule (see Vienna, Pestsäule) in gratitude.

MAUTHAUSEN

Mauthausen Concentration Camp: STAIRCASE OF DEATH

Once the quarries here provided the granite for the paving stones of Vienna, but in World War II this became one of the most notorious Nazi concentration camps, and on these stairs thousands died—forced by their captors to carry heavy boulders from the quarry up the stairs, and at the top to pick up other boulders and run down bearing them. It was even said that sometimes the steps were greased to assure that the prisoners would slip and either be crushed by their burdens, or fall to their deaths.

MAYERLING

Carmelite Convent (22 miles south of Vienna)

January 30, 1889, was not a happy day for Crown Prince Rudolf. Frequently at odds with his father, the emperor Francis Joseph, who disapproved of his liberal views as well as of his love affair with the eighteen-year-old baroness Marie Vetsera, father and son had argued angrily that afternoon. Rudolf, it is said, wished to marry Marie, but already married as he was to Stephanie of Belgium, that—without divorce—was out of the question; and divorce in Catholic Vienna was unthinkable. The subject of the meeting that day with Francis Joseph is believed to have been a pronouncement on the emperor's part that his son's affair must end, whether Marie was pregnant or not— and she was. After the meeting, the young man stormed back to the hunting lodge that then stood here to have dinner with his paramour and two male friends. Dinner over, the lovers retired. They were never again seen alive.

In the morning, blood was everywhere in their bedchamber—the lifeless body of the prince on the floor, his head shattered, a pistol in his hand; the body of Marie—a bullet hole through her head—beneath the sheets; farewell letters from the prince strewn about, suggesting that he preferred death to dishonor.

When word of Rudolf's death reached the court, it was quickly announced that Rudolf had gone temporarily insane. Indeed, his brain was subjected to examination to prove it. But many wondered then and have wondered since—would a bullet have so shattered Rudolf's skull? Could an enemy, deeming his affair unseemly to the state, have shot Marie and smashed the prince's skull? Or had Rudolf really tired of Marie and agreed that afternoon to his father's importunings? If so, had she turned on him when he told her of the end of their affair?

In any case, Francis Joseph tried to have all memories of the event erased and ordered the hunting lodge torn down and this convent built. But speculation has never ceased. The film *Mayerling* made much of it.

OBERNDORF

St. Nikolaus Memorial Chapel

The week before Christmas in 1818 there were worried discussions in the little church that then occupied this site. Always, on Christmas Eve, the schoolmaster-organist, Franz Gruber, gave a concert, but it looked that year as if it would be out of the question. A mouse, so the story goes, had chewed a hole in the bellows of the organ. Gruber didn't know what to do, but Joseph Mohr, the priest at St. Nikolaus's, had an idea. He had written a Christmas poem some time before. Perhaps Gruber could set it to music and a choir could sing it? A choral concert wouldn't be the same as the traditional organ concert, but it would be better than nothing at all.

So it was that Gruber took the priest's poem and "Silent Night, Holy Night" was written. A choir of villagers sang it that Christmas Eve to music from a guitar. It might have gotten no further, however, if the organ-maker who came from the Tyrol to repair the chewed bellows hadn't liked the sound of it, asked for a copy, and passed it on.

SALZBURG

Basteigarten

It shouldn't be here, but it is here all the same—the little summerhouse from Vienna in which Wolfgang Amadeus Mozart wrote *The Magic Flute*.

Since Mozart was a native son, the memorabilia of its great composer belonged here, Salzburg informed Vienna when it sought to acquire this house. Dutifully, Vienna acquiesced, and the little cottage was transported.

Dom (Cathedral)

Wolf Dietrich von Raitenau was a nephew of Pope Pius IV, and in his youth had spent many happy days with his uncle in Rome. So it was that when he was named archbishop-prince of this thriving Austrian community, he began dreaming of making it the Rome of the north. And it did not take him long to start accomplishing his aim, for in 1598 the medieval cathedral that had stood on this site burned to the ground. Wolf Dietrich soon had plans under way for a grand new cathedral—its designer, an Italian, of course.

As it turned out, however, though the foundation stone was laid within his lifetime, ambitious Prince-Bishop von Raitenau never saw the church he planned to rival St. Peter's completed, for desire conflicted with ambition, and he fell on hard times (*see* Salzburg, Friedhof St. Sebastian and Schloss Mirabell).

Friedhof St. Sebastian (St. Sebastian's Cemetery)

Wolf Dietrich von Raitenau (*see* Salzburg, Dom) did not endear himself to his people when he had the cemetery that had abutted the original Salzburg Cathedral moved here in the sixteenth century to make way for his *new* church. He was hardly solicitous of their departed. The unearthed bodies were simply left on their former doorsteps, or thrown into the river, though a few illustrious persons found a final resting place here. Wolf Dietrich himself is among those—in a splendid tiled mausoleum of his own design. In its day it was thought so grand, indeed, that there were those who whispered that he was not dead at all, but simply enjoying a quiet, private life—perhaps with Salome inside his mausoleum. (*See* Salzburg, Schloss Mirabell.)

Glockenspiel (Residenzplatz)

It was surely a fine idea to bring this carillon of thirty-five bells here from Antwerp in the seventeenth century. But for years after their installation they were silent, for no one in Salzburg knew how to play them. Finally, a Dutchman was imported to be carillonneur. Nowadays they play Mozart's music three times a day.

Hellbrunn: MONATS-SCHLÖSSL

On a bet, Marcus Sitticus built this villa above his gardens in a month in the seventeenth century for a visit by Duke Maximilian of Bavaria.

Hellbrunn: WATER GARDEN

Critical though the archbishop-prince Marcus Sitticus may have been of the morals of the uncle who was his predecessor, (*see* Salzburg, Schloss Mirabell) he, too, enjoyed his entertainments, and here on the outskirts of the city he built this summer palace in 1613 to indulge himself.

Guests invited to dinner parties in his Bacchus Court were, after one visit, not inclined to accept a second invitation. Once they had sat down at the stone table here, and dinner was progressing happily, their playful host would signal to have jets of water spurt up through the stools on which they sat. Since etiquette required that all stay in their seats until the prince had risen—and there was no jet of water driving him from his position—dinner, invariably, turned into a sopping and unfortunate affair.

Hohensalzburg

Archbishop Leonhard von Keutschach (whose coat of arms included a turnip) was hardly a benevolent despot. He expanded this imposing fortress-castle built into the rock face that towers above this city, begun in the eleventh century, to intimidate his flock. For the Salzburgers wanted freedom from oppression and he was not inclined to give it to them. When they finally succeeded, despite him, in obtaining the right directly from the emperor to be an independent city, the two-faced archbishop simulated great joy at their good fortune and invited the city leaders to a banquet here, on January 23, 1511.

But once they had arrived they were all bound onto sledges and hauled through the snow for fifty miles to the village of Radstadt high in the Hohe Tauern mountains. Then back von Keutschach came to Salzburg to warn the remaining citizens that if they kept on demanding freedom from his rule, the fathers and sons and husbands he had kidnapped would all be killed. That was the end of insurrection here. It is to this castle, too, that today's Salzburgers owe their nickname of *Stierwäscher*—"bull washers."

As the story goes, in time of civil war the peasants of this countryside were besieging the townspeople, who had taken refuge in this unassailable fortress. Although they could not conquer the castle itself, preventing those inside from going outside after food and water was quite another matter. Those besieged grew hungrier and hungrier. And soon, they knew, they would be forced to capitulate.

Then someone proposed that they parade their last remaining bull on the castle parapets, and as soon as they were sure he had been seen by the besiegers, bring him inside and paint him another color; then take him out, bring him back, and paint him still another shade.

Sure enough, their ruse worked well. The dumbfounded peasants watching below could not believe that there were still that many bulls left in this castle, but if there were, their siege was surely hopeless. And they all went home. Ever since, the people of Salzburg have borne the nickname of bull washer with good grace.

Schloss Mirabell (Mirabell Palace)

For his mistress, Salome Alt, the mother of his fifteen children, the archbishop-prince Wolf Dietrich von Raitenau had this pink and white baroque palace built in the seventeenth century, and he named it for her—Altenau. But as well as being his love and inspiration, Salome was the archbishop's undoing.

For a time, his attentions to her and the sizable family that he had by her were not criticized, but then they were, and his ambitious nephew, Marcus Sitticus, longing himself to be archbishop-prince, savored the criticisms. Von Raitenau was ousted; Marcus Sitticus acquired title, and promptly had his uncle incarcerated in Hohensalzburg Castle here. And there, after five years, von Raitenau died. (*See* Salzburg, Dom and Friedhof St. Sebastian.) As for Salome, she lost her palace, and it lost her name. Marcus Sitticus enlarged it and renamed it Mirabell.

TYROL

Lower Inn Valley

On damp days, it is said, a motherly spirit wafts through these valleys leading the souls of children who have died unbaptized through the villages. She is said to be Pontius Pilate's wife, given this task (apparently believed to be a pleasant one) for having done her best to dissuade her husband from condemning Christ.

VIENNA

Among the musical anecdotes of this lovely city is the tale of Johannes Brahms meeting Johann Strauss the Younger. An admiring Strauss asked Brahms for his autograph. An equally admiring Brahms transcribed the first few bars of the *Blue Danube Waltz* in the book, signing them, "Unfortunately not by Johannes Brahms."

Augustinerkirche (St. Augustine's Church) (Augustinergasse)

It was a political match, it was true—the marriage of Napoleon Bonaparte to seventeen-year-old Princess Marie Louise of Austria—that took place by proxy here in March 1810. But the middle-aged emperor waiting in France was impatient (*see* France, Compiègne) nonetheless to get a first genuine glimpse of his bride. A portrait of her had been sent to him and he found he was quite titillated by her heavy, slightly drooping Hapsburg underlip—a sure sign of the royal blood he hoped any offspring they might have would inherit.

Basiliskerhaus (House of the Basilisk) (7 Schönlaterngasse)

In the thirteenth century when workmen, digging a well in the yard of this house, were lifting their last clumps of earth, a cry rang out from them, it is said, for from the hole they'd dug emerged a terrifying beast with a tail, a beak, and a coxcomb, breathing deadly fumes. One by one, those who came in contact with this basilisk's breath as the day went on gasped and fell dead. And to this day, no Viennese child passes here without a second nervous glance.

The composer Robert Schumann, however, seemed oblivious to the stories of the beast with the withering breath, for in 1838–39, he took a room in the House of the Basilisk.

Belvedere Palaces

A generous and farsighted Prince Eugene of Savoy had these two handsome palaces begun in 1714 to provide jobs for the thousands who were left without them after that devastating plague year. Although he was not Austrian-born, Eugene was devoted to his adopted country, and the finest general it ever had—winning fifteen major battles for Austria.

As a youth, Eugene, whose father was in Louis XIV's Swiss Guards, had sought to enter the French army but was turned down because he was too short. And so he offered his services to Austria instead. When Austria accepted him, he made her proud that she had wanted him, and the French, who had sneered at his small stature and unimpressive looks, were eager to lure him back. (But they were notably unsuccessful in their efforts.)

Lower Belvedere

Often of an evening toward the end of his life, Prince Eugene of Savoy would climb into his carriage here and direct the coachmen who drove his cream-colored horses in pink harnesses to the home of his lady friend, the countess Lory Batthyany. And it is said that both the prince and his coach-men—also aging—were inclined to doze during the journey, but it was such a familiar route to the horses that they reached the countess's palace with-out direction.

Chancellery

In 1934, Adolf Hitler decided that Engelbert Dollfuss, the chancellor of Austria, must be eliminated. He was a man of too-independent spirit. It was true that Hitler, as he began thinking of conquering Europe, had promised Austria that he would always recognize its independence, but a chancellor who would not follow his lead could not be tolerated. On July 25, two men in army uniform arrived unexpectedly at the Chancellery. In no time they had gained entry to the room where Dollfuss was conferring and had shot him, refusing his whispered requests as he lay dying for the services of a priest.

Das Haus ohne Augenbrauen (The House without Eyebrows) (3 Michaelerplatz)

Poor Emperor Francis Joseph! Ever since the suicide of Eduard van der Nüll (*see* Vienna, Staatsoper) when he was told of the emperor's criticism of his work, the kindly monarch had made a point of saying of works of art he saw or heard only "It gives me great pleasure." But this curious house that faced the carriage entrance to his royal palace was more than even he could bear. Adolf Loos, who had designed it in 1910 after studies in Amer-ica with Louis Sullivan, had built it with straight simple lines and no lintels over its windows (hence the name). Its plainness in baroque Vienna was more than even understanding Francis Joseph could bear, and he tried to have it removed. He went to court over the matter, but lost the suit.

Donner Fountain (Neuer Markt)

Happily, this eighteenth-century fountain did not meet with the fate the empress Maria Theresa wished for it. Disturbed by the nude figures that represent the rivers on it, the straitlaced empress ordered it taken away to be melted down for lead in 1770. But it never hit the scrap pile. An artisti-cally inclined custodian had it shuffled between storerooms and it was forgotten until her reign was done.

Griechenbeisl (11 Fleischmarkt)

The year 1679 was a ghastly one here in Vienna. Thousands were being felled by the plague, and all who could were fleeing the city. As quickly as possible, the bodies of those who died were disposed of to prevent the spread of further infection. Some went into the Danube, others into a common grave on the outskirts of town. But because each day there would be more bodies, the burial squad tended to wait until a pit was filled before covering it with dirt. Here in the meat market, then as now, stood this café —a place of solace in most troubled times—and among its frequenters was Max Augustin, the cheery son of an innkeeper. Augustin played the bagpipe here while he drank his beer, and did his best with his songs to entertain his fellow patrons.

One night, it is said, Augustin, as he played and sang, consumed too much, and when the café closed, curled up outside to sleep off his excessive consumption.

And there he was—dead to the world, but not in actuality, when the burial squad came by. Assuming that, like so many of his fellow townspeople, poor Augustin had succumbed to the plague, the squad shoveled him into their cart and away he went to the common grave. Undisturbed, he continued his snooze through the night, and when morning came awoke refreshed—his companions in the grave notwithstanding. Indeed, at first, it is said, he assumed they were his drinking friends of the night before, like him in a hung-over condition, and proceeded to burst into song trying to waken them. But when they did not awaken, he climbed over them to reach the top of the grave, and was quite ready by midmorning to resume his singing and playing.

When he reappeared here no one knew what to do. The burial squad had let it be known that Augustin was dead. Had he risen from the dead? Should he be shunned or greeted? But there was no shunning Augustin. Full of song and laughter as always, he was soon playing his bagpipe once again to help Vienna weather that gruesome year of the plague. A popular song, "Ach, du lieber Augustin," recounts this adventure.

19 Haydngasse

Though French cannonballs were landing in his garden here in the spring of 1809, a gentle and devout seventy-seven-year-old Franz Joseph Haydn made nothing of them. He calmly soothed his servants with the words, "Don't worry. Nothing will happen to you while Haydn is here." But on May 26, he asked suddenly to be helped to his piano. There, with great emotion, he played his "Hymn to the Emperor" three times. The he went back to his couch. Never again did Haydn play the piano, and six days later he was dead.

Hofburg

Nine-year-old Wolfgang Amadeus Mozart endeared himself to the empress Maria Theresa on a visit here in 1765 when he asked for the hand in marriage of her little daughter Marie Antoinette. The pair were playing together. Wolfgang fell. The princess helped the tearful boy to his feet. To express his gratitude, the boy solemnly explained to the empress he wished to marry the princess. In later years as wife of Louis XVI of France (*see* France, Paris, Place de la Concorde), Marie Antoinette may well have wished her mother had accepted the offer.

❧

Clad only in her negligée, a jubilant empress Maria Theresa burst into the royal box at the theater here on February 12, 1768, and interrupted the performance to cry out that she just had had her first grandson. "Poldy—Leopold has a boy," the delighted grandmother shouted to her subjects below—who were equally delighted but somewhat astounded at seeing their portly empress décolleté.

Hofburg: SCHATZKAMMER

When young Adolf Hitler was a student at the Art Academy of Vienna, he would frequently come here to look with steely gaze at the Holy Lance that is part of this treasure. It is said to have pierced Christ's side as he hung from the cross. Young Hitler knew that the man who possessed that lance —the holy sign of imperial power—would be a mighty man.

When the school suggested that Hitler's talents could perhaps be better directed to architecture than to painting, the field that he wished to enter, he quit the academy in a tantrum—one of the first of those tantrums that were to destroy millions of people in Europe in the ensuing years.

The young man quickly forgot the art academy that he thought had failed to recognize his abilities, but he never forgot the Holy Lance, and in 1938 when his troops invaded Austria and made it a province of the Third Reich, he ordered the Holy Lance—and the rest of this treasure—taken to Nürnberg to assure his continued rule.

Hofburg: SPANISCHE REITSCHULE (Spanish Riding School)

To celebrate the capture of Prague in 1744, a splendid equestrian event was held here—a tournament with no one but women in the lists. The empress Maria Theresa, though expecting, was in the forefront of the tourney, clad in crimson and wearing a hat studded with precious stones.

❧

To help entertain the delegates to the Congress of Vienna in 1814, grand balls were held here, for one of which groves of orange trees were planted and 10,000 candles in silver candelabra flickered to light the floor for the dancers.

❦

It was thanks to Gen. George S. Patton that these handsome white horses, a Spanish breed with Arab blood that have been in Austria since the sixteenth century, were saved after World War II from the Russians. An accomplished rider himself, Patton had full sympathy for the Viennese, who feared that their prize animals, taken to Czechoslovakia as war threatened, would end up in the Russian Zone in post-war days. So in 1945, he engineered their return here before they fell into Russian hands.

Hofburg: ZUCKERBÄCKERSTIEGE (Confectioner's Staircase)

As a child, the boy who became the emperor Joseph II wheedled sweets from the servants on this staircase. Then he grew up but never forgot this favorite staircase. And when he tired of his wife and longed for an assignation, it was down these steps that he crept discreetly to share in adult sweets with his paramours.

Hoher Markt

Here, it is said, the Roman emperor Marcus Aurelius died in A.D. 180, when this was a Roman outpost called Vindobona.

Hotel Imperial (16 Kärntnerring)

This palace-away-from-home for visiting royalty was the scene of Adolf Hitler's triumphant return to Vienna on March 14, 1938. To the deafening cheers of a populace decked out in swastika armbands and lapel buttons, he appeared on the ornate balcony here to receive the homage of the former capital of Austria. For Austria became, by his decree, Ostmark—the Eastern Province of Germany.

Hotel Sacher (behind the Opera)

An illustrious pastry cook named Franz Sacher, the founder of this establishment, created the mouth-watering confection called "Sachertorte" in 1832 when he was a chef in the household of Prince Klemens von Metternich, the chancellor of Emperor Francis Joseph I. Metternich was continually pestering him for a new pastry, Sacher said, and so he put together chocolate sponge cake and apricot jam, thereby devising Vienna's most famous cake. Indeed, it is *so* famous and so popular that the recipe for it became a cause célèbre of Vienna's courts.

For seven years, a battle was waged to see who had the right to advertise his product as the "original" Sachertorte—this hotel or Demel's Café, which had bought the rights to produce it from Franz Sacher's grandson, Eduard. The court decided in favor of Sacher's. That, however, has not kept Demel's from selling its Sachertorte as the "first version" of the dessert.

❧

In the days of the emperor Francis Joseph I this was a popular spot, indeed, with his young officers. An early and rapid eater, the emperor was likely to be up and at the breakfast table well before 5:00 A.M. Not until he had been served was anyone else allowed to eat, and after he had stopped eating no one else at his table could eat. Since the table was large, and his company of officers considerable, it took some time for all to be served, and by the time the last few had been, the emperor was finished and his fork laid down—that unwelcome indicator of the fact that breakfast was over for all.

At such times, as soon as they had quit the imperial dining room, the officers would hasten here for a breakfast that they could enjoy.

Italian Embassy (formerly the Metternich Palace) (27 Rennweg)

How happily they were all waltzing—Admiral Lord Nelson of England, Talleyrand of France, Alexander I of Russia, and many more who had gathered in this Austrian capital for the Congress of Vienna. Franz II's chancellor, Prince Metternich, was holding a party here to chat amiably about how Europe would be divided up now that Napoleon was a prisoner on Elba and out of the political scene (*see* Vienna, Schönbrunn). Suddenly a messenger entered. He hurried to the host and whispered news in his ear that, when announced, stopped all the dancing. The messenger's news that sent shudders down the spines of the princes and plenipotentiaries was that Napoleon had escaped from Elba and was on the loose in France again.

Judenplatz (The Jews' Square)

This asymmetric plaza is one of the oldest squares in Vienna. It was the residence of the Jews, who were considered the property of the crown until the year 1421, and, as such, protected. But in that year, 210 were publicly burned for their sin of denying Christ. Number 9 is the site of the synagogue of that time, where the rabbi of that day would help those who wanted to avoid public burning to die with his slaughtering knife. Ultimately, he killed himself.

Kahlenberg Heights

Vienna's aristocracy had a grandstand view here, in the summer of 1809, of Napoleon's army fighting the Battle of Wagram. And they took full advantage of it—sitting beneath their parasols and drinking wine while 40,000 Austrians and 34,000 Frenchmen died below them.

Kapuzinerkirche: KAISERGRUFT (Imperial Crypt) (Neuer Markt)

In this imperial vault, all the Hapsburgs since 1619 are buried. But entrance —even for an emperor—was not easy.

The funeral procession would arrive at the door of the vault, and the master of ceremonies would knock three times. The priest within would inquire, "Who is it who desires admission here?"

"His Apostolic Majesty the Emperor."

"Don't know him."

More knocking, another question: "Who is it that wishes to come in?"

"The highest emperor."

"Don't know him."

The third time, the master of ceremonies would answer, "Your brother, a poor sinner."

Then the doors were opened and the coffin containing all but the heart of the deceased was admitted to its resting place. The hearts are kept in St. Augustine's Church. (*See* Vienna, Augustinerkirche.)

❧

For the fifteen years that remained to her after her husband Francis's death in 1765 (*see* Innsbruck, Triumphpforte), the empress Maria Theresa mourned his passing, calling him the joy of her life. All of the month of August each year after his death and the eighteenth day of every month, she remembered him especially with prayers and ceremonies and visits here where he lay. But in those last years of her visits she had grown so fat that descending and ascending stairs was virtually impossible for her, so she came here in an armchair lowered and raised by ropes. And when, on the last visit she was ever to pay, one of the ropes broke, she cried out so the story goes, longingly, "Ah, he wishes to keep me. I shall come soon." And only a short time later, she did.

Kapuzinerkirche: KAISERGRUFT (Imperial Crypt), *Tomb of Countess Fuchs*

Though many an eyebrow was raised when the empress Maria Theresa announced that her children's governess and her confidante, Charlotte,

Countess Fuchs, was to be buried here, the empress went right ahead with her plans. It was true that the governess was not a member of the royal family, but, as the empress tartly—but loyally—put it, "Since she was with us during our lifetime, why shouldn't she be with us during her death as well?"

Kunsthistorisches Museum (Gallery of Painting and Fine Arts)

Presbyterian Oliver Cromwell found aesthetic Charles I's rich art collection quite distasteful. And after he was instrumental in having Charles executed in 1649, he saw to it that the voluptuous Flemish nudes—and all the rest of the king's art—were carted off to an auction house in Antwerp. There Archduke Leopold Wilhelm of Austria bought them, and they became the basis for this fine art collection.

Lainzer Tiergarten

To help entertain the dignitaries at the Congress of Vienna in 1814–15, wild boar hunts were organized here. The dignitaries were ranged in order of importance: emperors first, then kings, then princes; and the boars were driven past, all closely herded together. The idea was that if the emperors failed to fell an animal, then the kings would have a chance at it, and if the kings failed, surely the princes would succeed.

Parkhotel Schönbrunn (Hietzing)

This is the site of Dommayer's Restaurant, where on October 15, 1844, the rivalry between the elder Johann Strauss and the younger climaxed in the debut of the son.

The elder Strauss had left his family by then, was living with a milliner, and taking little interest in his legitimate children—except trying to prevent their studying music. He objected particularly strenuously to his nineteen-year-old namesake's plan to have his own concert. All Vienna knew that, so all Vienna drove out to Dommayer's to see if the son was worth listening to. They came to ogle but stayed to cheer, for the youth's music was even more infectious and passionate than his father's. Ever after he was known as "the Waltz King."

Pasqualati House (8 Mölker Bastei)

In the days when Ludwig van Beethoven lived here, between 1805 and 1808, the street below was a marching ground for the imperial troops, and it is said that their trumpets and bugles can be heard in the *Eroica* symphony, which he composed at this address.

Pestsäule (Plague Column) (Grabon)

In the face of the Black Death, Leopold I, to whom a son had just been born, fled Vienna in the great plague year of 1679, praying as he went for an end to the disease that was felling thousands (*see* Vienna, Griechenbeisl and Mariazell, Gnadenkirche). And when it had abated, a grateful emperor had this column erected to thank God for his city's deliverance.

Piaristenkirche (Church of the Faithful Virgin) (Piaristenplatz)

When countrified composer Anton Bruckner, in his clothes that did not fit, sat down self-consciously at the organ here in 1861 to be tested on his abilities, his judges looked on disdainfully. But when his recital was finished, the awed church organist whispered quietly, "He should be testing us."

Prinz Eugen's Schloss (Palace of Prince Eugene) (8 Himmelpfortgasse)

Vienna had never known such a funeral. On the night of April 21, 1736, after a pleasant dinner and a game of cards with lady friends, the bachelor prince, Eugene of Savoy, the hero of the Turkish invasion, the builder of Belvedere Palace (*see* Vienna, Belvedere Palaces) died here in what is now the Ministry of Finance, but was then the prince's city dwelling.

For three days after his death was known, his body lay in state, and on the day of his funeral the church bells of all Vienna tolled for an hour. When his funeral bier left this house, 2,776 friends and admirers, it is said, gathered in the narrow street to pay their last respects by joining the funeral procession. First came all the residents of the Poor People's Home; then 19 limping officers who had been wounded under his command; then monks from all the hospitals of this city, bearing their crosses and tapers; then 587 monks of varied orders; then 130 Jesuits; and finally the military: 145 drummers with two black-muffled drums each, infantry, and six cannon. As for the prince himself, he was carried by pallbearers who were completely hidden from view by the gold and velvet covering of the bier.

Riesenrad (Giant Ferris Wheel) (Prater)

To express the emperor Francis Joseph's faith in technology, and to provide a symbol of Vienna that would be popular in the same way that the Eiffel Tower has been in Paris, this 210-foot-high ferris wheel was constructed in 1897. In *The Third Man,* the Graham Greene film that later became a novel, one of the classic chase scenes was filmed in a car of the Riesenrad.

Sankt Marxer Friedhof (Saint Mark's Cemetery)

A blizzard of rain, sleet, and snow so blinded the handful of mourners who set out to accompany the body of Wolfgang Amadeus Mozart to an unmarked grave in this cemetery in December 1791 that all but the bearers had turned back before the grave was reached.

Schönbrunn

It is to thirsty Emperor Matthias that this lovely seventeenth-century palace owes its equally lovely name: Beautiful Spring. Mathias, legend has it, was hunting one day when, hot and tired, he came upon a bubbling spring near where this palace now stands. Delighted, he drank from it, and named it. Later a hunting lodge was built nearby and given the spring's name—and ultimately, this palace itself was constructed.

☙❧

From all across Europe, the heads of state assembled here in 1814 to decide the future of the continent at the end of Napoleon Bonaparte's ravages, when he seemed safely put away on the island of Elba (*see* Vienna, Italian Embassy). But when they were not working, they were dancing and dining, spying and wooing, if not here in the palace, elsewhere in the city. Vienna had never seen so many masked balls and concerts and parades. Among the most notable for their enjoyment of the social life here during the congress were Czar Alexander of Russia and the sizable king of Württemberg. The former was said to have gone dancing for forty consecutive nights. As for the latter, who reveled in the pleasures of Viennese cuisine, a semicircle had to be cut into the dining table to make room for his considerable girth.

☙❧

The wedding gifts for the emperor Francis Joseph and his bride, the pretty Elizabeth of Bavaria, were all laid out here before the young couple's nuptials on April 24, 1854. Prominent among them was the diamond crown that the bridegroom had had fashioned for his bride-to-be. But while the gifts were being admired, the crown was accidentally swept to the floor and several of its points broke. They were quickly repaired before the wedding day, but there were those who said the incident bode no good to the royal pair, and in later years (*see* Mayerling, Carmelite Convent) these same prognosticators were inclined to nod sagely and say they had predicted the unhappiness that attended the couple.

☙❧

A royal scolding was given to thirteen-year-old Franz Joseph Haydn and several of his fellow Vienna Boys Choir members here by the empress Maria Theresa in 1745. The empress had caught the youths climbing on the scaffolding during reconstruction.

Schönbrunn: GLORIETTE

Although they loved each other, there were long periods of time when the emperor Francis Joseph (who chose to sleep on a hard iron bed) and the beautiful but distraught empress Elizabeth were estranged. At such times and, indeed, at others, the emperor would quit this garden through a special gate for an early morning visit with the actress Katharine Schratt. They would share coffee and the emperor's favorite cake, *Gugelhupf,* for an hour or two before he'd return here to the affairs of state.

Schönbrunn: NAPOLEON ROOM

Brought here by his mother when his father was exiled to Elba, the duke of Reichstadt—the only child of Napoleon Bonaparte and Marie Louise of Austria—grew to manhood, but little more, in this lovely palace. When he was twenty-one, in 1832, a little more than a decade after his father's death during his second exile on the island of St. Helena, the handsome, blond young duke succumbed to tuberculosis in this room, where his father had slept contentedly in 1809 after taking possession of Vienna. There had been few joys in the son's short life, but among them were the pet birds with which he played here and the occasional afternoons he spent painting pictures.

Schubert Park (Währinger Strasse)

Among the mourners at the funeral of Ludwig van Beethoven, here in March 1827, was his admirer Franz Schubert. After the funeral, Schubert led his friends to a café to drink a toast to the departed—and a second toast to "him who will go next." That was Schubert himself, who, nineteen months later, was dead at thirty-one. His devoted friends, who for so many years had offered their homes for his *Schubertiaden*—evenings of music and merriment where the compositions that he wrote but no publisher would publish were played—saw to it that he was buried here, as he had wished, near Beethoven.

Sigmund Freud Museum (19 Berggasse)

From 1891 to 1938, when he fled to England to escape the Nazis, Sigmund Freud and his family, including his wife's devoted spinster sister, Minna, lived in this house, and Freud carried on his practice here. Busy as he was with it, he let the women handle the household, to such an extent, indeed, that his wife, not infrequently, would even apply the paste to his toothbrush!

◆◆◆

In 1938, when the Nazis had raided the safe in his office here and Freud returned to find it empty, he is said to have remarked with a good-humored sigh, "I have never taken so much for a single visit."

7 Singerstrasse

Wolfgang Amadeus Mozart and the archbishop of Salzburg just didn't get along. The twenty-three-year-old Mozart came here in 1779 in the archbishop's employ. But their relations went from bad to worse until, in a fit of pique, the archbishop, so the story goes, instructed one of his servants to physically kick Mozart out the door here.

Staatsoper (Opera House) (Opernplatz)

Good, kind Emperor Francis Joseph was simply echoing the sentiments of his fellow Viennese when he happened to remark one day in 1868 during the construction of this magnificent opera house that it lacked a grand outside staircase for the arriving and departing audience to sweep up and down. But that was the finishing touch for architect Eduard van der Nüll, who had already heard the people's complaints. Van der Nüll committed suicide (*see* Vienna, Das Haus Ohne Augenbrauen). And within a few months the fellow architect for this structure, August von Siccardsburg, died too—it is said of a broken heart. The devastated Francis Joseph, feeling responsible, was never again known to comment publicly in any way but positively.

Stephansdom (St. Stephen's Cathedral)

It looked, at last, in the fifteenth century, as if this great Gothic cathedral would be completed. It had been under way, in the Gothic style, since the preceding century, replacing a Romanesque structure that had been largely destroyed by fire. Its nave was finished. It was roofed over, and one of its steeples was up. But there was still the second steeple to be completed. Plans were that it would equal the first, and a young builder named Hans Buchsbaum was assigned to see that it did. Hans, so the story goes, fell in love with a pretty girl named Mary and asked her father for her hand. Mary's father was not averse to the idea, but—like the rest of Vienna—he wished to see the second steeple finished, so he set a condition. If, within a year,

Hans had the second steeple as high as the first, and crowned as the first was crowned, then he could marry Mary.

There was nothing Hans wanted more, but as he left Mary's father's house that evening and looked up at the first cathedral steeple towering above him, he sighed. It was an impossible task his prospective father-in-law had set him. But he heard someone call his name. It was the devil offering his aid, the legend has it. He volunteered to be of help in Hans's time of need provided Hans at no time during the building of the tower used the name of Christ, the Virgin, or any saint, or entered the church to pray. A lovesick Hans readily agreed.

All Vienna was soon amazed at how quick and skillful Hans seemed to be. Taller and taller the tower grew. But then one evening working late Hans saw a shadow on the street below that he thought was the Mary he would soon be marrying. "Mary," he cried. That was just what the devil had been waiting for, and to the ground he hurled poor Hans. And that is why, to this day, there is one tall and one shorter tower topping this cathedral.

Votivkirche (Votive Church) (Rooseveltplatz)

The emperor Francis Joseph always enjoyed a constitutional, and he was taking one one February day in 1853, when a disgruntled Hungarian thrust a dagger deep into his neck. Fortunately, his thick military collar helped somewhat to deflect the blow, but not enough. The dagger pierced even the collar, inflicting a wound that was deep. And it might also have been poisoned, the emperor's aide-de-camp, Count O'Donell feared, so, spreading open the wound, he tried to suck out any poison. Happily, Francis Joseph recovered and lived to rule many years more. And a loving and grateful brother, Ferdinand Maximilian Joseph, later Emperor Maximilian of Mexico, had this church built in gratitude for his brother's narrow escape.

Zur Blauen Flasche (6 Domgasse)

It was midsummer of 1683. For two months, the Turks had been besieging this Christian city. Although Austrian forces were not far away, no messengers seemed able to reach them to let them know that—without help—a hungry Vienna would be forced to capitulate. And then one day a patriotic twenty-three-year-old Polish shopkeeper, Georges Kulczycki, appeared before Count Ernst Rüdiger von Starhemberg, who was directing Vienna's defense. He knew that others had failed, Kulczycki said, but he wished to try to reach the Imperial Army. The count's inclination was to scoff, but he held his tongue. The Pole clearly knew what dangers he faced. Several of those who had already tried to reach the Imperial Army had been captured and executed by the Turks. Count von Starhemberg asked what reward the young man wished for his efforts. Kulczycki replied that serving Vienna was enough reward for him. And that night he and a companion, both dressed as Turkish merchants, quit this city and headed toward the Turkish camp.

Of course they were apprehended, but their story was that they were merchants from Belgrade, and they were allowed to spend the night among the Turks. While there, they learned the precise whereabouts of the Austrian army, and one of them managed to sneak away and communicate with the Austrians, telling them of the dire plight of Vienna. By morning, however, the spy was back to share in the delicious aromatic brew the Turks were preparing from small hard beans they kept in sacks in their camp and roasted and steeped. Two days later, the "Belgrade merchants" returned here to Vienna with the welcome news that the army knew of the city's condition and would rout the Turks.

And so they did. Bombarded from virtually all sides—thanks to the information Kulczycki had passed on—the Turks fled in great disorder—in such disorder, indeed, that they left behind their sacks of aromatic beans. A grateful Count von Starhemberg begged Kulczycki to let him, in some way, reward him for having saved this city. Kulczycki, remembering the Turks' delicious morning brew, said he had one request: could he have the sacks of hard green beans the Moslem horde had left behind.

And so it was that coffee came to this city. And with the coffee, crescent rolls soon were served—invented as an affront to the Turkish enemy. What better way, after all, to insult the enemy than to eat the crescent that adorned his flag while drinking the coffee that was his favorite drink?

VIENNA WOODS

To these wooded hills Ludwig van Beethoven would often come to walk as his hearing failed and interchange with other people became difficult. It is said that his Sixth Symphony—the "Pastoral"—was conceived while walking here during a storm. The storm passed, as it does in the symphony, and in the clear, cool evening that followed, vintners came out to dance.

Belgium

ANTWERP ✥ ─────────

Handschoenmarkt

In ancient days a giant dwelled near the river Schelde here, it is said, and would cut off the right hand of any ship's captain who refused to pay him a toll, and toss it into the river. Finally, a brave descendant of Julius Caesar named Silvius Brabo had had enough of it and slew the giant. This tall tale accounts for the name Antwerpen—"thrown hand"—and this fountain honors the giant's killer.

Museum of Fine Arts

The painter-blacksmith Quentin Massys is represented here by the "Entombment" that he painted in 1508. A favorite adopted son of Antwerp, Massys came to work here from Louvain, and promptly fell in love with an artist's daughter. But in those early days it was as a blacksmith that he made his living, and his beloved's father had a better match in mind for her, so Massys was turned down. Unable to keep the young woman out of his fancy, Massys continued to visit her. One day, so the story goes, chatting with her in her father's studio, Massys picked up one of his brushes and painted a fly on a canvas that her father had left to dry. Some days later, when the father returned to the studio for the painting, he tried to brush off the fly. It would not move. Examining it more closely, he realized it was painted, asked his daughter who the artist was, and promptly gave his permission for her to marry Massys.

Rubens's House (Rubensstraat)

By four in the morning Peter Paul Rubens was always up for mass. Then he set about painting in his studio here. But not without entertainment. While he painted, he was read to, and, between brush strokes, would comment enthusiastically or critically on whatever it was that he was hearing.

This was a house of accomplishment and joy and entertainment till the untimely death here of his first wife, Isabella Brandt, in an epidemic in 1626. Together they had planned this house, which was built soon after they were married. To assuage his sorrow, after selling many of his paintings, he went abroad as a diplomat—painting, too, wherever he went, for the royalty with whom he was negotiating. But he returned here three years later to marry the youthful Helena Fourment, and joy again reigned in this handsome house.

BASTOGNE

McAuliffe Square

The weather was bad here, those weeks before Christmas in 1944. It snowed and the visibility was unfailingly poor, making it impossible for the American Air Force to drop food or munitions to the 101st Airborne holding out against 25,000 Germans. And the Germans, knowing that, decided that the time was right to ask for an American surrender. Gen. Anthony McAuliffe felt differently. And when the German negotiators came bearing their white flag and made their commander's proposal that McAuliffe's troops give up fighting, the general sent them back with a one-word reply: "Nuts."

BRUGES

Basilique du Saint-Sang (Basilica of the Holy Blood)

When Dierick of Alsace, count of Flanders, proved exceptionally brave in the Second Crusade, he was given a phial said to contain a drop of Christ's blood washed from His side on the cross. His chaplain brought it here, and this church was built to honor it. But in the fourteenth century, during an invasion by Gent, it was tossed into the river. Happily, a few days later, the nuns of the Beguinage, walking in their garden, noticed something gleaming in the water—and rescued the phial.

Cranenburg House (Rue St. Amand)

For twenty-two days in 1488 the archduke Maximilian of Austria was kept prisoner here by the burghers of Bruges, who were angered at his high-handed ways. Finally, when they had extracted a promise from him that he would entrust the upbringing of his son, the heir to the throne of the Netherlands, to the king of France, they let him go. But he did not keep his word. Returned to Austria, he left the ruthless Pieter Langhals to govern in his stead. And when Langhals' tortures and executions got to be too much for the burghers, they revolted again and chopped off his head.

That wasn't the end of the matter, though. When Maximilian once again was in command, he made sure the people of Bruges would not forget their murder of Pieter Langhals and ordered them forever to keep swans on their canals—a reminder of Langhals, whose name means "long neck."

Grand 'Place

Dressed in their most elegant gowns, the ladies of this city came out to greet Philip the Fair of France in 1301, when Flanders was annexed to France and Philip came to see his new acquisition. Philip's proud queen, Jeanne, covetous of the wealth she saw displayed on every hand, is said to have remarked haughtily, "I alone am queen. I will not have hundreds of others as splendid as I around me."

⟡

Though Philip IV had been warmly welcomed here in 1301, a year later it was a quite different story. Guildsmen annoyed by monies they were being asked to pay—some of them for the king's reception of the previous year—gathered in this marketplace to decry the taxes. Town officials broke up the meeting, arrested its leaders, and imprisoned them. That fanned the flames of revolt still more. The angry citizenry stormed the prison and released the leaders. The leaders then set out to rouse the whole countryside to the cause of freedom. Off to Gent and to Damme the men rode.

And while they were away, begging their neighboring towns to join the cause of freedom from the French, a French army arrived at the gates here and asked that it be allowed to enter. The city officials hesitated. A French army inside the city was hardly a welcome addition, but neither was a French army battering outside, so they agreed that a small number of the troops might enter, and opened the gates. In thundered some 2,000 soldiers. The nervous citizenry sped a messenger out to find the guild leaders at Damme and tell them that their city now really *was* in serious danger.

Though the men of Damme had been hesitant before to take arms against the French, they willingly did when word of the invasion reached them. By daybreak their army was in Bruges. Mass slaughter of the sleepy Frenchmen ensued. Any man on the streets, or inside a house, who could not properly pronounce the Flemish words *Schilt ende vriendt* (shield and friend), was murdered on the spot.

Groeninge Musee (Groeninge Museum)

The horrifying painting here by Gerard David of a man being skinned alive was commissioned by the archduke Maximilian at the height of his difficulties with the burghers (*see* Bruges, Cranenburg House). Presumably, it was a warning to the good people of Bruges to mind their *p*'s and *q*'s, for it was destined to hang in the Court of Justice.

Notre Dame (Church of Our Lady) (end of the Dyver)

Twenty-five-year-old Mary of Burgundy loved horseback riding. It did not matter to her that she was expecting. The weather was fine, the park at Wijnendale was an inviting place for a ride, and so one day in 1482 she mounted her horse there for a gallop. But the beloved wife of Archduke Maximilian of Austria fell from her horse on that ride, and both she and the unborn child she was carrying died. Her untimely death not only threw her husband into deep mourning but made the heavy-handed Hapsburg Maximilian regent of the Low Countries. And the Hapsburgs and the French had many long and bloody conflicts as time went on. Standing by Mary's tomb here some years later, Louis XV of France remarked: "There lies the cradle of our wars."

BRUSSELS

De Sterre (The Star) (Grand'Place left of l'Hôtel de Ville)

This statue of the heroic fourteenth century Everard 't Serclaes and his dog commemorates the time when an invader seeking to become the ruling duke here established himself in this house. Citizen Serclaes, furious at seeing the invader's standard flying on the square, tore it down. His valiant act led others to take up arms and drive the invader out. But just a few days later, Serclaes was found murdered. And so this statue was erected in his honor.

Grand'Place

No one could believe that June day in 1568 that the two heroes, Lamoral, count of Egmont, and Philip de Montmorency, count of Horn, were about to be beheaded. Both had served with honor in the armies of the emperor Charles V and his son Philip II. But Philip's bloodthirsty Spanish governor-general, the duke of Alva, had ordered torture and death because they had decried his persecution of the Protestants. To honor them, a statue depicting them was erected in the Place du Petit Sablon in 1890.

※

In 1695 when Brussels was a Spanish possession, Louis XIV, during the War of the League of Augsburg, gave orders to bombard this beautiful flamboyant Gothic market square. Above all, the enemy cannons sought to demolish the soaring tower of the Hôtel de Ville, but miraculously, they missed. They did, however, do much damage to the other buildings of the square. Dedicated town fathers and the guilds whose houses had been destroyed quickly saw to it, when the cannons of war were gone, that their lovely square was reconstructed.

Manneken-Pis (Rue de l'Etuve)

There are at least three tales they tell to explain the presence on a busy street for more than six centuries of this two-foot-high statue of a naked little boy wetting into a fountain. As one tale has it, the original child was the son of a prominent burgher. One day, dressed in finery, he got lost, and all Brussels turned out to find him. His frantic mother promised that—were he found—wherever he was found she would have a statue of him erected, doing whatever he was doing when he was discovered. And it was in this street that he was come upon—all of his elegant clothes stolen—but happily wetting into the gutter and smiling impishly, undismayed by his day's wanderings and by all the people searching for him. True to her word, his mother had this statue erected.

But then there is the tale that says he was a child who saved this city by extinguishing, by natural means, the wick of an enemy powder keg that he discovered and that would have set the whole of Brussels on fire.

The third story has the child hero after which the Manneken-Pis was modeled standing in a second-story window once when enemy troops were occupying the city, and wetting on the head of one of the officers.

Ever since he was fashioned, probably of sandstone in the original, he has been overwhelmingly popular—with Belgians and with foreigners alike— so popular, indeed, that he has been kidnapped five times. The first time was in 1745 when the British soldiers tried to carry him away, but were apprehended before they had left the city. The second time, in 1747, it was French soldiers who plotted to make off with him, but their plot was uncovered before it was played out. The saddest kidnapping of all was in 1817 when an ex-convict pulled him from his place and broke the little figure up. The pieces, however, were found and recast.

In 1956, after a kidnapping attempt, he was bolted in place and equipped with a burglar alarm, but a few years later, during a snowstorm, the alarm bells froze and students from Antwerp were able to make off with him. That theft, however, was simply a prank, and the next day he was returned. But then there was a 1966 theft, and there are those who say the Manneken who performs at his post today is a stand-in for the one that disappeared that year.

To make recompense in 1747 for his soldiers' seizing of him, Louis XV bestowed on him the title Chevalier of Saint Michael and Saint Louis and presented him with a court dress, sword, and hat to wear on festival days.

It wasn't long before other European royalty were providing him with more clothes for chilly Brussels nights. The wardrobe from which his clothes can now be chosen includes a Chinese mandarin's garb, a cowboy suit, a Boy Scout uniform, and a Scottish kilt. All are on display in the Maison du Roi on the Grand'Place.

Palais de Justice (Palace of Justice)

It took seventeen years in the mid-nineteenth century to build this enormous structure which, two-and-a-half acres in area, is larger than St. Peter's in Rome.

On September 3, 1944, the Germans set it on fire, and before the blaze could be extinguished, the 345-foot-high dome had fallen. It has, however, been reconstructed.

Palais de la Nation (Rue de la Loi)

In the senate chamber here, a steely German tribunal condemned the courageous English nurse, Edith Cavell, to death in 1915 for helping some 130 Allied prisoners to escape across the border into Holland. When the war began, and the Germans occupied Belgium, she and a friend, Marie Depage, who went down on the *Lusitania,* were running a training school for nurses. Uncowed by threats, Nurse Cavell had willingly harbored those seeking to escape from the German occupation. On October 12, 1915— efforts of the United States minister to Belgium notwithstanding—she was taken to the Tir National Rifle Range here, bound to a chair, and shot.

GENT

A merry tale is told of native-born Charles V of the Holy Roman Empire in the days when he was still a popular figure here—the early sixteenth century. To please him, the families of Gent decided one day to prepare his favorite dish—rice pudding—for him. The king was so informed and waited expectantly for the puddings to arrive. The procession of burghers, led by the lord mayor, entered the banquet hall of the Prinsenhof (no longer standing), but the lord mayor slipped, fell, and spilled the rice pudding. Following suit obediently, all the bearers of rice pudding behind fell to their knees, cursing with the same curse. It is said that Charles took the misadventure in the best of humors.

Beffroi (Belfry)

Although he was a native of this city, and his birth in 1500 was heralded with much acclaim, Charles V became less and less popular with his fellow citizens here as he sought to exert his control over them. For centuries the great bell Roland had pealed from this belfry to announce victories, to warn of dangers, and to call citizens to defend their city. So, in 1540 when Charles was especially annoyed at Gent's independent spirit, he ordered six-ton Roland removed to humble the proud burghers of this city. It has, of course, been replaced many times since.

❦

Legend has it that the gilded twelve-foot-long dragon that gleams from the spire top here was booty taken from the Church of Hagaia Sophia in Constantinople by the emperor Baldwin of Flanders and brought here as a gift to Gent in 1204.

St. Bavon: THE MYSTIC LAMB

It has had an extraordinary history, this fifteenth-century altar screen of the Mystic Lamb, painted by Jan and Hubert van Eyck.

In the mid-sixteenth century an ultraconservative Calvinist movement swept the country. Church after church was destroyed or their contents mutilated. At this time the screen was hidden high in this cathedral's tower. In the eighteenth century, Napoleon's forces took it home for their emperor, and it remained in Paris until 1815. Next, it found its way into the hands of the king of Prussia, and was not returned until the Treaty of Versailles. But the strangest episode occurred in 1934, when the panels of the Righteous Judges and John the Baptist disappeared one night. Then word came that one panel could be found in a luggage locker in Brussels' Gare du Nord—and it was. But the Righteous Judges still are missing, and the only clue to their whereabouts came in a dying man's inaudible whisper to his priest: a well-to-do burgher of Gent had, so the story goes, fallen on hard times. Also a canon of this cathedral, he slipped in one night and stole the panels, seeking ransom money. It was he who had left John the Baptist in the railroad station locker, he confessed to his priest on his deathbed. The priest strained to hear where the Judges had been concealed, but the burgher's final whispers could not be heard and the whereabouts of the panel, to this day, are a mystery.

St. Bavon: ADORATION OF THE MYSTIC LAMB

The Hapsburg emperor Joseph II was a very correct man, and the side panels of this van Eyck masterpiece that depict a nude Adam and Eve being expelled from the Garden of Eden offended him, so he had them both removed, and a clothed Adam and Eve substituted. Now, however, two centuries later, the originals are back.

❦

Among the elegant appointments in the interior of this cathedral are two Italian candelabra that Henry VIII had ordered for his tomb, but that Oliver Cromwell sold to a church official here.

NAMUR

The Citadel

What fierce fighting has gone on around this citadel. In 1577, Don Juan of Austria, the illegitimate son of the emperor Charles V (*see* Germany, Regensburg, Gasthaus zum Goldenen Kreuz), died after besieging it—from wearing, so one story goes, a pair of poisoned boots. It was his half brother, Philip II of Spain, who is said to have had him done in. And in 1692, Louis XIV looked on while his soldiers captured it, and the writers Racine and Boileau-Despréaux, on hand as war correspondents, wrote an ode in honor of the French victory.

Place d'Armes

Sadly, the jousts on stilts that for centuries were held here have been discontinued, but older residents still tell fond tales of the great event. It had its origin, so the story goes, in an angry duke's refusal to hear the pleas of the citizens who were forever protesting to him. It did not matter, he said, whether supplicants came on foot, by boat, or on horseback, he would not listen to them. So a town father devised the idea of their making their pleas on stilts. The duke was so dumbfounded that he listened.

WATERLOO

It is said that at this battle the British commander, the duke of Wellington, spared the life of Napoleon. When a British marksman sighted the emperor within range of his fire, so it's told, he informed the Iron Duke, asking if he should shoot. But Wellington forbade him, remarking that generals in battles had better things to do than shoot one another.

⚜

When the Prussians and the English were acclaimed the victors here on June 18, 1815, the French fled pell-mell for their border. Detractors of Napoleon Bonaparte have him leaving by coach, carrying with him a spare uniform with mounds of diamonds sewn into its lining. His admirers, on the other hand, have the emperor walking along with his defeated army, weeping for the dead and wounded and crying out that he wished he, too, had died on the battlefield.

Château de Rougemont

The British were inside; the French determinedly attacked the outside of this farm-castle in one of the bravest and bloodiest encounters of Waterloo. Though they had no artillery, the French made their way into the courtyard here while the English barricaded themselves inside what remained of the château itself. Before the battle ended, 6,000 French and English officers and troops are said to have died. Three hundred of them who were believed dead were dropped into the well here. But there were those who insisted, for days after the Battle of Waterloo ended, that they could hear moans and wails issuing from the well.

L'Auberge de la Belle Alliance (Inn of the Beautiful Alliance)

The Battle of Waterloo was over. After eight hours of bitter fighting, some 11,000 British, French, Prussian, Dutch, and Belgian soldiers lay dead, some 37,000 wounded. Here the two exhausted commanders of the victorious forces—Lord Wellington and Prussian general Gebhard Leberecht von Blücher—met, kissed, and congratulated each other.

Lion Monument

This 148-foot-high mound, built of soil carried from the battlefield on which, on June 18, 1815, Napoleon Bonaparte was defeated and the course of European history altered, was erected to mark the spot where the Dutch prince of Orange was wounded in the shoulder. Watchfully atop the mound, the enormous cast-iron lion looks toward France.

Tombe Jambe d'Uxbridge (Tomb of the Leg of Uxbridge)

Virtually without flinching, the brave Lord Uxbridge allowed his wounded leg to be amputated in a farmhouse kitchen here. The shot that struck the limb on the battlefield had just missed Wellington's chestnut horse, Copenhagen, so the story goes, and the wounded man calmly remarked to Wellington that he believed the injury meant he must lose his leg. Wellington, equally coolly replied that that, indeed, did seem so. And after the amputation occurred, the leg was buried in the farmhouse garden and this monument erected to it.

Wellington Museum

His monumental victory won, the duke of Wellington wearily returned to this little post house where he had made his headquarters to write his dispatches and to eat his dinner. The table, it is said, had been set for both Wellington and his staff. He waited and he waited, but no one came to join him, for they were all among the dead or wounded. When he finally gave up waiting, ate, and climbed the stairs to bed, he found that a wounded soldier occupied his cot. So he made the floor his bed.

Denmark

AALBORG ❦ ————

Swan Apothecary Shop (Østergade)

Although, technically, this shop was closed during World War II, behind its locked doors the Resistance fighters planned sabotage and the escape of many a refugee. When, from time to time, the Germans jailed one of their number, fellow patriots meeting here would plot the best way of getting the captive out to participate in an evening escapade. Then they would return him to the jail before he was missed by his captors.

BORNHOLM

Gudhjem

When cholera swept through this island in 1684 virtually the entire population died. But in this town there were three lonely survivors—two old fishermen and one youth. Gloomily, they went about the tasks of life, trying to decide what future lay ahead. And then one day they heard a church bell pealing in the distance. Somewhere else on the island someone was alive! The youth hurried to the top of the belfry here and rang its bell. Then he descended and ran toward the sound of the distant bell. Bornholmers today insist that they are all descendants of that youth and the young woman who had rung that distant bell.

Hammershus Castle

In 1660, when this ruin was a castle, Leonora Christine, the most intelligent and the most talented daughter of Christian IV, was imprisoned in it with her husband, Corfitz Ulfeldt. They had plotted to overthrow Leonora Christine's half brother, Frederick III, and been discovered. (*See* Copenhagen, Christiansborg Castle, Blue Tower.)

Always deeply in love, the pair managed—though they were in different quarters—to talk to each other out of their windows, till the governor of the prison learned they were communicating and had a rattling machine installed to drown out their voices.

COPENHAGEN

Amalienborg Palace

On April 9, 1940, the German army marched into Copenhagen. The next morning, quite as usual, Christian X left these palace gates on his horse to calm and greet his people. And every fair morning after that—the German occupation notwithstanding—he rode forth, much to the dismay of the Germans, for he was an imperious figure. He would smile at his people and nod to them, but omit to offer even the most perfunctory of greetings to any Germans he passed.

Caritas Fountain (Gammeltorv)

Ever since 1892, when Christian IX and Queen Louise celebrated their golden wedding anniversary, imitation golden apples have been set out to bob on this fountain each year on April 16, the official royal birthday of the ruling monarch.

Carlsberg Brewery

It may be said that Carlsberg beer owes its original quality to the ingenuity and determination of a Dane in 1845. That year, Jacob Christian Jacobsen, a young brewer, set out for Munich on a very special mission. The thirty-one-year-old Jacobsen had been in Germany earlier studying beer-making techniques, and had concluded that only with proper Bavarian brewer's yeast could he produce in Denmark a beer of a quality equal to the Bavarian. But Bavaria, understandably, wanted to keep its yeast to itself, so Jacobsen went to Munich to smuggle some out.

He managed to acquire two quarts of the marvelous yeast and take it home by coach. It was no easy task. He not only had to keep stopping along the way to pump water on the yeast to keep it alive, but was obliged to conceal it in his top hat at border crossings.

Christiansborg Castle

Modern Copenhagen began in the twelfth century when the warrior-bishop Absalon built a castle here. Patriot that he was, he would surely have been pleased that, in World War II, Resistance fighters kept a cache of explosives in the ruins of his original castle that lie beneath the present one. When, in 1944, there were virtually no more explosives to be had to sabotage the German occupiers, this supply, hidden in 1940, proved valuable, indeed.

Christiansborg Castle: BLUE TOWER

For twenty-two years in the seventeenth century, Leonora Christine, the brilliant, talented daughter of Christian IV and Christine Munk, his monganatic wife, was imprisoned in the tower that stood here.

Leonora Christine had been married when she was fifteen to ambitious, energetic Corfitz Ulfeldt, who became steward of the realm. Life was supremely happy for the young couple until Christian's death. Then Leonora Christine's half brother Frederick III inherited the throne. Neither Leonora Christine nor her husband thought him fit to rule, and together they plotted to overthrow him and install Ulfeldt as king. When the plot was uncovered, Frederick had Ulfeldt and Leonora Christine imprisoned on Bornholm (*see* Bornholm, Hammershus Castle). Although they managed to escape the tower, they were recognized and rearrested when they sought to hire a boat. Ultimately, Ulfeldt died in exile in Switzerland and Leonora Christine was shut up by her brother in the Blue Tower. There she wrote a moving account of her life, "My Sorrow," and poetry to her pet dog. She fashioned pottery, played the piano and the lute, and embroidered, until her nephew finally released her.

Danish Royal Theater (Kongens Nytorv)

When he was fourteen, Hans Christian Andersen donned new shoes that were too tight for him and a new hat that was too big for him, put a few other belongings in a sack that he carried over his shoulder, and set out for this capital city. He thought he wanted to be a ballet dancer. Like the Ugly Duckling of his fairy tale, he was awkward and unattractive—tall, long-nosed, gawky—and very much the country bumpkin. When he reached the city and stood in front of the original of this theater (it was rebuilt in 1874), a ticket touter offered him a ticket to the day's ballet. Andersen grinned his appreciation, accepted the ticket, and was about to go in to the performance when the touter realized the boy did not understand he was supposed to pay for it and yanked the ticket back.

But somehow the hopeful youth managed to obtain an interview with a ballerina. There are two stories of this meeting. One tale has him insulting her by asking if he could take off his pinching shoes in her presence. In the other, he performed a one-man ballet of his own devising—so bizarre and so dreadful that the ballerina thought him mad and screamed for help.

Andersen's determination finally won him a walk-on role as a troll, but it was soon clear to him that there was no future for him in ballet. Yet he continued to dream of success on the stage. Perhaps he could use the soprano voice his Odense neighbors praised so highly (*see* Odense, Fyn,

Andersen's Fairy Garden). But this hope too was short-lived—his voice changed. And it was then that he decided to become a writer.

The Little Mermaid

Ever since this statue of Hans Christian Andersen's "Little Mermaid" was unveiled here in 1913, the little sea princess who quit her father's underwater palace for love of a human prince has graced the harbor front, a cherished landmark. One April morning in 1964 Copenhagen awoke to find that the bronze statue's head had been sawed from her body. No one claimed possession of it. No ransom was asked. Some have speculated that the thief was an avant garde artist voicing a protest at such traditional art. Others suggest the head was taken by a sailor enamored of her. (Dutch and Brazilian sailors believe that kissing her brings good fortune. Perhaps one wanted such fortune always.) There are even a few romantics who propose that it was the spirit of the prince for whom she painfully split her tail and quit the ocean who came to claim her at last.

Happily, the original molds for the casting still existed, and by June the mermaid had a head again.

Museum of the Danish Resistance Movement (Amaliegade and Esplanaden)

With calmness and efficiency, Danish Resistance forces succeeded in saving 7,000 Jews from the Nazis in World War II, quietly hiding them in homes and smuggling them by night across the Øresund Strait to Sweden. And in 1943, when the Nazis began arresting policemen who were opposed to them, the Resistance hid and shipped out three-fourths of those who were in danger all over the country. A frequent disguise was the white coat and stethoscope of a doctor. Hospitals readily accepted these new "physicians" on their staffs.

National Museum (Gammel Strand): THE GOLDEN HORNS

The originals of these golden Viking horns lay in a field in Gallehus in Jutland for more than ten centuries. Dating from A.D. 500 and inscribed with runic writing, the first of them was found in 1639 by a country girl whose name has been recorded as Kristine, daughter of Svend. A century later a farmer, whose name is not recorded, unearthed the second in the same field. Both finds were greeted with excitement, and both horns went to the Copenhagen Art Gallery. There, many admired them—including a skilled and unscrupulous goldsmith's apprentice.

Niels Heidenreich envisioned all of the saleable items that could be fashioned from the gleaming gold, and one day in 1802, he slipped into the museum and stole the golden horns. By the time the theft was traced to him, he had already melted them down. Heidenreich was imprisoned, and is believed to have confessed that a bit of the horns had been turned into earrings. These are now on display at the Ringe Museum in Fyn. And the rest? No one knows. The horns here are copies of the originals, fashioned of gilded silver.

6 Strandgade

For a time in the eighteenth century, this was the home of Adm. Peder Wessel Tordenskjold, a naval hero who, it is said, kept two cannons at his main doorway and gave orders that whenever he shouted "*Skoal*" at a dinner party, the cannons were to be fired.

Osterbro Park

Søren Kierkegaard, the hunchbacked nineteenth-century philosopher who has been called the father of existentialism, frequently strolled here—always elegantly dressed—and stopped passersby (or took them walking with him) while he explained his philosophy.

Outer Harbor

Anything less than total victory was never enough for Horatio Nelson of the British navy. In 1801, to prevent assistance being given to Napoleon by other powers, England began inspecting cargoes of neutral countries on the Baltic Sea. When this nation bristled at having its vessels boarded, two divisions of British ships were sent here. Admiral Sir Hyde Parker was in command.

With fury, the British vessels attacked the anchored Danish fleet. For three hours the cornered Danes were bombarded. Finally, it seemed to Parker, the Danes had suffered enough. It had been prearranged with Vice Admiral Nelson that Parker would raise a signal flag when he wished the firing to cease. He ordered it raised. An officer on Nelson's ship alerted his commander that it was flapping. Nelson put his telescope to one eye—his blind eye—and remarked to the officer, "I see no flag," and continued his ruthless bombardment.

Rosenborg Castle

In the garden of this Renaissance summer palace, Christian IV angrily denounced Christine Munk, his morganatic wife of fifteen years, and the mother of twelve of his children. Before his council, he accused the pretty and passionate Christine of having tried to poison him in the aftermath of a love affair with a German count. The king's council acquitted her, but

Christian never believed her protestations of innocence. He banished her to her mother's home in Jutland and refused thereafter to tolerate even her children's affection for her.

⚜

The crown jewels are on display here. Twice in their history these magnificent jewels, including the largest amethyst in the world and a jewel case with 2,000 diamonds decorating it, have been spirited away in time of danger. In the nineteenth century, they were slipped out from under the eyes of the invading British and put into a sarcophagus in the crypt of a nobleman in the monastery of Søro. In World War II on April 8, 1940, the very day the Germans invaded Denmark, the jewels were again whisked out of their cases so swiftly and hidden so cleverly that the Germans never found them. To this day, no information has been released about that particular hiding place.

But it is not just invading armies, the Danes know, who might wish to abscond with the rich royal collection. To protect them from all thieves, the glass cubicle that holds the jewels will sink beneath the castle floor if tampered with in any way, it is said.

The Round Tower

No one is certain why a broad spiral ramp rather than a stairway leads to the top of this seventeenth-century observatory. Some speculate that it was constructed in this way so the observatory instruments could easily be transported to the top; others that Christian IV, for whom it was built, suffered from rheumatism and could more easily be carried on a ramp than stairs. But the ramp was put to spectacular use in 1716 when Peter the Great visited here and rode up and down on horseback, while his wife Catherine drove along in a horse-drawn carriage.

Royal Copenhagen Porcelain Showrooms (6 Amagertorv)

In this sixteenth-century house, now the showrooms for fine Danish china, "Dyveke," Christian II's Dutch wife is believed to have been poisoned in 1517 by a gift of cherries from the governor of Copenhagen, Torben Oxe, whose advances she had rejected for love of the king.

⚜

In existence since 1779, this porcelain works has had many a famous customer. Among the most renowned in its early days was Russia's Catherine the Great, for whom the company's most delicate and most famous design, Flora Danica, was created. (It took twelve years to make it, however, and the empress died waiting.) Admiral Lord Nelson's Lady Hamilton fared better, though the factory—thanks to the admiral—did not.

In 1807 Nelson's relentless bombing nearly laid waste this entire city. Among the accidental targets of his cannonballs was the Royal Copenhagen Factory, and he was chided for the damage he had done. Not only finished pieces, but patterns were destroyed by the British attackers. So, as if to prove that there was plenty of fine china left, he made a careful selection of items to present to his paramour, Lady Hamilton.

Shell House (2 Kampmannsgade)

The Shell Oil Company headquarters that stood here in 1945 was the site of an extraordinary air attack by the British RAF. Throughout the war, the building had been used by the Gestapo as a center for interrogating, torturing, and imprisoning Danish Resistance fighters. Since it was on its top floor that the arrested Danes were kept, the RAF Mosquitoes swooped in low, using a precision strike to hit only those floors occupied by the Germans. The approach was so successful that almost all Danes escaped, while the Gestapo on the lower floors were killed.

Tivoli Gardens

"When people amuse themselves, they forget politics," playboy Georg Carstensen told King Christian VIII when, in the 1840s, he sought permission to build this amusement park. Since those were times when revolutionary ideas were making the monarch nervous, Christian agreed to Tivoli's construction, but he insisted that the buildings be made only of wood, canvas, and glass so they could be easily removed, if it were necessary, to make way for the cannons of war.

ELSINORE

Kronborg Castle

Neither Hamlet nor his father's ghost ever walked the walls of this great sandstone castle, but the twelfth-century chronicler Saxo Grammaticus— who first wrote down the tale of the unhappy prince—may have. For Saxo Grammaticus was born here in Elsinore. The chronicler's account of Prince Amleth, whose mother married his uncle, has a Jutland setting. But this sixteenth-century fortress, built and rebuilt, has seen its share of anguish all the same. Here Queen Caroline Matilda, the sister of George III of England, was imprisoned for adultery by her husband Christian VII.

Nervous and high-strung (some say he was insane), Christian had employed a German physician, Johann Friedrich Streunsee, to look after him. King, queen, and physician frequently traveled together, and while the physician became the king's confidant, he became the queen's lover. By 1770, he was so much in the king's good graces that he was virtually ruling the land, and he ordered the king's council dismissed. In 1771, when the queen gave birth to a daughter, no one accepted the baby as the king's. Streunsee had been in Holstein with the royal family nine months before.

Finally, the nobility had had their fill. They demanded Streunsee's head and the queen's imprisonment. They got both. Here, after her lover's execution, Caroline Matilda was kept until her royal English brother, George III, persuaded Christian to release her to him. When the arrangements finally were made, an English naval squadron sailed here to get her. Although she was allowed to retain the title of queen, she was forbidden ever to return to Denmark.

◆◆◆

Whenever Denmark is in danger, it is said, the huge white statue here of Holger Dansk, the old warrior who fought for Charlemagne, will rise from the table where he sits, his beard growing into it, and fight again for Denmark. And in World War II, during the German occupation, Holger Dansk did, indeed, rise up: the crack Danish Resistance force took his name.

FÅREVEJLE

Dragsholm Castle

It is a complex tale, the story of the love of Mary Queen of Scots for the swashbuckling earl of Bothwell, who died, insane, chained to a rock wall here.

Bothwell, the twenty-five-year-old queen's third husband, had been accused in Scotland of the murder of her second husband, Lord Darnley. Bothwell was acquitted and he and the queen were wed, but their joint complicity in the gunpowder plot that had killed Darnley was widely rumored. There was a rebellion against Mary. Bothwell deemed it wise to quit the country.

He boarded a vessel bound, via the Shetland Islands, for the continent. Scarcely had he left before his enemies were in pursuit. His knowledge of the islands helped him to evade them while, at the same time, luring them to wreck their vessel on the rocks.

Then Bothwell sailed on to what he hoped would be a safer port in Norway. It would have been, except for a youthful folly. Years earlier, when he had needed money, he had married a wealthy Norwegian woman, then abandoned her. News of the earl's arrival in Norway spread quickly. So, too, spread the news that he was the husband of the Scottish queen. Furious when she learned that he had taken a new bride, his Norwegian wife charged bigamy. While the court weighed the case, Frederick II of Denmark (then king of Norway, too) considered the possible value of his prestigious visitor.

In the previous century, Denmark had lost the Shetland and the Orkney islands to Scotland. Perhaps the Scots' queen's husband could be exchanged for them, Frederick reasoned. So Bothwell was taken prisoner and transported to the castle at Malmö (then Denmark). There his surroundings befitted a royal prisoner. He was well kept while negotiations were planned with Scotland. (*See* Norway, Bergen, Bergenhus Fortress.)

Then Frederick learned that Mary had been imprisoned by Queen Elizabeth. That made the earl of Bothwell virtually valueless. From Malmö he was brought here to Dragsholm. This time, his surroundings were of the crudest. The once dashing earl grew thinner and thinner. He began to fail mentally as well as physically. But before he failed entirely he made one last gesture for the queen whom he had loved and wed. He wrote an account of the murder of Darnley that cleared Mary of knowledge of the plot.

In 1578, nine years after he had quit Scotland, Bothwell died here, raving mad, and was buried in the church graveyard. There he remained until the nineteenth century when grave robbers stole his skull and cut off locks of hair as souvenirs. Not until 1949 were the scattered bones reassembled.

FAKSE, ZEALAND

Gisselfeld Castle (two miles south of Haslev)

Lonely Hans Christian Andersen roamed from manor house to manor house visiting his friends, telling his stories, and drinking tea. It was here at Gisselfeld Manor, with its moat and ducks and wild swans, that he found his inspiration for "The Ugly Duckling."

FYN

Egeskov Castle

For five years, in the seventeenth century, Rigborg Brockenhuus, the pretty young daughter of this castle's owner, was kept in a bricked-up room here after she had given birth to an illegitimate child.

Rigborg had been sixteen when she'd gone to the court of King Christian IV to be a lady-in-waiting. There she'd fallen in love with the king's chamberlain, Frederik Rosenkrantz. When she'd found she was expecting, she'd left the court. After the baby was born, her enraged father walled her up, leaving an aperture just large enough to pass food in to the unfortunate girl. Her rescue came only after her father's death, when her brothers let her out.

JELLING, JUTLAND

Burial Mounds

On this site in the tenth century stood the castle of Gorm the Old (he lived to be over one hundred) and his wife, Thyra the Beautiful. Apparently they were a loving family. Gorm's funeral monument to his queen (prepared before her death) acclaimed her as the pride of the Danes. When one of their sons, Knud, died in battle, Thyra, fearful of how Gorm would take the news, could not bring herself to tell him directly of it. Instead she draped the main hall of the castle in black. Clearly, the king understood, for he died of shock at the sight.

KØGE

Church of St. Nicholas

In the days when pirates from Saxony raided this coast, it was from the tower of this church that any caught were hanged. The unhappy raiders were euphemistically dubbed "Køge chickens," and children from all around were brought to see them and take note of the fate of those who attacked Denmark.

NORTH ZEALAND

Frendensborg Castle

At this cozy summer palace on the shores of Lake Esrum, Christian IX, just before the turn of the century, liked to entertain his extensive family in homespun ways. So many monarchs were related to him that he was familiarly—and warmly—known as "the father of Europe." Here the boy who would one day marry Christian's daughter Alexandra, and become Edward VII of England, threw bread pellets at the dining table.

ODENSE, FYN

St. Canute's Cathedral

It was only because of his kindly brother, Eric, that Canute, whose remains are buried here, became a saint. Tough and brutal, eager to conquer England, he tried to assemble a naval force for the battle, but a mutiny broke out and the project was abandoned. Pursued by his rebellious subjects, he sought refuge in St. Alban's Church here, but his enemies slew him at the altar. His brother, horrified by the deed, walked barefoot all the way to Rome to plead for his canonization in 1103.

Andersen's Fairy Garden

Here, while his washerwoman-mother did laundry in the Odense River, young Hans Christian Andersen sang songs that earned the boy the nickname of "the Nightingale of Odense," and here he learned the love of nature that was to serve him so well in fairy tales like "Thumbelina" and "The Snow Queen" and "The Little Mermaid."

Birthplace of Hans Christian Andersen (39 Hans Jensenstrade)

No one is certain, but it is generally believed that it was in this little plastered cottage that the king of the fairy tales, Hans Christian Andersen, was born on a makeshift bed put together with wood from the frame of a funeral bier. His father was a shoemaker, his mother an alcoholic washerwoman. His paternal grandfather was the village madman who sported chicken feathers and flowers in his hair and was always followed about by a troupe of jeering children. Was it his grandfather's appeal to children—macabre though it was—that inspired his grandson to write fairy tales that would appeal to them, too?

RANDERS

Clausholm Castle

King Frederick IV "fluttered like a butterfly" from pretty woman to pretty woman during his reign in the seventeenth to eighteenth centuries. And although he had bulging eyes, an extravagantly long hooked nose, and a pinched mouth, the women succumbed to him. Among them was nineteen-year-old Anna Sophia Reventlow, the daughter of the king's grand chancellor, whose home was Clausholm Castle. The couple met at a masked ball. A few months later, though he already had a queen, the king declared his intention to marry Anna Sophia. Her mother wouldn't hear of it and forbade her daughter to see the king again so he decided on a more forceful course of action; with the aid of Anna's servants he spirited her away through a side door here one night and secretly married her. For the next ten years, the king kept two wives, Queen Louisa and Anna Sophia. Within two days of Louisa's death, he married Anna properly and made her his queen.

It was not to have a storybook ending, however. When Frederick died, his son Christian VI banished her, sending her home to Clausholm. Twelve years later, she died of smallpox.

RIBE

The Cathedral: THE CAT DOOR

Once upon a time a local merchant had a cat and a private island. When the cat ate all the mice and rats on the island, its owner was so pleased that he paid to have her portrait emblazoned over this door. So goes one story explaining the cat here. Another, less charming one, says the cat marked an entrance reserved for the devil.

ROSKILDE

Viking Ship Museum

In 1962, a fisherman dragging in the shallow fjord here hauled up a piece of ancient wood in his net. He hastened to the National Museum with his find, and divers were sent into the fjord to investigate. There the five Viking trading ships now in this museum were found. They are believed to have been sunk by the Danes in the eleventh century to keep marauding Norwegians from entering the harbor.

SKAGEN

Buried Church of Højer

A strong northeast wind one day in 1775 whipped up the dunes here into a wild sandstorm that—despite the best efforts of parishioners—buried all but the steeple of this little church.

SØNDERBORG

The Castle

A rut in the flagstones here was worn by the pacing of Christian II, who was imprisoned for ten years in this castle in the sixteenth century. The combination of his interest in the Lutheran faith and the influence of his unpopular Dutch mother-in-law (see Copenhagen, Royal Copenhagen Porcelain Showrooms) were his downfall. He went into exile in Holland, and later was invited to return—only to be waylaid, captured, and imprisoned here.

Finland

HÄMEENLINNA ❧ ─────────

When the composer Jean Sibelius was growing up here in the 1870s, some of his favorite excursions were to the nearby shores of Lake Vanajavesi where he would walk and listen to the lapping waters and the wind you can still hear in the symphonies he later wrote. (*See* Imatra, Järvenpää.)

HELSINKI

Sweden's king Gustavus Vasa should have been content (*see* Sweden, Mora), but he wasn't. He lacked a prosperous port city in his domain. He looked around and thought he had found the perfect site for the town he wanted here, where the Vantaa River flows into the Gulf of Finland. But he needed citizens to people it. He issued a royal life-or-death decree to the burghers of Porvoo, Rauma, Ulvila, and Tammisaari: they were to move or be executed. And so, grimly, they moved. Whether because their hearts remained behind or because the time simply was not right, Helsinki failed to prosper and, in time, Gustavus let the burghers all go home again. And that—for a time—was the end of Helsinki. What there was of it, indeed, burned to the ground in 1808. But in 1809 Finland became a grand duchy of Russia, and at about the same time the wooden structures of the Finnish capital of Turku succumbed to a fire. Czar Alexander I might have had Turku rebuilt, but like Gustavus Vasa, he had always liked the site of Helsinki, so he rebuilt the capital here.

Arabia Ceramics Factory (Hämentie 135)

In the 1800s, when Finland was a grand duchy of Russia, a general returned from the Near East and settled here on the outskirts of Helsinki. Wistfully, to remind him of his travels, he called the villa that he built Arabia. Little did he know that one day that name would be borne by one of the world's great ceramics firms. But about one hundred years ago, Rörstrand, a Swedish ceramics company, eager to sell wares in Russia, began to look around for a good location for a branch. They happened on the general's estate. The name Arabia was appealing, so Rörstrand adopted it for their Finnish ceramics, which, with Finnish designers fashioning them, soon led all Rörstrand ceramics in popularity.

The Cathedral (Senate Square)

From all over Finland, men, women, and children came to this cathedral by the busload in January 1951, to mourn the death of Field Marshal Carl Gustaf Emil von Mannerheim who, thirty-three years before, had been the military leader in the civil war that brought Finland its independence. Twelve generals carried his coffin and 2,000 of his officers marched in the procession that took him, Finland's greatest modern hero, to his grave.

Helsinki City Museum

It was a poverty-stricken refugee from the Russian Revolution who gave this museum its handsome collection of bejeweled Easter eggs, but for years before that he had kept them stuffed in a box under old clothes in his Helsinki apartment.

The Russian-born giver of the gift, a quiet, shy retired engineer, had lived a hand-to-mouth existence for years in a barely adequate apartment in this city's Munkkiniemi district. Then one day he was hurried to the hospital, terminally ill. There was one last message he must leave, the man whispered to his nurses, and he begged them to ask the caretaker of his apartment house to come to the hospital. The caretaker came. The old man said there was a box in his apartment that must be brought to this museum. He told its whereabouts. He said inside it was a gift of gratitude to Helsinki for having been his refuge in time of trouble. The gift, it turned out, was these priceless Easter eggs.

Olympic Stadium

How joyous all Finland was when it was announced that this city would host the 1940 Olympics. Track star Paavo Nurmi who, between 1920 and 1932 had set twenty world running records and received nine Olympic gold medals, was especially pleased, even though he had retired to become a haberdasher, to see his country so honored. But then the long shadow of World War II fell over Europe and the games were cancelled. It was to be a long twelve years—and many of the fine young athletes who would have competed here would be dead on the world's battlefields–before there was an Olympics in this stadium.

State Council Building (Senate Square)

It would have been hard to have been more detested than was Russian governor-general Nikolai Bobrikov, appointed to govern here by Nicholas II of Russia in 1898 when Finland was a grand duchy.

As Bobrikov saw it, Finland had to be absorbed into Russia and lose all self-identification. But, as it turned out, the fates allowed him only six years to accomplish this objective. For in June 1904, a twenty-eight-year-old patriot named Eugene Schaumann shot the governor-general and then killed himself. In his pocket Schaumann was carrying a letter to the czar explaining that he felt the murder and suicide necessary—in order to bring the czar's attention to Finland's unhappy state.

Suomenlinna

The whole Finnish army proudly assisted in the building of this immense fortress in 1748. So enormous it was, and indestructible as it was thought to be, it was known as "the Gibraltar of the North." But its day was a short one. Briefly, Helsinki, feeling safe, prospered with it guarding the entrance to its harbor. But in 1808 when the Russians attacked, Suomenlinna was surrendered without a fight by its commandant, Carl Olof Cronstadt, a sea officer, disgruntled at having been shunted off to Helsinki from Stockholm by the Swedish king who ruled over the Finns then. (Defenders of Cronstadt maintain that he may well have thought his garrison greatly outnumbered, for legend has it that the wily commander of the Russians marched his troops out of town each night under cover of darkness and back in the morning, to suggest that more soldiers were arriving each day.) Then in 1855, during the Crimean War, when it was under fire by the cannons of the French and British, and again in Finland's war of independence, it became evident that it could not withstand the sophisticated weaponry of the nineteenth century.

ILOMANTSI

World War II Battlefields

It is said that because the Soviet Union had such trouble fighting a small group of Finns here in the winter war of 1939–40, Adolf Hitler decided that the Russians would not be hard at all to conquer. So he altered his strategy, which would have concentrated all his military efforts in the west, and invaded the Soviet Union—as it turned out, to his great sorrow.

IMATRA

Järvenpää (23 miles north of Helsinki)

The composer Jean Sibelius built this hillside villa in 1904, and here, smoking his beloved Cuban cigars and listening to the soughing of the wind in the pines, he did much of his composing.

KANGASALA

The Church: BLEEDING STONE

Beautiful Kaarina so charmed the young men of this town in the sixteenth century that it was whispered she must be a witch. And when a nobleman's son named Klaus became enough enamored to wish to marry her, his father decided, once and for all, he would put a stop to her evildoing. And so, being a powerful member of the king's court, he saw to it that Kaarina was put on trial as a witch and sentenced to death. Her execution took place on this stone, and up to the very end she pitifully kept shouting, "I am innocent and for your killing me, this rock, on which I stand, will bleed forever."

No sooner was Kaarina dead than blood trickled from this rock, and, simultaneously, the bells of this church began to toll and would not stop. The frantic townspeople tore the bells from the churchtower and threw them into Ukkijärvi Lake across the road. And they lifted the accursed rock and put it into the facade of the church hoping that, somehow, incorporating it into the structure would make the red stream cease to flow. But their hope was in vain and the narrow red stream still flows from this granite rock. And during still summer nights there are those who insist one can still hear the churchbells ringing in the lake.

KAUKOPÄÄ (near Lake Saimaa)

At his seventy-fifth birthday celebration here in 1942, Carl Gustaf Emil von Mannerheim (*see* Helsinki, The Cathedral) had an unexpected guest —Adolf Hitler—who came to tell the marshal how greatly he admired him. After all, a Finnish-German union against the Russians could be extremely useful. The elegant and aristocratic Mannerheim was somewhat taken aback, according to accounts of the time, by the wild-eyed German leader, who asked for a vegetarian plate and tea and water at the meal they shared together.

LAPLAND

Rovaniemi: ARCTIC CIRCLE COTTAGE

When Eleanor Roosevelt announced in 1950 that she was coming on a visit to Lapland this little cottage that stands on the Arctic Circle was built in just one week to welcome her.

LUOMO

Hvitträsk (18 miles west of Helsinki)

In 1902, three young Finnish architects, Eliel Saarinen, Armas Lindgren, and Herman Gesellius, decided to build their dream studio and adjoining dream living quarters for themselves and their families on the rocks here overlooking shimmering Hvitträsk Lake. This structure that they fashioned, its design based on the shape of the rocks on which it stands, helped to revolutionize Finnish architecture and design.

Although life proved more profitable for Finnish-American architect Eliel Saarinen in the bustling United States than here in his quiet native land, his love of this home he and his friends had built among the tossing birches and granite boulders and spruces and pines never diminished. And this designer of the music shed in Tanglewood and the great red granite railway station in Helsinki asked that he be buried here. He died in 1950.

PORVOO

Runeberg House (at the corner of Runeberginkatu and Aleksanterinkatu)

When Finland's most famous poet, Johan Ludvig Runeberg, came here in 1852, he didn't like Porvoo. He was annoyed at having lost his post in Latin at Turku University (largely because of a light-hearted escapade in which he had thrown a snowball at the hat of another instructor). And it was pouring rain the night he arrived. But, as it turned out, he remained in Porvoo for the next forty years. For the first twenty, he walked from here each day up the hill to the old city to teach in the high school. For the next twenty, he lived in this house, writing and superintending the care of his garden and house plants.

SAVONLINNA

Kerimäke (3.5 miles to the south)

As many as 3,000 people can assemble in this enormous wooden church—reportedly, the largest wooden church in the world. The Finns like to say that its size was a mistake: the architect failed to explain whether his measurements were in meters or centimeters and, as a result, the building got out of hand.

Olavinlinna Castle

Surely the Finnish defenders of this castle through the centuries have been valiant in keeping marauders away, but important, too, has been the mermaid—so the story goes—who dwells in the dark waters that surround Olavinlinna, playing her melancholy music on her harp at night to warn those seeking to approach that they will be in danger if they dare to attack.

◆◆◈◆◆

In the heyday of this castle in the sixteenth century, a stocking-footed watchman made the rounds of these ramparts each night to assure himself that no guards were sleeping at their posts. And if they were, into the icy waters below they were mercilessly hurled.

Olavinlinna Castle: SMALL COURTYARD

For centuries from the southwest wall here, though there was no earth from which it could have grown, a rowan tree flourished in a crack. It is said that it grew from the heart of a pretty maiden who had been immured here unjustifiably for a treasonable act.

TAMPERE

Finlayson Mill

Incongruous certainly, but it is to an eighteenth-century Scottish Bible salesman that this city today owes its prosperity.

In 1819, John Patterson of Glasgow came to Tampere selling Bibles for the Russian Bible Society of St. Petersburg. It was his sixth visit here and, astute Scot that he was, he had seen other prospects besides Bible sales here where the Tammer Rapids thunder. And so he brought along on that sixth journey a Scots engineer named James Finlayson who was working in St.

Petersburg. Surely, Patterson said, there was some purpose to which the waterfall—if harnessed—could be put.

It didn't take Finlayson long to see the waterfall's possibilities, and to ask the national treasury for an interest-free loan to build a cotton mill here. He also obtained the right to import the machinery he needed and raw cotton tax-free for ten years.

In no time at all the little village of Tampere was a bustling city—its population swelled by Scots and Englishmen imported to assist in running Finlayson's cotton mill machinery. Ever since, this has been a city of mills.

TURKU

It is said that with bricks stolen from Turku, the first structures in St. Petersburg (Leningrad) were constructed.

❦

It was in 1827 that this former capital went up in flames when a milkmaid cleaning a barn, so the story goes, tipped over her lantern and the straw in the barn caught fire. Within an hour the whole of this then-wooden city, including Finland's first university, was ablaze. Only the castle and the cathedral remained. (*See* Helsinki.)

The Castle (at the mouth of the Aura River near Kanavaniemi)

Dazzling was the word for sixteenth-century life here when Duke John, who became John III of Sweden, lived in this castle with his Polish wife, giving balls and dinners and inviting neighboring royalty to join him here on hunting parties. But his brother Eric XIV grew jealous of him and put an end to it all, capturing the castle and clapping its occupants into prison. Not to be outdone, when John got out and obtained the throne himself, he imprisoned his brother Eric XIV here for two years. And in a hut outside, Eric's devoted wife, Karin Mansdotter, lived, doing her best to keep her husband company. (*See* Sweden, Mariefred.)

❦

The sixteenth-century duke, Charles, who became Charles IX of Sweden, could not believe that his greatest enemy, Klaus Fleming, the rebellious governor of this provincial castle, was dead. Charles had been besieging the castle for days and there had been no sign of capitulation. Then a traitor substituted sand for cannonballs in Fleming's artillery and Charles was victor. His good fortune dumbfounded him—he now possessed this most important stronghold in Finland. Better yet, Fleming was dead. To make certain, though, he demanded a look at the body. Viewing it, he tweaked the dead man's beard for assurance while Fleming's wife looked on in horror.

The Cathedral (at the beginning of the Aninkaistenkatu)

Zealous and pious Eric IX of Sweden, who became Saint Eric, decided in 1155 that it was about time that the heathen Finnish tribes who inhabited the land to the east of his became Christians. With a Scottish missionary named Henry in tow, he set off to convert them. And it was here in Turku, it is said, that Henry baptized his first Finns.

Neither Eric nor Henry lived long enough to see a church constructed here to further their work. Eric returned home to Sweden where he was killed by a Danish prince in 1160; Henry stayed on to devote himself to conversions.

Unfortunately, he took his task too seriously, covering the countryside on horseback seeking converts among the peasantry, and in 1160 he, too, met a bloody death. Traveling near Lake Koylio in snowy January, he sought food for himself and his hungry men at a manor house. Lalli, the lord of the manor, was not at home, but the Scottish missionary burst in anyway and asked for food. Lalli, it is said, was not at all taken with the christianizing going on in his neighborhood and among his serfs, and his wife declined to feed the intruders. They paid no attention to her, and helped themselves, leaving three gold pieces in payment when they had had their fill and were ready to face the outdoors again.

When Lalli returned home from his afternoon hunt and found his larder bare, in a rage, he went after the departing Christians. On the shore of the frozen lake he caught up with them and whacked Henry in the head with his battle-axe. Legend has it, further, that he cut off his victim's finger so he could have the ring he wore on it. (Eric had made Henry the bishop of Uppsala in Sweden; thus he wore a bejeweled bishop's ring.) But the finger—and the ring—slipped from the murderer's hands and disappeared in the wet snow covering the lake. It was not until spring that it was found—and not by Lalli, but by a blind man and his son rowing on the lake. The boy saw the grisly memento of the bishop frozen into a cake of ice that floated by and told his father what he had seen. The father urged him to go after it, and when they had hacked the finger with the gleaming ring out of the ice cake, the father, who was among Henry's converts and had heard the story of the martyrdom by Lalli, put the finger first to one eye, then the other, and his sight was restored.

A finger with a bishop's ring on it has, ever since this cathedral's construction, been part of its seal.

❧❦

Beneath the stained-glass window that depicts her, her son, and a page, Karin Mansdotter, the Swedish country girl who became Denmark's queen in the sixteenth century (*see* Sweden, Mariefred), is buried, the only member of royalty to be buried in Finland.

The Cathedral: TOTT FAMILY CHAPEL

Although Åke Tott was a splendid general and distinguished himself in the service of his native land of Sweden during the Thirty Years' War, he was apparently not a popular husband. For his second wife had this chapel built —in honor of her predecessor—and in recognition of all she had gone through.

France

AIGUES-MORTES ⋅✿⋅ ————————

What an exciting day it was in 1248 when Louis IX—Saint Louis—with 30,000 fellow Crusaders quit this port city on the Seventh Crusade. The devout king had had no port from which to leave, so he had bought a stretch of coast here—a bit of land known as Psalmody—and built this town where he could provision his fleet. Six years later, the successful Crusaders returned, having won many a victory in the Holy Land.

A few years later, Louis heard that 17,000 Christians had been massacred at Antioch. Back he came here to Aigues-Mortes in 1270 to embark on another crusade. This time, however, fortune failed to smile. The ships had just reached Tunis when the plague broke out, and it was only a matter of days before Saint Louis himself was dead of it.

Tour de Constance (Constance Tower)

It was a grim sight, indeed, that greeted the prince of Beauvais when he came in the eighteenth century with government permission to free three —at the most four—of the Huguenot women who had been imprisoned here for their faith. When the door to their dungeon was opened and they caught sight of a new and gentle face, fourteen gaunt prisoners fell to their knees and wept with joy. One of them, fifty-year-old Marie Durand, had been kept here from the time she was eight.

The prince of Beauvais was speechless at the pathetic sight of the women. There was no way he could choose only four of them to rescue from their dungeon. And so he ordered the prison commandant to free all fourteen. When the government in Paris censured the prince for freeing so many, the prince replied that if the king willed, he could, of course, relieve him of all responsibility but the king could never relieve him of the heavy conscience that would have been his forever had he left any of those beseeching women behind.

AIX-EN-PROVENCE

Atelier Paul Cézanne (Avenue Paul Cézanne)

Life was not easy for the artist Paul Cézanne. His wealthy hat-manufacturer father disapproved of him. He had expected him to become an established member of the business community. When, instead, the son chose to paint, fathered an illegitimate child, and altogether seemed a useless citizen, his father cut his allowance drastically. That forced the painter to turn for support for his mistress and child to his boyhood chum, the writer Emile Zola. Not until 1886, when Cézanne was forty-seven, did his eighty-eight-year-old father die, leaving his son—at last—with money to live decently and to paint. And after that, Cézanne would come each day to this studio to work.

Mont Ste. Victoire

At the base of this mountain which the painter Cézanne (*see* Atelier Paul Cézanne) so loved to paint, the Roman general Marius in the second century B.C. killed some 100,000 Germans migrating here from the Baltic. Despite the Germans' far greater stature and strength, the Romans completely stopped their advance. Indeed, so distraught were the German women as they saw their men fall that they strangled their own children rather than see them captured, and then killed themselves. Ever since this has been known as "Victory Mountain."

ALSACE

When spring comes to this northeastern French province, eyes are inclined to turn skyward to see if the storks are coming back. For, for more than a century, this has been a favorite nesting place for these long-legged birds that are said to bring good fortune. Hundreds of them, year after year, have returned to their favorite half-timbered houses and red-tile roofs. Only lately have their numbers diminished, for in Africa, where the storks winter, hunters have been shooting them.

It is said that God, after creating the golden sun and the white clouds, the blossoms of the fruit trees and the blue sky, admired His handiwork one spring and decided to create a harbinger to tell the world when spring was on its way. He took the white blossoms of the fruit trees and let them float in the air, and He created the storks from them. He touched their beaks and their feet with the light of the sun and made those golden. Each March, His white birds brought the news that winter was ending, and warm days were en route. The storks nested in the peak-roofed houses and laid their eggs and raised their young. Then, when mid-August came, they flew away.

One spring, as they flew back over the fields, there were bodies everywhere, for this fertile valley that lies between the Vosges and Germany's Black Forest has been tugged back and forth between the two nations ever since the Franco-Prussian War of 1870.

The storks, legend has it, were so saddened to see dead and dying Alsatians on the battlefield that they flew to God and asked for a band of black on their wings, so they could be in perpetual mourning—a tale vividly demonstrating the Alsatians' special affinity for the bird that has become almost a mascot in this region of France.

AMBOISE

The Château

It was Palm Sunday, 1498, and the young Charles VIII took his wife, Anne, strolling in the garden he loved so well. Beauty was all-important to him, and much of what is beautiful here is beautiful because he made it so, hiring the finest of architects and the most talented of landscape gardeners to embellish his surroundings.

And on this Palm Sunday, the royal pair admired the ornamental terrace the king had had laid out and then proceeded to a tennis match that was being played in the castle moat. To enter, it was necessary to pass through a broken down old door (no longer standing), for Charles's builders had not yet repaired everything in the castle. Charles struck his head on the lintel, expressed understandable surprise and some pain, and went on to the matches with his queen. He watched them for some time, chatting about them. Then suddenly he fell backward unconscious. To discomfort him as little as possible, he was laid on a straw mattress near at hand rather than being carried back to his chambers. Three times as the afternoon progressed, the king briefly regained consciousness and spoke, but at 11:00 P.M., on the straw mattress in the moat, twenty-eight-year-old Charles VIII died.

•⚜•

The impetuous future Francis I, as a playful teen-ager early in the sixteenth century, made himself distinctly unpopular with the servants by letting a wild boar loose in this ancient castle that served as royal residence to many French kings. His hope—which was realized—was to prove his heroism by knifing the raging animal single-handed on the castle's great staircase.

❦

It was a sight terrible to behold, but the crowd reveled in it—the execution just below these castle walls on March 30, 1560, of fifty-seven Huguenot noblemen whose only crime had been seeking to ask fifteen-year-old Francis II to allow them to worship as they pleased.

As one by one the condemned mounted the block, they sang together: "The Lord be merciful unto us, and show the light of his countenance upon us, and give us peace," and, each time another head fell, the chorus was one weaker until the last tremulous voice praised God and was extinguished.

So the audience could be assured of seeing the event in all its bloodiness, tiers of seats were erected for the public, while on the wrought-iron balcony off the king's apartments, comfortable chairs were placed for the royal family. Neither the youthful king nor his bride, the Scottish princess Mary Stuart, it is said, looked with favor on the mass execution. The king averted his eyes as often as he could, and grew noticeably paler as the headsman continued his horrid work. But his firm-willed mother, Catherine de Médicis, was there beside him to see that he behaved with kinglike dignity. Afterward, she provided Francis and Mary with diversion by taking them horseback riding and to a fete at Chenonceaux. (*See* Bléré, Château of Chenonceaux.)

This bloodthirsty event, which ever since has haunted this otherwise lovely and beloved castle, was set in motion when a group of Protestants —Huguenots—wishing recognition for their faith and angered by the control of the Catholic Guise family over the court (two of the most powerful Guises were uncles to the young queen), decided to go to Blois where the Estates General was to convene. There, the plan was, they would overthrow the Guises and have them impeached. Then they would seek permission of the king, whom they had no plans to harm, to be allowed their faith. But a traitor to the Huguenot cause informed the Guises of the plot. Quickly, the court quit Blois and hastened to Amboise. The gates to the town were closed. Guards were stationed everywhere.

Turning their attention to Amboise, the Huguenots continued with their plot. They had a goodly complement of men—upward of one hundred— who were in readiness to attack if a simple request for the ouster of the Guises and for recognition of the Huguenot faith failed.

But nothing happened as it had been planned. The Guises' army went out to meet the Huguenots, attacked them, and dragged their prisoners back to the castle, many of them tied to horses' tails where they died en route. Ordinary townspeople became part of the reign of terror: some joined the Guises so they could steal the finery of the plotters; others were indiscrimately seized simply because they were Protestants and were hanged, mutilated, and thrown into the river. If they were suspected of being Huguenots, they were suspected of a part in the plot.

The slaughter went on for days. The grand finale was the execution fete that Catherine smilingly oversaw, keeping a sharp eye on her less iron-stomached son and daughter-in-law.

Clos Luce

Sixty-four-year-old Leonardo da Vinci came to this manor house in 1516, invited by Francis I to be his painter, engineer, and architect, and here he died in 1519—in the arms, some say, of the king.

The aging painter did his best to fulfill his obligation to the French monarch. They frequently talked together, and the king found great enjoyment in conversation with the learned artist. Leonardo is believed to have worked on plans for the châteaux of Amboise and Chambord (*see* Chambord, The Château), and he did some painting. But in 1517, his right hand was paralyzed with a stroke. He reputedly drew with his left hand and painted with his right. He tried valiantly to paint with his left, but it never quite worked as he wished it to, so he spent most of his time here on scientific studies, especially on his flying machine.

LES ANDELYS

Gaillard Castle

Richard the Lion-Hearted erected this masterpiece of military fortification, which is now one of Normandy's most beautiful ruins, in just one year—an astonishingly short period of time. Richard is reported to have said of it in 1197, after its completion, "How beautiful is my one-year-old daughter!"

ARLES

Place Lamartine

In La Civette Arlesienne which stood here until World War II, the painter Vincent van Gogh, in a fit of madness, cut off an ear. When he had managed to staunch the bleeding, he slipped the ear into an envelope, wrapped up his wounded head, topped it with a beret, and went to a neighborhood brothel where he left it for a young woman. Some days before, laughing at his large ears, she had proposed that he give her one as a Christmas present. For the next fortnight, Van Gogh was kept in an insane asylum. Then he was released; then hospitalized again. From then on, his sanity seemed to come and go.

AVIGNON

Palais des Papes (Papal Palace): LE CONCLAVE

It was being bruited about in the fourteenth century that beautiful Jeanne des Baux, the twenty-year-old countess of Provence and princess of Naples, had strangled her husband, Andrew of Hungary. The rumors distressed Jeanne, who had taken a new spouse, her cousin, Louis of Tarentum, and adored him; she wanted the gossiping ended and her marriage sanctioned so she and he could live together in peace.

Pope Clement VI found himself especially interested in her situation. About four decades earlier, when Rome was in civil turmoil, the French pope Boniface VIII had moved his capital here to Avignon. It had been just a temporary measure, but as it turned out, French pope had followed French pope, and it had seemed convenient to have the seat of the church here in Avignon. There was only one problem. Although, by this time, it looked as if the popes were going to be here for a while, they did not own this city where their handsome fortress-palace stood. It would be more convenient if they did, Clement reasoned.

When he heard of poor Jeanne's dilemma—her longing to be absolved of complicity in the death of Andrew—he let it be known that he would consider her case. And so, here she came, radiant, it is said, on a white horse and dreaming of absolution. The fatherly Clement readily gave it—on condition that, in exchange for a most nominal sum, she sell him this city of Avignon. Possession of it really mattered very little to Jeanne, anyway— it was Genoa that she wished to rule, and soon did. Meanwhile Clement at last had a home that was truly his own.

Pont St. Benézet (St. Benézet's Bridge)

To the bishop of this city in the Middle Ages, Benézet, a twelve-year-old shepherd from neighboring Viviers, came one day with a strange request. An angel, he said, had told him that a bridge should cross the Rhône at this point, and he had come to ask that it be built. The dumbfounded bishop, annoyed at being interrupted by the scrawny child, ordered a guard to take him away and punish him, but the child stood his ground. Christ had sent him, he said firmly to the guard. "Then prove it," said the guard, according to the ancient story, "by lifting this stone." The stone in question was thirteen feet long and seven feet wide; under normal circumstances, even thirty grown men would have had difficulty raising it. Murmuring a prayer, the shepherd boy knelt and carried it to the riverbank where the angel had told him the bridge should be built. Whereupon, guard, bishop, officials, and townspeople all fell to their knees, worshipping the child. They dubbed him a saint, and this bridge was built.

As the angel had predicted, the bridge did, indeed, bring prosperity and fame to Avignon. Soon merchants across the river preferred the bridge to ferrying their goods across the Rhône. And the canny officials of Avignon began charging tolls to those using it—tolls that quickly enriched the coffers here. Indeed, so important did this bridge, now in ruins, become that a nursery rhyme, "Sur le Pont d'Avignon," was written about it.

LES BAUX-DE-PROVENCE

In the fourteenth century, this hilltop village was a grim place indeed, for the brigands of Raymond de Turenne—the Scourge of Provence—scoured the neighboring countryside, kidnapping all for whom they thought a good price would be paid. And if it wasn't—with black-mustachioed Raymond looking on, laughing gleefully, the victim was tossed from the walls of this castle into oblivion. It was all a far cry from the previous century, when this had been a much-beloved gathering place for troubadours.

In 1632, Louis XIII's powerful cardinal, Richelieu, tired of having this village a stronghold of feudal lords, had it destroyed. But that was hardly the end of Les Baux-de-Provence. In 1822, the discovery of the mineral bauxite here—to which it has given its name—assured Les Baux of immortality.

BAYEUX

Ancien Évêché (Old Bishop's Palace) (opposite the Cathedral):
BAYEUX TAPESTRY

Fortunately, in 1792, when the churches and monasteries all over revolutionary France were being stripped of their religious heritage, an army officer, noticing that this embroidered linen strip that recounts William of Normandy's conquest of Britain was about to be used as a wagon cover, managed to save it from such an ignominious end.

BLÉRÉ

Château of Chenonceaux

When in 1526, Henry II acquired this splendid château as payment for back taxes, he immediately turned it over to his beloved Diane de Poitiers, who would be his mistress for twenty-three years. Although she was twenty years older than he, he remained devoted to her throughout his life and bestowed many administrative duties on her. (She is said to have been both beautiful and intelligent. At the age of sixty-seven she reportedly could have passed for a woman thirty years younger.) An energetic gardener, she spent much of her time among her plants and flowers, always in mourning clothes of black or white for her dead husband, Louis de Breze. The raising of silkworms became one of her special interests.

Alas, the sportive Henry's reign came to an untimely end when he was mortally wounded by a lance thrust through his eye in a jousting tournament. His long-suffering queen, Catherine de Médicis—as forceful a woman as Diane de Poitiers—wasted no time in evicting her competitor from this exquisite château.

◄◊►

Extravagant indeed were the celebrations Catherine de Médicis arranged here to keep the court a festive place, especially after the bloody executions at Amboise (*see* Amboise, Château of Amboise). To help her son Francis II and his teen-age bride Mary Stuart forget the death throes they had witnessed there, she brought them here to Chenonceaux where she had had a triumphal arch erected with the king's name emblazoned on it. Flags flew and drums sounded to greet the royal pair. The river Cher had been stocked with fish that—quite entering into the spirit of the fete—jumped and played, much to the amusement of the guests at the extravaganza.

Also erected for the festivities was a tower with sides of colored glass through which candlelight danced. The Queen Mother's *escadron volant,* her "flying squadron" of pretty girls, who accompanied her everywhere, were dressed as sea nymphs for the occasion and they kept the wine cups filled with the best of claret. To especially delight the king and his Scottish consort, a cascade of exquisite flowers, decorative leaves, and sonnets to their majesties were tossed down onto them from the balcony above the main gate to the castle. History does not say if the pale king, so wretched at the executions he had watched, felt cheerier, as his mother hoped he would, at the merriment she had prepared for him, but it would have been hard not to have enjoyed such spectacles.

Three years later, in 1565, this was the setting for another of Catherine's fashionable fetes. By then Francis was dead, and his brother Charles had become Charles IX. For this gala occasion, his mother dressed (or undressed) her "flying squadron," making them mermaids. On the edge of the moat they sat and welcomed guests with their songs and décolletage. And in the garden, more pretty girls posed as wood nymphs, hiding and giggling in the shrubbery till they were scattered by court gentlemen masquerading as satyrs.

There was even a mock naval engagement staged for the fifteen-year-old king's enjoyment and a boar hunt was so arranged that Charles—with no danger to himself—would give the death thrust. And for one of the first times in France, fireworks blazed in the sky.

But nine years later Charles was dead. Again, scarcely was the mourning over when Catherine had a fete arranged to honor her third son, Henry III. This time the king was clothed as a woman in a low-cut doublet with pearls around his neck as he greeted his guests. All around him were his *mignons,* the favorite men of his retinue, similarly garbed and powdered and perfumed. As for the flying squadron, they wore gentlemen's dress, but with their shoulders bare, covered only by their flowing locks.

For another sixteen years there were, on and off, extravaganzas here. Then Catherine died, and Henry, a few months later, died of wounds from an assassin's dagger. It was at this château, rich in so many happy memories, that his widow, Louise of Lorraine, learned the sad news. She draped her room in black and put on the white widow's weeds she was never to take off. Indeed, ever afterward, this gentle, heartbroken, charitable lady was known as "the White Queen."

BLOIS

The Château: FIRST FLOOR, FRANCIS I WING

For seven years, Marie de Médicis ruled as regent of France while her son, who would be Louis XIII, at first contentedly played childish games with his comrades. Louis was just nine when his father died, but when he was sixteen, it was time, he decided, to become king. He was aided and abetted in that desire by Charles d'Albert of Luynes, to whom the young king's father had entrusted him as a child so he could learn to hunt.

Between them, the young king and the aide plotted to kill the queen's favorite, Concino Concini, a Florentine to whom she entrusted many of the affairs of state. In 1617, they succeeded, and Louis could rule at last. Virtually his first act as ruler—to ensure that it would, indeed, be he who was king—was to send his mother to this château at Blois. He gave her these lovely first-floor rooms, but the king's friend, Luynes, made sure all exits from her apartment were guarded—all exits but the windows.

For two years, the queen's friends planned her escape. Admittedly, it was a hazardous one. The only escape route from which she could not be seen was a window on the north side of the château overlooking the town. In those days—happily for the queen—a terrace built from the ground below stood halfway up the château wall. But there were two considerable drops, to the terrace and below the terrace, if she were to get to safety. Middle-aged and plump, the queen peered out that window now and again in those last days before her escape, contemplating dangling from it on a rope ladder. But it was that or nothing.

On the day finally set for her departure, her maids tried to dissuade her from the escape attempt. Her enthusiasm seemed to be waning, till a co-conspirator arrived with the news that 300 armed men were awaiting her some distance away and had sworn their lifelong fealty to her. So honored, the queen looked back into her room; then out the window toward the town. And grimly, she asked her ladies-in-waiting to hoist her to the sill. Because of her size, it took a bit of doing to fit her through the window, but then down the first ladder she went.

By the time she had reached the terrace, she had had enough of flimsy rope ladders. She was not going any farther, she said, and plunked herself firmly down. Clearly there was no going back. It was essential to talk her into going on. But she was adamant. Finally the last half of the descent was made by seating her on a cloak on the terrace and pulling the cloak down a gulley that the rain had washed into the terrace's sloping side.

Once Marie reached the bottom, there was a short run to a waiting carriage. Halfway there the queen stopped short. She was missing a precious bundle, she said, and someone must go back for it. There on the street corner, the discussion went on—her rescuers warning that sending someone back might mean recapture. But Marie was as adamant about having her parcel as she had been about not descending the second ladder. So a runner was sent after it. As it turned out, he found the queen's packet in the street, and it was precious indeed. It contained the jewels that were to finance her and her fellow conspirators in the months to come.

The Château: SECOND FLOOR, FRANCIS I WING

It was a gruesome deed, even in a time of gruesome deeds—the murder of the duke of Guise, the lieutenant general of France—in the king's bed chamber here.

December 22, 1588, dawned cold and gloomy. Rain fell alternately with sleet. The Estates General had been summoned to meet the following morning at this château. Nervous, insecure Henry III had not wanted the meeting, but his powerful enemy the duke of Guise had insisted—500 councilors were to assemble, virtually all of them supporters of the duke, and thereby enemies of the crown, or so the king saw it. While the rain pelted this cold château, Henry paced and pondered. The Estates General, he felt sure, would depose him. The only way he would ever feel secure again was if there were no duke of Guise. And so he laid his plans that grim gray day. He explained them to twenty hired killers.

The following morning, the duke was summoned to the king's study. He had been warned before he arrived at Blois that he was in danger, but he had smiled and remarked on his hardihood and perennial good fortune. It is even said that when he was handed a warning note as he mounted the stairs toward the king's chambers, he simply crumpled it in his fingers and smiled assuringly. His assurance failed a little, however, when he noticed that the king's Scottish archers had closed in behind him on the stairs.

But he shrugged his shoulders and moved on. He warmed his back before the fire in the great council chamber and, not having breakfasted, he munched a few plums he found there in a comfit box and put the box with a few still in it into a pocket for later eating. His brother, the cardinal of Lorraine, and several members of the Estates General were already in the council chamber. An aide informed him that the king was ready to receive him in his old study. To reach it in those days required passing through the king's bed chamber, thence down a narrow corridor.

As the duke passed through the bedroom, he politely greeted eight of the king's armed henchmen, who simply seemed to be lounging there and chatting. On the duke went, down the corridor. Again, as on the stairs earlier, there were armed men behind him. And suddenly there were men ahead of him in the corridor, too—their swords and daggers drawn. Trying to return to the bedroom the duke found that it was the eight who had politely saluted him a moment before who were now behind him in the corridor, and advancing toward him as the group from the king's study was also advancing.

Strong as well as courageous, the duke of Guise was not about to die in the dim corridor squeezed between two bands of assassins. He tried to draw his sword but was encumbered by the cloak he had kept on because of the chill in the damp castle. And so, without arms, he fought off his attackers, struggling to get back out into the light of the bed chamber, struggling to get closer to his friends in the council chamber. Incredibly, he succeeded in knocking down several of his assailants; into the face of one he smashed the comfit box of plums he had carried with him for a snack.

Back to the bed chamber he struggled, flailing out this way and that. After him came the hired killers. Although, in the open bed chamber, the duke managed, at last, to draw his sword, it was too late. He had been stabbed too many times and fell, mortally wounded, at the foot of the king's bed.

A moment or two later, the hanging at the far end of the room moved, and the haggard king cautiously emerged.

"Is he dead? Is he dead?" he asked. Assured that he was, Henry was emboldened. He strode to the body of his rival, remarked on its size, and kicked the prostrate form.

Six months later, Henry, too, was dead, assassinated by a monk seeking to do away with tyrants.

CAEN

Abbaye aux Dames (Place Reine-Mathilde) and ***Abbaye aux Hommes*** (Place du Lycée)

Theirs was a stormy courtship—that of William the Conqueror, of Normandy, and his cousin, Matilda of Flanders. Reportedly, when William's emissaries sought her hand for their lord, she turned them down, vowing that she would prefer becoming a nun to marrying a bastard (*see* Falaise, The Château). Thereupon, William mounted his horse and galloped off to her father's castle in Lille to do his own wooing—albeit hardly in an acceptable manner. Forcing his way into her chambers, he grabbed the proud Matilda by her long hair, dragged her round the room, flung her to the floor, and beat her into submission. Politically wise though the the union was, the church was displeased because of the close blood tie between the royal pair, and they were excommunicated. It was only when they promised to build hospitals in Normandy's major towns—and this convent and this abbey—that they were reinstated in the church.

CALAIS

Monument to the Burghers of Calais (opposite Parc St. Pierre)

For eleven months, in 1346–47, Edward III of England blockaded and besieged this port, finally agreeing to lift the siege only if the six leading citizens of the town surrendered themselves to him with halters around their necks and put themselves totally at his disposal. The six burghers did. But for all their heroic offering of themselves, an angry Edward, tired after the months of siege, prepared to have them killed. Happily, his wife, Philippa, intervened, and the heroic burghers were saved. François Auguste Rodin memorialized them with this statue.

CANNES

In November 1834, an incensed Lord Brougham, chancellor of the exchequer of England, was stopped at the border between France and Sardinia and told that he could proceed no further. Cholera was widespread in Provence and every effort was being made to keep it out of Sardinia. No travelers who might be carrying it were allowed across the border.

What was holiday-bound Lord Brougham to do? He fussed and fumed to no avail. Then he went to Antibes.

In 1813, Napoleon had stayed for a time at a château there, and Brougham decided it might be inviting, but the price being asked for the house—because of the former emperor's stay—was exorbitant, and the residents of Antibes had learned of the English chancellor's interest and were not pleased. An official of the government of England in Napoleon's former house? They wouldn't hear of it! So Lord Brougham came here to Cannes—no posh resort then—simply a quiet fishing village. The longer he stayed, the more he liked it. Soon he had bought land and built a house, and was inviting his friends to his seaside paradise. Thanks to cholera and Lord Brougham, Cannes today is the star of the Riviera.

Île Ste.-Marguerite

To this little island one spring day in 1687 a boat came bearing a man in a sedan chair so draped with a black oilskin that the man could not be seen. The sedan chair was off-loaded by guards and for the next eleven years the mysterious stranger occupied one of the dank cells here. Never identified, always masked, he has become known in history as "the Man in the Iron Mask." (Accounts suggest, however, that the mask was of velvet, rather than

iron, and was worn not to prevent his being recognized, but because scars
had left his face so grotesque.)

Who was he? Clearly he was an aristocrat (*see* Maincy, Vaux-le-Vicomte).
Was he a twin brother of Louis XIV? Was he an indiscreet doctor who had
attended Louis XIII and gossiped that the king could not father children?
Was he Louis XIV's chancellor of the exchequer, maligned to the king and
so incarcerated here? And could the Man in the Iron Mask have been the
father of Napoleon Bonaparte? (According to this rumor the prison governor, to alleviate his high-born prisoner's loneliness, conducted a search for
a woman of quality to keep him company. And one came, and a child was
born of their union, and was sent to Corsica and became Napoleon I.)

The mysterious prisoner did not remain here forever, though. In 1698,
his warder, tired of this distant outpost, asked for a transfer to the Bastille
in Paris, and when he left, the Man in the Iron Mask left, too. It was in the
Bastille in 1705, still unidentified, that the illustrious prisoner died. Not
even in his final illness, it is said, was he unmasked. The doctor who treated
him remarked on the beautiful timbre of his voice, but he never laid eyes,
he admitted, on his patient's face.

CARCASSONE

During the Middle Ages, this walled city was besieged for five years by
troops of the emperor Charlemagne, for it was a Saracen stronghold. By
then, hundreds of inhabitants were dead—including the governor of the
city—and more, it was certain, would die soon if the siege continued. It was
then that the governor's widow, Carcas, hit on the plan that saved the city.

One pig and one sack of grain were the only foodstuffs left inside the city
walls, but Carcas ordered that the pig be fed the sack full of grain, and when
it was stuffed, she had the animal hurled from the battlements. Striking the
ground, the pig burst—and the grain it had been fed scattered before the
amazed Franks. How could it be that there was still so much food inside the
walled city that even the pigs were being fed on grain? Dumbfounded and
discouraged, Charlemagne's army prepared to retire. Just then a triumphant trumpet sounded from the battlements. *"Carcas sonne"* (Carcas calls)
the soldiers cried. And that is how, legend has it, this city acquired its name.

CHAMBORD

The Château

It gave every indication that it was a theatrical flop—even though Molière had written the play and Jean Baptiste Lully the music. Happily, Molière was sick, so at least it would be awhile before he would know about it. Louis XIV, for whom it had been written, and who was watching it in the little theater behind the staircase, was bored. He never laughed or smiled. Obediently, his courtiers, watching their liege lord attentively, followed suit. After awhile, it was more than Lully could stand.

Taking matters into his own hands, he leaped from the stage, on which he was playing a role, onto a harpsichord in the orchestra pit. He broke the harpsichord and the ice. The king, amused at the idiocy of the composer's action, began to laugh. His courtiers laughed with him. And then everyone began to enjoy the play, *Pourceaugac,* and the king remarked that it was the funniest play Molière had written.

CHARTRES

The Cathedral

It was an incredible feat: the construction of this towering cathedral in just twenty-five years in the twelfth and thirteenth centuries. A fire in 1194 had destroyed its predecessor, and it was important that the Virgin not be left long without a cathedral here in her honor. It was believed that this was where she wished her greatest cathedral to be. It had seemed that way to the early Christians when they found a statue to a pagan mother goddess here. And later, Charlemagne's grandson, Charles the Bold, had given a veil believed to have been the Blessed Virgin's to this church. There was no time to lose. The Cathedral at Chartres quickly had to be rebuilt. Those who had money gave it to help in the construction; those who had only strength of limb gave that. From all over France the builders and sculptors and stone-carvers and woodcarvers came to assist. It is even said that when they were short of animals to do the hauling, men yoked themselves in large numbers to blocks of stone so they could haul them here from the quarries more than six miles away. And by 1228 the new cathedral had been completed.

❦

When the sculptor Auguste Rodin first laid eyes on this magnificent Gothic cathedral, it is said, he swooned at the beauty of it.

LA CHÂTRE

Château de Nohant (4 miles north of La Châtre)

Everybody who was anybody visited George Sand at this ancestral home at one time or another in that novelist's life: her beloved Chopin and Franz Liszt, the writers Balzac and Théophile Gautier, Turgenev and Gustave Flaubert. At one festive occasion Flaubert was called upon to don a dancing-girl's costume and entertain the assembled company with a fandango.

Until midnight, George Sand would stay with her company—doing womanly things like embroidering. After that—in her later years when she had returned here after the exotic adventures of her youth—she would retire to her study to write until dawn.

CHAUMONT-SUR-LOIRE

Château of Chaumont

Dusk was falling that October day when the Queen Mother, Catherine de Médicis, fearful of the future, came here to the dark donjon room where her astrologer, Cosimo Ruggieri, plotted horoscopes and studied the heavens, stirred strange brews and produced medicaments. Only a few months widowed, she was frightened by the curious malady that had suddenly afflicted her son, the new king, Francis II. It had reddened his face and covered it with pustules. He was losing weight; his eyes had lost all luster. Surely Ruggieri could tell her what the future held.

The astrologer nodded and handed her the horoscopes for her four sons. The queen might have been pleased, but the mother gasped, for Ruggieri's horoscopes showed all four as kings of France, but all dying without offspring and two dead by violence.

The terrified Catherine asked what more might lie in store, and Ruggieri showed her to a mirror in his dark room. In it, he said, she would see the faces of the coming kings of France and how long each would reign.

The quivering Catherine looked. She saw Francis, her firstborn, pale and shadowy, and almost as soon as he was in the mirror, he was gone. Then came her secondborn, Charles. Thirteen and a half times he turned before her eyes. Then he was gone. Next Henry came and he spun fifteen times before he faded from his mother's sight. And next it was a son-in-law, Henry of Navarre, who crossed the mirror before her eyes. Twenty times he turned before her and was just beginning on his twenty-first when a little child appeared—Henry of Navarre's son Louis—and spun and spun.

Catherine could bear it no longer. She closed her eyes and turned away.

There was only one error in the astrologer's predictions: only three of Catherine's sons—not four—achieved the throne.

◆❀◆

Briefly, in 1810, when Napoleon ordered the critical woman of letters Madame de Staël to quit Paris and stay away, she came here with her children. But country living was never to her liking. She longed to be back in her beloved Paris and remarked that lovely though the countryside was, she missed her gutter in the Rue du Bac.

CHINON

Château de Milieu: RUINS

France was in a sad state, indeed, when Joan of Arc, the dark-haired peasant girl from Domrémy, came to Chinon to conduct Charles VII, king of Bourges, to a proper coronation at Reims as king of all of France. The English held the northern part of the country and much of the south, and Charles had taken refuge in the château with a few retainers.

Into the great hall the eighteen-year-old Maid was finally led after much interrogation one wintry evening in 1429. Fifty torches lit the room. Three hundred courtiers milled about in the flickering light, and Charles, ill-clad as was his wont, milled among them. He was the least likely one to be king —small, knock-kneed, ugly, unkempt, a large head on a small body. But in a trice, the country maid with the mission had singled him out and knelt at his feet. He swore he was not the king and pointed out a better-clad gentleman, but Joan remained prostrate at his feet. Finally, Charles acknowledged that he was, indeed, the dauphin whom she sought. The Maid begged a private audience. She said she had important information for him, and finally the skeptical dauphin acquiesced.

They drew aside and talked, and the dauphin's face lit up. Much later it was learned that Joan won Charles's acceptance by assuring him he was, indeed, the true king of France, for he had doubted it. His mother, Isabella of Bavaria, had led a questionable life with many men, and until Joan reassured him, it is said, Charles never was quite certain that he was the son of Charles VI. But, overwhelmed to be so reassured, the dauphin warmed toward the soft-voiced peasant maid. He ordered that she be lodged in the abutting Château du Cordray.

A few weeks later, after she had presented her plan to save the besieged

Orléans, and after further interrogations (*see* Poitiers, Palais de Justice), Charles gave her men to lead. Properly clad in armor, her white banner in her hand, she rode off with her troops to rout the English and fulfill the dauphin's—and Joan's—destiny. (*See* Reims, The Cathedral, and Rouen, Place du Vieux-Marché.)

COGNAC

For 400 years cognac has been distilled from the white wine of St. Emilion in this little village—ever since, so the story goes, le Chevalier de la Croix Marron (Chevalier of the Brown Cross) discovered in 1574 that his wife was unfaithful and killed her and her lover. Nightmares reportedly disturbed the murderer's sleep—dreams in which the chevalier was being burned twice in Hell for this misdeed. But, in time, his conscience bothered him no longer. Instead, he wondered what *other* meaning there might be to the double burning. Being a drinking man, the legend has it, the chevalier's thoughts turned to his brandy. Perhaps the nightmares were a suggestion that he should be distilling his brandy twice. And so he did. Thereafter cognac became the most renowned of all the brandies.

The brownish tinge on all the cognac storage buildings here results when the cognac, for which this town is famous, evaporates from its oak barrels during the distillation process. As much of the brandy evaporates each year as is exported to the United States. But the distillers never complain. Instead, they call the cognac that disappears into the air "the angels' share" and point out happily that more angels hover over this little town and guard it than over any other town in France.

COMPIÈGNE

The Château

The dauphin who would be Louis XVI shyly met his Austrian affianced, the princess Marie Antoinette, here in 1770. Indeed, it is said he was so shy he dared not raise his eyes to meet those of his pretty bride-to-be.

Napoleon was too impatient to wait at this appointed place to meet his second bride, the princess Marie Louise of Austria in March 1810, so he rode out—despite a driving rain—to greet her with affection. But it was here that the gentle teen-age princess and the emperor nearly twice her age —whom she had been reared to view as a monster, but grew to love— shared their first meal together.

Église St. Jacques

The devout Joan of Arc knelt here to receive communion in May 1430, the night before the capture in battle that led, almost exactly a year later, to her trial and execution for witchcraft. *(See* Rouen, Place du Vieux Marché.)

Forêt (Forest): CLARIÈRE DE L'ARMISTICE (6 miles north of Compiègne)

At 5:15 on the morning of November 11, 1918, the armistice ending the First World War was signed in the special railway car of French marshal Ferdinand Foch on a siding in this quiet glade.

In August 1940, an exuberant Adolf Hitler demanded a surrender from the French in the very same railway car in this same spot, and danced a jig with delight—so, at least, photographs of the event suggest. Then the railway car was proudly taken off to Berlin—a trophy of war—to be displayed. But its days of glory as a German trophy were short-lived. In an Allied air raid, it was bombed to bits. The railway car now on the siding here is a copy.

DUNKIRK

German General Karl Rudolf Gerd von Rundstedt saw no great need to push his men on without a pause for regrouping in those late May days of 1940. In three days, his Panzer tanks had traveled 300 miles to the English Channel. They could take their time pursuing the enemy up the coast. And in any case, the Luftwaffe wanted to play a role in vanquishing the Allied army. So the Panzers simply rested for seventy-two hours before heading north in an onslaught. It may have been those three days, war historians have since speculated, that made possible the miraculous rescue from Dunkirk.

The Allied troops had been pushed to the Channel. Their German attackers, but for the water, had them surrounded. But there *was* the water, and there was the gift of fog—as well as the efforts of courageous English ferryboat captains and fishermen and yachtsmen who undertook under cover of that fog, when the Luftwaffe had trouble seeing what they were bombing, to rescue 338,226 men and ferry them to safety in Britain across the Channel.

ÉPERNAY

Hautvilliers Abbey

It was here that the blind seventeenth-century monk, Dom Pérignon, blessed, it is said, with an especially sensitive palate in compensation for his blindness, skillfully blended the juices of Pinot Noir, Pinot Chardonnay, and Pinot Meunier grapes that grow in this chalky soil to make the finest of champagnes. Although there had been bubbly wine produced here before, none of it had the subtlety that the blind monk introduced.

And without Dom Perignon, there might never have been corks in French wine bottles. Until his day, bottles were plugged with wooden stoppers wrapped in oil-soaked hemp. Then two Spanish monks stopped here one night, and Dom Perignon discovered that corks were the stoppers of their water gourds. From then on, corks stopped champagne bottles and, eventually, all French wine bottles.

FALAISE

The Château

From one of this castle's windows, the young Norman duke, Robert le Diable, first glimpsed Arlette, the tanner's daughter, washing clothes in a stream—and, bedazzled, took her into his bed. And that first night, Arlette, mother of William the Conqueror, is said to have dreamed that from her body a giant tree would grow that would overshadow not only Normandy, but England as well.

FONTAINEBLEAU

The Château

Three major events in the life of Napoleon Bonaparte occurred in this—his favorite—château. Here the decree of divorce was pronounced, in 1809, separating him—as his need for an heir, not the dictates of his heart, instructed—from his beloved Josephine. Here on April 6, 1814, in the Salon Rouge, he signed his first abdication, and here, at the foot of the horseshoe-shape staircase in the White Horse Court he bade a moving farewell fourteen days later to his devoted guard before leaving for exile on Elba.

Hyères

It was in a chalet here called "La Solitude" that tubercular Robert Louis Stevenson learned that a book he had written and called *Treasure Island* was to be published. He had been sent here in the early 1880s by his physicians to profit from the fresh sea air. Later he wrote, "I was only happy once, that was at Hyères."

LOCHES

The Château

It seems incongruous, somehow, that this enormous, gloomy castle was the home of one of the most delicate and beautiful ladies of the fifteenth-century French court. The legendary loveliness of Agnès Sorel, beloved of Charles VII, and the first royal mistress to be acknowledged publicly, was matched by her intelligence. Her influence over the king was considerable. Although the king was something of a rake, he never ceased to love this lady-in-waiting of his queen. Agnès, in turn, urged Charles to restore the greatness of a France emerging from the crippling Hundred Years' War. At her behest in 1449, he set off to reconquer Normandy for his kingdom.

At the same time, Agnès readily accepted jewels and palaces (including the Château de Beauté sur Marne—a gift that gave this beauteous lady the title Dame de Beauté) even though funds in the national treasury were extremely low. So her attractiveness and charm notwithstanding, she was not popular with the people, and when, at twenty-eight, she died mysteriously, it was rumored that she had been poisoned on orders of the dauphin (who became Louis XI), who was jealous of her power over his father. Her black marble sarcophagus lies today in the New Dwelling here.

The Château: MARTELET

For eight years in the sixteenth century, Ludovico Sforza, duke of Milan and patron of the arts (particularly of Leonardo da Vinci), was held captive in the first of these dark dungeons by Louis XII. Louis insisted that he himself had a claim to the throne of Milan and, allied with the Venetians, readied for war against the duke. Before there was any combat, however, the duke was betrayed, captured, and carried here in one of the infamous cages for which this castle was notorious.

Even in prison, Ludovico's devotion to the arts did not desert him and he kept his sanity by painting the frescoes still to be seen on his cell's walls. But his physical health was a different matter, and on the day of his release, emerging from the darkness of this dungeon into the light, from excitement or illness—no one knows—the duke of Milan fell dead.

Another notable prisoner here—but one whose sojourn in captivity ended more happily—was the count of St. Vallier, father of Diane of Poitiers, who later became Henry II's mistress. (*See* Bléré, Château of Chenonceaux.) Accused of a plot against Henry's predecessor, Francis I, the count was confined to the dismal quarters here that are even below Sforza's. Though he denied his guilt, he was condemned to death, and it is said that on the eve of his execution, every hair on his head turned white. The count was led to the place of execution and mounted the scaffold. Only then did Francis I—at the pleading of Diane and her husband—issue a pardon. Victor Hugo commemorated the event in his play in verse, "Le Roi S'Amuse."

The Château: TOUR RONDE (Round Tower)

Guillaume de Haraucourt, bishop of Verdun, was indeed, "hoist on his own petard" here in the fifteenth century when, accused of a plot against the king, he was imprisoned in one of the eight-foot-square wood and iron cages he had, himself, gleefully designed as a means of punishment for prisoners. For fourteen years he was so confined. Some say these cages (others were kept in them, too) dangled from the ceiling, but that added fillip has never been confirmed.

LOURDES

One midwinter day in 1858, Bernadette Soubirous, the sickly fourteen-year-old daughter of a poor miller of Lourdes, was sent with one of her sisters and a friend to gather wood near the Grotto of Massabielle here. Suddenly a beautiful lady appeared before Marie. She was dressed in white with a blue sash and a golden rose on each of her bare feet, Marie, who was to become Saint Bernadette, reported.

On seventeen ensuing occasions Bernadette saw the lady, who eventually identified herself as the Virgin Mary. It was at their ninth meeting, which was witnessed by many curious neighbors, that the Virgin instructed the girl to scratch at the soil by one of the grotto rocks. Bernadette did as she was bidden. Suddenly water trickled from the earth. It is that trickle that is today's gushing spring beside the Basilique de Rosaire. To it more than a million pilgrims come annually from all parts of the world, hopeful of cures from its holy waters.

Bernadette herself entered a convent when she was twenty and lived there quietly. She suffered severely from asthma, but bore her affliction without complaint. She also quietly bore the skepticism of her convent sisters, and at thirty-five, she died. Her canonization, which took place in 1933, emphasized not her visions, but her deep faith and her long-suffering nature.

MÂCON

His wines, Claude Brosse knew, were exceptionally good—far too good not to be brought to the attention of the king. It was true it was 250-odd miles from this Burgundian market town to Paris, but it was time Louis XIV tasted his wine, so Brosse filled up his wagon with barrels of his best vintage and off he set for the capital. It was an arduous journey that took him a month, and when, at last, he reached Paris he was told the king was at Versailles. So on to Versailles he went. There, somehow, he managed an audience with Louis, offered him a sip of his crisp white wine, and the king—as Brosse could have predicted—wanted more. Ever since, Mâcon wines have been among France's favorites.

MAINCY

Vaux-le-Vicomte

Had he not seen this spacious château, an hour's drive today from Paris, Louis XIV might never have had Versailles built.

In the early days of his reign, he had as his superintendent of finances Nicholas Fouquet—charming, brilliant, attractive—patron of the arts, close friend of the fabulist La Fontaine, close friend of the prime minister, cardinal Mazarin.

While discharging his duties by keeping Louis XIV's royal coffers filled, Nicolas Fouquet is believed to have sometimes pocketed a little for himself. In any case, he thrived financially, and in 1656 he decided to build the handsomest house in France. To achieve this end, he hired the architect, Louis Le Vau; the decorator, Charles Le Brun; the landscape artist, André Lenôtre—all rising young men in their respective fields.

The sandstone château that they produced, set on terraces and surrounded by a moat, by statues and ponds and patterned walks, by a sweeping garden of clipped hedges and pruned trees was, indeed, and still is, a masterpiece of architecture. Fouquet was justly proud of it.

So, when the king's advisor, later finance minister, Jean-Baptiste Colbert, suggested that he have a party to show it off, and invite the king, Fouquet happily agreed. He did not know—or chose not to remember—that Colbert was no friend of his.

Graciously and gracefully, Fouquet planned his party and invited the court. Eagerly, the king came to the sumptuous banquet in the exquisite château. Three weeks later, the jealous king, infuriated that one of his "servants" was living more stylishly than he, sent the captain of his musketeers to arrest Fouquet.

For more than three years, Fouquet's trial on charges of embezzlement continued, and while it did, the king made plans for his own grand palace to outshine Vaux-le-Vicomte. Lenôtre, Le Brun, and Le Vau were to build his palace too. Fouquet was sentenced to life imprisonment.

And Versailles went up, its nucleus a favorite hunting lodge of the king. Inside, highlights included tapestries and furniture he had taken from Vaux-le-Vicomte. In the king's garden, orange trees from his former finance superintendent's effulgent gardens were planted.

Meanwhile, Fouquet languished. Where? Most of the time in the Fortress of Pignerol in the Savoy Alps. But some believe that he was the mysterious Man in the Iron Mask, imprisoned for a time on the lonely Ile Ste.-Marguerite off the shore from the city of Cannes. (*See* Cannes, Ile Ste.-Marguerite.)

MARSEILLE

Château d'If

Though the Count of Monte Cristo, who escaped this prison in a coffin, was purely a figment of novelist Alexandre Dumas's imagination, many a genuine prisoner has languished on this rocky island. Not the least of them was the stormy orator of the Revolution, Honoré Gabriel Riqueti, count de Mirabeau, sent here for assault and battery.

As the story goes, Mirabeau was attending a dinner party at his sister Louise's home in Grasse, when she told him that one of her neighbors, the baron de Villeneuve, had been speaking ill of her. Just at that moment, the baron himself happened to go for a stroll in his garden next door. Louise pointed him out and, being an outspoken woman, made it clear what she would do to him if she were a man. Taking the hint, Honoré quit the table, crossed to the baron's garden and went after him. The baron, fat and flabby and over fifty, was keeping cool under a parasol. The young defender of his sister's honor seized the parasol and belabored the baron with it, smashing his hat and giving him a nosebleed. As punishment Mirabeau was sent here for a time, but he was well cared for and even provided with an opportunity to seduce a guard's wife.

Vieux Port (Old Port)

It was unfortunate, surely, that there were cases of plague aboard the vessel from Syria that put in here in 1720, laden with goods that Marseille businessmen planned to sell at the Beaucaire trade fair. But in view of the money to be lost if the ship were not unloaded, the chance of the plague being brought ashore along with the goods just had to be taken, the businessmen said.

So the goods—and the fleas on them—went to the fair, and the plague visited Marseille and Aix and Arles and Toulon. At the height of the disease, 1,200 people a day died in Marseille; in two years, the population had been reduced by 50,000.

❧❀❧

In the rabbit warrens of this old part of the city, Underground activities flourished in World War II. The occupying Germans never knew who, in the narrow streets running up from the waterfront, was a black marketeer or a pimp or a plotter against the invaders, and so, in 1943, 40,000 residents of this area were moved out and the buildings they had inhabited for generations were blown up. The Germans said the destruction of the old city was "for health reasons."

MONTIGNAC

Mont-St.-Michel

To this rock promontory rising from the sea, the souls of the dead were brought by boat, the pre-Christian Celts believed.

❧❀❧

In 1064, Harold of England—either as an emissary from the court of Edward the Confessor, or simply on an outing across the English Channel—was driven ashore by a storm in unfriendly territory with some of his men. The French count on whose lands they landed held them for ransom—and it was William of Normandy who demanded, and received, the Englishman's release forthwith. Then the pair, who two years later would be arch-enemies in a battle for the throne of England, enjoyed each other's company. They hunted together; they applauded tournaments held in honor of Harold together, and, finally, William suggested that they be companions in a little foray against one of his enemies. So off they galloped toward this site, for the lord they were intent on fighting was just over the frontier in Brittany.

Well in advance of their men the pair rode. Suddenly there was a cry from behind them. Some of the Normans had been caught in the quicksand here. Harold turned, and was at the spot in a trice. Laying a long Norman shield on the sand, he crept out onto it and one by one pulled the sinking men out of the quicksand and to safety. His valiant rescue is depicted on the Bayeux Tapestry. (*See* Bayeux, Ancien Évêché, Bayeux Tapestry.)

During the 1880s speculators interested in land reclamation wanted to reclaim the land surrounding Mont-Saint-Michel by extending the polders all the way up to the island. But in 1884, the year before he died, Victor Hugo appealed to his countrymen that "Mont-Saint-Michel is for France what the Great Pyramid is for Egypt. It must be guarded from mutilation. It must remain an island. At whatever cost this double work of Nature and Art must be preserved." And so an association was formed to see to its preservation forever.

NANTES

The Protestant theologian John Knox was a galley slave here from 1547 to 1549.

From 6,000 to 9,000 suspected Royalists were sent to their deaths by drowning here during the revolutionary Reign of Terror. Although Nantes was generally in sympathy with the Republican cause, Jean Baptiste Carrier, the grossest and cruelest of men, was sent here to make absolutely sure that this city would be a Republican stronghold. And when the executioner operating the guillotine collapsed under Carrier's relentless orders, and shooting loyalist suspects seemed too time-consuming, Carrier devised the idea of *noyades* (drownings)—or "Republican Weddings"—in which pairs of alleged transgressors were stripped, tied together in pairs, and put aboard barges that were then scuttled midstream in the Loire. But in the end, his cruelty proved too much even for those who had hired Carrier and he, too, was felled by the executioner.

The Château

One of the most notorious (and perhaps most wronged) criminals in the history of France was burned at the stake here in 1440. Gilles de Rais, a baron, a devoted supporter and defender in battle of Joan of Arc, returned here to Brittany after the capture and execution of the Maid of Orleans. De Rais had extensive landholdings and increased them still more by marrying well. Then his life seemed to change. No longer was he the Spartan soldier. He lived lavishly, entertaining frequently, employing many servants. He decorated and redecorated his magnificent château and—his wealth notwithstanding—eventually went into debt. He tried to sell some of his lands. When he could not, he turned to alchemy. Surely, if he worked at it hard enough, he could transform base metals into gold.

But those efforts seemed to fail, too. And that was when de Rais allegedly began seeking the aid of the devil—and in those satanic pacts he was soon, so the story goes, sacrificing children. He reputedly murdered so many young girls—as many as 140—that he is said to have inspired the fairy tale of Bluebeard, murderer of many wives.

In time, he was brought before both an ecclesiastical and a civil court here; the former threatened excommunication unless he confessed to the crimes of which he was accused. Continually, he denied any evildoing. All the same, he was found guilty of heresy by the ecclesiastical court and of murder by the civil court and condemned to death.

Then, in the face of torture, de Rais confessed and repented. Indeed, in his day, his confession was touted as an outstanding example of Christian contrition. But his contrition did not cancel his death sentence. There are those, to this day, who insist that he was never fairly tried.

Maison de Guigny (3 Rue Mathelin-Rodier)

The duchess de Berry didn't like Louis Philippe and openly plotted against him. In 1832, her plotting took her here to Nantes where she thought to find friends and accomplices. But her whereabouts was revealed, and to this house government officials came in search of her. Although there was no sign of an occupant when they arrived, the officials decided to stay awhile. The house was cold. They lit a fire. In so doing they smoked the duchess out of the chimney where she had been hiding.

NICE

Among the famous English devotees of this resort city were Queen Victoria, who was a frequent visitor to the Hotel Excelsior, and the writer Tobias

Smollett. It was he, it is said, dwelling here in 1763, who wrote so invitingly of the therapeutic qualities of the sea that travelers began to swarm to Nice for their health.

Promenade des Anglais

The winter of 1822 was disastrous for the orange trees here. Ordinarily, they thrived, perfuming the air with their blossoms and fruit, but frost that year killed them, putting much of Nice's population out of work. To help alleviate the unemployment problem, the English residents here proposed —and financed—the construction of this lovely waterfront promenade.

NÎMES

Maison Carrée

How men have longed to possess this exquisite Roman temple built by Agrippa in 20 B.C.! An admiring Italian cardinal proposed that it be set in gold like a precious stone. Louis XIV's finance minister, Colbert, wanted it taken apart stone by stone and moved to the gardens at Versailles. Napoleon, too, was enamored of that idea.

Even Thomas Jefferson marveled at this building's simplicity and beauty. He acquired the plans for it, and they are reflected in his design for the Virginia State Capitol.

NORMANDY INVASION BEACHES

Dawn was just lightening the horizon here on June 6, 1944, when the first of some 200,000 Allied soldiers, sailors, and Coast Guardsmen waded onto this uninviting shore. Operation D-Day—the Allied invasion of war-torn Europe—was beginning. All that day, the flood of troops kept coming from the 5,000 barges, landing craft, troop transports, warships, and minesweepers assembled here. Before the operation was over, 6,603 Americans were dead, wounded, or captured; 946 Canadians; and some 3,000 British. But the beginning of the end of World War II had also come.

PAIMPONT

It was in the forest around this village in medieval days that the sorcerer Merlin and the enchantress Morgan le Fay were said to dwell, casting their spells in the depths of these dark woods that were then known as Brocé-liande. To witness the fury of a storm, to this day, it is said, the traveler need only splash a drop or two of water from the Fountain of Barenton onto Merlin's stone that lies below it.

Le Val Sans Retour (Valley of No Return) cuts through this forest and in its deep crevasse faithless lovers used to be lured by Morgan le Fay. Clear pools and lakes that some say are still enchanted shimmer here where the sun peeks through the trees. Many a hermit has worshipped God in these mystical surroundings and it was here, fending off wild boars in its thickets, that the fourteenth-century warrior Bertrand Du Guesclin developed the endurance and military sagacity that made him a terror to the English. Hiding in the bracken and behind the trees, he perfected the art of ambush.

It was to these woods, too, so the stories say, that the Holy Grail from which Christ sipped at the Last Supper was brought by Joseph of Ari-mathea, who had offered his tomb as Christ's burial place. And here King Arthur and the Knights of the Round Table came seeking—but never finding—that Holy Grail.

PARIS

Arc de Triomphe

In 1940, Adolf Hitler made his one visit to Paris. It was this monument—Napoleon's triumphal arch—that he ordered his driver to bring him first to see.

Basilique du Sacré-Coeur (Basilica of the Sacred Heart) (Montmartre)

Unlike most churches, which are conceived in thanksgiving to God, the Sacré-Coeur was built as an act of contrition by France, which had just lost the Franco-Prussian War so resoundingly that it caused Napoleon III to abdicate. The church was not opened until the end of another war, the First World War.

Champ-de-Mars

This beautiful formal garden was, in the days of revolutionary Paris, the site of the Festival of the Supreme Being. The festival was designed by the neoclassical painter Jacques-Louis David and organized by Maximilien de Robespierre, the leader of the second Committee of Public Safety and the instigator of the Reign of Terror. By establishing the worship of a supreme being, Robespierre attempted to foist his deism on his colleagues, many of whom were atheists.

Earnest in all things, Robespierre, originally a lawyer, had been appointed to a judgeship before the Revolution. But he'd resigned because —in those days—he was opposed to capital punishment!

Château de Bagatelle (St. Cloud)

So that Marie Antoinette might rest on her journeys between Paris and Versailles, her brother-in-law, the count of Artois, built this little pavilion for her in 1777. The count wagered that it could be built in a few weeks time, and so it was. It is said that when the queen thanked the count for his gift, he gallantly replied, "Madame, it is only a bagatelle." And so the Château de Bagatelle was christened.

Cité Berryer

This little mews filled with exquisite shops, tucked away just off the Rue Royale, is said to have been the site of the original stables of the Three Musketeers, renowned seventeenth-century fighters fictionalized and made popular by Alexandre Dumas *père*.

Comédie Française (Place du Théâtre-Français)

On February 17, 1673, Molière was playing the title role in his own play, *Le Malade Imaginaire*, when he suddenly collapsed. Some tales say he died on stage, some that he was taken to his home around the corner at 40 rue de Richelieu, and died there. He was fifty-one years old. The chair he was sitting in as he spoke his last lines is still in the foyer of this theater.

Concièrgerie (Quai de l'Horloge)

A last-ditch attempt to rescue Marie Antoinette from this final place of imprisonment failed because of the queen's ingenuousness. The plot had been hatched by a young adventurer who talked the director of prisons into taking him on a tour of the prison facilities one day. When they reached the queen's cell, the adventurer dropped inside it a carnation carrying details about his escape plan. He whispered to the queen that when he was gone she should retrieve the flower. Marie Antoinette managed that and even—skillfully—pin-pricked a reply onto a scrap of paper. But then she made her fatal mistake. She asked her guard—for the love of God—to deliver her pin-pricked note to the man who had visited her cell. That was the end of any escape plan. Alexandre Dumas wrote *Le Chevalier de Maison Rouge* about it.

Les Deux Magots (170 Boulevard St. Germain)

The eccentric nineteenth-century satirist Alfred Jarry is said to have pulled a pistol out of his pocket here one day and shot at the mirror on the wall directly opposite a woman who had been staring into it. Then he reportedly said, "Now that the mirror is gone, can we talk to each other?"

Fouquet's (Champs-Elysées)

An example of the extravagance of the aristocracy of the nineteenth century's Belle Époque: the duchess de Gramont used to buy fresh trout from the tank at this restaurant and take them to the zoo at the Botanical Garden to feed the seals.

Harry's Bar (5 Rue Danou)

A favorite watering hole for American expatriates for decades, this is also the birthplace of many a famous cocktail. The first Bloody Mary is said to have been stirred up here in 1921, the first Side Car in 1931, while the Black Velvet and the White Lady were reportedly the best-loved drinks of composer George Gershwin. It was bartender Harry MacElhone who shook up these immortal concoctions. Other notable habitués were F. Scott Fitzgerald, who gulped martinis here, and Ernest Hemingway, who liked to talk of sports. In more recent years, the philosopher Jean Paul Sartre was among its customers.

Hôtel d'Alsace (13 Rue des Beaux Arts)

Exclaiming against the flowers on his wallpaper, the poet Oscar Wilde died here in poverty and disgrace in 1900.

Hôtel des Invalides

Into the underground arsenal that was here in 1789, when this was a home for the wounded, stormed a riotous rebel mob bound for the Bastille on the morning of July 14. When they left, they had with them 28,000 rifles, with which they took the infamous political prison. (*See* Paris, Place de la Bastille.)

◆❖◆

Napoleon Bonaparte's body lay in the Chapel of St. Jerome here for more than twenty years before his magnificent tomb was completed in 1861. Part of the reason for the delay was the decision to carve the tomb from red porphyry, the stone used for Roman imperial tombs. It took six years just to find it—in Karelia in Russia—and another three to finish the work. He now rests in his guardsman's uniform inside six coffins. Near him is his son, *l'Aiglon* (the Eaglet) who died in Vienna at the age of twenty-one. Adolf Hitler returned his body here as a gesture to France in 1940.

Hôtel de Sens (Rue de l'Hôtel de Ville)

From a window here, fifty-two-year-old Marguerite de Valois, divorced by Henry IV in favor of Marie de Médicis, watched one young lover killed for having killed another.

The middle-aged former queen, for whom Henry had supplied this dwelling, was being helped from her carriage by her eighteen-year-old page (and lover) when an earlier wooer of her affections set upon and killed his successor. Marguerite was both heartbroken and in a rage and demanded of the king swift retribution. He granted it and the next morning Marguerite watched the execution that was held on the very spot where her youthful page had been slain.

Hôtel de Ville (Place de Hôtel de Ville)

To the Hôtel de Ville that preceded this structure, the revolutionary leader Maximilien de Robespierre fled with a number of his fellows as his Reign of Terror was drawing to an end in 1794. Attackers pursued them, throwing one adherent out a window, frightening two others into jumping, a third into committing suicide, and shooting Robespierre himself in the jaw. The jaw remained dangling grotesquely until he lost his head the following day, July 28, on the guillotine to which he had sent so many. (*See* Paris, Place de la Concorde).

Jardin des Plantes (Botanical Garden) (Left Bank end of the Pont Austerlitz)

During the short reign of Charles X (1824–30), the nation received a most memorable gift from Egypt—the first giraffe ever to be seen on French soil. It walked all the way to Paris from Marseille, accompanied by the French army. Its arrival here at the Botanical Gardens created such a stir that in no time there were giraffe china patterns, giraffe wallpaper, giraffe jewelry, clocks, boxes, songs, and even a giraffe flu epidemic. That was in 1827. No one knows what became of the giraffe, but by 1870 all the animals of the zoo had been eaten by local citizens whose supplies had been cut off in the Prussian siege of Paris during the Franco-Prussian War.

The Louvre

In 1750, the Louvre was in such poor condition that Louis XV wanted to tear it down. In the seventy years since Louis XIV had moved the whole court to Versailles, the old palace had become a slum, filled with squatters. Fortunately, Enguerrand de Marigny, the brother of the king's mistress, the marquise de Pompadour, talked the king out of it, expelled the ragpickers and itinerants, and had it cleaned up. By the time Louis XVI took it over, the building was in good enough condition for him to put some of the royal art collection on display and to open it formally to the public.

◆◈◆

Nobody could believe it. On August 11, 1911, Leonardo's *Mona Lisa* disappeared from this museum. Surely it had been misplaced, taken out to be cleaned, not stolen. It was inconceivable that the *Mona Lisa* was actually gone. But it was gone. And for the next twenty-seven months, though French police scurried everywhere pursuing clues, interrogating workmen, following suspects, there was no sign of the lady with the enigmatic smile.

And then one November morning in 1913 in Florence, the art dealer Alfredo Geri found a letter on his desk from Paris. Its writer described himself as an Italian patriot who felt that since the *Mona Lisa* was an Italian painting, it belonged in Italy. It was in his possession, he said, and he would like—for a sum—to bring it back. Geri thought the story unlikely, but felt it would do no harm to take a look at whatever it was the letter writer might have to show. And so he wrote back suggesting that "Leonard," as the writer called himself, come to Florence with the painting.

Much to Geri's surprise Leonard did. They met in Leonard's hotel room and from a box under his bed he drew forth what, indeed, proved to be the missing *Mona Lisa.* As the story unfolded, it turned out that the thief, actually named Vincenzo Perugia, was a housepainter who had worked at the Louvre. He had also assisted in putting the famous painting under glass at a time when officials felt that was the best way to preserve it. At that time, he had studied how it was hung and discovered how simple it would be to remove it. And so, one day in his workman's clothes, he entered the Salon Carre where the *Mona Lisa* was then kept, took it from the wall, removed its frame, and hid it under his long workman's blouse. His plan all along, he said, was to return it to Florence. Under questioning, however, it turned out his motives were not purely patriotic. The money he was asking for it was not a minor sum, and Perugia had a criminal record.

Briefly, the painting Francis I had bought for France in the sixteenth century was exhibited in Florence, Milan, and Rome. Then it was returned here to the Louvre. As for Perugia, he spent seven months in jail for his "patriotism."

Luxembourg Gardens

Having decided to leave journalism behind and instead try to support his family by selling stories, Ernest Hemingway fell upon hard times. During one very lean Paris winter, Hemingway decided to fend off starvation by eating pigeons that he found in these gardens. Every afternoon at four, he discovered, the gendarme on duty would disappear into a café for a glass of wine. It was easy enough for Hemingway the hunter to lure his unsuspecting prey—all it required was a pocketful of corn. He would snatch up the birds and twist their necks with one deft movement, then toss them under a blanket in his son Bumby's baby carriage, and take them home for cooking.

La Madeleine (Rue Royale)

Because Frédéric Chopin had wanted Mozart's Requiem to be played at his funeral, it took nearly a fortnight after his death on October 17, 1849, to have the burial. Women's voices were essential for the piece and the archbishop of Paris refused to allow them to participate in the service. Not until the end of the month did he relent. Meanwhile, Chopin's body rested in one of the vaults here, and the 3,000 invitations that were to go out to the event could not be sent.

Montmartre

Legend has it that this hill—the Martyrs' Mount—was the site of the beheading in the third century of Saint Denis, the first bishop of Paris. But the decapitated bishop somehow managed to retrieve his head and, carrying it under his arm, walk as far as the suburb of St. Denis, where he finally collapsed and was buried.

Notre-Dame (Île de la Cité)

In this great Gothic cathedral, completed in the middle of the thirteenth century, the coronation of Napoleon as emperor took place on December 2, 1804. It was perhaps the most elaborate spectacle ever staged in Notre-Dame. Napoleon's sisters, Maria Anna Elissa, Maria Paulina, and Maria Carolina, resented their brother's wife Josephine bitterly and refused to carry her train, until the emperor himself intervened. After Napoleon and Josephine entered the cathedral, the graceful Josephine discovered that she could no longer walk; the Bonaparte sisters were standing on the train! The procession was put in motion again, however, with one stern glance from Napoleon.

Thanks to Napoleon Bonaparte this great Gothic cathedral still stands today, for it came close to demolition shortly after the Revolution. Briefly, it had enjoyed a moment of revolutionary glory as a Temple of Reason, with the high altar used as a stage for a live Goddess of Reason, one Mademoiselle Maillard, a dancer from an opera troupe. But soon the church was sacked, inside and out, the gutted building used for storage; finally it was sold to a local contractor for building material. Fortunately, Napoleon needed someplace to receive the pope at his own coronation as emperor, so he took the building back for the government in 1804. The cathedral remained in a sad state of repair, however, until the 1820s, when twenty-nine-year-old Victor Hugo wrote his novel *Notre-Dame-de-Paris* about it, and piqued public—and eventually government—interest in its restoration.

Palais Royale

The spendthrift duke of Orléans, Philippe-Égalité, had these covered colonnades of shops and cafés built in 1781 around his palace in hopes that renting them would get him out of debt.

Palais Royale: 57–60 GALERIE MONTPENSIER

On July 12, 1789, the fiery orator Camille Desmoulins leaped to a tabletop outside the Café Foy that then stood here and urged revolt against Louis XVI. He tore leaves from the tree above his head and pressed them as badges on those who endorsed his cause. And so the French Revolution, to which so many thousands—including the fiery orator himself—were to fall victim, was born.

Panthéon (Rue Soufflot)

Built as a church in 1789, the Panthéon has been secularized and then reconsecrated many times. In 1791, when the revolutionary statesman Honoré Gabriel Riqueti, count de Mirabeau died and his admirers were considering appropriate places to have him buried, they hit upon this structure that had been built two years earlier as a church dedicated to Paris's patron saint Geneviève. Already, with the onset of the Revolution, it had ceased to be a church. And so it became a burial place for this nation's great. For that first funeral here, a crowd of more than 400,000, led by Lafayette, assembled to pay their respects and to lay the body to rest in the sepulcher by candlelight while stirring music played.

But that was not the end of the matter. Mirabeau remained at rest here only two years; then correspondence he had had with Louis XVI was unearthed that suggested he had tried to aid the monarchy. The furious

Republicans had him disinterred, and, where his bones had lain, those of the bloodthirsty revolutionary leader Jean Paul Marat (see Paris, Rue de l'École de Médecine) were put instead. But not for long. Two months later, Marat was in disfavor, and his remains went to a common grave.

Also interred with much pomp were the writers Rousseau and Voltaire. But, like Mirabeau and Marat, they were not to lie undisturbed. When the monarchy was restored and the Panthéon again sanctified, they were removed. The finishing touch in Napoleon III's day was the request by the archbishop of Paris to remove even the tombs that had held the two writers' remains, because, he told Napoleon III, they made his devout flock uncomfortable since both men had been atheists.

"Come now," Napoleon III is said to have replied, "how do you think those atheists felt in the presence of your believers?"

Père Lachaise Cemetery (northeast Paris)

When, in the nineteenth century, an enterprising Paris prefect sought to make this a popular cemetery, he did it by having the remains of four notables moved here with great fanfare. The playwright Molière, the fabulist Jean de La Fontaine, and the star-crossed lovers Héloïse and Abelard were the four selected to bring this cemetery up in the world. And with what success! It is said that the upper middle-class Parisian of that century had a single desire for the years after death: "To nourish the same vegetation that those immortals nourished."

Place de la Bastille

On this site stood the infamous political prison whose storming on July 14, 1789, marked the start of the French Revolution. But much to the surprise of the attackers, the only inmates whom they found to free were four counterfeiters, two madmen, and a count whose family had asked to have him imprisoned for an unspecified crime.

◀☙▶

One of the last of the many famous political prisoners to be held here was the mysterious Man in the Iron Mask. He had been imprisoned for many years on Ste.-Marguerite, one of the Îles de Lérins, off the coast at Cannes (*see* Cannes, Îles Ste.-Marguerite), and when that prison's governor became the governor of the Bastille, he brought his most important prisoner with him. They arrived in Paris in the same carriage—the prisoner's face covered with a black velvet mask. The guard who accompanied them remained at the Bastille as personal servant and jailer to the masked man for five years, until the prisoner, his identity still a mystery, died.

Place de la Concorde

What joys have been celebrated and what sorrows suffered on this hand-some seventeen-acre square. On May 30, 1770, the marriage of the dauphin who became Louis XVI to the Austrian princess, Marie Antoinette, was cause for a fireworks festival that brought thousands to watch. (But even then it was the site of death; several rockets went awry, and fleeing onlook-ers trampled each other.)

Twenty-three years later, it was the setting for the execution of the very pair whose wedding the fireworks had announced. On January 21, 1793, Louis XVI was guillotined where the Obelisk of Luxor now stands. On October 16, Marie Antoinette met her death on the same spot. Altogether, between the guillotining of the king in 1793 and May 3, 1795, when the guillotine stopped its work here, more than 2,800 men and women perished. It is said that by the end of this period the carnage had been so great that oxen refused to cross the square because of the odor of the blood.

After the revolution, it was proposed that a fountain be erected to the memory of the martyred king exactly where the guillotine had stood, and the square was renamed for him. But the idea of the fountain came to nothing, the novelist François René de Chateaubriand remarking that it would be most inappropriate—that no amount of water could wash away the bloodstains on this terrible place.

Time healed even those wounds, and there was festivity here again in 1836 when the Obelisk of Luxor, a gift from the khedive of Egypt, Mo-hammed Ali, to Louis Philippe was set in place. It had been over two years in transit—from the Temple of Luxor, where it had stood, to the Nile; then 600 miles down the Nile to the Mediterranean, then to the Atlantic. The story of its journey is recounted on its pedestal. More than 200,000 people eager to see it at last after its long travels attended its inauguration, the horrors of the Revolution long forgotten.

Place Vendôme: THE COLUMN

Many have been the vicissitudes of this column that Napoleon had fash-ioned after Trajan's column and decorated with bronze from cannons cap-tured from the Russians and Austrians at Austerlitz.

In the beginning, a statue of Napoleon dressed like a Roman emperor crowned it, but that was knocked down by Royalists; in its place Louis XVIII had a giant fleur-de-lis put up. Then when Louis Philippe became king, he restored Napoleon—but dressed him this time, more properly, in soldier's uniform.

The next turn was Napoleon III's. He preferred his uncle back in the Roman emperor attire. And then there was the Commune of 1871, which knocked the whole column down. (Among the organizers of that venture was the painter Gustave Courbet, who ended up in prison for it.) Not until 1875 did the column rise again—this time to stay. Once more a Caesar-like Napoleon was on top.

Pont-Neuf (New Bridge)

Restored many times, the "new bridge," finished in 1607, is the oldest of the bridges of Paris. In its heyday, it was a busy place, indeed, and tradition had it that one could not cross it without meeting a soldier, a white horse, and a woman of the streets. For a time, booksellers plied their trade here, but the previously established booksellers on the Île de la Cité angrily forced them out—to the bookstalls along the Left Bank of the Seine where ever since they have carried on their business.

Le Procope (13 Rue de l'Ancienne-Comédie)

The patrons of this seventeenth-century café, reputedly the oldest in the world, have surely been a widely assorted lot. In the eighteenth century, the revolutionary leader Georges Jacques Danton and the philosophers Denis Diderot and Voltaire frequented it; in the nineteenth, its devotées included the poet Paul Verlaine and the decadent J. K. Huysmans. And Napoleon Bonaparte is said to have left a hat here, which is still to be seen, kept under glass.

Quai de New-York

Along the quay here, in what was formerly the village of Chaillot, Robert Fulton first demonstrated his steamboat in 1803. The first time the steamboat was floated, Napoleon scoffed and refused to look at it.

Quai Voltaire

This riverside street is named after its most famous inhabitant. Voltaire lived here, at number 24, both before and after his thirty-year exile from Paris. When he returned to his house at the age of eighty-four, he threw himself into the production of his last play, *Irène,* which was such a success that on its opening night the entire Quai was illuminated to welcome him home from the theater, and a boisterous parade of admirers accompanied him back across the Pont Royal to his home. He died there just a few weeks later, on May 30, 1778. (*See* Paris, Panthéon.)

Other well-known residents of the gracious homes along the Quai were the painters Delacroix, Corot, and Ingres. Ingres died at number 11. At number 19, Baudelaire wrote *Les Fleurs du Mal* in 1857, and Wagner, *Die Meistersinger von Nürnberg* in 1867.

Rue de l'École de Médecine (Street of the School of Medicine)

It was in a first-floor apartment here, when this was the Rue des Cordeliers, that the pretty Norman, Charlotte Corday, stabbed Jean Paul Marat, doctor, journalist, and revolutionary firebrand, one hot July night in 1793. The dedicated young woman assumed that the death of the great exponent of revolutionary death and destruction would mean an end to the death and destruction, too. And so she had written a letter to Marat, begging an audience and telling him she had secrets to impart that would help the cause of the Republic. When she arrived, she was ushered in to see him in the special bath he sat in almost constantly to relieve the painful skin condition he had acquired hiding in the city sewers.

She was not long about her business. Scarcely had she been left alone with him when there was a cry, and Marat's common-law wife, hurrying to see what was the matter, found blood gushing from his chest and the papers on which he had been working (he used his tub as an office, too) blood-soaked. While she tried to staunch the flow of blood, Charlotte Corday left the apartment but was stopped at the door, questioned, carried off to prison, and put to death on the guillotine (*see* Paris, Place de la Concorde). Unhappily, instead of ending the Revolution with her brave act, she made her victim a martyr and heightened the fury of the Republicans.

The Sorbonne

There were many acts of heroism at this university during World War II, but none quite equaled the theft by Resistance members of the records of 3,000 law school students slated for labor service in the Third Reich. Into the Paris sewers the records went.

La Tour Eiffel (The Eiffel Tower) (Champ de Mars)

The whole world was agog when this tower was inaugurated in 1889, and many a prince and potentate came to the celebration. Among them was the Shah of Persia, Nasser Addin, who had never seen an elevator before. Too skeptical to try it, he preferred to climb to the top on foot, followed by his retinue.

Then there was the courageous mayor of Montmartre, who made his impression by speeding down from the first level on his bicycle. Many romantic young couples launched love notes attached to balloons, from the tower's upper reaches, and one of these, it is reported, ended up in a Hungarian potato field.

Versailles: GALERIE DES GLACES (Gallery of Mirrors)

It was in this magnificent room of gleaming mirrors and windows that the Treaty of Versailles, ending the First World War, was signed on June 28, 1919.

Versailles: LE PETIT TRIANON

This miniature palace was a favorite hideaway for both Louis XVI and his queen, Marie Antoinette, to whom he gave it, and she liked to perform in the pretty theater here. In the English garden outside was the queen's "village" of country cottages where she amused herself raising chickens and churning butter.

POITIERS

Palais de Justice

Priests and archbishops, university professors and the dauphin's mother-in-law all rigorously examined Joan of Arc here to see if she was in the employ of God or of Satan.

Though the dauphin was well disposed toward her (*see* Chinon, Château de Milieu), her enemies still insisted that she be interrogated by churchmen before she was given an army to help free Orléans from British siege. Harshly quizzed, she answered straightforwardly and impressed her interrogators with her honesty. But then the accusers questioned her virginity. Only a virgin would have been approached by God, they insisted, and demanded that her virginity be attested to. This task was given to the dauphin's mother-in-law, who quickly assured all that Joan was indeed a maid. So approved, she was finally given the army for which she had begged.

REIMS

The Cathedral

Joan of Arc had two dreams: to see the dauphin Charles crowned Charles VII (*see* Chinon, Château de Milieu), and to drive the English from her native land. Here, on July 17, 1429, she accomplished that first goal, for Charles was crowned, and Joan fell to her knees at her king's feet and wept for joy.

La Salle du Guerre (War Room) (12 Rue Franklin Roosevelt)

In this map-lined room where Gen. Dwight D. Eisenhower had his head-quarters, the army of Germany capitulated on May 7, 1945, and World War II in Europe was over.

RENNES

Lycée Emile Zola (Avenue Janvier)

It was a dramatic event, indeed. Here on August 7, 1899, Alfred Dreyfus, a Jewish officer in the French army, imprisoned for life on Devil's Island on charges of passing military secrets to the Germans, went on trial for a second time.

Since the first trial years before, Dreyfus's case had become a liberal cause célèbre. The officer had always insisted on his innocence, but he was Jewish and a native of Alsace, which had been annexed by Germany in 1871. Though Dreyfus had quit Alsace then, there were many who murmured that, of course, his sympathies were German.

The matter had all begun when an unsigned note promising military secrets to Germany was found in the wastepaper basket of the German military attaché in Paris. The secrets promised could only have been known by a high-ranking member of the army. As it turned out, Dreyfus's hand-writing resembled that on the note, and he was arrested. The minister of war insisted that the army's good name must be cleared. And so it was— trying Dreyfus without allowing his lawyer to see all the data the army had accumulated in his case. Dreyfus was condemned to a life sentence.

But then it was discovered that another officer's handwriting also resem-bled that on the note. The news got out. Public opinion forced the army to try the second officer. Officials remained convinced of Dreyfus's guilt, however, and the trial of the second man was largely a farce. He was acquitted.

Incensed by what he considered the injustice of it all, the novelist Émile Zola took up the cause for Dreyfus. In a soon-famous letter in a newspaper he accused the army of having imprisoned an innocent man and having let a traitor go free.

In the aftermath of it all, one French intelligence officer committed suicide; the officer tried and acquitted fled the country. The army had no choice but to bring Dreyfus back from his imprisonment for the second trial that was held here.

Again, he was found guilty—but there were extenuating circumstances, it was also found, and he was offered a presidential pardon. A few years later, further evidence indicated his innocence, and Alfred Dreyfus was reinstated in the army, from which he retired as a lieutenant colonel after serving in World War I.

ROUEN

Place du Vieux Marché

Only six days after her trial was ended, and she had been condemned to life imprisonment, Joan of Arc was burned at the stake here. The English wanted it that way, for it was safer to have the inspiring Maid who had given France a king (*see* Chinon, Château de Milieu and Reims, The Cathedral) dead than alive. After the life sentence was given, Joan was issued a suit of men's clothes to wear in prison. She had promised to dress decorously in women's garb but since she had none, clearly she had no choice. And when she had to go outdoors to relieve herself, she was accused of having broken her word. Forthwith, on May 30, 1431, she was brought here and burned alive at the stake. When her heart would not burn in the licking flames, the nervous English shuddered and pondered whether they would be damned for having assisted in the killing of a saint.

ST.-GERMAIN-EN-LAYE

Château de Malmaison (9 miles west of Paris)

At this pretty château where Josephine raised roses, Napoleon said he was happier than any other place.

ST.-PAUL-DE-VENCE

Le Colombe d'Or

When hungry painters came to this Riviera inn in the 1920s, there was always food for them, even if they had no money to pay—Utrillo, Braque, Matisse were among the artists who came here and ate, and left paintings on the walls instead of francs on the table. By 1955, the walls of this little inn were rich in early twentieth-century French art. And then, one night in 1960 twenty of the paintings were gone.

No one really knows what happened next. Some theorize that Francis

Roux, this café's owner, after a tip from an unidentified caller, paid a ransom to get the paintings back. In any case, all but one were recovered from the baggage room of the Marseille railway station a little less than a year after their disappearance.

ST.-RAPHAËL

Pyramid on Avenue Commandant-Guilbaud

On October 9, 1799, a victorious Napoleon landed here after his conquest in Egypt. All along the shore the ebullient crowd gathered to hail their hero. It mattered not at all that he might be carrying the plague—much of his army had been felled by it, many men had been left behind. All the same, the crowd pressed toward him, wishing to hail him and touch him.

Fifteen years later, on April 28, 1814, it was a considerably less jubilant Napoleon Bonaparte who came here, accompanied by British, Austrian, Prussian, and Russian generals, who put him aboard a British frigate and sent him into exile on Elba. Exile, yes, but that did not prevent the military men whom he had defeated over those fifteen years from honoring him for his great military prowess. Hats in hand, they bade him adieu. And the British frigate he was to board welcomed him with a twenty-one-gun salute.

STRASBOURG

Banque de France (4 Place Broglie)

On this site, Rouget de Lisle, the composer of the French national anthem, was born in 1758. He grew up dabbling with poetry and playing the violin. When the Revolution broke out, he joined the army, and on the night of April 24, 1792, he was at a farewell party that the mayor of Strasbourg was giving for the volunteers leaving for military service. It was too bad, the mayor was exclaiming, that there was no inspiring song to urge the soldiers on. Turning to Rouget de Lisle, he asked why he, since he was both a poet and musician, didn't write one.

That night was a sleepless one for the young officer. There were no snores from his bed chamber. Instead, notes issued from his violin, and by the time the sun arose, he had both words and music for a song. He woke a companion and sang his composition. Recognizing its quality, his listener urged—despite the early hour—that they present the piece to the mayor. The mayor, delighted at what he heard, roused his niece from her bed to play the tune on the piano. It was only a matter of days before it was the marching song of the Revolution.

The night before the volunteers from Marseille were to leave the city to join the revolutionary forces in Paris in 1792, they were feted at a banquet. The marching song just composed with revolutionary fervor by Rouget de Lisle of Strasbourg was sung as encouragement for them. The volunteers liked what they heard, and the next day, as they set off for the capital, they sang it with enthusiasm. From then on, wherever they made a stop, they entertained townspeople with the song, and by the time they reached Paris were an accomplished choir. They sang with such gusto that Rouget de Lisle's song—which was to become the national anthem—was named "La Marseillaise" in honor of the Marseille volunteers who sang it so well.

The Cathedral

The poet Goethe, who suffered from vertigo, regularly forced himself to climb to the top of this 470-foot church tower when he was a student here. Across the street, in the thirteenth-century apothecary shop—the oldest in France—whose facade writhes with dragons and salamanders, Goethe learned of herbs and poisons from the old druggist. Was he thinking of *Faust* even then?

Despite its associations with Goethe, despite the fact that it is an exquisite example of medieval architecture, this soaring cathedral spire was marked for destruction in the anticlerical days of the Revolution. But a locksmith saved it by perching a red Phrygian bonnet—the sign of the Republicans —on its tip, thereby turning it into a symbol of the Revolution.

TOULON

Darse Vielle (Old Port)

In the seventeenth century, when Louis XIV and Cardinal Richelieu contrived to make this city an important naval base, the galley slaves who manned the vessels became a major tourist attraction. Ordinary criminals, political and religious prisoners were condemned to the galleys. One leg was chained to the deck, one wrist to an oar—and even when they were eating, the pitiful prisoners remained shackled to their posts.

❦

November 27, 1942, was a grim day in this port, for sixty French ships were scuttled by their crews to prevent their falling into German hands.

VAUCLUSE

It was on a knoll in this pretty village that the poet Petrarch, exiled from his native Florence on political grounds, met golden-haired Laura one Good Friday morning in the fourteenth century. Dressed in green, with violets at her breast, her hair tumbled provocatively by the breeze, Laura quite bewitched the young Florentine. From then on, though their love was never consummated, she was the source of meaning in his life, his inspiration.

VERDUN-SUR-MEUSE

Two million Frenchmen and Germans fought on this World War I battlefield from February to December 1916, in what has been called the bloodiest battle in all history. A determined Crown Prince Frederick William commanded the German troops. An equally determined Henri Philippe Pétain was in charge of the Allies, and firmly said of the attacking Germans, "They shall not pass." They didn't, though by December, when the French could claim a victory, one million of the two million soldiers who had fought here were dead.

Germany

AUGSBURG ❧ ————

To the Fugger family of Augsburg in the sixteenth century, the Hapsburg emperors Maximilian I and Charles V often sheepishly sent notes to request loans for their far-flung enterprises. In those days the Fuggers, who began making their money in the weaving trade and then became mine owners and traders in spices and wool and silk, were the wealthiest family in the world —five times as rich as Italy's Medicis. It was the Fuggers who invented the system of payment by check that still is in use today. In the original Hotel Drei Mohren (Three Moors Hotel) that was replaced by a modern structure in 1956, checks of the years 1513 through 1517 written by the emperor Maximilian were burned by Jakob Fugger in exchange for an unspecified royal honor.

Fuggerei (Kappeneck)

Here poor, respectable Catholic Franz Mozart, the great grandfather of Wolfgang Amadeus Mozart, was granted a house for a pittance in the seventeenth century, when no one was seeking him out any longer as a stonemason. To this day, for about a dollar a year, indigent, married, respectable Catholics are provided with dwellings in the Fuggerei—as long as they promise to pray for the souls of the Fugger family, who built these homes for the poor.

Rotes Tor (The Red Gate)

At the open air theater at the foot of this seventeenth-century tower, the works of native son Bertholt Brecht are frequently performed. In his lifetime, however, his avant-garde writings were looked at askance by most townspeople—especially those who remembered (and liked to gossip about) how, as a child, he had received failing grades in school.

Schaezlerpalais (Schaezler Palace) (Maximilian Strasse)

This palace where, today, Mozart Festival concerts are given in summer, was built to receive Austria's unlucky Princess Marie Antoinette when she was en route to France to marry Louis XVI and—ultimately—to lose her head on the guillotine. (*See* France, Paris, Place de la Concorde.)

BADEN-BADEN

To this fashionable spa in the Black Forest Feodor Dostoevski came in 1867. He had recently married the young stenographer to whom he had dictated *The Gambler*. She was pregnant; he was irritable. The combination drove him to the city's vast casino where he squandered money at the gaming tables.

Brahmshaus (5 Maximilianstrasse)

For ten summers, Johannes Brahms lived in two attic rooms in this little wooden cottage. His *German Requiem* and his First Symphony were both composed here. A devoted admirer, close friend, and—some suggest—lover of Clara Schumann, Brahms kept her company here where she came to recover with her children from her composer-husband Robert's anguished death after years of madness.

Lichtentaler Allee

Along this elegant promenade in the nineteenth century, Queen Victoria of England, Napoleon III and the empress Eugénie, the Russian writers Turgenev and Dostoevski, the composers Brahms and Liszt and Berlioz strolled and rode in their carriages. Here, Edward, the Prince of Wales, draped in white sheets, rode to a costume party where he was playing ghost. An imaginative horse breeder frequently traveled the Lichtentaler Allee in a cart pulled by billy goats. There was even one famous escapade in which an English duke, on a bet, tugged a calf on a blue ribbon leash along the promenade. A less happy event here was the attempted assassination in 1861 of William I, the king of Prussia.

BAMBERG

A visitor here in 1439 was so impressed with the quantity of beer consumed by the city's 4,000 residents that he made a survey of their annual consumption of that beverage and found that it was 460 quarts per capita. The fondness for brew seems to have continued down through the ages. Today there are twelve Bamberg breweries for 75,000 people.

Altenburg (outskirts)

In the little pavilion in the garden of the former bishop's palace here, E.T.A. Hoffmann, nineteenth century composer, opera director, and writer, is said to have languished in a love he never revealed for a sixteen-year-old music pupil, Julia Mare, and to have written some of his most compelling tales—perhaps one of the three adopted by Offenbach for *Tales of Hoffmann*?

BAYREUTH

Festspielhaus (Festival Theater)

When this theater—a life-long dream of Richard Wagner—was opened with a performance of *Das Rheingold* on August 13, 1875, the emperor was in the audience, along with composers from all over Europe—Saint-Saëns, Grieg, Rubinstein, Gounod, Tchaikovsky. Not all of them liked what they heard. Tchaikovsky remarked that the omelettes and baked potatoes and cutlets served were more interesting than Wagner's music; and the first festival was a financial failure, closing with a deficit of about $30,000. It remained closed until 1882, when it was the site of the world premiere of *Parsifal*.

Opernhaus (Opera House)

It was this gem of a baroque opera house with its unusually deep stage that inspired Richard Wagner to build his great festival theater (Festspielhaus) in Bayreuth. The Opernhaus was built between 1745 and 1748 by Wilhelmina, favorite sister of Frederick the Great, with the cooperation of her husband, the margrave of Brandenburg-Bayreuth.

Wilhelmina's marriage to the margrave had an unusual background. As an unhappy young prince, her brother Frederick had attempted to run away to England, and had been caught and imprisoned by their tyrannical father, Frederick William I. (As part of the punishment, prior to the imprisonment, the youthful Frederick was held to a window and forced to watch the execution of the best friend who had encouraged the running-away plan.)

To rescue her brother, Wilhelmina struck a bargain with their father: she would marry the man he had chosen for her—the kindly, but dull margrave —in exchange for Frederick's freedom.

For whatever else their marriage lacked Wilhelmina and the margrave shared a love of culture. He let her build the pretty little theater just as she wished it; act in it herself; paint; compose music; and encourage the arts among others as well as enjoying them herself.

Wahnfried (between the Hofgarten and Richard-Wagner-Strasse)

When he discovered Bayreuth, he had at last found the perfect place to live and work, Richard Wagner told his patron, Louis II of Bavaria (*see* Munich,

Bayerische Staatsoper), as he wrote to solicit financial support not only for a festival theater but for the erection of this dwelling place. As usual, Louis responded affirmatively to Wagner's request for money, and the composer got both the house and the opera house he wanted. Superintending house construction proved more than Wagner had bargained for, and midway through construction the composer began, angrily, to call this *Ärgersheim*— "Home of Annoyance." By the time it was finished, however, he was feeling considerably happier about it, and gave it its present name, *Wahnfried,* "Peace from Delusion." Here he completed *Die Götterdämmerung* and wrote most of *Parsifal.*

♦❀♦

There are those who say that it was Adolf Hitler's warm reception here in 1923 by Richard Wagner's widow, Cosima; son, Siegfried; English-born daughter-in-law, Winifred; and English son-in-law, Houston Stewart Chamberlain that convinced him that he was, indeed, a messiah. Hitler had long revered the music and the memory of Wagner. The fact that Wagner's family revered him, too, gave increased assurance to his thoughts and his actions.

BERCHTESGADEN

The emperor Barbarossa and his knights lay in a cave in the mountains here in an enchanted sleep, it was believed in the Middle Ages. When they awoke, they would bring peace and prosperity to Germany. But it was not Barbarossa who stirred in these mountains in this century, as students of Hitler note. It was, instead, Adolf Hitler, the apostle of death and destruction.

Adlerhorst (The Eagle's Nest) (Obersalzberg)

Hitler henchman Martin Bormann had this mountaintop retreat—now a teahouse—built for his master's fiftieth birthday. To assure that it would be a safe retreat, it could be reached only through a 124-foot-long tunnel at the end of which was an elevator that went the 124 yards up to the mountaintop. As it turned out, however, Hitler rarely visited Adlerhorst—perhaps no more than half a dozen times—for he found the air too thin for him. Most of his time in Berchtesgaden was spent in his chalet, Berghof, farther down the mountain.

BERLIN

Brandenburger Tor (Brandenburg Gate)

When Napoleon Bonaparte invaded Prussia in the early years of the nineteenth century, he took away with him to Paris the ten-ton bronze figure of Victory in her two-wheeled chariot pulled by four horses that adorns the top of this triumphal arch. He proudly set it up on the Place du Carrousel near the Tuileries. There it remained until Napoleon's defeat, after which, in 1814, it was returned here. But when it was reinstalled, it was turned around. Though the reinstallation preceded the division of Berlin into East and West by much more than a century, Victory, returned from France, was set to face Unter den Linden which is, today, the main thoroughfare of East Berlin rather than West Berlin's Tiergarten, which it had previously faced.

World War II brought about a second change in the famous bronze when, because of extensive bomb damage, the figure had to be recast. The work was not done until 1958, at which time there was a divided Berlin, and the Communist government of the East saw fit to remove both the Iron Cross and the eagle from the hand of Victory.

Charlottenburg Castle

In 1695 the humpbacked Frederick I of Prussia built this little castle, designed to resemble Versailles, in order to please his wife, Queen Sophia-Charlotte. Here she fostered the arts and the sciences while he, in red high-heeled shoes to make him taller, and wearing the long wig fashioned to hide his hump, sought to introduce French ways and the French language to the court.

But Francophilia died when, a little more than a century later, another queen, Louise, wife of Frederick William III, urged her husband to end his alliance with that "monster" Napoleon and ally himself instead with handsome Czar Alexander of Russia. Both a beautiful woman and a dedicated patriot, she was much beloved, and all Prussia suffered with her when, in an 1807 peace settlement with France, Napoleon made Prussia give up all land west of the Elbe, and endure other indignities. Louise went to visit him to see if she could make him change his mind, but her efforts failed. She returned to Charlottenburg Castle weary and discouraged, and died a few years later at the age of thirty-four.

◆❁◆

From an upper window of this palace, the fifty-six-year old Prussian crown prince Frederick William, about to be crowned Frederick III, sadly looked out on the funeral cortege of his father, Kaiser William I, as it passed by in 1888 en route to the family mausoleum, the Chopin "Funeral March" sounding. Suffering from cancer of the larynx, Frederick William was too ill to join the procession himself—and too ill to live more than ninety-nine days after his own coronation.

Charlottenburg Castle: STATUE OF THE GREAT ELECTOR

This equestrian statue, regarded by many as among the world's finest statues of a man on a horse, survived World War II without incident, for it was moved away from this site. It was when it was on its way back by boat from its safe hiding place that it almost didn't make it. The horse and rider were crossing Tegel Lake in 1948 when the boat carrying them capsized. It was two years before divers managed to retrieve the statue from the bottom of the lake.

Former Ministry of War (Stauffenbergstrasse)

This memorial stone marks the spot where Lieutenant-Colonel Claus Philip Schenk, count von Stauffenberg, and three fellow army officers, were shot in 1944 for their efforts to assassinate Adolf Hitler (*see* Berlin, Plötzensee Prison). As the order to fire was given, Stauffenberg, drawing to attention, cried out, "Long live our sacred Germany!" This street, formerly named Bendlerstrasse, has been renamed in his honor.

Kurfürstendamm

In the sixteenth century, this was a wooded path that the elector Joachim II took to get to his hunting lodge in Grunewald Forest. In 1870, when it had become a narrow sand road, the chancellor Otto von Bismarck rode horseback here in his dark blue coat with its yellow military collar, his sword at his side. But by 1872, Bismarck had decided that a growing Berlin needed a widened roadway that would accommodate carriages and pedestrians as well as equestrians. So soon the Kurfürstendamm began to have a new look and become fashionable. Coffeehouses sprang up along both sides of it. Thomas Wolfe was among the writers who often passed time in them, when he visited Berlin between the wars.

Plötzensee Prison (Gedenkstätte von Plötzensee)

In this prison, about one hundred German army officers were hanged in 1944 by order of the Fuehrer after an attempt to assassinate him in his forest retreat, Wolf's Lair, in East Prussia, had failed.

    Claus Philip Schenk, the count von Stauffenberg, a cavalry officer fearful of the future for a Germany under Hitler, had decided getting rid of

Hitler was worth the sacrifice of his own life. A number of other army officers agreed with him. And so on July 20, 1944, the count carried a briefcase with two time bombs in it when he went to a meeting with Hitler. Setting the bombs to go off in ten minutes, he left the briefcase on the floor near the table where Hitler sat, and excused himself to answer a telephone call. Five minutes were left before the bomb would explode.

But in those five minutes, the briefcase was moved—not because it was suspect, just because it was in the way. The result was that it was others, not Hitler, who suffered the consequences of its detonation. The explosion rocked the room. Four men died of its effects; three others were injured. But the only damage to the Fuehrer were a few leg burns, a burn on one arm, punctured eardrums, and a scratch on one hand. Stauffenberg, meanwhile, had seen the puffs of smoke emerging from the conference room and was en route to the air base at Rangsdorf to report Hitler dead to his fellow conspirators. By nightfall, Stauffenberg himself was dead—shot after a brief court-martial, along with three fellow officers (*see* Berlin, Former Ministry of War). And then the retribution began. In the ensuing weeks, 2,000 were sentenced to death for having had a part in the conspiracy—or because they were believed to have had a part. Hitler ordered the prime conspirators hanged at Plötzensee. Today, the hall where they were executed is a memorial to them.

Reichstag (Parliament)

No sooner had Adolf Hitler become chancellor in 1933 than he declared that the opposition Communist party would not be tolerated in Germany. Twenty-seven days later the nighttime Berlin sky glowed red with flames leaping from the dome of this seat of government. Clearly, Hitler and his henchmen said, the fire that destroyed the Reichstag's interior was the start of a Communist uprising which must be squelched. So that night, 1,000 Communist leaders were arrested and imprisoned. Within ensuing weeks, nearly 3,000 more Communists were hunted down. No longer did Adolf Hitler have opposition.

The necessary scapegoat was a twenty-four-year-old, almost blind, insane Dutchman named Marinus van der Lubbe, who was found wandering in the neighborhood of the burned-out Reichstag. Accused of being the one who actually had set the fire, poor van der Lubbe—too crazy to be able to defend himself—was executed. Two others were imprisoned. But before a decade had passed, Hitler's sidekick, Hermann Göring, was proudly admitting his own responsibility for the fire and applauding the ingenious way he had managed to get rid of the Communists.

Schöneberger Rathaus (Schöneberg Town Hall)

To help bygones really become bygones, seventeen million American citizens contributed toward this Freedom Bell that was given to Berlin in 1950.

Tiergarten

From behind the trees of this 412-acre park laid out with ponds and streams and bridges, gunfire frequently rang out during the long years of World War II. Soldiers' boots trampled the rose gardens. And even peace brought no beauty back to the Tiergarten. The winter of 1945–46 was bitterly cold with a shortage of coal, so shivering Berliners chopped down the Tiergarten trees for firewood. Not until 1949 did the Tiergarten begin to revive, when a million young shrubs were planted here.

BLACK FOREST

Schoenwald

It is said that it was the bellows working the church organ here that inspired Franz Anton Ketterer in the seventeenth century to invent the cuckoo clock mechanism. Two other Black Foresters are credited with having thought of adding the bird song.

BONN

Beethoven's Birthplace (20 Bonngasse)

This house where Ludwig van Beethoven was born and lived until he was four was saved from destruction in World War II when the caretaker, Heinrich Hasselbach, seeing that incendiary bombs had fallen on its roof, climbed onto it and knocked them off.

BREMEN

Dom (Cathedral Crypt)

Five centuries ago a workman from a nearby town fell to his death from this cathedral's roof. His fellow workers laid him to rest in an underground storeroom where they kept stained glass. Although they wrote to tell his family of their loss, they never received a reply and the workman's body was forgotten in the rarely used stained glass cellar.

Some years later a workman of an entirely new crew went to the cellar on an errand. He came running back pale and shuddering. In the cellar, he told his co-workers, there lay a body of a man.

On further inspection, it turned out to be the body of the workman out of the past—perfectly preserved. No one then—or now—is quite sure why. Some speculate that the lead of the cathedral roof is the answer; others that there are subterranean uranium deposits here. In any case, today there are more than three dozen mummified bodies in the cellar. After that first body was found, for a time it became the practice to put in this crypt unclaimed bodies of strangers who died in Bremen.

COLOGNE

On the banks of the Rhine River here the British princess Ursula, who became Saint Ursula, is said to have perished in the fourth century.

Betrothed by her father to a heathen prince, the Christian Ursula begged leave, before the marriage, to go to Rome on pilgrimage. In hopes of converting him, she asked to take her fiancé along with the entourage, too. The group (the ancient figures vary and can be read to suggest either 11 or 11,000 companions) arrived safely at Rome and were returning when the fleet of vessels was set upon by barbarian Huns. When Ursula shunned the advances of their king, he and his men plundered the ships and murdered their passengers. Suddenly the sky was awhir with angel wings (though a bit too late) and the Huns were driven off. The grateful people of Cologne, delighted to be rid of the barbarian attackers themselves, buried Ursula and her retinue, including the prince (the records do not say if he had succumbed to conversion), in a field here that is now the Cemetery of Eigelstein. Then they built St. Ursula's Church to honor the princess and her friends. In the seventeenth century, the bones of the martyrs were unearthed and put in the church's Golden Chamber as decoration. Also honoring them are the eleven flames that leap as part of the coat of arms of this city, and the many paintings of this martyrdom.

·✖·

Back in 1709 when it was invented, citrony Eau de Cologne, the product that surely has given this city international renown, wasn't a toiletry at all, but a patent medicine. When quaffed, it was said, it prevented corns, heart-ache, childbed fever, and bad breath. Made 86 percent of alcohol, it could be drunk diluted in water or in broth. What ill it cured depended on the quantity consumed. It was so valuable—or at least so popular—that by the end of the eighteenth century, there were 114 firms here producing it. The original Eau de Cologne was invented by an Italian resident here, a chemist named Giovanni-Maria Farina. When his aqua mirabilis became such a rage, one of his imitators sent an emissary to Italy to bring back anyone he could find named Farina, so his firm, too, could use the great "Farina" name on its labels.

When Napoleon occupied Cologne in the first decade of the nineteenth century, he demanded a list of all medicines produced in the city and their ingredients, but no producer of Eau de Cologne (called *Kolnisch wasser* at that time) wanted his secret formula known. Wilhelm Muhlens, for example, a merchant who was making a great success of his water, asserted that his recipe had been a wedding gift from a Carthusian monk. He certainly was not going to pass on a monk's secret to the conqueror. So Napoleon forbade the production of the "magic medicine." Not about to be outsmarted, its producers quickly dubbed it a "refreshing water" rather than a tonic and kept on selling it.

It was in Napoleon's day, too, that it acquired the name by which it is still known today. Since German street names were difficult for the French to pronounce, they gave each house in the city a number. It was in No. 4711 (the site today of the Eau de Cologne Museum) that the Muhlens firm made its fragrant, refreshing water. "Eau de Cologne," of course, was the French translation of the German *Kolnisch wasser*.

Among the most distinguished users of Eau de Cologne No. 4711 was Queen Victoria of England. "Though she never drank alcohol," Cologne residents gossip, "she ordered great quantities of 4711."

Seven firms here still make the "original" 4711, and the formula—now as then—remains a secret (all but the name of one ingredient—bitter orange). Is it still safe to drink? No one says, but certainly when it is rubbed in one's palms and held to the nose, a sniff of it clears the head and keeps the faint from fainting.

Church of the Antonites (Schildergasse)

The bronze figure of the Angel of Death here was first cast for the Cathedral of Güstrow in north Germany in 1927. The angel's features were those of the graphic artist and sculptor Käthe Kollwitz (1867–1945), champion of the oppressed; the sculptor was Ernst Barlach. Within ten years, however, the Angel was dubbed degenerate art, removed from the cathedral, and melted down. But a second casting secretly made from the original had been buried, survived the war, and was installed here.

Dom (Cathedral)

In the thirteenth century, when this edifice was started, it was to be the largest cathedral in the world. (Today, it has been outstripped by St. Peter's in Rome and St. John the Divine in New York.) It was built to shelter the remains of the Three Magi after they had been taken from a church in Milan by the emperor Frederick Barbarossa.

For three centuries work on it continued. Then the money ran out, and in the three centuries that followed, while work was at a standstill, the plans, as originally conceived, disappeared. No one knew if there would ever really be a great Cologne cathedral.

In the late eighteenth century, the monies to proceed with the building were acquired, but where were the plans?

One day a Cologne antiquarian, visiting in Darmstadt, was watching his hostess lay out peas and beans to dry on an old sheet of paper she kept for that purpose. Lines on the paper caught the antiquarian's eye. He squinted and moved closer. They were the outlines of towers. He moved closer still. The towers were surely those of Cologne Cathedral. The paper, it turned out, contained a major part of the original plans. The rest, after a search, were located in Paris. So by 1800, 600 years after work on it had begun, the lacy spires, the hunched gargoyles, the sculpted saints and virgins were, at last, in place. During World War II it was badly damaged in the bombing raids—but survived.

One night in 1975, a slender, dextrous thief slid through the air shaft into the cathedral's vault and stole what many consider the richest collection of ecclesiastical treasures in Europe. Thirteen hours after the theft, three men —two Yugoslavs and an Italian—were questioned about the crime. They disclaimed any knowledge of the incident, and since no stolen goods were found with them they could not be held.

A year later, however, one of the three—the mastermind of the project, Ljubomir Ernst—was arrested on new evidence. It turned out he had boasted of his plan to rob the church to a fellow inmate at Zurich Prison where he had served time on a stamp-stealing charge. This time, Ernst admitted the theft and told authorities that many of the treasures had been taken apart and sold piece by piece. Some of these have since been found and returned. Others are still being sought. Meanwhile, Ernst and his accomplices are serving prison terms.

Roman-Germanic Museum

The virtually intact Sepulcher of Publicius, a Roman legionnaire of A.D. 50, was unearthed after the end of World War II by a family seeking to expand its shirt-and-tie shop. The teen-age sons of the shop's proprietor were working on the addition in the cellar when they dug away rubble, and the statue of Publicius stood before them. The two youths hurried to the newly founded Roman-Germanic Museum to report their find. The curator scoffed and said obviously what they had found was nineteenth-century art nouveau, not ancient art. He urged them to forget any further excavation, leave the statue where it was, and get on with the shop expansion.

The youths were disappointed but not discouraged. They went on with their excavating, and in time, the entire sepulcher was revealed. Scorned as they had been by the Roman-Germanic Museum, the two young men opened the cellar of the family shop to the public, for a fee, and showed off their discovery by flashlight. Ultimately, the museum curator, too, came to take a look and was forced to admit that he had made a mistake. The funeral temple was then removed to its present site.

Sternengasse

The world of art and music owes much to this little street. Here Peter Paul Rubens lived as a boy in a house that stood where the telecommunications center now soars. It was an art collector, Everhard II Jabach, who also lived here, who commissioned from Rubens the painting of the crucifixion of Saint Peter that now hangs in the parish church that bears the apostle's name. Jabach's son, Everhard III, an art collector like his father, and ultimately director of the Aubusson tapestry works in France, spent so much on his personal collecting that he went bankrupt, and the art with which he was forced to part became the start of the Louvre in Paris.

And finally, it was at the Schuhmachergaffelhaus that once stood on this street that seven-year-old Ludwig van Beethoven gave his first public concert, on March 26, 1778.

DINKELSBÜHL

It was the gatekeeper's little girl, Lore, who saved this town from angry Swedish soldiers in the Thirty Years' War.

For days, the Protestant Swedes had been besieging the Catholic village of Dinkelsbühl. They had lost more men and munitions than anticipated as the valiant citizens fought to defend their town. But finally, there was no choice but surrender.

The Swedes, angry at their losses, wanted revenge, and their commander ordered his men to destroy Dinkelsbühl. As pillaging began, little Lore gathered her young friends together and they marched to the Swedish camp to beg that their homes not be burned, their belongings stolen.

The commander, who had a child of his own at home, heeded their tearful pleas and spared Dinkelsbühl. And the grateful townspeople feted the children afterward, giving them as much to eat and to drink as they could hold. Annually since 1897, the children's saving of Dinkelsbühl has been reenacted with much fanfare here each July.

DÜSSELDORF

In a fit of deep depression, Robert Schumann threw himself off a bridge into the Rhine here in 1852. The week before his suicide attempt, his mental unbalance had clearly gotten the better of him and he was imagining angels dictating his music to him, and tigers and hyenas that were really devils telling him that he was foredoomed to Hell. Rescued after his suicide attempt, he asked his wife Clara to commit him to an asylum.

Heine Birthplace (53 Bolkerstrasse)

Outside this house where he was born in 1797, little Heinrich Heine stood a few years later and watched Napoleon Bonaparte come in with his army and take over the town. The impression that the Little General made on the little boy, who was to become a famous German Romantic poet, was everlasting. From then on Heine was a Francophile.

Königsallee

The youngsters turning cartwheels for tourists along this main street are a reminder of the wedding day of the elector Jan Willem in the seventeenth century. It seems that a wheel of the wedding coach got loose and a little boy, noticing it, attached himself to the wheel in such a way that he could roll along with it and prevent its falling off. He was rewarded with a gold piece. Today's cartwheelers look forward to receiving money, too.

Malkasten (Artist's Club) (Jakobistrasse)

It isn't an American river at all that flows through the familiar painting of Washington crossing the Delaware. It is the Rhine here in Düsseldorf where the man who painted it, German-born Emanuel Leutze, made his home after spending his childhood and young manhood in Philadelphia. As for Washington's troops, their models came from this community. Leutze was the founder and first president of this artists' union, established in 1848.

Marktplatz (Town Hall Square): STATUE OF JAN WILLEM

Because they loved him so, the people of Düsseldorf erected this equestrian statue of the elector Jan Willem here in front of the town hall in 1711. But there was a problem. The sculptor, Gabriel de Grupello, discovered when he was doing the casting that he was short of metal. A plea went out to the townspeople to help out. And they did, hurrying to his studio with any table silver they could spare and throwing it into the mold.

FRANKFURT

In the now nonexistent ghetto here, Meyer Amschel Rothschild, the eighteenth-century founder of the Rothschild banking dynasty, grew up. With his tradesman father he often traveled from place to place carrying samples. In those days of the Holy Roman Empire, their travels took them through many states with many separate currencies. Young Meyer was fascinated by the money. And when his father decided to open a money-lending bureau, he often left Meyer in charge. The variety of coins that passed through his hands piqued his imagination, and, in time, he began a rare coin collection.

His interest in money notwithstanding, there were plans for him to become a rabbi. He soon seemed disinclined toward the scholarly life, however, so he was sent to Hannover to work in a bank. Where the prospect of the rabbinate had failed to take, banking took. The young man was delighted with it. And he was delighted with the friends he made—among them a general who was a fellow coin collector, and who, it turned out, was a close friend of William, the wealthy prince of Hesse-Cassel. The prince, like the general, was a numismatist and one day the general suggested that he look at Rothschild's coin collection. And so the pair met. The crown prince was impressed and bought coins. It was the beginning of a long association, and eventually Meyer became William's financial agent. Because of his skill in this role, his fortunes flourished, and his five sons went on to build the House of Rothschild into one of Europe's major financial powers in the nineteenth century.

Goethehaus (Goethe's House) (23 Grosser Hirschgraben)

In the original of this reconstructed house, Johann Wolfgang von Goethe was born in 1749 to a lighthearted young mother and a stern, demanding father twice her age. It was not a happy household. Only Wolfgang and one sister from among six children born to the couple survived, and those two were constantly under their father's critical eye. He even had a window cut in his library so he could watch them as they came and went. But young

Wolfgang—sickly after two years at Leipzig University—returned here all the same and took refuge in his puppet theater, in books of alchemy and mysticism, in dreaming and drawing, and writing. It was in this house that he wrote *The Sorrows of Young Werther.*

The River Main

The emperor Charlemagne found solace in this winding river during the eighth century. In a fog that hovered over its water, Charlemagne, legend has it, escaped a powerful enemy force. Safely on shore, he thrust his lance into the riverbank and announced that he would found a city here and call it *Franken Furth*—the "Ford of the Franks."

Rossmarkt

Once Frankfurt's place of execution, it was here that the actual Margaret —Margareta Brandt (whom Goethe transformed into Faust's Margaret)— was executed for killing her own child.

FREIBURG IM BREISGAU

In 1770, this was the last stop in Austria (of which it was then a part) for fifteen-year-old Princess Marie Antoinette en route to become the bride of Louis of France. He would become Louis XVI. She would become Queen Marie Antoinette. And both, in the French Revolution, would lose their heads on the guillotine (*see* France, Paris, Place de La Concorde). In May 1770, though, Marie Antoinette was still a shy innocent, and the people of Freiburg, in deference to her, carefully painted over the occasionally lusty names like "House of Brief Joy" that adorned some of their buildings.

GOSLAR

William Wordsworth shivered here in a rented room through the coldest winter in a century—the winter of 1798–99. That icy season on German soil helped to inspire the "Lucy" poems, it is said. "I travelled among unknown men,/In lands beyond the sea;/Nor, England! did I know till then/What love I have to thee."

HAMBURG

Reeperbahn (Rope Walk)

In this notorious red-light district, ten-year-old Johannes Brahms used to play the piano in the bordellos while simultaneously reading a book. Although the money he earned at the piano helped to support his parents—his aging, crippled seamstress mother (she was forty-one when she married the twenty-four-year-old double bass player who became his father), the sights he saw did psychological damage. Brahms never married (though he reputedly had a platonic love for his friend Robert Schumann's widow, Clara). He once remarked to a friend that his childhood experiences had hardly led him to think of honoring and cherishing a woman.

St. Katharinen (St. Catherine's Church) (Zoll Kanal)

It is from pirate gold that the original designers of this fifteenth-century church (reconstructed after World War II) are said to have fashioned the twelve-foot crown atop the tower.

HAMELN

It wasn't children whom the Pied Piper lured away from this town in 1284. It was young married couples. It seems neighboring communities needed population in those days, and the bishop was concerned about it. Hameln had more than its complement of citizens, so the bishop sent recruiters out to drum up residents for its less populous neighbors. The Brothers Grimm transformed the recruiters into the piper in his multicolored clothes and the young marrieds into boys and girls. They were piped away, the fairy tale says, when the town fathers failed to pay the piper, as per agreement, for ridding the town of rats and mice.

HEIDELBERG

When Louis XIV's soldiers were ordered to set fire to all the homes in this city in the seventeenth century, after they had destroyed its castle, they could not bring themselves to do it. But to make their commander think they had, they lighted bunches of wet straw. These smoked enough to satisfy the commander that his orders had been carried out and he moved on.

In the late nineteenth century, Mark Twain came here suffering from writer's block. But a raft trip down the Neckar, about which he found that he *could* write, cured him, and he was able to finish his manuscript of *The Adventures of Huckleberry Finn* about rafting on the Mississippi.

Elisabethentor (The Elizabeth Gate)

To surprise and please his pretty eighteen-year-old English wife, Elizabeth (her loveliness merited her the nickname, "the Queen of Hearts"), Frederick V had this archway erected overnight in 1615. As it turned out, there were to be few pleasures for the pretty princess, for although her husband was chosen king of Bohemia and she and he went off to Prague together to enjoy that new position, within a year he had lost the crown, his money, and his lands.

Scheffelhaus

This area was the home of Kathie, the pretty servant girl beloved of Sigmund Romberg's "student prince," in the operetta of that name.

HERRENCHIEMSEE

Here on Herren Island in Lake Chiem, Bavaria's largest lake, nineteenth century Louis II had this castle built out of adoration for seventeenth century Louis XIV of France. It was to be Louis II's Versailles, with its exquisite hall of mirrors and its flowing baroque facade. But as it turned out, Louis had little time to enjoy it. In all, Louis spent only twenty-three days here before his mysterious death. (*See* Starnberg.)

KLEVE

Schwanenburg (Castle)

In medieval days, Schwanenburg, now a ruin, was an impressive castle, and the home of the handsome, mysterious knight Lohengrin, on whom Richard Wagner based his opera of that name.

The ancient legend recounts how the mistress of the castle, the duchess Elsa of Brabant, was widowed and had scarcely buried her husband when the most powerful of his vassals demanded his lands and her hand and vowed to fight to the death any man who challenged him. The day came when he was publicly to make his claim.

In the courtyard below the castle, a crowd gathered, including a number of sturdily built knights. Surely one among them would come to her aid, the pale young widow hoped. Slowly, tremblingly—but still hoping for a champion—the duchess, dressed in her mourning clothes, descended into the courtyard. The knight who sought her hand and her castle laid his claim and asked once—twice—for challengers. There was no response. He asked a third time. The duchess, praying fervently, touched a silver bell on her rosary. As it melodiously tinkled, a barge drawn by a graceful white swan swept up the river and stopped below the castle. A knight stepped forth. The knight challenged the greedy usurper and forthwith defeated him in combat, thereby claiming castle, lands, and the delighted duchess, who was overwhelmed by his having championed her cause and by his handsomeness and gentle manner. He asked only that she not seek to learn his name. They were wed, had two sons, and lived for a while in great happiness. But as her children began to grow, Elsa longed to know what their ancestry might be. So, one night, she asked the fateful question—the knight Lohengrin's identity. Lohengrin sighed. Their happiness was over. She had broken her promise never to ask him about his past. Up the river came the swan boat; Lohengrin boarded it, and never again was seen.

LORELEI ROCK (St. Goar)

On this promontory, so the legend goes, a beautiful siren used to comb her golden hair and sing songs that so bewitched their listeners on the river below that they would forget to watch where they were going, and their boats would smash into the rock. Heinrich Heine retold the story elaborately in poetry, and Friedrich Silcher set it to music. Most believe that it is the remarkable echoes here that gave rise to the legend of Lorelei.

It is below this rocky promontory that the accursed gold of the thirteenth-century German epic poem, *The Nibelungenlied,* later made famous by Richard Wagner in *The Ring of the Nibelung,* is said to have been hidden.

LÜBECK

This city was the birthplace of marzipan, invented in the Middle Ages when Lübeck was under seige. In want of ordinary flours, the Lübeckers ground almonds to make it.

Buddenbrookshaus (on the Square)

Today the Volksbank occupies the old building where Thomas Mann and his brother Heinrich ran barefoot and played with their pet rabbits when they were children. In adulthood, Thomas made this the setting for his novel *Buddenbrooks,* the story of a merchant family—like his own—fallen on hard times.

The Cathedral

Its nave bombed out, its tower felled by bombs, its bells smashed by World War II, this cathedral seemed unlikely ever to be a functioning church again. But native son Thomas Mann saw to it that it was, by starting a collection to rebuild it—a collection to which he himself gave generously.

The Gänge

In the narrow old streets of this section of the city, many an Aryan Lübecker in World War II found a hiding place for Jewish friends.

St.-Marien-Kirche (St. Mary's Church)

Dietrich Buxtehude was the organist here at the start of the eighteenth century, and Johann Sebastian Bach walked the fifty miles from Arnstadt here with an eye, it is said, to inheriting the position. But he never obtained it. Speculation was that he did not because he declined to marry Buxtehude's daughter, who, he said, was too old for him.

MAULBRONN

Kloster Maulbronn (Cistercian Abbey)

When this Cistercian abbey fell on hard times in the sixteenth century, its abbot called on a learned alchemist from neighboring Knittlingen to help out. The dour alchemist (who had a reputation for dabbling in magic, too) was Dr. Johann Faust. He moved into what is now called the Faust Tower here with his candles and beakers, and sought, by day and by night, with much stirring and murmuring, to transform base metals into gold. The English playwright Christopher Marlowe learned of him; the alchemist inspired Marlowe's *Tragedy of Dr. Faustus* and, two centuries later, Goethe's *Faust.*

MUNICH

Bayerische Staatsoper (Bavarian State Opera)(National Theater, Max-Joseph-Platz)

One night in 1861, when he was sixteen, handsome Prince Louis watched and listened enthralled during a performance of Richard Wagner's *Lohengrin* in the old opera house here. The young man's dark eyes sparkled. It seemed to his fervid imagination that the opera actually had been written about *his* home, Hohenschwangau—as if *his* lake and *his* swans were in it. And, on the spot, a lifetime love for the opera's composer, Richard Wagner, was kindled. It was two years, however, before they actually met. The association between the young prince and the struggling composer proved immensely profitable for Wagner (*see* Bayreuth, Wahnfried), but contributed greatly to Louis's unpopularity. Bavaria was poor and the spendthrift king was giving more and more money to the extravagant, difficult composer. To mollify his outraged court, Louis suggested that Wagner go to Switzerland for a while. (It would be less obvious if he lived there at Louis's expense than in Bavaria.) And there Wagner went and continued to compose (*see* Switzerland, Zurich, Villa Wesendonck) thanks to Louis's devotion to opera and his largesse. Meanwhile the largesse led courtiers and advisors to begin to question the sanity of their ruler. (*See* Neuschwanstein.)

The English Garden (east side of Schwabing)

It was American-born Benjamin Thompson from Massachusetts who started this pretty garden in the eighteenth century. A sympathizer with the British, he had left the Colonies during the American Revolution, been knighted by the king, served in the British Colonial Office; then came to Munich where the elector of Bavaria made him a count, Count Rumford, and minister of war and police. Few of Count Rumford's enthusiasms were for projects as salutary as this garden. On New Year's Day in 1790, for example, he had the police round up all the beggars they could find in the city—2,500—and take them to the workhouse. "They were all made happy, because they were forced to become virtuous," said Count Rumford righteously.

Hofbrauhaus (Am Platzl)

Today they drink beer here, but for centuries they made it. This was the site of the court brewery, founded in 1589 when Duke William V decided he was spending too much money buying beer from monasteries to quench the thirst of the 700 to 800 people who were on his staff. He began producing his own brown barley beer, first near the Alter Hof, then here. The royal brew turned out to be cheaper than any other beer, and soon was the city's most popular drink. This retail establishment for the imbibers was built in 1897, and the brewery itself was moved across the river Isar.

Mariensäule (Marienplatz)

If only the Swedish invaders who had wrecked Magdeburg would spare Munich and Landshut, prayed the devout elector Maximilian of Bavaria in 1732, he would erect a soaring column in praise of the Virgin. Miraculously, his prayer was answered. Though Munich was occupied, it was not destroyed, and, true to his word, six years later, Maximilian fulfilled his vow. All Munich gathered for the solemn ceremony of dedication in which the gilded bronze Madonna on a column was set in place.

Schloss Nymphenburg (outskirts of Munich): AMALIENBURG (in the park)

The elector Charles Albert, a devoted spouse, had this hunting lodge built for his wife, Maria Amalia. To design it, he selected the dwarf, François de Cuvilles, whom his father, Maximilian Emanuel, had found in Brussels and had made his court jester—only to discover that the dwarf's architectural talents far surpassed his comedic ones. So Cuvilles was given architectural training in Paris, and then brought back to the Munich court to embellish the city with his rococo designs.

Schloss Nymphenburg (outskirts of Munich): SCHÖNHEITEN-GALERIE (Gallery of the Beauties of King Louis I)

So they would never age and he could always see them, Louis I of Bavaria had portraits painted of the prettiest women in his kingdom, and hung them in his Residenz. (They were moved here after World War II.)

A shocked Munich in 1827 whispered about the inappropriateness of the king's first selection for his gallery. It was a portrait he commissioned, not of royalty, but of Auguste Stroble, a bookkeeper's daughter. But the most famous sitter of all was Lola Montez, the Irish-born adventuress, singer, and dancer, with whom the king, at sixty-one, fell in love on sight. The black-haired beauty, turned down as a performer at the Court Theater on the grounds of lack of talent and a questionable reputation, had arranged, nonetheless, to have an audience with Louis. Immediately, the king ordered the Court Theater director to have her perform. And then Louis hired her to be his Spanish tutor—even though it was only her name that was Spanish.

Both Lola and Louis always denied that she was his mistress (he said she was his best friend), but surely she became powerful. She championed liberal causes and Protestantism. The king made her a naturalized citizen of Bavaria, and then a countess. His cabinet resigned over Lola. His sister offered to pay her to leave Bavaria. Students at Munich's university demanded her departure. Two hundred of them gathered outside the door of the house the king had given her, and Louis, paying her a visit, found them there. (They were on the street shouting at her; she was on her balcony taunting them by eating chocolates and sipping champagne.) An enraged Louis ordered the university closed.

Two thousand citizens of Munich protested by petition. Louis, regaining his senses a little, then announced the closing would be for the summer only. But it was already too late to stem the tide against Lola. On February 11, 1848, students and general populace, bearing arms, marched on the palace. Louis had no choice. Though he had promised he would never let her go, he told her she must quit Munich.

Lola could not believe that he meant it, but when it became clear that he did, she boarded a train for Augsburg. No sooner was she gone than the students stormed her house. The heartsick king who had gone there—perhaps to relive some of the joys of their time together—was hit on the head during the storming.

The next night, Lola tried to make a comeback. Dressed in men's clothes, she returned to Munich in an effort to reinstate herself with Louis, but she failed. At pistol point, the king had her taken to an exorcist who was to try to oust the devil within her. But clearly Lola did not want the devil ousted, and when it appeared that there was no chance of reconciliation with Louis, she escaped to Switzerland. She ended her days—at forty-three—in a sanitorium in New York. Louis, who outlived her, had long since abdicated in favor of his son.

Theresienwiese (outskirts)

When Crown Prince Louis (later Louis I of Bavaria) married the princess Theresa von Saxe-Hildburghausen on October 17, 1810, Muncheners celebrated the event in a gala way on this meadow. That year, there was no beer served, but on the first anniversary of the royal wedding the peasants asked the king if they could not honor the event with a *real* celebration. And the beer flowed. It has flowed ever since, each October, during this city's great Oktoberfest.

NEUSCHWANSTEIN

On this site, legend has it, the castle of the lyric poet Tannhäuser stood. Romantic Louis II liked the idea of having a new castle on the site where the troubadour of the Middle Ages was said to have lived, so he built this fanciful structure. Today, it is a small version of Neuschwanstein that is the trademark castle of Disneyworld.

❧❦❧

Before dawn on June 10, 1886, a commission from the Bavarian council arrived at this dream castle of King Louis II to inform him that he was no longer king. The bizarre behavior of the forty-year-old bachelor king who loved opera, worshipped Wagner (*see* Munich, Bayerische Staatsoper), and built extravagant castles (this one cost three million dollars) (*see* Herrenchiemsee) had led the council to act. They were placing Bavaria under the regency of Louis's Uncle Leopold, and Louis was to be incarcerated and watched.

The king reacted predictably. The commissioners, he announced, should be punished as traitors—their tongues should be cut out, they should be whipped and scalped. The threats were in his accustomed excessive vein, but in the end, the commissioners left, untouched.

The next night they were back, however, and the king was not so handsomely treated. This time there were armed men accompanying the commissioners, ready to take Louis away with them forcibly to Schloss Berg (*see* Starnberg), an old family castle near Munich on the Lake of Starnberg.

When it was clear there was no escape, Louis first requested poison, which was denied, then a key to his castle tower so he could throw himself from it. But the key was denied, too, and at four in the morning Louis II had his last glimpse of this castle he had loved so well. How many happier nights had he stood on the bridge crossing the gorge here and watched the windows of his fairy-tale marble palace being lighted, one by one, till 1,200 candle flames were dancing in the distance? How many nights had he sat alone but for his adored Wagner, who came here to play for him?

Louis looked longingly back as the coach rode off into the breaking day. He would never see the gleaming dream castle again.

NÜRNBERG

Albrecht-Dürer-Haus (39 Albrecht-Dürer-Strasse)

Hiding from his shrewish wife Agnes, who always wondered why he did not make more money, the artist Albrecht Dürer would climb to the second floor of his house and quietly draw. When she got to be entirely too much for him, he would flee to a neighboring sausage shop to eat and drink with his friend the poet, cobbler, and *Meistersinger,* Hans Sachs.

Dutzendteich (southeast outskirts of Nürnberg)

At this resort, Adolf Hitler planned construction of an enormous Congress Hall for Nazi party rallies. He had 22,000 cement pillars sunk into the earth for its foundation, but the great structure was only getting under way when Allied bombs destroyed it.

It was at the Soldiers' Field here that Nazi party members had enthusiastically hailed Hitler at rallies, and in 1935 had approved the Nürnberg Laws by which all German Jews lost their civil rights.

OBERAMMERGAU

When the plague was felling all of Europe in the seventeenth century, 600-odd residents here felt sure they were going to be able to keep it out by building a circle of fires around the village that no outsider would dare pass through. And no outsider did. But a villager who left and returned brought the dread disease back with him. Within a month there were eighty-four deaths. The frantic populace then gathered and promised God that if He would end the plague in their village, they would enact a play of the Passion of Christ every ten years ever afterward.

Miraculously, the plague stopped. The people of Oberammergau—except for the years of the Franco-Prussian War and World War II—have performed the Passion play every decade since 1634, living up to their part of the bargain.

In 1870 Mad Louis II of Bavaria was among those who attended the play. He was so delighted with his reception that he had a giant marble crucifix made in Munich for the villagers. It was so heavy that railway tracks had to be laid from Munich to Oberammergau so that it could be brought to its destination. It now stands above the village.

REGENSBURG

Gasthaus zum Goldenen Kreuz (Inn of the Golden Cross) (Haidplatz)

It was here one happy night in 1546 that the emperor Charles V and pretty Barbara Blomberg of Regensburg shared a bed, and Don John of Austria was conceived. (*See* Belgium, Namur, The Citadel.)

The recently widowed forty-six-year-old emperor was attending a meeting of Reichstag representatives from all over the country. His sister Maria, who lived here, knowing her brother had a fondness for music, arranged a concert for him and invited young Barbara Blomberg to be among the entertainers. Her voice had impressed Maria when she had heard her in the church choir. Since Barbara was not of a well-to-do family and Maria wished her to be properly dressed, the older woman had a blue silk gown delivered for the younger one to wear for the occasion. Proud Barbara, however, sent it back, remarking that if she was not good enough to sing for the emperor in her own clothes, she would not go.

She went—in her own clothes—and as she sang her eyes met those of Charles and she fell in love. Her repertoire was just five songs, but her eyes noticed that each time she sang, the emperor looked more interested. Barbara boldly whispered to the director that there was an extra air she wished to sing. It was a spring song she trilled then—about rebirth. The widowed king's gloomy spirits rose. And the next day he sent a message to ask if Barbara would like to see him. The message was no imperious demand for the favors of a pretty subject but a humble, shy man's request to see a woman he had found attractive—if she, too, found him attractive.

They met here in the emperor's chambers and spent their one and only night in each other's arms. They never again saw each other, but when, nine months later, Barbara was delivered of a son, Charles planned for his future, and when Don John was three, he was sent to his half brother, Philip II of Spain, for his education.

As for Barbara, Charles remembered her in his will with 600 pieces of gold.

ROTHENBURG OB DER TAUBER

Twice in its history this little community of half-timbered houses that architects call Germany's best preserved medieval town has narrowly escaped destruction.

In 1631, during the Thirty Years' War, the Protestant Germans were under attack from the Catholic Hapsburgs. The Hapsburg army of Johan Tserclaes, count of Tilly, had invaded, and it was announced that all Rothenburg councilors were to be hanged and the town itself razed. Mercilessly, General Tserclaes sent the mayor after the hangman. With little time to spare, the councilors, gathered at the town hall, tried to think of a way to escape. Here in the Franconian region the wine is exceptionally fine— and exceptionally strong. Perhaps a little wine, the councilors thought, would mellow the invaders.

And so they asked the town cellarmaster to fill up the town's great three-and-one-half-quart goblet with his best wine and pass it around among the Austrians. The invaders drank with gusto. And once it seemed to have gentled the soldiers a little, the wives and children of the councilors fell on their knees before the general and his men begging mercy.

As it had on his men, the brimming goblet had had an effect on the previously teetotaling general. He ordered the cellarman to refill the goblet and announced that if anyone in town could quaff the whole goblet at one gulp, Rothenburg would be spared.

For several minutes there was silence in the square. Man looked to man. Then a former burgomaster who had lost his son in battle that day stepped forward. History remembers him only as the former burgomaster Nusch. His son gone, he had nothing else to lose, and he knew he was a good drinker. Nusch lifted the cup. With one long draught (no one has recounted how long that draught took) Nusch drained the goblet of its three-and-one-half quarts. True to his word, Tilly sent the hangman away and gave orders that the town itself was not to be touched. As for Nusch, he is said to have slept for three days.

Three centuries later, in World War II, Rothenburg was targeted for shelling by American forces. Assistant Secretary of War John J. McCloy learned of it, and he immediately appealed to the general in command, begging him to try to negotiate a surrender. When he was a child, McCloy said, pictures of Rothenburg had hung on his mother's kitchen wall. For her sake, could the town be saved?

The proposed surrender was arranged, and McCloy was later given the title "Protector of Rothenburg" by its grateful citizens.

St.-Jakobs-Kirche (St. James' Church)

The Altarpiece of the Holy Blood here was carved by the masterful Tilman Riemenschneider in 1504. All of the figures in it are carved from the same piece of wood—except Judas. Riemenschneider took pains to assure that the betrayer of Christ, in wood as in life, would be kept separate from all the rest.

RÜDESHEIM

Brömsersburg

When Hans Brömser, the lord of this castle that is now a wine museum, was captured by the Turks during the Crusades, he promised his only daughter, Mechtildis, to the church should he be freed.

Almost immediately thereafter fellow Crusaders stormed his prison and obtained his release. Waiting enthusiastically here for his return was seventeen-year-old Mechtildis and the young lord of the neighboring Falkenstein family. The pair had fallen in love during the knight's absence. Hardly had Brömser stepped from his boat when Falkenstein asked for Mechtildis's hand. Brömser blanched. Such a liaison was out of the question, he explained, for Mechtildis was to be a bride of Christ. Falkenstein was ordered from this castle; Mechtildis, in tears, withdrew to her room. And when night fell, the heartbroken maiden flung herself into the Rhine.

SPEYER

Dom (Cathedral)

Seven-foot-tall Holy Roman Emperor Rudolph of Hapsburg, taken ill far away and sensing death, had himself bound to his horse so that he would not fall, and, accompanied by a handful of devoted courtiers, galloped here to the tomb he had prepared to receive him. When he arrived Rudolph—who had virtually crossed his kingdom to reach this burial place of Holy Roman emperors—fell from his horse and was untied. Then he stumbled inside and died—as he had wished—beside his tomb.

STARNBERG

Schloss Berg (Mountain Castle)

It was midmorning on June 12, 1886, when King Louis II of Bavaria was brought to this castle by coach, under guard, deposed by orders of the Bavarian council on grounds of insanity (see Neuschwanstein). The night had been arduous, the coach ride from his beloved Neuschwanstein understandably depressing. His spirits were hardly raised as, walking about this castle, he saw that the locks had been taken off all the doors and peepholes had been cut into the doors so he could be spied upon.

He said nothing to his captors. He quietly ate his dinner that evening and went to bed. He was up early the next day and he suggested a walk with one of the physicians sent to keep an eye on him. Neither Louis nor the doctor ever returned. A second doctor, disturbed by the length of their absence when morning turned into afternoon, afternoon into evening, went looking for them.

On the shore of the nearby Starnberg lake he found the doctor's hat and umbrella; the king's hat and his cloak fastener. The sand at the water's edge had been trampled. Clearly, there had been a fight, but there was no sign of the participants. Searchers in a boat later found the two men's bodies. Was the king escaping? Was his cousin Elizabeth of Austria across the lake trying to help him? No one will ever know which death was murder, which suicide. Or did the pair—the mad king and the state doctor—simply murder each other? (*See* Herrenchiemsee.)

TRIER

Amphitheater (outskirts of town)

In this Roman amphitheater, now a ruin, the emperor Constantine is said to have thrown thousands of Franks to wild animals in A.D. 308.

Karl Marx Museum (Brueckenstrasse 10)

Here Karl Marx, the social philosopher who is the father of modern socialism and communism, was born in 1818 to Heinrich and Henriette Marx. His father, born Hirschel, had converted from Judaism to Christianity to become a lawyer—a profession from which Prussian Jews were then barred. And when he was six—again because it was expedient (non-Christian children could not attend public schools) young Karl was baptized.

Porta Nigra

In 1028, when the Greek hermit Saint Simeon Stylites, after serving as a guide in the Holy Land to the archbishop of Trier, was offered as a gift his choice of homes in Trier, he chose not a palace but the east tower of this Roman gateway fortress. Furthermore, he asked to be bricked in and fed only bread and water through a small aperture, though on feast days he agreed to eat fresh vegetables. Much enfeebled by life in his self-imposed prison, Simeon died in it seven years later.

ULM

A daring experiment in flying took place here in 1811 when Albrecht Ludwig Berblinger, the Flying Tailor of Ulm, put silk sleeve wings over each arm and attempted to fly over the Danube in honor of a visit by the king of Württemberg. He started his flight from the town wall, and ended it in the Danube, but, happily, he survived and apparently was none the worse for his adventure. Good businessman that he was, he sold the silk from his wings to a parasol maker for a tidy price.

The Cathedral

Green lights affixed to the 530-foot spire of this cathedral (the tallest church spire in the world) are said to have signaled Allied air raiders in World War II that this was a famous churchtower. As a result, only two bombs fell and did minimal damage.

WINDSHEIM

Cathedral of St. Kilian

The hard-working councilor, mayor, and, above all, woodcarver of this city, Tilman Riemenschneider, proudly saw two of his finest works, the red marble tombs of two of Würzburg's prince-bishops, put in place here, before, in 1524, he took the peasants' side in their rebellion and fell into disfavor. Then he was imprisoned, tortured, and the means to his great art —his fingers—were broken.

Greece

ARTA ✦❀✦ ————

Across the river Arakhthos here tiptoe the arches of a great stone bridge. It has stood serene since the eighteenth century. The bridge builder had problems, however. At the beginning, the stonework kept falling apart and down. According to local song and story, an unidentified onlooker told him that only the incorporation of human bones would strengthen his materials against the stresses of existence. Along came his wife fetching his lunch. He shoved her into the foundation and resumed work. But the builder apparently had afterthoughts, for later he committed suicide.

ATHENS

The Acropolis

Although it is thanks to the fifth-century-B.C. statesman Pericles that this citadel that is Athens's greatest glory was built, his fellow Greeks turned on him during its construction and accused him of squandering their money. They charged him with turning Greek against Greek and of being a man of immoral character. And their attacks finally drove him to an untimely death.

Had he not, as a married man, fallen in love with another woman—and a foreigner at that—things might have been different. But there are also those who say it was the benign and cultured influence of the Milesian, Aspasia, that was responsible for his having had this splendid complement of buildings designed and constructed by his friend the sculptor Phidias. Aspasia, however, was distinctly unpopular, and finally she was accused of impiety toward the gods of Greece and brought to trial. Mustering all his eloquence, her lover defended her before a court of 1,500 jurors—and she was acquitted. But after that, proud Pericles seemed dispirited—shocked that those for whom he had done so much had treated him so badly—and within three years the master builder, master statesman was dead.

✦❀✦

It was no wonder that in 1801, Thomas Bruce, earl of Elgin, Britain's ambassador here, asked permission to take away some of the blocks of stone

144

scattered on this hilltop, for ever since the seventeenth-century bombardment by the Venetians there had been battles here. And when the Turks
were rulers of Greece, it is said that the military governor kept his harem
of forty wives in the Erechtheum. The likelihood of this fine architecture
and statuary lasting much longer seemed slim indeed. So Elgin asked to
make a few casts and drawings, and to remove a broken piece of pediment
here and there. The trouble was, as the Greeks saw it, he was not really
protecting their interests—or those of the Acropolis—and he overdid. By
the time he was through, he had removed a dozen statues, fifty-six pieces
of frieze, and more. Lord Elgin has sometimes been accused of greediness.
But backers have suggested that he saved great numbers of examples of fine
art from certain destruction. In any case, he made no money from his
purchases. Their cost to him was £50,000. When the British Parliament
agreed to buy them for the British Museum, they were willing to pay only
£35,000.

The Acropolis: PARTHENON

The Athenians have never forgiven the Venetians for the damage they did
to this ancient temple in 1687. Athens was then in Turkish hands and the
Venetians were besieging it. And it was in this temple that the Turks kept
each day's supply of ammunition. When the Venetian commander's spies
informed him of this, he fired directly at the Parthenon. One of the shells
hit the roof and this structure was severely damaged. But that was not the
total of the injuries that the Venetians inflicted. When they had taken over
the city, they tried to make off with some of the statues from the pediment
—and clumsily dropped and broke them.

The Acropolis: THE PROPYLAEA

While this great entrance gate was under construction, one of the most
indefatigable of the builders working on it fell from the roof and was
seriously hurt. And Pericles, whose project all this was, after all, was greatly
dismayed. Tossing in his sleep one night, legend has it, he was approached
by Athena, telling him of a cure for the worker. He followed her advice and
the workman recovered. In gratitude the statesman had a bronze statue to
Athena erected. Unfortunately, even with the industrious workman back on
the job, the Propylaea was never finished, for the Peloponnesian War
began.

The Acropolis: SOUTH SIDE

From this site, the broken-hearted Aegeus, mythological ruler of Athens,
is said to have flung himself into the sea that today bears his name.

For years, so the legend goes, Aegeus had been forced to send an annual tribute of young men and maidens to be eaten by the monstrous Minotaur that inhabited the island of Crete. But when Aegeus' son Theseus came of age, the young man determined to end the bloody tribute, and so informed his father. Thankful but fearful, Aegeus begged his son to take care. The youth promised that he would. Then taking the young men and women who were that year's tribute, he prepared to set off in a ship rigged with black sails. There was a last request from his worried father. When the boat returned, if Theseus had vanquished the half-man-half-bull Minotaur and was safe, would he be sure to raise white sails of victory so that Aegeus would know that all was well as soon as the ship hove in sight? Theseus promised.

Arrived on Crete, Theseus was about to enter the labyrinth of the awesome Minotaur when Ariadne, the princess of Crete, saw him. Smitten by his handsomeness and impressed by his valor and his willingness to sacrifice himself for others, the Cretan princess, so the story goes, gave him a magic ball of thread to help him find his way out of the labyrinth should he succeed in killing the Minotaur. Kill the creature he did, and out of the cavern Ariadne's thread led him. But then, without even a thank you to the princess who had made his victory and escape possible, Theseus reembarked for Athens.

Woeful Ariadne waded into the water in pursuit of him, but he abandoned her. Then, turning to prayer, she invoked the wrath of the gods against Theseus who had left her behind. And one of the curses was that he forget his promise to his father to raise white sails on his trip home, if he had destroyed the Minotaur and was safe. Aegeus, waiting here for his son's return, saw the black sails in the distance; he uttered a cry of anguish and, in despair at what he supposed was the death of his son, jumped into the sea.

The Agora

It was the cobbler Simon, who kept a shop here, who first wrote down the teachings of Socrates. The philosopher would come to have his shoes repaired, it is said, and while he waited would while away the time discoursing.

◈

The Roman, Paul, talked too much, the Epicurean and Stoic philosophers who frequented this marketplace decided when the apostle came here on a visit in A.D. 60–61. But they agreed to take him to the court on the Areopagus and hear him out. (*See* Areopagus.)

Areopagus (Hill of Mars)

Since on this hilltop, in ancient days, there was a court, it seemed an appropriate place to bring the Roman babbler, Paul (*see* Athens, The Agora), and let him talk away about the Christ and resurrection and then judge what he had to say. Some, it is said, mocked, and some suspended judgment, but Dionysus the Areopagite "clave unto him and believed."

The Hill of the Museum: PRISON OF SOCRATES

Solemnly, they assembled in 399 B.C. at this dungeon at the foot of this hill —the philosopher Socrates and his companions. Accused, tried, and found guilty of having corrupted youth by introducing them to new thinking, he was condemned to drink poison from the hemlock here. While his disciples stood by helpless, watching, he reported to them as limb after limb went cold, until he died.

Hotel Grande Bretagne (Syntagma Square)

In 1944 when Britain's prime minister, Winston Churchill, was on a visit here, a plot to blow up this hotel from the sewers was uncovered just in time.

National Archeological Museum (1 Tossitsa Street)

The Christmas he was seven, little Heinrich Schliemann, the son of a poor pastor in Germany, was given a gift of a *Child's History of the World.* There was a picture in it of Troy in flames, so the story goes, and of Aeneas carrying his old father and leading his young son by the hand. The picture captured the young German's imagination, and, then and there, he determined that one day he would find that ancient disappeared city.

For a long time, the prospect seemed highly unlikely. First young Schliemann worked in a grocery store; then he went to sea as a cabin boy. Next, for a while, he clerked in an Amsterdam office. But all the time he was studying indefatigably—both languages and books about the Greeks with whom he was so intrigued. Among the languages he learned was Russian, and when he was twenty-four he went to St. Petersburg to enter business. It was the mid-nineteenth century, the time of the Crimean War. The war made his business prosper and by the later years of the century, he was well off enough to move here to Athens, where he longed to be, and start his quest for Troy. His studies had convinced him that he should dig halfway between Corinth and Argos, at Mycenae, and there, at last, his childhood dream of uncovering the Trojan civilization came true. The treasures he unearthed are now in this museum.

Plaka (11 Aghias Theklas Street)

Enamored of the thirteen-year-old daughter of his landlady, Lord Byron wrote his poem, "Maid of Athens," here.

Theater of Dionysus (below the Acropolis)

It was in this theater (though not on this spot), it is said, that the play was born.

In 534 B.C., at the Festival of Dionysus, the poet Thespis suggested an innovation on the usual idea of having entertainment by an entire chorus. His suggestion: have one performer separate from the chorus who would converse with its leader. The idea took, and by 500 B.C. works by Aeschylus, the father of modern drama, were being performed. Soon Sophocles, Euripides, and Aristophanes were on the boards, and drama became so popular that by 400 B.C. an imposing stone theater had been built.

CORFU

Achilleion

To this Florentine Renaissance palace that she had built in 1890–91—it is now a casino—the Austrian empress Elizabeth (*see* Austria, Vienna, Schönbrunn) would often come to spend holidays alone to assuage her unhappiness. She named it, lovingly, for her favorite Greek, Achilles, and filled it and the grounds around it with the statues of that hero, some good, more bad, that still remain.

Mon Repos

It was a narrow escape. King Constantine I's efforts to bring back into Greece that part of Asia Minor that belonged to Turkey but had a large Greek population had failed with great loss of life. Constantine had abdicated. Generals and government officials who had been at all connected with the sad defeat were being executed. And among those slated for execution was Prince Andrew, brother of the king and father of Philip Mountbatten, the present duke of Edinburgh. Andrew was taken prisoner at this Greek royal summer palace in 1922 and condemned to death by a firing squad when his son Philip, who was born here, was barely a year old. Happily, British intervention saved him.

CORINTH

Life here in A.D. 51 and 52 was licentious, to say the least. Prostitutes abounded and riches seemed to be on every hand. Indeed, this was called the most sinful city of the ancient pagan world. The apostle Paul inveighed against it, after he had left, in his First Letter to the Corinthians.

CRETE

Saint Paul, visiting Crete, found little to recommend either about the place or the people, whom he criticized as slothful and lying. But some fifteen centuries later, Domenico Theotokopoulos—the painter El Greco—hardly slothful, was born here in the village of Fodhele and began his studies, it is believed, at the Church of St. Katherine in Heraklion. Though most of El Greco's life was spent in Italy and Spain, the stark landscape of this island seems never to have left him and is reflected in much of his painting.

Heraklion

It was probably the longest siege in history. For twenty-two years in the seventeenth century, when this was the Venetian city of Candia, the Turks cut it off. The pope begged the rest of the Christian world for help, and Louis XIV sent men to try to assist, but all were lost. Even the indomitable Francesco Morosini, who was in charge of Candia's defense, could think of no strategem to send the Turks away, and in 1669 this city—acquired by Venice as a pawn of war after the Fourth Crusade—became the property of the Turks.

Heraklion: VENETIAN WALL

In the Martinengo bastion of this fifteenth-century wall—in its day acclaimed as the strongest wall in the Mediterranean—the iconoclastic twentieth-century writer, Nikos Kazantzakis, was buried in 1957 when the church refused to have him lie in hallowed ground because of his beliefs. In keeping with the philosophy of this author of *Zorba the Greek,* his tombstone reads, "I hope for nothing. I fear nothing. I am free."

Knossos

No one knows what destroyed the great Minoan culture that once flourished here. Between 1700 and 1400 B.C. Crete was one of the great cultural and maritime powers of the Mediterranean world. But suddenly it was all gone, tumbled in a single night, by an earthquake, most speculate, but others suggest that invaders from the mainland overwhelmed this island citadel.

For centuries little was heard about Crete. Then, in the thirteenth century, Venetian explorers rediscovered it, wondering if it could be the Lost Continent of Atlantis. Now and again, amateur archeologists examined the ruins that protruded from the ground, but no one dug looking for more. Though Heinrich Schliemann tried to obtain permission from the Turks in 1886 to do some digging, they turned him down. Happily, in 1900, Arthur Evans, the British archeologist and keeper of the Ashmolean Museum at Oxford, came here. In Athens he had bought some engraved seals said to have come from Crete. He hoped to find more information—perhaps clay tablets with pictures on them—that would provide clues to the early civilization here. And this time, the government agreed to let an excavation site be bought. His discoveries went far beyond clay tablets. They led to the discovery of this enormous palace with its colonnades and graceful staircase, its bathroom with running water, its open-air theater with room for an audience of 500. For the rest of his life, Evans dug and restored here (though purists criticized his restoration). The British government rewarded him with a baronetcy for his efforts.

DELPHI

Zeus, the king of the gods, it is said, sent two eagles from either end of the world to determine where the center of the earth might be, and when the birds met here it seemed clear that this was the center, and it was so decreed.

Temple of Apollo

Among the notables who came here in ancient days, burdened with problems, were the Roman orator Cicero seeking to know how he could win greater fame, and the Roman emperor Nero. To Cicero's question, the Oracle reportedly replied sensibly that fame would come if his actions reflected his character rather than the opinions of others. And the Oracle's advice to Nero was to beware the number 73. Delighted, he assumed that he would live to be 73. But such was not to be the case. At the age of thirty-one, he was overthrown by a seventy-three-year-old.

◄◦§◦►

Because the climate here was so delightful, the god Apollo, so the old myths have it, chose this to be his home. But when he got here, he found the people terrified by a python dwelling in a cave of Mount Parnassus. Bravely, Apollo killed it. In gratitude for his valiant act, a temple was set up here to honor him in the sixth century B.C. Around his temple a religious city grew, and until the fourth century A.D. all those (women excluded) seeking to know what the future would hold, came to consult the Oracle who dwelt here in a cleft in the rock. Known as the Pythia, this interpreter of the word of the gods was always a middle-aged peasant woman. She would prepare herself for her sacred activities by bathing in a holy spring, and chewing laurel leaves; then, sitting near the stream that issued from the crevice here, she would make her pronouncements and the priests of Apollo's temple would interpret them.

Once the foreign king Croesus of Lydia sought her help, and though with his great riches he had helped rebuild the Temple of Apollo when it had burned to the ground, the Oracle was of no great help. When Croesus asked her whether he should invade Persia, she replied enigmatically that, by so doing, he would be destroying a great empire. Encouraged, poor Croesus duly attacked. The empire that was destroyed turned out to be his own.

❦

Rich in treasure as this temple was, it frequently suffered at the hands of the light-fingered. Nero, enraged when the Oracle condemned him for the murder of his mother, it is said, took away 500 bronze statues. The two Constantines—Christians with no use for pagan nonsense—also plundered here.

EDESSA

Philip II of Macedon, brilliant in war, generous in peace, conqueror of Greece and organizer of its city-states into a union, made one grave mistake. He angered his wife Olympias by his affairs with other women. And one day here in 336 B.C., her anger culminated in his assassination. At her urging, so the story goes, a former guardsman in Philip's army stabbed him as he walked in a procession. The father of Alexander the Great was dead, and Alexander became the king.

THE GREEK ISLANDS

When God, it is said, had finished fashioning the earth, a handful of rocks remained. And so he tossed them over his shoulder. Scattering, they formed these 1,425 Greek islands in the Aegean and the Ionian seas.

HYDRA

It was the ships of Hydra and their brave crews that made up the greater part of the fleet of Greece in its nineteenth-century war for independence from Turkey. Especially notable were the seamen for their kamikaze-like tactic of filling their ships with tar and setting them aflame as they rammed the vessels of the enemy.

ITHACA

Grotto of the Nymphs

Here, to this island grotto, the legendary Ulysses is said to have come with the treasure accumulated in his wanderings; he buried it in this cave and built his palace nearby.

KOS

Plane Tree of Hippocrates

This tree, it is said, is a descendant of that plane tree under which Hippocrates, the father of medicine, treated his patients some 2,400 years ago. His precepts—the divinity of the body; the need for exercise and the importance of sun and air and rest rather than drugs and potions; the confidentiality of the patient-doctor relationship; his dictum to do no harm—are the basic principles of medicine today.

LESBOS

Here the poet Sappho, the world's first and one of its greatest women poets, wrote passionately and vividly in the sixth century B.C. of women's love—so passionately, indeed, that to protect good Christians from the poems' influence, many were burned by the church in 1073.

As for Sappho, wife and mother, lover of men as well as women, it is said that she leaped from the rocks on the island of Lefkas when she fell in love with a handsome young boatman who did not return her affection.

LIVADIA

Clock Tower

It was a nice gesture—Lord Elgin's presentation of this pretty clock tower as compensation to Greece for his having carted much of the Parthenon away to England—but the gesture, as the years have gone on, has sat less and less well.

MARATHON

Mound of Marathon (26 miles northeast of Athens)

It looked like an impossible battle that summer day in 490 B.C.—9,000 Athenian militia pitted against some 100,000 Persian infantry and 10,000 cavalry. So the runner Pheidippides was sent to summon aid from the Spartans as the Persians landed for a march on Athens. For two days and nights, Pheidippides ran toward Sparta—only to find when he reached there that the Spartans were celebrating a religious festival and hardly in the mood—or condition—to help out. So back he hastened to the battlefield to take his place in combat. And when, joyously, the Athenians put the enemy to flight, he took it upon himself to run to Athens as the bearer of good tidings. But he never made it. On the outskirts of the city, Pheidippides fell dead of exhaustion, gasping out, however, the news of the victory with his last breath. Today's marathon—a difficult race—takes its name from Pheidippides' feat.

MISSOLONGHI

Monument to Lord Byron

It seemed an ill-fated trip from the beginning. Romantic that he was, however, the English poet Lord Byron wished to offer his services on the side of Greece against its despotic Turkish overlords, and in this village those most opposed to the regime were gathering. A gypsy had warned that he would be in danger in his thirty-sixth year, and Byron was then in his thirty-fifth. It was likely, since he was leaving late in the summer, that he would be celebrating his January birthday in Greece. But he shrugged his shoulders at the idea of misfortune and went ahead.

The first part of his voyage, from Venice, was easy enough. But once arrived in Greece, internal conflicts among the insurgents kept him on the island of Cephalonia almost until the first of the new year. Then, when finally he set sail to join some of the revolutionaries on the north shore of the Bay of Corinth, his little vessel was almost shipwrecked. After that, it narrowly escaped being attacked by the Turks. And when he finally landed here at Missolonghi, he found the life of a soldier uncomfortable; the weather wet and cold; his companions less heroic than he had envisioned. He had a seizure of some sort in February, and never seemed to fully regain his strength.

The post he undertook was as a supplier to the insurgents, and even when the weather was foul and his own spirits low he would ride out into the field to try to buoy the spirits of the Greeks. And on one of these trips Byron caught cold. A fever followed. He was bled by his doctors, with greater weakness resulting. On April 18, 1824, Easter Sunday, George Gordon, Lord Byron, age thirty-six, was dead—as predicted.

THE METEORA

God created these rocky pinnacles, that soar like needles as much as 1,820 feet into the sky, expressly as a sanctuary for the most ascetic of His monks, so the story goes. And in the fourteenth century, the first such monks took advantage of His architectural offering and built their first monastery here. At the height of enthusiasm for this hermitlike religious life, there were twenty-four monasteries perched precariously on these rocks that could be reached only by nets and ropes. But never, even in the direst of circumstances, was a woman allowed to ascend to these rocky heights. Not even a dying, starving woman could be offered help and sustenance here.

MONEMVASÍA

Called the "Gibraltar of Greece," this place was famous for the wine it exported, which the French called *vin de Malvoisie.* In Britain it was known as "Malmsey," a white wine, strong and sweetish, and very highly esteemed. In the fifteenth century, the duke of Clarence gave it quite a testimonial.

Sentenced to die by his brother, Edward IV, he asked to be drowned in a butt of Malmsey.

MOUNT ATHOS

Surely neither the Virgin nor Saint Helen would be jealous, but it is because they are said to have helped in the founding of this mountaintop monastic community that began 900 years ago that no other women ever have been allowed to enter here.

MOUNT OLYMPUS

Here in this highest mountain range of Greece, the ancient gods were said to live, eating ambrosia and sipping nectar, listening to the lyre of Apollo and the songs of the Muses.

But in later times, this was not such a soothing place. In the nineteenth and early twentieth centuries, bandits skulked in these mountain fastnesses awaiting unwary travelers and mountain climbers whom they would capture and hold for ransom.

MYCENAE

The Citadel

So enormous are these unearthed walls that it is said only the one-eyed monster, Cyclops, would have been strong enough to have constructed them.

❦

A joyous King Agamemnon returned here after successfuly vanquishing Troy, so Homer tells it. In his bath, preparing for the dinner to celebrate his victory and his homecoming, he was murdered by his wife Clytemnestra and her lover Aegisthus.

MYKONOS

Because so many of the men of this little island have faced the dangers of the sea, hundreds of them who have survived the waves have built chapels of gratitude. One could, it is said, worship in a different chapel or church each day of the year, there are so many of them.

NAUPLIA

The night of April 26, 1941, was grim at the mouth of the harbor here. The British transport *Ulster Prince,* seeking to evacuate 6,685 British soldiers who had gone to the defense of Greece against the Germans, and 150 nurses, ran aground in the darkness. While aground, the ship was bombed. Four vessels trying to assist her—along with many men—were lost.

Fort Palamedes

To be an advisor to Otto I, the first king of Greece, required stamina, for in 1832 when, for a time, he made this fortress his castle, those who served him had an 857-step climb for their audiences.

Port of the Passage

As everywhere in the world, executioners were not held in high regard in Greece, and the less said about them—or seen of them—the better. So it was here, far from everyone, that a home was established for them in their retirement.

NÁVPAKTOS

Out of this port, when it was called Lepanto, the previously unvanquished Turkish fleet set sail in 1571—its admiral sure as always that he would be victorious against all foes. But this time the foe was the combined forces of Spain, Genoa, Savoy, Venice, and the Knights of Malta, all determined, with religious fanaticism, to vanquish the infidel fleet. And the Christians did. Among the fighters who undoubtedly wished he had not come, however, was the young Spaniard Miguel de Cervantes Saavedra, for in the Battle of Lepanto the aspiring writer lost an arm.

NAXOS

On the beach here, scene of twentieth-century composer Richard Strauss's lush opera *Ariadne auf Naxos,* the homeward-bound Athenian Theseus put ashore the adoring Ariadne, with whose help he had destroyed the terrible Minotaur. (*See* Athens, The Acropolis, South Side.)

Apollon

Disgruntled sculptors of 2,600 years ago apparently abandoned this thirty-five-foot-tall statue of Apollo when they discovered a crack in its marble.

Gateway to the Temple of Dionysus

Probably Ariadne of Crete did far better being abandoned here by Theseus (*see* Athens Acropolis, South Side) than she ever would have done had he kept her with him. As the myth has it, Dionysus, the god of wine and revelry, was captured by unknowing pirates soon after Ariadne's misadventure, but when ivy miraculously sprouted from the mast and rigging of their ship, the terrified pirates jumped overboard, leaving Dionysus in command. He soon sailed here, found weeping Ariadne, feted her with wine and song, and married her. Richard Strauss wrote the opera *Ariadne auf Naxos* about it. In time the temple, of which this gateway is the remains, was built in the wine god's honor.

OLYMPIA

Successful at the ancient games held on this site was the Roman emperor Nero. Expert horseman and charioteer though he was, he fell from his chariot twice during the race in A.D. 67. Both his falls and his subsequent victory were attributed to his racing with ten teams of horses, while other contestants had only four.

Excavations

For more than 1,000 years beginning in 776 B.C., here on the lush, green plain between the rivers Arpheus and Kladeos, the great Olympic Games took place. They were more than athletic contests. They were part of the worship of Zeus, whose statue done in gold and ivory by Phidias presided over the proceedings in a shaded grove sacred to him. The games were a summer conference of intellectuals, at which poets and playwrights read their latest works. They were exhibits of graphic arts and sculpture. They were the occasion of the Ekecheiria, or Olympic Truce, during which any fighting among the Greek states was recessed until the more important business of the games was concluded.

The interval between games was four years, and this span of time, the Olympiad, became the basic unit of the Greek calendar. Only men of pure Greek descent were permitted to compete. Barbarians, being persons whose mother tongue was not Greek, were admitted as spectators; slaves excluded; and married women barred. The games were suffused with religious significance, the Greeks devoutly believing that the body as well as the spirit was divine and that *both* could be improved by exercise.

◆⚜◆

In the days of the original Olympic Games, death was decreed for any woman attending them, but once, one proud mother, disguising herself as her son's trainer, managed to get inside. When her son was declared a winner, the mother cried out in delight, thus disclosing her sex. But because she was not only the mother of an Olympic champion, but also the sister of several, she was pardoned and was not hurled from the Typaean Rock here—the accustomed punishment for trespassers at the games.

Gymnasium

Here in this gymnasium is the altar and the eternal flame from which the Olympic torch of today is lighted, to be carried across the world to the city in which the next Olympic Games will be held. The ancient games were forbidden by the Byzantine emperor Theodosius in A.D. 393. Under Roman rule, competition had become professionalized and bitter, and the Christian emperor did not approve of pagan festivals.

PASS OF THERMOPYLAE

Monument to the Spartans

This monument honors Leonidas and the Spartan band who perished trying to block the pass to the Persians in 480 B.C. When told by a spy that the Persian archers were so many that the sun would be blocked by their arrows, Dieneces (a laconic Laconian) said, "At least we shall fight in the shade."

PATMOS

To this island in A.D. 95 Saint John the Divine is said to have been banished by the Romans, who used it as a prison isle. And here, it is believed, he received the vision of the Apocalypse and wrote the Book of Revelation.

PHILIPPI

As a result of fighting on the plains here in 42 B.C., between the assassins of Julius Caesar—Brutus and Cassius on one side, and Mark Antony and Octavian, great-nephew of Caesar, on the other—both Brutus and Cassius committed suicide: Cassius after the first battle because he feared he had failed as a general; Brutus after the second when he realized he would not be victorious.

Basilica

In a cave just north of here, it is said, Saint Paul—who preached his first sermon on European soil in Philippi—and his companion Silas were imprisoned by local authorities. But as they prayed and sang, so the Book of Acts tells it, an earthquake was felt; the doors of their prison burst open and the pair were free. When their terrified jailer tried to commit suicide, they changed his mind by converting him and baptizing him instead.

PIRAEUS

Odos Filonos (Filonos Street)

A workman busily repairing a cellar here one July day in 1959 suddenly felt something cold and metallic beneath his hand. Alerting his fellows, they unearthed a bronze hand buried deep in the soil, and further digging brought to light statues of a helmeted Athena, a Hellenistic girl, and a young man. Were they perhaps stolen in the Roman attack on Athens in 87 B.C. and hidden here for shipment later? In any case, they now are to be found in the archeological museum here.

PÓROS

Ruins of the Temple of Poseidon

The great Athenian orator Demosthenes poisoned himself here in 322 B.C. to avoid being captured by the Macedonians. He was the orator who started life with a stutter but overcame the impediment by filling his mouth with stones and shouting at the waves on the shore.

Trizin

In ancient days this was Troezen where Theseus brought Phaedra, the sister of the Cretan princess Ariadne, whom he had abandoned despite her having aided him in destroying the Minotaur (*see* Athens, The Acropolis, South Side).

Theseus, so the myth has it, married Phaedra, but the marriage was doomed, for the pretty young bride soon met Theseus' son Hippolytus, handsome and charming like his father, but—in addition—her own age. Here, she threw herself at the attractive youth, but was turned down by him and in despair hanged herself. Both Euripides and the French dramatist Racine based tragedies on her love affair.

RHODES

In the third century B.C. this was the site of one of the Seven Wonders of the World—the Colossus—a 120-foot-high bronze statue of the sun god Helios which, it is said, stood astride the entrance to the harbor. But it only stood in place for 50 years. Then an earthquake sent it shuddering into the sea—and there it remained, untouched, for the next 800 years, for it was believed that it would bring death to all who touched it. Finally, however, Saracen pirates—who forgot all superstition when there was money to be had—hauled it out of the water and, using 900 camels, lugged it away and sold it to a dealer in scrap metal.

❦

Here, to Rhodes, renowned for its orators, the eloquent Roman, Cicero, came as a budding public speaker to perfect his art.

Palace of the Grand Master

In World War II this was chosen to become a summer palace for Mussolini and King Victor Emmanuel III. It was restored so that—externally—it resembled the palace built here at the end of the fourteenth century when the Knights of St. John of Jerusalem were headquartered here. But the refurbished palace was barely ready for occupancy when Italy was forced to give up Rhodes.

SKYROS

On Shakespeare's birthday, April 23, in 1915, the twenty-eight-year-old English poet-naval officer Rupert Brooke died here of blood poisoning. He had been put ashore when he took ill en route to combat in Gallipoli. Presaging that he would die before the First World War had ended, he had written in his famous poem "The Soldier": "If I should die, think only this of me;/that there's some corner of a foreign field that is for ever England."

CAPE SOUNION

Poseidon's Temple

The poet Byron loved it here, high above the blue Aegean. He carved his name on one of the pillars of the temple and wrote of this site: "Place me on Sunium's marble steeps/Where nothing save the waves and I,/May hear our mutual murmurs sweet;/There, swan-like, let me sing and die." Byron did die in Greece (*see* Messolonghi), but not at this beloved place.

SPARTA

Amyclae: THE AMYCLAEON

In 1925, German archeologists excavated the sanctuary surrounding the tomb of Hyacinthus, a beautiful mortal beloved of Apollo, who was killed by a discus either sloppily hurled—by Apollo himself—or by the jealous west wind's whipping it off course. Where the young man fell, Apollo caused hyacinth flowers to spring from his blood.

THESSALONIKE

It was a ghastly reprisal. In A.D. 390, the emperor Theodosius the Great, Christian convert though he was, one day invited 7,000 of the citizens here to attend games in the circus, and when they had all assembled, killed them. The reason: retaliation for the people's having hanged the military commander of Thessalonike and several of his men for what they considered undue harshness to one of their best-loved athletes.

Agios Demetrios (Basilica of St. Demetrius)

Although the original of this basilica was burned virtually to the ground in 1917, this reconstruction marks the ruins where Thessalonike-born Demetrius was killed without trial for having preached Christianity. It was said thereafter that he guarded the city by raising storms as enemies approached, and—with the wind's help—hurling attackers from the city ramparts.

White Tower

A massacre here by the Turks in the early nineteenth century when this was a prison gave this seafront structure the name of "the Bloody Tower." To help the heinous deed be forgotten, the tower was whitewashed toward the end of the century, and given its present name.

THEBES

Oedipodeia Spring

Almost nothing remains here now of this once thriving city where the legendary Oedipus ruled. He had unwittingly slain his father, the king of Thebes, then equally unwittingly married his mother. It is said that Oedipus washed away his father's blood at this spring.

THÍRA (SANTORIN)

One day in 1450 this island trembled in a volcanic explosion, and its whole center sank. Over that center—seven miles long and four miles wide—the waters of the Bay of Santorin now toss. Is this seven-mile-long center, then, the lost continent of Atlantis, that happiest of isles that the ancients reported was suddenly, mysteriously, engulfed by the sea—the lost paradise for which generations of explorers sought in vain?

Italy

ASSISI ❧🎋❧ ————

Convento di San Damiano (Convent of St. Damian) (1½ miles
south of Assisi): CRUCIFIX OF ST. DAMIAN

In 1206 this village church was in sad repair. Giovanni Bernardone, the son
of a prosperous Assisi merchant, had passed it many times without paying
much attention to its condition. He himself was well-off and it was that,
principally, that mattered to him. He liked to dress well and enjoy himself
and though, in 1203, he had gone off to war, been captured, gotten sick,
reenlisted and gotten sick again, so that he was somewhat subdued, he
remained largely the attractive, fastidious merchant's son who looked forward to a life of as great ease as his father's.

But then one day, returning from a fair where he had made a most
profitable horse sale for his father, he passed the little chapel here. Inexpli-
cably, he stopped and knelt and prayed before this crucifix, and later he
insisted he had heard Christ urging him to rebuild this aging church. The
dumbfounded Giovanni Bernardone did the only thing that he could think
of doing. He took the purseful of money made from the horse's sale and
gave it to the priest of the chapel. The priest declined the offer, but asked
his would-be benefactor if he cared to spend the night.

Many more nights than one passed before Giovanni's father discovered
where he was and went after him—and after the money he had made at the
fair. Along with him the father took the bishop, to convince his son that the
money he had offered the priest was hardly Giovanni's to give. The young
man agreed and readily returned it. And along with it he gave his father his
handsome clothes and relinquished the name his father had given him. He
took, instead, the name of Francis. He would have no need of his fine
clothes or his family's name, he said, for he had decided to become a
missionary.

And so he did, founding the order of the Poor Brothers of Assisi. One
Palm Sunday night in 1212, a pretty young woman fled to him and begged
him to save her from a marriage she did not wish to enter and to let her
join the religious life instead. Francis cropped her hair and received her
into his order, and soon the Poor Clares, a sister order to Francis's Poor
Brothers of Assisi, had been founded.

164

St. Francis Basilica: LOWER BASILICA

Because he so feared the theft of the precious bones of his beloved Saint Francis, the saint's devoted follower Brother Elias conceived of this lower basilica as a hiding place for them. Although this was considered an accursed site, for it was an execution ground, Francis had asked that he be buried here. In 1228, two years after his death, construction of the basilica began, and this hill, previously known as the Infernal Hill, was renamed the Hill of Paradise.

CALABRIAN COUNTRYSIDE

The rural parts of this rocky province at the toe of Italy's boot are rich in lore of bandits who doubled as revolutionary guerrillas and vice versa, but none cut quite so complex a figure as Fra Diavolo—Brother Devil. Born Michele Pezza to poor parents in the town of Itri, he was in turn a monk, brigand, anti-French and pro-Bourbon guerrilla fighter, and duke of Cassano here in Calabria before he ended his days in front of a firing squad.

When Napoleon's troops overran the Kingdom of Naples in 1799 and forced Bourbon King Ferdinand IV to flee to Sicily, Neapolitan Cardinal Ruffo stayed behind and organized bands of jailbirds and brigands to reconquer the lost territory. Fra Diavolo's band was the most notorious of these, cutting off isolated detachments of French troops and executing summary "justice" on villagers who sympathized with the French. On one occasion, the good monk had seventy men, women, and children shot; on another, he threw captives over a cliff. He was finally captured and shot in 1806 by troops of Joseph Bonaparte. A once-popular opera by Auber and an always-popular lobster dish are named for him.

CAMPO IMPERATORE

In 1943, World War II was not going well for the Italians. The Allies had invaded Sicily and Benito Mussolini's alliance with Germany was falling out of favor, even within the Fascist party. So Victor Emmanuel III ordered his arrest. Pietro Badoglio became premier and Mussolini was held prisoner at this winter sports resort. But from the top of the 9,958-foot-high Gran Sasso, one of the highest peaks in the Apennines, he was rescued by German airmen, and flown to northern Italy. There he established a puppet government under German domination, which lasted until his capture by partisans two years later.

COMO

Villa Olmo

This neoclassical villa, part of the eighteenth century flowering of villas on Lake Como, was the focus of nineteenth-century patriot Giuseppe Garibaldi's greatest personal humiliation just as he was celebrating his greatest public victories.

Here in early June 1859, Italy's fifty-two-year-old liberator—victorious on his entry into Como—fell in love with eighteen-year-old Giuseppina Raimondi, whom he had met when the girl crossed enemy lines to deliver a message to the revolutionaries a few days earlier. In his diary, Garibaldi recounts the exciting days he spent by the lake here with Giuseppina, the daughter of the owner of this villa. Head over heels in love, Garibaldi proposed, but Giuseppina turned him down, for she was in love with and soon to be secretly married to a young nobleman. In December, however, she wrote apologetically to Garibaldi and reversed her decision. Apparently she was under pressure from her father to marry the nation's greatest hero. The wedding was held in the private chapel here a month later. But scarcely was the ceremony over when Garibaldi was handed an anonymous note telling him that Giuseppina had become his bride under protest.

Raging threats against the family that had forced her into the marriage, he stormed away from the villa. The hapless Giuseppina, meanwhile, was confined here by her father.

As for her first choice—her true love, whom she had wished to marry—he was captured in subsequent fighting with Russian troops and died in Siberia.

FLORENCE

The year 1505 was an extraordinary year for the Renaissance city of Florence. In Florence then the following artists were working on various projects: fifty-nine-year-old Il Perugino (painting his *Assumption* in the Church of the Annunciation): fifty-three-year-old Leonardo da Vinci and thirty-year-old Michelangelo Buonarroti (both doing cartoons in the great hall of the Palazzo della Signoria); twenty-two-year-old Raphael (painting his *Madonna del Gran Duca* now in the Pitti Palace, *Madonna del Cardellino* now in the Uffizi, and his *Last Supper* in the monastery of St. Onofrio). Also at work that year in Florence were Lorenzo di Credi, Fra Bartolommeo, and Sandro Botticelli.

Bargello (National Museum) (4 Via del Proconsolo)

In the days when this thirteenth-century sculpture museum was a prison, its history was bloody indeed. In the sixteenth century when Cosimo I obtained the throne, much to the amazement of all who had watched him pass a desultory boyhood in which he evinced little interest in anything but hunting and sports, he began his reign as a firm, indeed, a merciless ruler. When, in 1537, he defeated an army assembed to dethrone him, the eighteen-year-old Cosimo made sure that there would never be a plot against him again by having all involved—even if they had been among his closest friends—tortured and executed here.

Battistero (The Baptistery): THE NORTH AND EAST DOORS

In the fifteenth century, artists from all over Italy were invited to compete for the commission to fashion these two doors. Even Brunelleschi and Donatello were among them, but the fifty-four judges unanimously agreed that the finest handiwork was that of the youthful Lorenzo Ghiberti—not yet twenty. So it was he who fashioned these great doors—the high point of his career, as it turned out. Michelangelo, seen looking at the East Door one day, was asked what he thought of it. The great sculptor sighed and remarked, "It is so beautiful that it would grace the entrance to Paradise." And the East Door has been known ever since as "the Gate of Heaven." In 1966, when floods inundated this city, several of its panels were dislodged, but they were recovered and have been reinstalled.

Casa Guidi (8 Piazza San Felice)

Soon after their marriage, Robert Browning brought his wife, Elizabeth Barrett, six years his senior, to this house. Here the poets lived and loved, espoused causes, and wrote for the next fourteen years. Here, too, their son Penini spent his childhood, dressed by his mother like a little girl with golden curls of hair reaching to his shoulders.

Galleria dell'Accademia

When another sculptor working with Michelangelo in the cathedral workshop turned down a piece of marble he did not like, Michelangelo fashioned it into the *David* that stands here.

House of Livia (Piazza San Marco)

The garden on the right side of this house is what remains of the great garden of Lorenzo the Magnificent, the Medici ruler who in the late fifteenth century surrounded himself with the best examples he could find of sculpture and painting. The place became an academy for young artists, especially those of noble birth. But Lorenzo also provided food, housing, and clothing for students who were poor, and he encouraged a spirit of competition among all.

Around 1590 Lorenzo began complaining that there were no great modern sculptors, and asked the artist Domenico Ghirlandaio if he had any students in his workshop with special ability as sculptors. The teen-age Michelangelo was the student Ghirlandaio sent. Before he could go on to spend four happy years in this garden, Michelangelo had to overcome the usual problem of the new boy in school—coping with the resident bully, a jealous young sculptor named Torrigiano, who had a habit of damaging the work of others if it was too good. In their final fight, Torrigiano broke Michelangelo's nose.

Michelangelo's first effort here was an imitation of an ancient statue of an old faun, which he "improved" in his version by opening the mouth and showing tongue and teeth. When he inspected the work, Lorenzo was deeply impressed, but thought to tease Michelangelo by gravely admonishing him: "You should know that old men never have all their teeth, but have always lost some," he reportedly said. Lorenzo then walked away, but the young sculptor took the admonishment so seriously that he broke off a tooth and changed the gums.

Loggia dei Lanzi (Piazza della Signoria): STATUE OF PERSEUS

The sixteenth-century sculptor Benvenuto Cellini had worked long and hard preparing the mold for this impressive statue; exhausted, he contracted a fever and took to his bed during the fusing process. Those whom he had left in charge suddenly woke him. Something had gone wrong, they said. His *Perseus* was ruined.

Cellini leaped from his bed and raced into the foundry. To melt properly, more tin alloy and more heat were needed. Shouting to his assistants to add wood to the fire, he began adding tin. The immense heat generated by the additional wood burst the furnace, but the metal was melting. Now it was still more tin that was needed and all that he had was gone—except that there was tin in his pewter plates. Two hundred of them were hurled into the pot of metal, and his statue was saved. Cellini fell to his knees and thanked God.

Museo di San Marco: CLOISTER BELL

This bell, a gift to the convent from Cosimo de' Medici, had been tolled as a warning to Savonarola that enemies were about to attack his convent, and so, to punish the convent after the friar's execution (*see* Florence, Piazza della Signoria), the bell was taken from its place and whipped by the public executioner as it was pulled out of the city to a place of exile.

Palazzo Medici-Riccardi (Medici Palace) (Via Cavour)

Florentines on the eve of the Renaissance held themselves in very high esteem, and their paeans to their own greatness often ended not with God but with Cosimo de' Medici, who established his powerful line in this palace.

"I praise God that of all the times I could have lived," wrote wealthy Florentine Giovanni Rucellai, "I have lived in these times that are the apex of history, and in Italy which is the jewel of these times, and in Tuscany which is the jewel of Italy, and in Florence, which is the jewel of Tuscany, and among men like the illustrious citizen Cosimo de' Medici."

Cosimo himself returned the compliments, adding to his favor among the citizenry. His favorite saying was, "Give me two yards of red cloth and I will make a gentleman of any Florentine."

❧⚜☙

Here, from the time he was sixteen until he was nineteen, Michelangelo lived as a member of the household of Lorenzo the Magnificent. He sculpted. He participated in family affairs. When he yearned to have a violet cloak, the sensitive Lorenzo saw that the color-conscious youth got one.

❧⚜☙

The Medici rulers of Florence had their ups and downs, but things looked especially bleak in 1527. While the inept Medici pope Clement VII hid in the Castle Sant'Angelo in Rome and watched that city sacked by German troops here, the illegitimate Medici brothers, Alessandro and Ippolito, who had assumed rule of Florence, cowered in this palace while angry mobs thronged the Via Larga outside demanding a new government.

Suddenly a litter appeared, bearing a legitimate Medici who valued the old family honor more than she valued what was left of the family. She was Clarice de' Medici. Storming into the palace, she harangued the brothers in a voice loud enough for the mob outside to hear. She noted how things had been managed differently by her ancestors, who were *true* Medici, and ended her speech by demanding the illegitimate pretenders' departure. The Medici Palace, she told them, had not been built as a "stable for mules." After the frightened brothers had left the palace and the city, the people wanted to raze the building and rename the area "the Piazza of the Mules."

❧⚜☙

Shortly before his death in 1464, paterfamilias Cosimo de' Medici lost his favorite son Giovanni. The heartbroken old man had himself carried through this palace he had built, sighing that it was now too big for such a small family. Cosimo spent most of his last months in his monk's cell in the Church of San Marco nearby, reading Plato and communing with the saintly painter Fra Angelico.

Palazzo Rucellai (Via della Vigna Nuova, in quarter of Santa Maria Novella)

Giovanni Rucellai, founder of the great merchant family who lived here in the fifteenth century, was rumored in his later years to be trying to usurp Medici greatness with this palace, the loggia across from it, and the family chapel in nearby Santa Maria Novella, all done by the Renaissance architect Alberti. But the old man knew that the best way to win power was to buy it or marry into it, so he married his son Bernardo Rucellai to Cosimo de' Medici's niece Nannina. Giovanni, known also for his willingness to spend large sums of money, produced a wedding to top all weddings.

As crowds gathered on Sunday, June 8, 1466, at dawn, servants brought quartered bullocks; casks of Greek wine; capons hanging on long staffs; bars of buffalo cheese; turkeys in pairs; barrels of ordinary and choice sweet wine; baskets of pomegranates; hampers of sea fish and crates of smaller freshwater fish from the Arno; birds; hares; cream cheese wrapped in fresh green rushes; baskets of sweetmeats, tarts, and other pastries. The street was hung with tapestries and insignia of the Medici and Rucellai families, and the feasting continued from Sunday morning to Tuesday night. At three giant tables 500 guests ate two meals daily: Sunday morning's menu included boiled capon and beef tongue, a roast of meat and another roast of baby chickens garnished in sugar and rosewater. Sunday evening saw galantine, another roast of meat and chickens with fritters. Monday's breakfast was blanc mange (a flavored milk pudding), boiled capons and boiled sausages, and roasted chickens. Monday evening's meal was a repeat of Sunday's as well as sugar and almond tarts. Tuesday's breakfast was roast meat and platters of quails; on Tuesday evening the satisfied and plumpened guests finished with another roast and galantine.

Palazzo Vecchio

When the reprobate Fra Filippo Lippi, too zestful and lustful to stay long a friar, turned painter, he was still much too distractable. So his patron, Cosimo de' Medici, gave him a room here to do his painting in—and locked him into it. That arrangement was short lived, for after only a day or two desire got the better of the erstwhile priest/painter, and he escaped out a window on a rope of bed sheets. It was some days before he had had his fill of excesses and let Cosimo find him. He continued to keep his studio, but was never again confined in it. The English poet Browning wrote a famous dramatic dialogue about him.

❧❀❧

After the assassination of Giuliano de' Medici and the attempted assassination of his brother Lorenzo (*see* Santa Maria del Fiore), the conspirators sought to take over this palace. But they failed and, indeed, found themselves locked inside. A new self-locking mechanism of which they were unaware had just been installed, and it was only a matter of hours before a dozen plotters were swinging from this palace's windows, another two dozen from its walls.

Piazza della Signoria

The Piazza della Signoria was the site both of the great victories and the great defeats of the fiery fifteenth-century Dominican friar Girolamo Savonarola.

Horrified by the excesses and the immorality of Florentine life under the Medicis (not only did Lorenzo and his retinue enjoy art and literature, but wine, women, and lascivious song), Savonarola roused the people to burn in bonfires here all that he deemed immoral. He organized the children of this city and had them go from door to door collecting lewd books and pictures, toiletries, fancy dress, cards, and dice. All these "vanities" were stacked in the center of this piazza and put to the torch while the children sang hymns of joy and the crowds applauded. That was in 1497. The next year, on this same spot, Savonarola was challenged by a Franciscan monk to endure an ordeal by fire. If he were genuinely on the side of the Lord with all his rigid righteous teachings, then he would not suffer from the flames, the Franciscan averred.

Savonarola refused the challenge. His devoted aide and friend Fra Domenico accepted, however. A crowd gathered here eager to see the outcome of the ordeal. But there was one delay after another. First, the Franciscans said that Fra Domenico's red robe was under Savonarola's spell and would have to be removed. Then they took away his crucifix, protesting that it, too, might be charmed. When Savonarola proposed to give his friend the Sacrament to guard him in the flames instead, the Franciscans insisted that must not be.

Next there was a thunderstorm. By then, it was too dark for any audience to enjoy the projected ordeal, and it was postponed—never to be held. But the crowd had been looking for a Savonarola miracle and had been disappointed. Enthusiasm for the demanding, ascetic friar diminished overnight, and his opponents had the upper hand.

The next night they came to the Convent of San Marco after him. Some of his fellow friars, foreseeing that danger lay ahead, had hidden arms inside the cloister. When the enemy pounded at the convent doors, the friars decked themselves in their helmets and prepared for battle. Savonarola told them they must lay down their arms. They did, but this did not prevent them, when the attackers finally broke through and found them at their prayers, from fighting back with their candles and crucifixes. And many of the enemy fled, thinking it was angels fighting back.

Next, the Dominicans were warned that unless Savonarola and Fra Domenico were surrendered, artillery would destroy their convent. Although their fellow friars begged Savonarola and Fra Domenico to try to escape out a window, they elected instead to surrender.

There followed days of torture for the two men and a third friar. Savonarola's inquisitors insisted that he deny that he had ever seen visions urging correction of Florentine morals. Ultimately, under the extreme torture, he said that he had not, though later it was reported that his confessions and the other friars' had been falsified.

Finally, on May 22, 1498, a gallows for hanging and burning of the friars who had been sentenced as heretics was erected here. It was built beam across beam, and the crowd that had gathered the night before to be sure of the best seats for the morning execution began to whisper, "They are going to crucify him." Quickly city officials ordered some of the cross pieces cut away so there would be no resemblence to a crucifix. That done, on the twenty-third, first his two friends, and then the outspoken reformer-friar, were hanged and burned.

21 Piazza Pitti

Here Feodor Dostoevski wrote *The Idiot* while on a visit in 1868.

Pitti Palace and Uffizi Museum

"On condition that it should never be removed from Florence and that it should be for the public of all nations," the last of the Medici, the electress of the Rhine Anna Maria Ludovica, left the works of art she and her forebears had gathered here to the state of Tuscany when she died in 1743. By then, Tuscany was in Austrian hands, but she made sure the Medici art collection never would be.

San Miniato al Monte (Piazzale Michelangelo)

In 1530 when the army of Emperor Charles V was attacking here, the ingenious Michelangelo, in charge of the defense of the city, ordered mattresses brought to this Romanesque church and laid against it to protect it from enemy artillery fire. Without him, it would almost certainly have collapsed under the enemy blasts.

Santa Croce (Church of the Holy Cross) (Piazza Santa Croce)

When Michelangelo died in Rome, there was a grand funeral for him, and burial in the Church of Santi Apostoli, but it didn't seem right somehow to Cosimo I that such a famous native son should be buried so far from home. And so two merchants smuggled the body out to a second burial here. And what a grand affair it was! Though efforts had been made to keep it secret, word had gotten out, and artists, craftsmen, clergy, and ordinary citizens flocked to pay tribute to the great artist.

With native son Dante Alighieri, however, the Florentines were not so successful. He died in Ravenna in 1321 and despite centuries of efforts to have his remains returned to the tomb that awaits them here, Ravenna has adamantly refused to let them go. (*See* Ravenna, Dante's Tomb.)

Santa Maria del Fiore (Cathedral)

In the chancel of this cathedral, Lorenzo the Magnificent and his brother Giuliano were set upon by members of the rival Pazzi family and their hirelings on April 26, 1478. Giuliano was killed. Lorenzo escaped with a wound in the neck. The instigator of the plot, it was said, was Pope Sixtus IV, eager to give the Florentine state to one of his nephews. The Pazzis participated—not to help the pope or his nephew—but to gain greater power for themselves.

The original plan was to poison the Medicis at a banquet they were giving. But Giuliano was not well the night of the banquet and failed to attend. The murderers' next plot was to assassinate the pair the following morning during the elevation of the Host at mass here. That moment was selected since it was the holiest moment in the celebration of the mass, and a time when all heads would, therefore, be bowed. It would be easier to lop off a bowed head, and, in addition, no one would see the executioner.

But the mercenary hired to do the murdering recoiled at the prospect of committing the evil deed at such a very holy time. Two bungling priests had to be substituted. Although Giuliano was done in quickly by one of the Pazzis, the two priests were slow in their attack on Lorenzo and, despite his initial wound, he drew his sword and fought them off. Then he raced toward the sacristy, followed by several of his friends, who slammed the heavy bronze doors shut and locked them in the faces of their pursuers. (*See* Florence, Palazzo Vecchio.)

Santa Maria del Fiore (Cathedral): MICHELANGELO'S PIETÀ

Work on this magnificent *Pietà,* destined, some say, for his own tomb, was abandoned by Michelangelo when he was eighty, when he found a flaw in the marble.

Uffizi (off the Piazza della Signoria): TRIBUNA

This frescoed ceiling crashed to the floor when the Germans were blowing up the Ponte alle Grazie in World War II. But thanks to prewar German art historians who had painstakingly photographed the ceiling piece by piece, it was possible to put it all together again.

LAKE COMO (Lakeside Villages of Dongo, Mezzegra, and Menaggio)

As the Nazi and Fascist worlds collapsed in April 1945, Benito Mussolini vowed to defend this little finger of land—the Valtellina—reaching north from Lake Como into Switzerland with "3,000 loyal Blackshirts." Little did he know that in a few days he and his young mistress would face death alone on a roadside above the lake.

An angry Mussolini in a caravan of thirty-eight vehicles manned by Germans left Milan on April 25, heading in this direction. He spent the night of April 26 in Menaggio, which was still held by Fascists, but partisan guerrillas were pouring down from mountaintop hideouts and liberating the lake's villages one by one from German occupation.

On the morning of April 27, his caravan headed north along this lake. The partisans, however, alerted to the presence of Germans in Menaggio, set up roadblocks in Dongo and north of the village of Musso. The Germans, though armed, stopped at the first sound of gunfire outside Musso and let themselves be surrounded. But the caravan was given permission to go on to Dongo where it would be checked for escaping Italians before being allowed to pass on through the Valtellina toward Germany.

During the long stop at Musso, Mussolini managed to slip out of his Italian clothes and into a German uniform, as well as out of his armored car and into the back of a truck where he hid under canvas. Dongo searchers went through the truck—the first time without seeing Mussolini. But a partisan named Giuseppe Negri, making a second search, noticed the shape of a man covered by the material in back. The Germans laughingly said it was a drunken friend of theirs. Looking under the canvas, however, Negri recognized Il Duce and reported the news to fellow partisans. Mussolini was hauled out from under the canvas and brought to the Dongo town hall. There he joined his mistress Clara Petacci, who had already been discovered.

The partisans wanted to keep Mussolini out of the hands of the rapidly advancing Americans, who had talked about putting him on trial in the United States. He was to be punished as they chose, so they brought Il Duce and Clara to a small house in the hamlet of Bonzanigo. At 3:00 A.M., partisan Walter Audisio arrived at the house with a squad of three men and orders from partisan commanders in Milan to execute Mussolini.

Waking Il Duce and Clara, Audisio pretended he had come to free them from the partisans stationed at the house. Actually he wanted to make sure there would be no escape attempt and that the execution would be swiftly done. He hurried the pair to a jeep and had them driven to a preselected execution spot in the hamlet of Mezzegra. Suddenly Audisio said he thought he'd heard a noise and ordered the jeep to stop. Then he told Mussolini and Clara to get out and walk quietly toward a gate in the wall along the road. It was only when Audisio uttered the first words of the one-sentence condemnation—"In the name of the Italian people"—that Mussolini realized what was about to happen. Young Clara (whose rival, Rachele Mussolini, was then safely with her children in nearby Como) threw her arms around Mussolini.

"Get away from him unless you want to be killed too," said Audisio. And the first shot rang out. Mussolini fell to his knees. No one knows what happened next. Perhaps it was just because she was in Audisio's way that Clara was killed, too, in the volley of shots that followed.

The spot is marked today by a small cross and a small Italian flag.

LAKE GARDA

Village of Malcesine

The German poet Goethe was one of many people charmed by the panoramic views from the shores of this subalpine lake. But Goethe was treated a bit more harshly than most tourists. He was surprised by suspicious local constables one day in September 1786, as he sketched the fourteenth-century castle of the Scaligeri family of Verona, which is visible from this point. Goethe was arrested and locked up in jail.

LERICI

San Terenzo

In May 1822, Percy and Mary Shelley took up residence in the Villa Magni here, where the sea roared at their terrace. Shelley enjoyed the drama of it, but the Shelley houseguests, Captain and Mrs. Edward Williams, were not so sure. Something in the wind boded evil, they felt, as summer progressed. All the same, Williams sailed with Shelley when Shelley asked him to, and early in July when they had word that the poet Leigh Hunt was in Leghorn, off they sailed to visit him. It was on the return here, after a happy two-day stay, that the pair was drowned. (*See* Viareggio.)

MANTUA

Palazzo Ducale (Ducal Palace): APARTMENT OF THE DWARVES

In this precious miniature set of rooms, the Gonzaga duke Vicenzo I, who ruled from 1587 to 1612, kept one of his favorite mistresses—a dwarf. Many of the apartment's scaled-down furnishings are gone, but a tiny stairway remains. Vicenzo, who was tall and thin, had to bend deeply every time he came through the doorway to this apartment.

MILAN

Biblioteca Ambrosiana (Ambrosian Library) (Piazzo Pius XI)

The romantic poet Lord Byron, visiting here in 1816, mused over a lock of Lucretia Borgia's hair (*See* Rome, The Vatican Museums) and found it lovely enough to steal a single strand and to remark on his wretchedness at not having been born soon enough ever to have seen her.

Duomo (Cathedral)

Although he went on to become a saint of the church, it took some doing on the part of the people of Milan to persuade their Roman governor, Ambrose, to become a Christian at all.

In the fourth century, the worshippers in the basilica that stood on this spot (tile and foundations of which can still be seen) were sharply divided between Arians who accepted Christ, but not as the Son of God, and Orthodox Christians. At the height of the controversy, Ambrose was sent from Rome to govern here. Some years later, when the reigning bishop died and his successor had to be chosen, the controversy between the Arians and the Orthodox Christians came to a head. When bishops from elsewhere in the Christian world assembled to weigh the problem, an angry populace rushed into the nave, shouting, ready to come to blows among themselves. Only Ambrose could calm them. No sooner had he done so than a child's cry was heard from the multitude, "Ambrose bishop!"

No one would have believed it. Suddenly there was peace between the factions as Arians and Orthodox Christians alike echoed the child's cry of "Ambrose bishop." But Ambrose didn't want to be bishop. Ahead of him lay an inviting career in the Roman government. He thanked his admirers, and fled.

The enthusiasm for his selection would not be quelled, however. For days, representatives of both sides wheedled and cajoled. But to no avail. Indeed, to turn his admirers against him, Ambrose ordered several accused criminals viciously tortured and invited prostitutes to his house. But the people still followed him everywhere, assuring him that his misdeeds would be forgiven as soon as he was baptized.

Finally, exasperated, Ambrose tried to escape the city. He fled at night and in the darkness his driver lost the way. And so, at dawn, Ambrose found himself back at the gates of Milan. There, he was captured and locked inside his own house. Finally, deciding that it was *some* god's will that he surrender to the people's wishes, Ambrose made the necessary arrangements with his superiors in Rome and agreed to be baptized here. Eight days later, he was consecrated bishop.

❧⚶☙

With the crown with an iron rim said to have been made from a nail from the True Cross, Napoleon I crowned himself king of Italy here in 1805, remarking that God had given him the crown and he who tried to take it from him had best beware. In using the Iron Crown for his coronation he put himself in noble company—both Frederick Barbarossa and Charles V had been crowned emperors of the Holy Roman Empire with it.

Grand Hotel (29 Via Manzoni)

On January 21, 1901, the eighty-eight-year-old composer Giuseppe Verdi suffered a stroke in his hotel room here while sitting on the edge of his bed. Few composers have been more loved by their own nation in their own lifetime than Verdi, whose early operas were inspiring political allegories for Italy's nascent independence movement and whose later works were the summit of narrative opera. As news spread that his right side was paralyzed and death imminent, a death vigil was started outside the hotel, which was draped in black. Straw was placed on the Via Manzoni to muffle the sound of carriage traffic, and much of this business center's everyday activity stopped until Verdi died on January 27, without ever having regained consciousness.

Piazzale Loreto

Partisans bearing the bodies of Benito Mussolini and Clara Petacci (*see* Lake Como) arrived in the early dawn hours of April 29, 1944, here in Milan, and quietly laid out the corpses. As the Milanese began waking on this day after their liberation by the Americans, word spread through the city that the bodies were on display, and a crowd gathered. It soon turned into a mob that gave the world one of the last grisly sights of World War II in Italy. People kicked, stabbed, and shot at the remains of Il Duce and his mistress as they hung by the feet above this square.

Santa Maria delle Grazie (Church of St. Mary of Grace)

The distraught prior of this Dominican monastery hurried one day in 1497 to see duke Ludovico Sforza and complain that the painter Leonardo da Vinci, from whom the monastery had commissioned a fresco of *The Last Supper*, was lying down on the job. He had done all the apostles, the prior said, but the heads of Christ and Judas Iscariot remained undone; Leonardo sometimes would waste half a day just looking at the work he had already done—never picking up his brush at all! Could the duke get him to complete his job? the prior asked.

To satisfy the plaintiff, an amused duke did call Leonardo in to see him, making it clear, however, that he understood the artist was not malingering. Leonardo admitted he was having a problem with both heads. He said he could not conceive of painting the beauty of Christ. As for Judas, perhaps if he were *really* stuck, he teased, he would use the annoying prior as his model. There were no more complaints.

NAPLES

Castel dell'Ovo (Port of St. Lucia)

In medieval days magical powers were sometimes ascribed to the beloved Roman poet Vergil. For example, it was said that he gave this castle its name when he placed an enchanted egg within its walls. As long as the egg did not break, people believed, Naples would be protected from all calamity.

In 1370, a severe storm damaged this seaside castle. The city's rulers averted a riot among the panic-stricken populace only by assuring them that a new egg—also enchanted—would be put inside the walls when the damaged structure was rebuilt.

Palazzo Real (Royal Palace)

Through a secret corridor that led from this palace down to the water, Naples's King Ferdinand, his wife Maria Carolina, their children, and Lord Nelson and Lady Hamilton fled to the sea—and safety—as the French approached Naples in 1799. Maria Carolina, sister of Marie Antoinette, feared that the guillotine would be her fate, too, when the French invaders arrived. Close friends of Lady Hamilton, mistress of England's Lord Nelson, the king and queen prevailed upon the admiral to arrange an escape.

And in a fierce December storm—so fierce that even Nelson was dismayed by it, and one prince died of exposure—the royal family sailed for Sicily aboard Nelson's flagship.

PADUA

Capella degli Scrovegni (Chapel of the Scrovegni)

The poet Dante was traveling on diplomatic missions from Ravenna to Padua in the early fourteenth century, legend has it, when Giotto was painting his famous frescoes here. One morning the poet met the painter and his sons on the street. Dante was struck by the ugliness of Giotto's sons and, with the same bluntness that helped get him exiled from his native Florence, is reported to have said, "My friend, you make such handsome figures for others—why do you make such plain ones for yourself?" To which Giotto replied, "I paint for others by day."

PALERMO, SICILY

Chiesa di Santo Spirito (Church of the Holy Ghost)

On Easter Monday morning in 1282 as the people of Palermo were leaving church, they suddenly found French soldiers in their midst, searching them for hidden weapons. For more than a dozen years, Charles of Anjou, the brother of the king of France, with the endorsement of the pope, had ruled this city. But his rule was severe and the French troops of occupation had become increasingly unpopular. Revolt was, indeed, in the offing. And all it took to start it was the ill-advised act of one of the French soldiers.

Taking advantage of his orders to search for weapons, the soldier fondled the breasts of a pretty Sicilian girl. Within seconds, his sword had been wrested from him and he was run through with it. Then the enraged congregation turned on the other soldiers. Leaving them dead and dying, the people rampaged on through the city streets, shouting "Death to the French." Before night fell, several thousand French men, women, and children had been slaughtered. Stopped on street corners, approached in their houses, the test was their ability to pronounce "ceci"—"chick-pea." Those who could not, clearly, were of French origin, and fell to the sword. History remembers that frightful night, mournfully, as the Sicilian Vespers.

PISA

Torre Pendente (Leaning Tower)

It is hard to understand why this city, renowned above all other medieval turreted Tuscan cities for its tower building, had so much trouble constructing this central tower. After all, medieval estimates of the number of towers here range from 10,000 to 16,000. One eighteenth-century French visitor went so far as to theorize that it was purposely built to lean by a hunchbacked architect, who wanted the structure to resemble himself.

In any case, the tower, started in 1174 by the architect Bonnano Pisano, seemed cursed from the start. After Pisano had built to a height of forty feet, he found his tower sinking through the loose soil on one side. Hoping to correct the problem, he placed second, third, and fourth stories successively nearer the perpendicular, and when these measures failed, in despair he left the tower unfinished. Sixty years later, another Italian architect approached the task but also abandoned it—after adding a fifth story, which only made things worse.

Then a foreigner named William of Innsbruck managed to restore the tower to the perpendicular by making the pillars of the first and sixth stories taller on one side than the other. But the tower started sinking once again, and William abandoned the work in frustration.

One hundred years later, Tommaso Pisano crowned the tower with a bellhouse that would have toppled the whole thing had it been a few feet higher.

POMPEII

At last in the summer of A.D. 79 this prosperous city of 25,000 seemed to be returning to normal. An earthquake sixteen years before had disrupted life for a time, but Pompeii, a favorite resort city, was enjoying a comeback. And then on the morning of August 24, the city shuddered as if there were to be another earthquake. But instead, a curious cloud appeared in the sky and hovered over 3,900-foot-high Mount Vesuvius that rose above the city. People went to their doorsteps to look at it. By afternoon, ash was falling, and there had been more explosions. Then as cinders began to fall, dwellers in villas at the base of the mountain frantically put out into the Bay of Naples in their boats. Before the volcano had subsided, 2,000 people were dead, buried beneath ash and pumice that covered the rooftops by as much as eight feet. In their very tracks they were buried—or killed by poisonous gases.

Not until the seventeenth century was Pompeii ever seen again. Then road builders found it. A century after that, excavation began by awed archeologists. But even today, a third of the city still remains to be uncovered.

PORTOFINO

The body of Saint George, it is said, was brought here from Palestine after his martyrdom, and his bones still are believed to lie in the little chapel that bears his name. In gratitude for his reception here, legend has it, he aided the Crusaders embarking from this port for the Holy Land. Richard the Lion-Hearted was among them.

RAVENNA

Dante's Tomb

Time and again the bones of Dante have been unearthed and reinterred since his death here in 1321. First, it was said that they should be removed and burned because he was a heretic. To forestall that, the bones were stolen by Franciscan friars. Then, when all seemed safe again, they were restored.

Next the Florentines sought them, insisting that after all—even if they had treated him shabbily by exiling him—Dante was one of theirs. But Ravenna would not hear, that time, of having him taken from them. In 1692, when it was reported that repairs were about to be made on the chapel, the bones were spirited away again by the Franciscans who wanted to make sure that they would not—valuable as they were—be stolen during the repairs. It was two centuries before they were found again.

This time, a festival honoring Dante was being held in Florence, and Ravenna, not wishing to be outdone, decided to clean this tomb—empty though it apparently was. And in the process, when workmen removed a piece of wall to repair a pipe, they found a wooden box. A note inside identified the box's contents as the poet's bones. Oh what a grand celebration *that* turned out to be!

Pineta (Pine Woods) (outskirts of Ravenna)

Here Dante, exiled from Florence for his outspokenness, often walked, and is said to have composed much of the *Divine Comedy*. And here the poet Byron and his mistress (and one true love, it is said), the countess Teresa Guiccioli, would come riding after she had coerced him into quitting Venice to be at her side.

RIMINI

The beauteous thirteenth-century Francesca da Rimini made the mistake of falling in love with her handsome young brother-in-law Paolo—an understandable mistake because her husband, Giovanni Malatesta, the ruler here, was both cruel and ugly. But, of course, Giovanni learned of the romance —and with one blow of his sword killed both his wife and his own brother. Dante tells the story in Canto V of the *Inferno*. Gabriele D'Annunzio wrote a tragedy about it. Jean Auguste Ingres made the murder the subject of a painting, and Tchaikovsky of an overture.

Tempio Malatestiano (Malatesta Temple)

Although, ostensibly, this striking Renaissance church was built in honor of Saint Francis by Sigismondo Malatesta during the fifteenth century, in reality it was in adoration of his mistress Isotta degli Atti, and the inscription on her tomb reads "Sacred to the deified Isotta." Brilliant and handsome, a patron of the arts, himself a poet, Sigismondo was also so violent and cruel that Pius II actually publicly condemned him to Hell. The process was not unlike a canonization and an investigation by a cardinal preceded it. The pope's edict said, in part, that Sigismondo should be committed to Hell and "to the companionship for eternity of devils and the damned." Among his evil deeds are said to have been the murders of two wives—one by poison and one by strangulation with a napkin—and the rape of his own daughter.

ROME

It was the abandoned twins, Romulus and Remus, whose cradle was washed up by the Tiber at the foot of the Palatine Hill (*see* Rome, Palatine Hill), who founded this city in the eighth century B.C. Legend has it that the pair was discovered and suckled by a she-wolf, and then set about establishing a city here. Romulus outlined its boundaries by digging a furrow with his plow and announced that anyone who crossed the boundary would be put to death. In defiance of his brother's order, Remus did. Accordingly, Romulus killed his twin, and, alone, as had been prophesied, became the first king of Rome.

To people his city, he accepted foreigners fleeing their countries for one reason or another, but there were few women among them. The neighboring Sabine women, however, were unusually attractive. So one day Romulus declared that there would be a festival in Rome and all neighboring tribes were invited to attend. The Sabines readily accepted, and—men, women, and children—all came to enjoy the entertainment. Then, suddenly, the entertainment ended. The playfulness of the Roman men with the Sabines' daughters became something more. Fighting ensued. The happy festival ended in bloodshed, and the vanquished Sabines were forced to return home minus their young women.

Back home, they organized for full-scale combat and returned here, but by the time they got back, their daughters had already been wed to the Romans and—quite satisfied with them as husbands and lovers—declined to return. The women sought, instead, to unite their Sabine fathers and brothers with their Roman husbands. Many a painter through the centuries depicted the rape of the Sabine women and the subsequent attempt at reconciliation.

Arch of Septimus Severus (Roman Forum)

Happily, it is for the beauty of his baths (*see* Rome, Terme di Caracalla) not the cruelty and jealousy of his nature that the emperor Caracalla is remembered. But this arch, built by his father, Septimus Severus, in A.D. 203 in honor of Caracalla and his brother Geta, clearly shows the dark side of his nature. On the death of their father, the sons were to have shared the rule of Rome, but Caracalla wanted all the power for himself. No sooner thought of than done. Geta was murdered and to wipe the memory of him from his own and his people's minds, Caracalla had Geta's name expunged from the arch and in its place, after his own name, "Greatest and Most Powerful of Princes" was inscribed.

But it wasn't quite that easy. A trace of Geta's name, no matter how hard the workmen worked, remained to haunt his usurping brother—and still remains. It can be seen in the fourth line of writing on this arch.

Castel Sant' Angelo

When the emperor Hadrian, patron of the arts that he was, had this immense marble tomb built in A.D. 135, he decorated it with the finest of Greek and Roman statues. But most of them were yanked from their walls in the sixth century and hurled below to stop the progress of invading Goths.

◄◦◊◦►

Thousands of Romans were dying of the plague in A.D. 590 and Pope Gregory the Great, just elected to office, was determined to do something about it. Carrying a cross, he led a procession of praying citizens around the city for three days. On the third day, as the group crossed the bridge that leads to this ancient mausoleum, Gregory looked up. In the sky above this enormous tomb he said he saw the archangel Michael sheathing his flaming sword. Surely that meant the plague would end. And it did. In remembrance, Bernini carved the statue of an angel with a sword that stands atop the tower here today, and the name of Hadrian's ancient sepulcher became Holy Angel.

Castel Sant'Angelo: CORRIDOJO DI CASTELLO

Down this corridor between the Vatican and the Castel Sant'Angelo scurried Pope Clement VII in 1527 as Charles V of Burgundy, with an army of Germans and Italians and Spaniards, stormed into Rome. At his prayers in St. Peter's when the invasion was announced, the well-meaning but somewhat baffled Holy Father was at a bit of a loss as to what to do. Should he stand and face the enemy courageously or flee? His aides suggested that the latter course was surely the wiser, so through this passageway he came, all dressed in papal scarlet. Halfway down this passageway, with its many windows, someone thought better of his attire—he was surely an obvious target in his brilliant plumage—and flung a dark cape over the scarlet robes as camouflage.

It wasn't just the pope who fled the invaders. A complement of cardinals joined him—one of them, late in seeking to escape, was hauled to the protection of the castle in a wicker basket. The goldsmith Benvenuto Cellini was among the notable escapees—and also among the defenders of the pope, shooting his arquebus valiantly at the invaders.

For eight days the siege of the city went on. Women were raped; cardinals held for ransom; tombs and palaces plundered. The holy veil of St. Veronica, used to wipe the brow of Christ on the cross, was discovered by the German Lutherans and casually tossed about. As the battling continued, the besieged clerics in the castle grew hungrier and hungrier, and finally, surrender seemed the only way out. Then as now, however, the enemy would not accept surrender unless a ransom was paid. Happily, the clever Cellini had taken the papal crown apart and sewed its jewels into Pope Clement's robes—and it was those jewels that bought the pontiff's freedom.

Castel Sant'Angelo: HEAD OF THE STATUE OF POPE PAUL IV

Not only did no one mourn on the day in 1559 when this hated pope, who was the father of the Inquisition and the founder of the Roman ghetto, died, but a joyous populace pulled down his statue from the Campidoglio and threw it into the Tiber. This head is from that Campidoglio statue and—much later—was fished from the river.

Catacombs (Via Appia Antica, Via Ardiatina, Via Aurelia, Via Latina, Via Nomentana, Via Salaria Nuova, Via Tiburtina)

For centuries, all but one of this city's catacombs lay forgotten. Then one spring day in 1578, a man digging volcanic dust for his vineyard on the Via Salaria found that he had dug his way into a tunnel—and on both sides of the tunnel were the dead. Fascinated by his discovery, he made his way down the first tunnel and discovered that it was crossed by another; that by another, and on and on. After historians started descending into these Christian tombs dug on the outskirts of Rome, they began to be frequented by curious sightseers and still are today.

It was in the days of the early Christians, who insisted on burying rather than burning their dead, as was the Roman custom, that these catacombs were constructed in the only place the Romans would allow burials—the outskirts of the city. Looted in the Dark Ages by invaders, the popes decreed that all the bones of martyrs that were in them should be brought into the city for safekeeping. And so, as generations came and went, no one remembered that the underground tombs were there—until the energetic farmer dug too deep.

Church of St. Paul (Via Nazionale)

This is Rome's major Protestant church, established by Americans and Britons shortly after Italian independence in the nineteenth century. It is also the home of the only carillon bells in all of Rome. For that reason, it was loved by the young king (then prince) Humbert II.

Before World War I, the young prince, then living in the Palazzo del Quirinale, used to listen to the carillon and learned the words to its hymns from his Protestant nurse. His favorite was "Pull for the shore, boys, pull for the shore." One day he sent his royal equerry to the church to request the hymn, and Catholic Rome rang with a royal command performance of Protestant music.

The Coliseum

For one hundred days, the people of Rome celebrated the dedication of this amphitheater in A.D. 80, and in the course of the celebration, the bloodthirsty populace watched 9,000 animals being slaughtered. Between times, the arena was flooded so that mininaval battles could be held to entertain the festivity-hungry Romans.

❦

Here, thousands of men—both Christians and gladiators—met death at the hands of each other or in the jaws of wild animals—until the day in the fifth century when the monk Telemachus, sickened by the sight of so much bloodshed, strode into the arena. Seeking to separate two gladiators, the brave monk turned to the assembled crowd and begged them to put an end to gladiatorial combats. The audience, at first intrigued by the change from the usual program, listened to the zealous monk, but they quickly grew bored at his harangue and began to shout insults. When he continued his pleading, they were no longer insults that were flung at him. Instead, the crowd pelted him with stones, and Telemachus died here in the arena.

The spectators left the Coliseum that day, however, never to return. Telemachus' martyrdom spelled the end of gladiatorial combats.

❦

In the eighteenth century, in the reign of Pope Benedict XIV, it looked as if there would soon be no Coliseum left. The Normans, in 1084, had virtually destroyed it in an attack on Rome. In the thirteenth and fourteenth centuries, earthquakes had further devastated it and, in the fifteenth century, Romans had started taking the stones from it as though it were a building quarry. This worried Benedict, for the Venerable Bede in the eighth century had warned that if the Coliseum fell, Rome would fall, and if Rome fell, so would the world. So Benedict had a cross erected in the center of this amphitheater where so many thousands of Christians had met death as martyrs and thereby saved this ancient pagan monument as a holy Christian place.

Collegio Romano (Roman College) (Piazza del Collegio Romano)

The porter here in the 1880s was a man who allegedly enjoyed his drink. Since, in those days, this was the storehouse for the books and manuscripts collected from monasteries all over Italy during the disestablishment of the church, he had a heyday selling rare works to satisfy his habit. But then one day a scholar bought some butter from a market-woman and undoing it at home, discovered that its wrapping was a letter signed by Christopher Columbus. An investigation followed, and the porter was relieved of his post. Today, the books and manuscripts he might have sold had he not been found out are the base of the Biblioteca Nazionale Centrale Vittorio Emmanuele II.

Domus Aurea (Golden House) (off the Forum—Esquiline Hill)

The Renaissance painter Raphael, it is said, risked his life descending on a rope through the roof of the enormous underground palace that Nero had built in A.D. 64. The object was to sketch the curious birds and animals and people—most in erotic poses—that decorate these walls. And because they were underground—in grottoes—they were called *pittura grottesca* and the word *grotesque* eventually entered the language.

In Nero's day, this palace—one square mile in area—featured perfume showers for its guests; a 120-foot-high statue of its owner so enormous that it took two dozen elephants to move it; a lake; and both seawater and sulfur baths. When Nero moved in here, he happily sighed that at last he was housed like a man. But his joy was short-lived. Though he was resident in it, the Golden Palace was not even finished when he committed suicide (*see* Rome, Santa Maria del Popolo) and his successors largely dismantled it. Vespasian gave its lake to be the site of the Coliseum, and Trajan destroyed much of it to build his baths.

Fontana della Barcaccia (Fountain of the Big Boat) (Piazza di Spagna)

This boat-shaped fountain was commissioned of Giovanni Bernini by Pope Urban VIII about 1624, soon after a disastrous flooding of the Tiber that had drowned several thousand people. The flood had reached to the steps of the piazza, and when the waters receded, they left behind a boat. It was this which gave Pope Urban the idea for a fountain in the same shape, on the same spot.

The clever Bernini went one better than the pope, however, in his inventiveness. Because the water pressure here was not sufficient for great jets of water, the fountain he designed is a leaking boat.

Fontana dei Fiumi (Fountain of the Rivers) (Piazza Navona)

When Pope Innocent X decided he wanted a fountain here in the seventeenth century, he called on the baroque sculptor Francesco Borromini to do the work, but Borromini's design failed to satisfy the pope.

When the sculptor's rival, Giovanni Bernini, learned of Innocent's dissatisfaction, eager to have a crack at the commission himself, he saw to it that a model of the fountain he had designed was placed where the pope was sure to see it. The pope did see it, liked what he saw, and commissioned Bernini to do the job. Borromini, understandably furious, kept as close an eye on his rival's chiseling as he could. Just as the work was nearing completion, Borromini learned that there were fatal flaws in Bernini's calculations that would prevent the water's rising forcefully enough to fill the fountain reservoir. Gleefully, he told a group of his friends of his discovery. Among them, as it turned out, was a friend of Bernini's, who quickly passed the word along to the sculptor.

Bernini redid his calculations time and again, but he could not find his error. Whereupon he bribed a maid in Borromini's household to seduce one of his students who revealed what the problem was.

On the day the fountain was to be inaugurated, both sculptors were on hand. Borromini strolled happily to the event, convinced the fountain of his rival would be a failure. It was much to his anger and surprise that the fountain spewed and bubbled perfectly. Bernini smiled triumphantly at Borromini as the fountain reservoir filled.

Fontana di Trevi (Trevi Fountain)

The water that bubbles from this famous fountain is said to be the finest in Rome. It was thirsty Roman legionnaires who were led to it one hot summer's day centuries ago by a little girl who knew its source. In her honor, the water here is known as "virgin water."

Just how the legend grew that tossing a coin into this fountain would assure a return to Rome, no one knows, but as long ago as the 1860s it seems to have been the custom, for Nathaniel Hawthorne described it in *The Marble Faun.* How to do it remains a question, however. Some say the coin must be tossed into the water in the moonlight; others say it must be thrown over a shoulder; still others insist (but the prospect is not very inviting) that taking a sip of the water, too, is essential to working the spell.

◆◆◆

Time was when this was a simple little fountain in the neighboring Piazza de Crociferi, but Pope Urban VIII moved it here in the seventeenth century and Pope Clement, in 1730, decided it was not grand enough for his tastes. So he announced a competition to improve the fountain. Nicolo Salvi won, and for the next thirty years as the spirit (and his imagination) moved him, he added horses and ocean waves and arches and gods and goddesses to make this the elaborate baroque creation that it is today.

The Forum: BASILICA EMILIA

Business centers like this basilica (first building on the right as you enter the Forum) were certainly the coolest places to be on a hot August day in ancient Rome, and maybe that is why the money changers who worked in the Basilica Emilia went about their business as usual even as an army of Goths bent on sacking Rome appeared at the city gates on August 23, A.D. 410. The money changers' ill-conceived optimism is recorded forever in the green spots on the marble pavement of the basilica: These are copper coins that melted into the pavement when the Goths set this building—and the rest of Rome—on fire that night.

The Forum: MAMERTINE PRISONS

In these horrible dank cells the apostles Peter and Paul are said to have spent several months during the first century A.D. The misery of their surroundings notwithstanding, they succeeded in converting forty-seven fellow prisoners and two guards to Christianity, and when there was a water shortage, Peter struck one of the rocks and water trickled forth. So here, in the fifteenth century, the Church of St. Peter in Prison was built.

The Forum: TEMPLE OF ANTONINUS AND FAUSTINA

Theirs was a true love affair during the second century A.D., and many was the time during their life together that the emperor Antoninus was heard to remark that he would rather live in a desert with Faustina than in a palace without her. When she died, the heartsick emperor had her deified and built this temple in her honor.

The Forum: TEMPLE OF JULIUS CAESAR

A tearful crowd burned the body of Julius Caesar here according to the custom, on March 15, 44 B.C. The bereft Romans took anything that would burn—including the magistrates' chairs and the robes of the musicians and actors in the funeral procession—to construct the funeral pyre. It was Augustus who built this temple to the assassinated leader.

The Forum: TEMPLE OF SATURN

This ancient temple, dating back to 497 B.C. (though it was rebuilt in the fourth century A.D.), was chosen by the Romans of the early Republic to be their treasury. Their gold and silver was hidden in a room dug into the side of the stairs.

When Julius Caesar came to power and ended the Republic, he opened the room and took the 50,000 gold pieces, 30,000 silver pieces, and 30 million bronze coins that were there. Many objected, saying he had no right to confiscate the money, since some of it had been salted away to use if there were an attack by war-prone Gauls. But Caesar, with characteristic pride, responded that he had earned the right to spend the money as he chose, since he had guaranteed that the Gauls would never attack Rome again.

Keats-Shelley Memorial House (26 Piazza di Spagna; Spanish Steps)

The English romantic poet John Keats lived here in the autumn and winter of 1820–21. The young poet was gravely ill with tuberculosis and subsequently died here (*see* Rome, Protestant Cemetery). But in those last days passersby would occasionally see him throwing the spaghetti that his cook had made for him out his window, so eminently unsuited was this hearty dish to the frail Englishman's appetite.

Museo di Villa Borghese: STATUE OF PAULINE BONAPARTE

This nude statue of Napoleon's sister Maria Paulina was fashioned by the sculptor Canova soon after the emperor's sister became Prince Camillo Borghese's wife. Envisioning herself as Venus, she insisted on posing—with nothing on—as the love goddess. And no one thought much of it till she and her husband were separated. Then she wrote Camillo to tell him that even if he continued to admire her unclad form, she hoped he would do her the courtesy not to show it to others.

Palatine Hill

Because he saw twelve vultures sitting on this hill, the twin Romulus, who, with his brother Remus (*see* Rome) founded this city, was accorded the honor of naming Rome and chose to call it for himself.

Those ugly vultures, were, perhaps, an omen of things to come atop this hill. Although this was selected as the building site for many a king's and emperor's beautiful palace, more than one of them also died an anguished death here.

Fearful Domitian had his palace built with a portico whose walls were of shiny stone (some say mica, others a rare marble)—so shiny that he could readily see anyone who passed behind him. A cruel and unpopular ruler, he was certain if he did not take this precaution he would be assassinated. His "Hall of Mirrors" notwithstanding, Domitian fell victim to an assailant's knife. It was not, however, on that mirrored portico but in his bedroom walled with burnished gold (clearly not reflective enough).

Among the thousands delighted at his death were the Roman leaders he had invited to a palace banquet one evening who found their placecards tombstones with their names engraved. Throughout the dinner party, Domitian regaled his guests with grisly tales of murder, and the assembled company waited for the executioner to arrive. Domitian, meanwhile, glee-fully pressed food and drink upon them and chided them for their lack of appetite. Then, suddenly, the "practical joke" was at an end and all the guests, unharmed, were sent home. Domitian's banquet was not the sort to inspire loyalty and affection in his guests.

And it was here as the mad emperor Caligula returned home for dinner during the intermission of a theatrical performance that he was pierced with a sword as he approached his palace.

Here, too, Livia, the wife of the emperor Augustus, a woman reputedly well schooled in the art of poisoning, mixed her potions and plotted the way she would make sure her son became the heir to the Roman throne.

The twelve vultures of Romulus' day, and their descendants, surely had their fill here.

Palazzo Pamphilj (Pamphilj Palace) (Piazza Navona)

On his ascension to the papacy in 1664, Innocent X gave this palace that is now the Brazilian embassy to his powerful widowed sister-in-law, Olimpia Maidelchini. Some say it was a gift of love from the seventy-two-year-old pontiff, who was known to have been enamored of Olimpia. Others say it was a simple thank-you for her having helped arrange his election. In any case, from here she virtually controlled the papacy. And in death, as in life, Olimpia continued to control Innocent. When he died, she denied that she had money for the interment, so the body was taken to a toolroom at St. Peter's. Only a kindly workman paid attention to the remains of the poor pontiff, lighting a candle beside the body and trying to keep attacking rats away. The dead pope's plight finally came to the attention of one other kindly soul, a church canon who offered what little he could manage for the burial service of Innocent, the pope who, in life, had ordered the grandest of monuments built in this city by the greatest of artists. (*See* Rome, Fontana dei Fiumi.)

Palazzo del Quirinale (Quirinal Palace) (Piazza del Quirinale)

One pope, aged and ill; another in tears; a third in disguise—all were forced to leave this much-loved palace in their time. Now the home of the president of Italy, for centuries this was the summer residence of the popes. In 1798 when Napoleon's troops were entering Rome, eighty-two-year-old ailing Pius VI was told he must surrender all temporal authority and quit Rome. When the pontiff refused, his papal ring was wrenched from his gnarled finger and he was hustled into a carriage and out of the city. Frail Pius VI was dead a year later in France.

In 1809, there was virtually a reenactment of that departure scene. This time it was Pius VII who was told by Napoleon to surrender all temporal power. When he refused, he was whisked away in tears, gently extending his arm from the carriage to bless his people.

And one dark night in 1842, a priest heavily wrapped in a muffler, accompanied by a servant carrying his belongings, left this palace stealthily. This time it was Pius IX who was leaving, fleeing after the assassination by revolutionary forces of his prime minister and his secretary.

Unlike his ousted predecessors, Pius IX at least had a chance to return to this home of which he was so fond. But his joy was short-lived, for Victor Emmanuel II invaded Rome and established it as his, not the pope's, capital, and Pius IX sadly quit the Quirinal again, this time for good.

Palazzo di Spagna (Spanish Palace) (Piazza di Spagna)

Bearing a letter of recommendation to the Spanish ambassador, an attractive young man with high hopes for a diplomatic career came to Rome in 1743. The young man—Giovanni Casanova—did not yet have the amorous reputation that would forever be attached to his name, but a misadventure in this palace soon set him on his way. Ironically, Casanova was completely innocent in this first escapade, which nevertheless put an abrupt halt to his budding diplomatic career.

Casanova was hired as the ambassador's personal secretary and given living quarters in this palace. One night a girl disguised as a priest burst into Casanova's room. Casanova knew the girl and was, in fact, enamoured of her, but she came to his bedroom with other problems. She had been caught trying to run away with her lover, and the police were after her seeking to return her to her family. Casanova convinced her to seek asylum from the ambassador. She did, it was granted, and eventually she made peace with both her family and the police. But unlucky Casanova was accused of having dallied with her while she was in his bedroom. Though it was a totally unjust accusation, he was fired from his job and forced to leave Rome.

It was more than a quarter of a century, and many adventures later, before he returned, but when he did, he had more ill fortune.

He took rooms in the Hotel Ville de Paris and fell in love with Teresa Rolland, the daughter of the proprietor. Lover par excellence that he was by then, he should have known better, but he made the mistake of introducing her to his brother Francesco, who fell in love with her too and married her. As for Casanova, he ended his days alone at 32 Piazza di Spagna.

Palazzo Scarpucci (Via dell'Orso where it becomes Via dei Portoghesi)

A preview of *King Kong* was enacted around this crenellated tower in the seventeenth century when it was part of a fortress belonging to the powerful Frangipani family.

One day a pet female ape picked up one of the family's infant sons and carried him outside, trying to nurse him. To the top of this tower it climbed, gently cradling the infant. A crowd gathered, crying for help, and shaking angry fists at the ape. The animal froze in fear at the pinnacle.

At the height of the outcry, the infant's father arrived home. Silencing the crowd, he uttered a prayer to the Virgin. Then he called the ape in a normal voice. Gently it rearranged the baby's swaddling clothes to keep him warm and carefully climbed down from the pinnacle with its young charge, entering the tower through a window. The grateful father vowed that he would have a statue of the Virgin placed at the tower's top and would keep a light lit there eternally. And there it is today, the light still burning, though nowadays it is electrified. (Nathaniel Hawthorne based a short story on this incident.)

The Pantheon (Piazza della Rotunda)

One pope saved this ancient temple; another disrespectfully dismantled it, and for the burial of Italy's first king after independence, much of what had been taken away was returned.

In A.D. 609, Pope Boniface IV convinced the Roman emperor Phocas to agree to have this temple of the days of Hadrian consecrated as a Christian church, and thereby, it was preserved. But Urban VIII, the Barberini pope, in order to supply cannons for the Castel Sant'Angelo and an altar canopy for St. Peter's, had part of the bronze portico melted down. This act gave rise to a bitter saying: "What the barbarians didn't do, the Barberinis did."

When Victor Emmanuel II was buried here in 1878, however, history made a full circle. To help make his tomb's ornaments, the bronze cannons of Castel Sant'Angelo were melted down.

Pincio

It was on this hill overlooking the capital that the Roman general Lucius Lucullus had his villa and dined in style. Once when he was dining alone, his chef, knowing there would be no guests, prepared a simple meal. He was called to the table and taken to task for a dinner not up to his usual standards. When he explained apologetically that he had understood there was to be no company that evening, Lucullus, drawing himself erect, replied, "Did you not know that this evening, Lucullus dines with Lucullus?"

Ponte Sant'Angelo

On a September morning in 1599, beautiful, golden-haired, twenty-two-year-old Beatrice Cenci walked unbowed to the scaffold that had been erected here, and was beheaded for the murder of her father. Beheaded, too, was her long-suffering stepmother and one of her brothers, while a second brother was forced to watch the bloody proceedings.

No sooner had the cruel punishment been carried out—by order of Pope Clement VIII—than a grieving Rome honored the dead with an enormous funeral procession. Virtually the whole city was aghast at the severity of the sentence imposed upon a family that had suffered years of indignity and abuse from the violent Francesco Cenci, whom they were convicted of having murdered.

Cenci was notorious for beating both his family and his servants. Once banished, he had also been in and out of prison for his excesses. He had refused to provide a husband for his beautiful daughter, nor had he been willing to send her to the peace of a convent. Instead, when she wrote beseeching letters to relatives begging them to intercede for her, and he learned of them, he beat her and imprisoned her. It was even rumored that he had made sexual advances to his daughter and been rebuffed. When his wife took issue with him, he struck her in the head with a spur.

So Rome understood—where the pope did not—how the Cenci family had been driven to plot Francesco's murder. Servants were talked into doing the deed, and afterward it was made to seem that Francesco, actually bludgeoned in his bed, had fallen from a balcony on his head. But when the dead man's wounds were washed, it was clear that his death had not been accidental. Ultimately, torture led to confessions, the confessions to the Cenci family's execution.

And on that September morning, poor Beatrice's severed head was blanketed with flowers. A compassionate procession, bearing lighted candles, accompanied her body to its final resting place beneath an unmarked slab in the Church of San Pietro in Montoro on the Janiculum Hill, for it was she, especially, whose pathetic story touched the hearts of Rome. And not only Rome, as literature and art attest, was touched by Beatrice Cenci's story. Percy Shelley wrote *The Cenci* about her; Guido Reni painted her.

Protestant Cemetery (Via Caio Cestio)

Though he deeply mourned the death of his friend and fellow poet John Keats in the poem *Adonais,* Percy Bysshe Shelley comforted himself on Keats's loss with the thought that "It might make one in love with death to think that one should be buried in so sweet a place." A year later, Shelley was dead (*see* Lerici and Viareggio), and his ashes were brought, too, to this "sweet place."

St. Peter's Square: OBELISK

How completely should a pope's command be obeyed? The question was put to the test in 1586 when Pope Sixtus V ordered the architect Domenico Fontana to transfer this ancient Egyptian obelisk from its site to the left of St. Peter's to its present location in the center of the piazza. It took 900 men and 140 horses four months to move the massive structure.

On the day of its raising, the pope ordered that all attending the ceremony, on pain of death, maintain total respectful silence. After all, the cross on top contained relics of the true cross. As all strained to raise the obelisk to a vertical position, ropes started to fray and give way. But nobody dared to say a word. But finally a voice cried out in the Genoese dialect, *"Agua ae corde!"*—"Put water on the ropes!" The advice, a common nautical command, came from a sailor named Bresca, who had left his home in Bordighera near Genoa to work on the job.

His command was carried out, and a thankful pope ordered that, ever afterward, the palms used in Palm Sunday masses at St. Peter's were to be prepared by members of the Bresca family of Bordighera.

San Giovanni in Laterano (Basilica of St. John Lateran) (Piazza San Giovanni in Laterano)

This basilica—Rome's official cathedral and traditionally the site of the pope's temporal power—has been destroyed and rebuilt by man five times since the emperor Constantine built the original in the fourth century. But a sixth act of destruction was the most dreadful. That took place in 897 in an earthquake. Pope Stephen VI took the event as a sign of divine wrath against the macabre sacrilege he had committed against his predecessor, Pope Formosus.

When Formosus had died in 896, the emperor Lambert had elevated Stephen to the papacy. But he shouldn't have and Pope Stephen knew he would feel more secure if he could discredit his predecessor. To do so he had Formosus' body exhumed, dressed in papal vestments once more, carried before a tribune of bishops, and placed on a throne. The chronicler Gregororius wrote: "The lawyer for Pope Stephen rose, turned to the horrible cadaver and . . . [listed the accusations] and the living pope, in a mad rage, asked the dead one: 'Why ambitious man, did you usurp the apostolic seat of Rome?' " Of course Formosus did not answer, and so was duly convicted and stripped of his vestments. The three fingers of his right hand used to give papal blessings were also cut off. His corpse was thrown from the hall, dragged through the streets of Rome, and thrown into the Tiber.

And it was then that the earthquake leveled this church, and Stephen's fortunes began to turn. He himself was stripped of his pontifical insignia and strangled in prison. Shortly after Stephen's execution, fishermen pulled in the body of Pope Formosus and, now rehabilitated, the corpse was borne in a procession through the streets of Rome back to its sepulcher in St. Peter's.

San Paolo alle Tre Fontane (St. Paul's at the Three Fountains) (Via Laurentina)

It was here, tradition says, that Saint Paul was beheaded in A.D. 62 and in the three places where his head bounced, fountains spouted from the ground. This fifth century church marks those three springs. Here, too, stands the pillar to which he was reputedly bound before the execution.

San Pietro in Vincoli (Church of St. Peter in Chains) (near the Coliseum): MICHELANGELO'S STATUE OF MOSES

The haughty Renaissance pope Julius II commissioned this work to be part of the monumental tomb he was planning for himself in St. Peter's. He got there, but it never did, and the proud pontiff's resting place is virtually unmarked, for the creation of this work of art was beset by delays.

Delighted when he received the commission and determined to do well by it, Michelangelo spent six months in the Alps looking for suitable marble. Once the sculptor had found it and made the arrangements to buy it, he notified the pope. But Julius wasn't interested just then. He declined to supply the money for the purchase because he needed funds for a military campaign. Michelangelo tried to get an audience with him to plead his case. When he couldn't, he left Rome for Florence in high dudgeon.

After a while, the pope's military campaign ended, and he began to think about his tomb again. He asked Michelangelo to return to Rome. It took considerable persuasion, but when he finally did come back, Julius took advantage of the artist's presence to ask him to paint the ceiling of the Sistine Chapel.

By the time Michelangelo got back to the statue, Julius was dead and long buried. Ultimately, Moses was installed here, with Leah and Rachel at his sides—all three a goodly distance from the bones of the pope they were originally supposed to have memorialized.

A footnote: So impressed was Michelangelo with this masterful statue, it is said, that when it was finished, he commanded it to speak—and when it didn't, struck it on one knee with his chisel, a mark that may be seen to this day.

Sant'Agnese in Agone (Piazza Navona)

In the days of the emperor Diocletian, the pretty Christian girl Agnes declined the advances of a Roman official's son, and so was condemned to stand, unclothed, in the Stadium of Domitian. Miraculously, so the legend goes, her hair grew to cover her nakedness. Clearly, that meant she was a witch, and she was consigned to the flames. But they would not consume her. Finally, she was beheaded. This church marks the site.

Sant'Angelo in Pescheria (Via del Portico di Ottavio)

Rome's Jews in the sixteenth century were forced to sit through Saturday church services here and in nearby St. Gregory's while Dominican fathers railed against them and prayed for their conversion. But they heard barely a word. To make sure that they didn't, they plugged their ears with wax before leaving home. Though the forced church attendance continued until the end of the eighteenth century, not a single Jew is reported as having been converted by these efforts.

Santa Maria d'Aracoeli (Church of the Altar of Heaven) (Capitoline Hill)

In ancient days, some say, this was the site of a temple to Juno and here her geese were kept and used to predict good and evil fortune. And once they saved the day for Rome when enemy Gauls were stealthily climbing the hill. The geese cackled with such fury that the Romans were alerted to the invasion in time to stop it. Geese, ever afterward, were honored by the Romans as the saviors of the city while dogs, since they had not barked a warning, were shunned.

In the days of Caesar Augustus, Rome prospered, art flourished, and there was peace in the land. Indeed, so impressed was the Roman Senate with the emperor's wisdom and good works that the senators suggested that he be declared a god.

Not certain himself of the wisdom of that suggestion, Augustus consulted a soothsayer. It was not Augustus who was to be a god, she foretold on this site, but nevertheless a god was coming. As she spoke, it is said, the heavens parted and the emperor had a vision of a mother and child; a voice from the heavens proclaimed that the child was the Son of God.

So Augustus ordered a new altar built to that god who was coming—hence the name of this church: the Church of the Altar of Heaven.

Sitting in this church one autumn day in 1764, listening to Franciscan friars singing at vespers here where once a Roman temple had stood, twenty-seven-year-old Edward Gibbon conceived of writing his *History of the Decline and Fall of the Roman Empire.* It was nearly a quarter of a century later before his monumental work of history was done.

Santa Maria d'Aracoeli: THE STEPS

These 132 steps leading to the church were built in 1348 with contributions from a grateful populace delivered from the plague. But in the eighteenth century, there was no deliverance of the peasant farmers from the arrogance of a neighborhood prince.

On market days, the peasants came here from outside the city to sell their produce and would stretch out to sleep on the steps at night. But Prince Caffarelli, who lived nearby, found the sleeping country folk unsightly and ordered them away. When they refused to go, he sent men to eject them forcibly. But the next night, the farmers came again, and the next. And so the prince and his men, to end the matter once and for all, filled barrels with rocks and rolled them down the precipitous steps, crushing to death all those who were in the way.

Santa Maria del Popolo (Church of St. Mary of the People) (Piazza del Popolo)

On this site the cruel first-century emperor Nero was buried after his suicide, and demons thrived in a walnut tree that grew near his grave. To counteract their evil influence, Pope Paschal II in 1099 cut down the walnut trees and had the original of this pretty little church erected.

It was no wonder that exorcism and a church were needed to rid this area of evil spirits, for Nero had seen to the murder of his mother (with whom he had committed incest), his aunt, and his wife Octavia. And he had been responsible for the death of his second wife, Poppaea, whom he had kicked when she was pregnant.

When after Poppaea's death he sought the hand of his cousin and foster sister, Antonia, and she refused him, he had her executed. Because he found Rome an ugly city in need of rebuilding, he had it set on fire, according to the historian Suetonius.

Always delighting in music (Nero loved to sing and played the lyre), he is said to have sat in a high tower and watched the city's buildings crumble and fall, its people run screaming. And while they did, he sang a song of the destruction of Troy, remarking from time to time on the beauty of the leaping flames. When after nearly fourteen years of such atrocities, the Romans revolted against him, Nero fled in disguise to the outskirts of the city, where, when he learned his captors were near at hand, he tried to commit suicide, but lacked the courage to, until he persuaded a scribe to direct the dagger to his throat.

Santa Maria in Cosmedin (St. Mary's in Cosmedin) (Piazza della Bocca della Verità)

In medieval times, the *Bocca della Verità*—"the Mouth of Truth"—at the end of the left portico here served as a lie detector. An accused criminal making an oath would place his or her hand inside this mask's mouth. If the person was lying, the mouth would chew off the hand of the offender. It has been said that the Mouth had a fearfully efficient helper in its judgment—an executioner armed with a sword who was hidden behind the massive stone mask. On signal from a hidden judge, the executioner would slice off the hand of a suspected liar.

One medieval adulteress, however, outwitted both her husband and the Mouth. As her husband led her through a crowd of onlookers to the judgment place, the woman's lover—by prearrangement—broke through the crowd dressed and acting like a madman, and embraced her while laughing hysterically. The poor "lunatic" was chased away by the onlookers, and the woman went on to put her hand into the Mouth. "I swear before God," she said solemnly, "that in my entire life I have been embraced only by my husband and by that poor soul whom you just saw."

Scala Santa (Holy Stairs) (Piazza di Porta San Giovanni)

It was up these stairs that Jesus climbed to his condemnation by Pontius Pilate, tradition says. In those days, these twenty-eight marble steps were in Jerusalem and led to the palace of Pontius Pilate. Today, they lead to a private chapel of the popes. Because of their role in holy history, Saint Helena, the mother of Constantine, had them sent here to Rome. All those who climb, climb on their knees in veneration to the Christ. Not so Martin Luther, however, who rose to his feet when he was halfway up, turned, and walked back down.

Another famous climber here was Pope Pius IX, who, on September 20, 1870, when the army of Victor Emmanuel II was on the march here to relieve him of his temporal authority and make Rome the capital of a united Italy, asked to be brought here for one last sad climb. Then he secluded himself—his temporal power gone—in the Vatican for the remainder of his life.

Sinagoga (Synagogue) (2 Lungotevere Cenci)

In October 1943, the orders went out. Any Roman Jews who were likely to defy the Nazis were to be rounded up and deported to concentration camps. There was only one way they could be saved, the Germans said: they could pay their way out of their dilemma if, within thirty-six hours, they provided fifty kilos of gold. In war-torn Rome that seemed unlikely, but the Jewish community gathered frantically, and the collection began. It was nearing deadline time, and the Jews were still slightly short of their goal. Then Catholics began to appear, too, awkwardly, hesitantly; they came here to ask, if they, too, could help. And thirty-six hours after the Gestapo's either-or threat, the Germans received their fifty kilos of gold.

Except that it did no good. Three weeks later, the Germans broke their promise and more than 1,000 of Rome's Jews were sent to Auschwitz.

Sistine Chapel

It is said the Michelangelo, after having spent four-and-a-half years on his back painting this chapel, could never again read without holding the article he was perusing above his head.

◆⟨⟩◆

Though the name Michelangelo has lent itself for centuries to heroic legends, one nearly superhuman feat is almost certain. The third and final section of the ceiling here, including the four creation scenes, was painted in little more than one hundred days.

Sistine Chapel: THE LAST JUDGMENT OF MICHELANGELO

As the painter painted this monumental work in the early sixteenth century, Pope Paul III would often come to watch him. One day he brought along his master of ceremonies, Biagio da Cesana, and asked his opinion of the fresco. Michelangelo's work, the master of ceremonies haughtily replied, was fit for an inn perhaps, but certainly not for a chapel. The painter was silent, but when Biagio da Cesana next visited he found, to his horror, that he had been incorporated into the work as Minos, one of the three judges in Hades. Appalled, he appealed to the pope to insist that Michelangelo paint him out. Paul smiled. "If Michelangelo had painted you in Heaven, I might have been able to do something about it," he reportedly said, "but down below I have no power."

Statue of Marcus Aurelius (Piazza del Campidoglio)

Had Rome's rulers in the Middle Ages not believed this horseman's head was a representation of the Christian emperor Constantine, it is unlikely that this second-century equestrian statue would have been preserved. When Michelangelo was designing this piazza in the sixteenth century, he asked that it be placed here. Acquiescent Pope Paul III not only had the statue placed where Michelangelo asked, but authorized a keeper for it and established an annual salary for him of ten pounds of sealing wax, three pounds of pepper, six pairs of gloves, three pounds of nuts, sugared almonds, and two flasks of wine.

Teatro Argentina (Argentine Theater) (Largo Argentina)

It was approximately where this theater now stands that the emperor Julius Caesar fell, mortally wounded by twenty-three stab wounds inflicted by his friends and associates, on March 15, 44 B.C. As he fell, he discreetly pulled his toga about the lower half of his body to assure—even in death—that he would be decently covered. Caesar had had ample warning of an impending assassination but had disdained the warnings and gone, as usual, to attend to public matters in the Senate.

As the ides of March approached, his soothsayer had urged him to beware. The morning of his assassination, when he rose from bed, he had told his wife Calpurnia that he had dreamed of being in the heavens and clasping the hand of Jupiter. She, in turn, told him of her dream, that she had held him, dead, in her arms. At first, Caesar had been inclined to pay heed to these ill omens, but by the time, at midmorning, that a young conspirator had come to accompany him to the Senate meeting—to make sure that he was there to die—Caesar had changed his mind and decided to go. And when, en route to the gathering, he passed his soothsayer, he had laughed at him, and told him his prognostications were not up to their usual quality, for the ides of March had come, yet all was well.

It is said the soothsayer offered still another warning, noting that the ides had come, but not yet gone. But Caesar, regardless, boldly entered Pompey's curia, where the Senate was meeting, and, as Calpurnia had feared, minutes later was dead.

❦

When the world premiere of Rossini's *Barber of Seville* was performed here in 1816, it was received with hissing and catcalls—partly, perhaps, because one singer tripped during the performance and a cat wandered on stage and stole the show. In any case, the chastened composer crept away to his rooms in the nearby Via de Leutari. The following night, when a second performance of his opera was scheduled, he discreetly stayed at home. But that night, the *Barber of Seville* was acclaimed, and a delighted audience, eager to honor him, made its way by torchlight to his lodgings and carried him off to a banquet.

Tempietto (San Pietro in Montorio Convent Yard, Janiculum)

An aged, weary Peter, condemned to death by Nero's courts, was led here from the Mamertine Prison to be crucified. Not only was he too old and weak to carry his own cross, as was the custom for those condemned, but he was too exhausted by the climb to reach the top of the Janiculum Hill, so his executioners performed their function here, just halfway up, crucifying him, as he had wished, upside down. For he was not worthy, Peter said, to be crucified as Christ was.

Terme di Caracalla (Baths of Caracalla)

In these extensive baths that were opened in A.D. 217, and that gleamed in their heyday with precious metals and colored marbles, 1,600 Romans could bathe at one time, or they could read poetry, or enjoy art in the art galleries. Though largely destroyed by invading Goths, enough remained to be an inspiration to the poet Shelley, who composed much of *Prometheus Unbound* here.

Theater of Marcellus (near the Portico d'Ottavia)

This much-altered Roman theater was begun by Julius Caesar and completed under the emperor Augustus, who arranged lavish festivities for its inauguration in 13 B.C. Six hundred wild beasts were killed by gladiators during the ceremony. But the pomp and circumstance was undercut when, during the middle of the festivities, the emperor's chair collapsed and he fell to the ground.

The theater's interior is now a labyrinth of private apartments, which provided an excellent hideout for Italian Resistance fighters during the German occupation of Rome in 1943–44.

Torre dei Frangipani (also called Torre della Scimmia) (Via dell'Orso—also called Via dei Portoghesi)

The family who gave this tower its original name earned their own name —and a reputation as beneficent landlords—during a Roman flood in the late 700s. Family members made regular trips on their boat through city streets, distributing bread to the starving people. As they were doing this, people would cry out, *"Frange nobis panem!"* (Give some bread to us!).

The Vatican: LAOCOON ROOM

Working his vineyard one day in 1506, a simple peasant, Felis de Fredis, uncovered this ancient Greek statue, and the court of Pope Julius II was beside itself with delight. To honor him for his discovery—and his reporting of it—de Fredis was given a tomb in the Church of Santa Maria d'Aracoeli.

The Vatican Museums: BORGIA APARTMENTS

In these six rooms, the handsome Spanish pope Alexander VI (Rodrigo Lanzoly Borgia), dubbed in his day "the most carnal of men," plotted and planned for the success of his notorious illegitimate children: Caesar, the cardinal who was deft and murderous, and golden-haired, thrice-married Lucretia, maligned (but history suggests unjustly) in literature and music by Victor Hugo's drama *Lucrèce Borgia* and Donizetti's opera *Lucrezia Borgia.*

Literature and legend would have Lucretia a murderer like her brother, even the mistress of her brother and father. But there is more reason to think she simply failed to interfere in Caesar's death-dealing and never took issue with her father's political conniving in which she was used as a marriage pawn.

But in these rooms Duke Alfonso of Aragon, Lucretia's second husband, recovering from wounds suffered in an attempted assassination, was suffocated by henchmen of his brother-in-law on August 18, 1500.

For a month, Lucretia and Alfonso's sister Sancha had been tending him —ever since the evening when three heavily cloaked figures had set upon him in St. Peter's Square. Though severely wounded, the duke managed to fend off his attackers. But he finally fell; they fled, and his squire screamed so loudly that the Vatican gates were opened and the bleeding duke carried inside.

Slowly Alfonso mended. Papal guards were placed outside his door to protect him from further attack. Lucretia, herself, saw to the preparation of his food to insure that it would not be poisoned. The pope expressed his sorrow at the incident; Caesar did, too: ostensibly, though, once on a visit to his brother-in-law, he reportedly commented that undertakings that fail at lunch can still be successful at supper—a comment later interpreted to mean that though he had once failed to murder Alfonso, he would not fail a second time.

And he did not. For a little while that August 18 evening Lucretia and Sancha left Alfonso alone, but they made sure before they left that his guards were outside the door. When Caesar's hired killers came, however, the guards, curiously, simply disappeared. An hour later, Lucretia returned to find her way barred and Alfonso dead. Was it politics or jealousy that was responsible? No one has ever known, though many speculate it was the latter, as they speculate that it was an incestuous attachment to his sister that had led Caesar, a little earlier, to murder his younger brother, Juan, who also is said to have loved the beauteous Lucretia with more than brotherly love. The charm that so affected her brothers and perhaps her father can be seen in Pinturicchio's painting of Saint Catherine in the fourth room here, for the radiant Lucretia is said to have been its model.

Via dei Banchi Nuovi

This elegant street housed both princes and prostitutes in the seventeenth and eighteenth centuries, and often the homes of the courtesans were just as lavish as those of the courtiers. Laura Bona and Imperia were two of the wealthiest courtesans living here in the seventeenth century. One day the Spanish ambassador came to enjoy the favors of Imperia as a respite from his duties. While he waited for her in an anteroom, he felt obliged to spit. He looked around: the room was filled with superb pieces of furniture, expensive vases and plates from Urbino and Faenza, and silver basins with work of the most famous engravers of the time. Disconcerted just for a moment, the ambassador called his valet and spat on the poor man's face, judging him the least valuable thing in the room.

Via del Corso

In the Middle Ages, horse races took place here. In the seventeenth century, Pope Innocent X's greedy sister-in-law, Olimpia Maidelchini—though she said she hadn't the money to bury the pope (*see* Rome, Palazzo Pamphilj) —surrounded herself with fine works of art in the Palazzo Doria that stands on this fashionable main street. In the nineteenth century, Maria Letizia Ramolino Bonaparte, the mother of Napoleon Bonaparte, was given sanctuary here by Pope Pius VII when he returned to Rome after Napoleon's exile to Elba. The pope's kindness to Madame Bonaparte was generous, indeed, for it was Napoleon who had taken away Innocent's temporal powers and forced him from Rome.

Madame Bonaparte lived quietly and frugally here. Always in black, she was a familiar figure on this street. And she tried to repay her debt to the pope, too. A shrewd businesswoman, she lent him money when he needed it at a lower rate of interest than ordinary bankers would.

As the century closed, among those who frequented this street was the poet Robert Browning. He set the wedding of Pompilia in "The Ring and the Book" in the Church of San Lorenzo in Lucina here.

Villa Borghese (Borghese Gardens)

Twice in their history the avariciousness of the owners of these gardens and their buildings have threatened their continued existence. And once, indeed, avariciousness actually did lead to a great loss. That was when Prince Camillo Borghese married Maria Paulina, the sister of Napoleon I, and sent to the Louvre in Paris more than 200 works of art from the Casino here in exchange for land Napoleon had and Camillo wanted. The papal government protested, but to no avail. As it turned out, they were more than right in protesting. Not only did Rome lose art, but Camillo never did get the land he had been promised for it.

The founder of the art collection and the builder of these gardens was seventeenth-century cardinal Scipione Borghese, familiarly known as "Rome's Delight" for his elegant manners and enjoyment of the best in life. But the cardinal—in contrast to some of his descendants—wanted others to enjoy these lovely park lands, too. He so informed the public in a statement engraved on a marble block, noting that his gardens were made "more for others than for the owner."

In the late nineteenth century, Prince Marcantonio Borghese, greedy like Camillo, sought to sell this land for development. The mayor of Rome contended that he couldn't because of Scipione's statement on the stone. And to the delight of all Romans, the mayor and his lawyers—for all time —won these marvelous gardens for Rome.

Villa Farnese (opposite Palazzo Corsini)

A lovesick young Raphael could not seem to complete the frescoes Agostino Chigi had commissioned for this palace, and he was having trouble, too, with his work at the Vatican. Each morning, he would make a detour to visit Margaret, the baker's daughter, who lived in the neighborhood and who would be waiting to wave a greeting to him from her window. When he finally reached work, it was clear that his thoughts were still back at the bakery. Sometimes he would even pause to compose a love verse or two.

His two employers, the banker Chigi and Pope Leo X, met to discuss what could be done to hurry his work to completion. Chigi proposed that Margaret be sent out of the city for a time. On the grounds that her departure was essential to the artist's completion of his work, she agreed. Raphael was not to be told of her whereabouts for fear he would follow her.

When Margaret first disappeared, the painter was beside himself with grief and worry. But Chigi promised he would look for her, and soon was feeding Raphael with tidbits of news about her and bringing assurances that she would soon be back. The painter returned to his frescoes with energy and enthusiasm.

But when she did not return as promised, his energy again evaporated and he made no progress. There seemed only one answer. Chigi brought Margaret back and discreetly installed the baker's daughter and the master painter in a room of their own here in this villa. Raphael's painting then prospered and he produced his *Galatea* with its lovely maiden riding in a shell surrounded by cupids aiming arrows at her.

❧❀☙

When the wealthy sixteenth-century banker Agostino Chigi had outdoor dinner parties here overlooking the Tiber, for simplicity's sake, the dishes and cutlery were simply tossed into the river as each course was done. But appearances were deceiving. The host was, after all, a banker. Neither silverware nor cutlery ended up lost forever in the mud of the Tiber bottom. Chigi had his servants set nets below the surface before each party.

Villa Giulia (on Viale delle Belle Arti, near Porta del Popolo)

An old Roman expression for a warm, hospitable house in which guests happily toast their host is *la vigna di Papa Giulio*—"Pope Julius's vineyard." It recalls the grounds of this lavish villa, built by the genially corrupt, feast-loving pope Julius III, pontiff from 1550 to 1555. A man who never went anywhere without his jesters, who scandalized even jaded Rome by appointing a seventeen-year-old male favorite a cardinal, Pope Julius built this villa and lived here during most of his pontificate. He completely opened the gardens to the city's populace, even allowing them to partake freely of the grapes in his vineyard. The statues of cavorting, naked nymphs that grace this landscape were transported here from the Vatican after the pope's death by officials who deemed them not fit for the eyes of the next pope. Also, after the death of Julius, his heirs tried to revoke the decree opening the grounds to the people, but the city's official art curators won a court battle upholding that right.

VENICE

Venetians are not proud of the fact that Adolf Hitler liked their city, but like it he did—enough, on a visit, to leave behind his entourage and guards to explore the city by himself early one morning.

Arsenale (Shipyard) (Calle del Pestrin)

It was an exciting day for Venice when twenty-three-year-old Henry III of France came for a visit in 1574. To greet the attractive young king as he was rowed ashore, an escort of fourteen galleys was sent out along with a raft full of glass blowers to entertain him with their fanciful creations. And while he was at dinner (*see* Venice, Palazzo Ducale), Arsenale shipwrights put together a galley for him and cast a 16,000-pound cannon to show what they could do. Though today little remains here, in the heyday of Venice this was the greatest shipyard in the world—protected from spies and intruders by two miles of high walls and sending a new vessel down the ways every one hundred days. Although the secrets of Arsenale shipbuilding were carefully guarded, the poet Dante apparently seemed innocuous enough to be allowed to visit. He went away shaking his head and promptly condemned some of the evildoers in his *Inferno* to being boiled in pitch like that which was used to caulk the galleys and galleons here.

Basilica di San Marco (St. Mark's Basilica)

Among the thieves who have stolen from this treasury are two worthy of special note. One, in the fifteenth century, bored a hole in the ceiling, entered the treasury, and departed with a sizable quantity of gems. But he was apprehended. And when he was, and death decreed, he asked—since he had grown accustomed to precious objects—if he could be hanged with a golden cord. Napoleon Bonaparte is the other thief—said to have taken diamonds from here to adorn the empress Josephine's crown.

Basilica di San Marco (St. Mark's Basilica): BRONZE HORSES

From nation to nation for centuries these handsome horses have passed as the spoils of war. Greece is believed to have been their place of origin; then off to Trajan's Arch they went. Next, conquerors carried them to Constantinople. Then when the riches-hungry Venetians proposed a fourth Crusade to topple Constantinople (Christian though it was), the horses were part of the loot this city acquired when the Byzantine capital fell. Proudly, they were installed atop this basilica.

When Napoleon took over Venice in the eighteenth century, he coveted the horses for Paris's Place du Carrousel, and off they went again—for only a brief stay, however. The Austrians returned them to Venice when Napoleon put this city under Austrian rule.

In World War I they were sent to Rome. In World War II they were simply packed away in crates.

Campanile

In July 1902, plaster suddenly began to tumble into St. Mark's Square from the precursor of this belltower. It had stood for nearly ten centuries virtually without mishap (though in 1900 when there was a little crumbling, a commission of inquest suggested that "The urinary discharges of visitors onto the interior walls may be rendering the mortar inconsistent").

Sensible Venetians roped off the area below the tower and forbade entry. And a few days later, the whole belltower crumbled and fell. Thanks to the advance warning of the falling plaster (Venetians believe that it came from the Virgin Nicopeia whose statue is part of the treasure of St. Mark's), only a cat and three pigeons were killed. Contributions from around the world helped to rebuild the Campanile, which was inaugurated on April 25, 1903, exactly 1,000 years after its original had risen.

Campo del Getto Nuovo (Ghetto)

In the sixteenth century, this city was the home of the wealthiest Jew in Europe, Asher Meshullam. Thanks to him and his wise money-lending practice, the Jewish population was not evicted from Venice, though it was confined to this *getto nuovo*—new foundry area.

Oust the Jews, the senators were warned, and they would lose the money Jews lent and the taxes they paid to the city. The Senate thought about it only a little while, for they were clever businessmen. The Jews were invited to stay on, though after dark they were confined within this ghetto area, until Napoleon rescinded that order in 1797. And today's word *ghetto,* it is said, had its origins here.

Canal Grande (Grand Canal)

Gay blade and indefatigable swimmer that he was, the poet Byron is said to have swum home along this canal many a night after a party. He did, however, insist—for safety's sake—that a servant follow in a gondola behind him.

Case dei Mocenigo (right bank of the Grand Canal)

It was a shocking seventeenth-century spy story. A well-known, highly placed Venetian named Antonio Foscarini was executed for allegedly plotting against the Venetian government with the English ambassador, Lord

Arundel, who occupied one of these houses decorated with lions' heads. Foscarini had been a frequent visitor here, and it was against the law for a Venetian of his rank to visit privately with a foreign ambassador for fear state secrets might be exchanged.

A year after the execution, Lady Arundel returned here alone. It was not to buy state secrets from her husband that the handsome Italian had visited her home, she said. Indeed, her husband never had been there when Foscarini was, for it was for love trysts with her that he had come.

But theirs was not the only assignation here. The poet Byron lived here from 1816 to 1819, and there was many a tête-à-tête with many a lovely lady during his tenancy. On one famous occasion, a cast-off mistress arrived to find the poet dining with a new paramour. In a rage, she pulled a knife from the dining table and was on the verge of attacking the pair when she was forcibly removed. She continued to seethe, however, and the story is that she jumped out the window into the Grand Canal in her fury—or in her lovesickness.

Corte Seconda del Milion (Second Court of the Million)

The tablet here marks the spot where the home of the Polo family stood and from which the traders Maffeo, Niccolò, and fifteen-year-old Marco set out in the thirteenth century for the court of Kublai Khan. It was nearly a quarter of a century before they decided to return to Venice. The city had almost forgotten them. When they knocked at the door that this plaque marks, the servants who answered were wary. Surely these three grizzled men from the East in their strange garb could not be Polos! It took a while, but finally the Polo household was convinced. It still remained to convince the rest of Venice, however.

Maffeo and his two sons gave a party for their fellow traders, the story goes. When the guests arrived all three Polos were in crimson satin brought from the East. After the guests were seated, the Polos took off these robes and put on others of crimson damask, meanwhile ordering the ones they had just shed to be cut up and distributed among the servants. When the first course was over, the Polo family rose again and repeated the process, this time changing into robes of red velvet. Finally, dinner ended, they retired a third time, and returned to the table in the threadbare, sorry garb in which they had come home to Venice and which had made their fellows skeptical of their identity. No sooner were they back among their guests than they began to cut the linings of their suits and coats. Out tumbled diamonds and emeralds and pearls and rubies—all the jewels of the East that they had carried with them. And their disbelieving guests were no longer disbelieving. The Polos were hailed and honored. And it is because of the wealth with which they returned and because of the great wealth they described that this court where they lived was called "the Court of the Second Million."

Danieli Royal Excelsior (Riva)

It took some doing to obtain permission to build this hotel addition, for here some 800 years ago Doge Vitale Michael I was murdered, thereby cursing this otherwise most desirable site. The government at the time of the murder decreed that the stone houses where the deed had been done must be torn down and thereafter only temporary wooden quarters could be constructed here. Not until the end of the Second World War did they relent and allow this Danieli addition to rise. After 800 years, the curse, happily, seems to lie dormant.

La Fenice Theater (The Pheonix Theater) (Campo San Fantin)

During the Austrian occupation of Venice in the first half of the nineteenth century, agitators for independence would throw bouquets of red, white, and green flowers from the balcony onto the stage after a performance, thus taunting their overlords with the colors of the flag of independence. Sometimes a bouquet would be tied with ribbons of the Austrian colors, so the Venetian audience would have the pleasure of seeing a performer kick it aside. Giuseppe Verdi's operas, rich in revolutionary symbolism, gave those in the balcony another chance to taunt the Austrians, for the Venetians would chant "Viva Verdi"—which stood for *Vittorio Emanuele Re d'Italia* (Victor Emmanuel King of Italy). He was the Piedmontese ruler who was the rallying point for a united Italy.

Giudecca

Many have sought peace on this once-quiet little island. Here Michelangelo took refuge after being exiled from Florence. The French poet Alfred de Musset wrote of wishing to live here forever. In troublous times the city's Jewish population was sent here (hence the island's name, derived from the Latin *Iudaica*—"district reserved for the Jews"). And here the architect Palladio designed the Church of the Redentore in gratitude for the end of the plague of 1575–76.

Lido

Here Goethe gathered seashells, Byron liked to ride horseback and swim (he raced an Italian and another Englishman once from the San Nicola end of the Lido to the farthest end of the Grand Canal and won), and Shelley's infant daughter Clara is buried. Byron, too, longed to be buried in this favorite spot, but he lies, instead, in England.

Mercerie

The tablet in the pavement here just before the clock tower marks the spot where the old crone, Giustina Rossi, peering out the window above one day in 1310 to see why there was such commotion in the street, accidentally knocked a piece of marble window sill onto the head of a rebel standard-bearer—one of the followers of Bajamonte Tiepolo who was seeking to overthrow the government. The soldiers behind him, interpreting the accident as an evil omen, immediately took flight and the aged crone overnight became a national heroine.

Murano

It was the danger of fire that brought glassmaking here in the fifteenth century. The craft was a popular and profitable one from the very beginnings of Venice, but the heat from the glassmakers' furnaces worried the government sufficiently to have it decree that henceforth, all glassmaking would be here. And so profitable a business was it, and so beautiful the glass, that any glassworker who quit the Venetian Republic was considered a traitor and—if found—was to be punished by death. On the other hand, so valuable was a good glassblower that one of them, although condemned as a murderer, was pardoned so that he could return to work. It was said in the Middle Ages—when poisons were greatly feared—that if any drop of poison touched a Murano glass, it would immediately shatter.

Palazzo Ducale (Doge's Palace)

It was from these cells high under the roof of the Doge's Palace that the gentleman-adventurer and notable lover Giovanni Casanova managed an extraordinary escape in 1756. He had been imprisoned by the state inquisitors on grounds of not attending mass, not observing Lent, and being reluctant to invoke the name of the devil when he cursed. For about a year he remained in this prison, but ultimately managed an escape onto the roof of the palace, thence into an empty room, and finally out into the street, and, ultimately, to freedom abroad. He later detailed his adventures in his entertaining many-volumed *Memoirs*. (*See* Rome, Palazzo di Spagna.)

Palazzo Ducale: GRAND COUNCIL CHAMBER

Marino Falieri is the doge whose portrait is missing here, and the tale of whose crime is written here instead. When he was eighty, this fourteenth-century doge married a pretty girl whose charm and attractiveness were the talk of all Venice. One evening, twenty-year-old Michael Steno was among the guests at a ducal banquet. Like all the rest, he was much taken with the lovely duchess. Indeed, he paid enough attention to have the doge order him out of the palace. The furious Steno could not be so insulted without retaliating. So he managed to sneak back here when this council chamber was empty and to inscribe on the back of the doge's chair "Old Marino Faliero is a cuckold who keeps his beautiful wife for the benefit of others."

Enraged, Falieri demanded punishment for the youth. The judges of the Grand Council, taking the whole affair lightly, however, simply sentenced Steno to two months in jail and to a year's banishment from Venice. This was hardly enough to satisfy the doge. The only answer, as he saw it, was a new government that would inflict a more severe punishment. He knew others of his age who were equally dissatisfied with the too-liberal rulings of the Grand Council (doges really had relatively little power themselves), and with them he began to plot an overthrow of that council and the installation of another. But the plot was uncovered—and Falieri was beheaded at the top of this palace's main stairs. Here where he had taken the oath of office, his severed head fell rolling the length of the stairs.

Palazzo Moro-Lin (Moro-Lin Palace) (left bank of the Grand Canal)

Othello, gondoliers are inclined to say, lived in this palace in the sixteenth century. In actuality, this was the residence of a Venetian nobleman who paid a visit to Cyprus in 1508 and returned well bronzed by the sun and full of stories that may have given rise to Shakespeare's tragedy.

Palazzo Rezzonico (right bank of the Grand Canal)

Visiting his son Pen here in 1889, the poet Robert Browning caught a cold and died. A financially profitable marriage two years earlier had enabled young Browning to restore this exquisite seventeenth-century dwelling, and his father had looked forward to spending his declining years here.

Palazzo Vendramin-Calergi (Grand Canal)

Now the winter casino, here Richard Wagner died in 1883, vacationing, exhausted after the completion of *Parsifal.*

Palazzo Venier dei Leoni (Peggy Guggenheim Museum) (left bank of the Grand Canal)

In this eighteenth-century white stone palace where, it is said, lions were once kept in the garden, the heiress and art collector Peggy Guggenheim made her home and opened a museum of her collection after World War II. In her garden, she displayed her sculpture—among the pieces a Marini horse and rider, cast for her by the artist. The rider's phallus was erect to show his ecstasy. The statue was so cast that the phallus was detachable—a feature that proved especially valuable to Miss Guggenheim when, on holy days, a group of nuns regularly passed by the garden.

Piazza San Marco (St. Mark's Square)

The boat of Saint Mark the Evangelist, it is said, on a voyage out of Alexandria, was caught in a terrifying storm within sight of these Venetian islands. But while the storm raged, suddenly there was a clear patch in the sky, and an angel appeared to Mark and wished him well, heralding him as God's evangelist. The angel told him that, as God was saving him from that day's storm so, on another, later day, he would find refuge from his cares here. And sure enough, as predicted, 800 years later, Venetian merchants trading in Alexandria found the saint's remains there and smuggled them back here to make this the evangelist's final resting place.

The smuggling took some doing. There was a guard around the clock at Saint Mark's sepulcher, but the Venetians persuaded one of the guards—a man named Theodore—to assist them. Being well acquainted with the Moslems' distaste for swine flesh, Theodore proposed covering the basket in which they had put the saint's remains with cabbages and pork so port officials would take no notice of it. And, to keep the disappearance of the body a secret as long as possible, Theodore and the merchants substituted another corpse for Mark's in his sepulcher.

As Theodore had hoped, the theft went undetected and the vessel bearing the relics of the saint quit Alexandria easily. But the trip back to Venice was another matter. Again, a storm caused the sea to seethe, and the winds one night drove the ship perilously close to submerged rocks. Mark, legend has it, stirred in his basket and rose to warn the captain of the imminent danger. The vessel's course was altered, and—as foretold eight centuries earlier—Mark returned here. To house his relics, construction of the first St. Mark's began in 830.

Not quite yet, however, was there an end to Mark's vicissitudes. A fire destroyed the first St. Mark's in 976, and when rebuilding began, there was no sign of the saint's relics. Desperately, a fast and prayers and a procession were ordered. His remains were found. So with great celebration the church was completed. There had to be a third rebuilding in the eleventh century, however. And finally, as promised, Saint Mark lay at rest.

❧❦☙

Had it not been for pigeons, Venetians say, there would be no Venice, and so, for the most part, they tolerate the thousands that strut here.

When in the ninth century barbarian invaders from the north were threatening the residents of Malamocco, one of the outer islands here, pigeons with crosses in their beaks appeared and led the refugees to these islands, the Rive Alto—today's Rialto—where the refugees built their homes on stilts and founded Venice.

Piazza San Marco (St. Mark's Square): FLORIAN'S CAFÉ (south side of the square)

A discouraged Richard Wagner, in Venice to complete *Tristan and Isolde,* took time to drink coffee here and complain that his music was not sufficiently appreciated.

Piazza San Marco (St. Mark's Square): QUADRI'S CAFÉ (north side of the square)

During the Austrian occupation in the early nineteenth century, patriotic Venetians snubbed this previously popular café, for its reputation was one of catering to the invaders.

Ponte dei Sospiri (Bridge of Sighs)

Across this bridge, it is said, the condemned of Venice walked over the water to torture, imprisonment, or death in the adjoining prison. One among them, for whom two lamps are lit eternally, was a poor baker who, leaving work late one night, happened upon the body of a nobleman and reported it. The unoffending baker was charged with the noble's murder and condemned to death, despite a petition in his behalf. Since the judgment of the Council of Ten—a body of stern, always dark-clad guardians of the public safety—could not be challenged, the baker was duly hanged. Later, another nobleman confessed to the crime, so the poor baker was memorialized with the lamps.

Rialto Bridge

Although this hump-backed bridge has spanned the Grand Canal here for four centuries, it is far from being the first on this location. Once there was a pontoon bridge. Next came a series of wooden ones. (One fell when the marchioness of Ferrara's wedding procession was crossing over it. Another simply wore out.) So in the sixteenth century, the government decreed that stone must be the bridge material and a competition was announced for the best design. Michelangelo submitted a proposal. So did Palladio, but it was this Antonio da Ponte bridge with shops along it that was the prize-winner in the competition. Shakespeare helped make the Rialto famous in *The Merchant of Venice*.

Santa Maria della Salute (Church of St. Mary of Salvation)

In the fifteenth century a plague here in Venice took 50,000 lives; in the sixteenth century, the painter Titian was a plague victim. In 1630, again there was a visitation of the dread disease, and a frightened Senate decreed that when the illness had passed, the city should give thanks to the Virgin by construction of a handsome (but not too costly, the Senate advised) church.

Santa Maria Gloriosa dei Frari (St. Mary's Church) (Campo dei Frari): TITIAN'S TOMB

Although no one else among the thousands who died of the plague that desolated Venice in 1576 was given church burial, the painter Titian—who had lived to the remarkably old age of ninety-nine—was. It was here that his body was brought to be entombed. And it was here, many decades earlier, that he had painted his wife Celia as the Madonna in the Pesaro Altarpiece. And that real-life Madonna had died in childbirth afterward, desperately clutching at the strong hand of her painter-husband, Titian.

VERONA

Castelvecchio (Old Castle)

The poet Dante was known for his caustic wit, and he was ready to use it even on the mighty, as when he was a guest of the della Scala family, who ruled fourteenth-century Verona from this castle. Apparently Dante did not receive the attention he felt he deserved from the head of the family, Can Grande della Scala. A gentleman of the court took note of this and, to humiliate Dante, commented that Can Grande seemed to prefer the company of his jester to that of the poet.

"Like will associate with like," replied Dante tartly. It was a rash statement since, for speaking his mind in his native Florence, he had been exiled and was under double sentence of death if he ever returned there. Yet amazingly, the poet managed to finish his visit to Verona with his head intact.

Casa di Giulietta (Juliet's House) (Via Cappello)

Those who maintain that William Shakespeare's Juliet was a real person point out this balconied medieval house as where she lived. Not Shakespeare, but a sixteenth-century Italian novelist, Luigi da Porta, first recounted the tale of the unhappy lovers.

VIAREGGIO

On the beach of this fashionable resort the body of the poet Shelley was washed ashore in July 1822.

Two days before, on an uncommonly hot summer day, Shelley and two companions had set sail from Leghorn aboard a small schooner (*see* Lerici). Though the sultriness of the weather might have presaged some sort of storm activity, no one expected the fury of the tempest that suddenly blackened the sky and leadened the waters, bringing with it wild wind and pouring rain, lashing lightning and thunder that shook masts and stays.

Though it was ferocious, the storm quickly subsided, and the return of the poet and his fellow sailors was expected—that night, then into the next day. But the little schooner *Ariel,* named for Keats's poem, did not return. The first news those waiting had was word that a body—apparently an Englishman's—had been found along the harbor here. Edward Trelawny, a friend of the poet's and often a fellow sailor with him, hurried as quickly as he could to the site. There was no mistaking whose body lay on the sand, even though it had suffered from the effects of the water. In one jacket pocket was a copy of Sophocles; in the other, pressed open as if he had just been reading it, a book of Keats's poems.

It remained for Trelawny to inform Mary Shelley, and then to dispose of the body as she wished. Her wish was to have it back in Rome where their young son lay buried in the Protestant Cemetery (*see* Rome, Protestant Cemetery). But Italian authorities insisted on burial in quicklime on the spot and were not inclined to disinter and rebury. Trelawny begged and cajoled. He asked that the body be burned so that its ashes could be interred in a proper graveyard. Eventually, officials acquiesced; the funeral pyre was built, and the body dug from the sand. Everything burned except the heart. Trelawny waited. The heart remained untouched. Suddenly, impetuously, Trelawny reached into the flames to save it and take it back to Mary. And so, today, the poet's ashes are in Rome, his heart in England.

Netherlands

ALKMAAR ❧

Stadhuis (Town Hall)

In the seventeenth century, the tulip was worth far more than its weight in gold in the Netherlands. On February 5, 1637, in the Guards' Room of this town hall, there was a bulb auction that resulted in sales of 90,795 gulden —well over half a million dollars in today's terms. That was the height of the *Tulpenmania*—"tulipmania"—that brought the price of certain rare single bulbs as high as $4,000. Houses and businesses were mortgaged for the cash to buy more bulbs. The painter Rubens, it is said, could only afford to give a single bulb to his wife as a birthday present, and the entire dowry for the daughter of a wealthy family was often a single bulb.

AMSTERDAM

Anne Frank House (263 Prinsengracht)

Here thirteen-year-old Anne Frank, her older sister Margot, their mother and father, two friends and their teen-age son, and, for a time, another friend, hid in the attic from 1942 till 1944. And then one August day the Gestapo came and took them all away to concentration camps. Only Anne's father Otto survived.

Until the rise of Adolf Hitler, the Frank family had lived prosperously and contentedly in Germany, although they were Jewish. Merchandising was the family business and, as a young man, Otto Frank's parents had sent him to New York to study American merchandising methods. For a time, he had worked at Macy's Department Store. But, his training over, he had returned to Germany. He had served as an artillery officer in the First World War, and was a proud German with a successful pectin-making business. But then the shadow of nazism loomed, and the Frank family deemed it wise to quit Germany for this neutral neighbor.

Here in Amsterdam the Franks for a while lived as comfortably as they had in Germany. But then neutral Holland was invaded. In Germany, the Franks had learned enough about the Nazis. There was no time to lose. Quickly, they shut up their spacious Amsterdam apartment. Otto Frank wrote a note explaining that he and his wife and daughters had left for Switzerland. Mrs. Frank bundled up her daughters in as many layers of clothes as they could wear without being conspicuous—there was no telling how long the clothes would have to last. Then the family set off across the city to the pectin company headquarters from whose attic, for the next two years, none of them would emerge.

Anne Frank recounts the story in her *Diary of a Young Girl,* written on scraps of paper, which were left behind that August day when the Gestapo raided the apartment.

Through those two years, four friends had brought food after dark when the doors of the business below closed. Laundry had been taken away by the same friends. By day, there could scarcely be whispering upstairs, no flushing of toilets, no running of water to give away the hideaways' whereabouts. But by night, it was quite a different story. When the employees downstairs were gone, there could be singing and laughing—and joy at being alive and undiscovered another day.

But one night, Otto Frank heard footsteps downstairs when there should not have been footsteps. He silenced his family and friends. They waited. There were no more sounds. All the same, a nervous Frank and Peter van Daan, who shared the attic with them, crept below to investigate. They found nothing. Relieved, the pair came back upstairs to sing joyously again.

But this time their joy was short-lived. There had been a burglary downstairs, the Franks learned from their friends the following night, and a sizable reward was being offered for the apprehension of the burglar. And it was just after that that there was the tramp of boots on the stairs and harsh-voiced German invaders filled the little attic shouting epithets and ordering the attic dwellers out. Apparently the burglar had seen or heard the hideaways and claimed his own reward. The Gestapo sent Anne and Margot to Bergen-Belsen, their father and mother to Auschwitz. The girls were never heard of again. But Anne's diary lives—a monument to hope.

Looking out the attic window on February 23, 1944, she wrote, "As long as this exists . . . and I may live to see it, this sunshine, the cloudless skies, while this lasts, I cannot be unhappy."

◆◆◆

In 1954, playwrights Frances and Albert Hackett and director Garson Kanin visited here in preparation for the Hackett play, *The Diary of Anne Frank.* Led by Otto Frank, they mounted the secret staircase to these attic rooms to find Anne's decorations on the walls—a photograph of Sonja Henie, another of Ray Milland, and one that brought tears to Garson

Kanin's eyes. It was of Ginger Rogers—Anne's favorite actress—in the Kanin-directed film, *Tom, Dick and Harry.*

Begijnhof (Nun's Court) (near the Floating Flower Market)

Shortly before Catholic lay-sister Cornelitgen Arents died in 1654, she asked to be buried in a gutter here rather than in the chapel, for in 1578 this chapel—like all Catholic churches here in the Netherlands—had been made Protestant. She wished, Sister Cornelitgen said, to be buried out of doors where the falling raindrops would be the tears to remind her, even after death, of her sorrow that her Catholic church was in the hands of Protestants. Today, she would be happier, for her chapel has become Catholic again.

Canal Banks

The name "Dutch elm disease" was given to that fungus infection that has stricken so many elm trees here and abroad, not because it began in Holland, but, rather, because the Dutch have studied the disease more diligently than others have. City-supported specialists now inspect and treat the trees lining this city's sun-sifted canals regularly, aided by infrared aerial photography in which the foliage of healthy trees shows bright red, while that of sickly ones appears pale pink.

Dock Worker Statue (Jonas Daniel Meijerplein)

On February 24, 1941, following a Nazi roundup of 400 young Jews for deportation to Germany, workers of all religions here in Amsterdam met to discuss a protest, with the dock workers in the forefront of the action. A general work stoppage was begun the following morning. No trains ran. No garbage trucks appeared. No mail was delivered. Every single factory, office, and workshop in Amsterdam emptied, and the city fell silent. By afternoon, the strike had spread to a fifteen-mile radius around this city. In response, the Germans sent troops all over town, arrested or shot strikers, and within a few days suppressed the work stoppage. The Amsterdam action was the first and only time that the entire population of a city in occupied Europe in World War II went on strike—a capital offense against the Reich—in support of their Jewish fellow citizens. This statue by Mari Andriessen stands as a permanent memorial to the city's brave action.

Hearing of the strike from her exile in England, Queen Wilhelmina resolved that Amsterdammers should be presented with a lasting memento of their worthy stand. After the war, the queen had the words "Heroic, Determined, Merciful" added to the municipal flag.

I. J. Asscher (127 Tolstraat)

In 1908, Joseph Asscher of this house painstakingly set to work to cut the Cullinan diamond, at 3,025 ¾ carats and about a pound and a half in weight, the world's largest diamond. Asscher cut the two largest pieces—516½ and 390 carats—for the crown and scepter of England, as a gift from the Transvaal government to Edward VII.

4 Jodenbreestraat

Rembrandt van Rijn bought this house in the Jewish quarter, where many artists of his day chose to live, and spent here the dashing, luxurious years of his young married life. But buying it and joyously filling it with the collectibles he so loved to purchase at auction—art, weapons, the resplendent velvets and silks in which he dressed his models—also led to his financial ruin.

It was the wealth of his adored wife Saskia that enabled him to buy 4 Jodenbreestraat. But after only eight years of marriage, Saskia died, leaving Rembrandt with a year-old son, Titus. Then came the financial problems. Though he continued to paint indefatigably and tried to make money teaching, there was never again enough money. A heartsick Rembrandt was forced to dig into the estate Saskia had left for their son. When even that wasn't enough, this handsome house and all of its contents, acquired with such enthusiasm over the years, had to be sold at auction. Rembrandt, Titus, and Titus's nurse, Hendrickje Stoffels, who became the artist's beloved mistress, model, and companion, had to move to the considerably less fashionable neighborhood of the Rozengracht. And for the next seventeen years, until her death, Hendrikje managed the household finances. Money management, clearly, was never Rembrandt van Rijn's forte.

26 Kloveniersburgwal

In seventeenth-century Amsterdam, those who could afford them built great canal-side mansions. The Trip brothers, who were merchant princes, built such a stately residence at what today is 29 Kloveniersburgwal (occupied by the Dutch Royal Academy of Sciences) that their coachman is reputed to have said, somewhat facetiously, "I wish I had a house as wide as their front door."

He got his wish. This house at 26 Kloveniersburgwal, almost directly across the canal from number 29, is the narrow house—just the width of the master's door—that was soon tenanted by the coachman.

Koninklijk Paleis (Royal Palace) (Dam)

Meindert Hobbema was among the last-born of the great seventeenth-century Dutch artists. But he painted almost all his rural landscapes when he was a young man. Marriage changed the painter's habits. His wife, who was an excellent cook, was hired in that capacity by the burgomaster of Amsterdam, who entertained in grand style here when this was the town hall. And Hobbema got the easy job of wine-measurer for the city. Life became too comfortable for him to take up the brush much after that, though toward the end of his life he probably should have, for both he and his wife died paupers.

◆❄◆

In 1806, Napoleon Bonaparte made his brother Louis Napoleon king of Holland, though Louis—who didn't want the job—even pleaded that the Dutch climate would injure his health. Napoleon's wishes prevailed, however, and in 1808 Louis took over this building, them Amsterdam's Stadhuis (town hall) as his royal palace. Being a conscientious king, with the well-being of his subjects at heart, Louis frequently found himself quarreling with his brother, who believed that Holland existed only for the glory of France.

After two years, Louis had had enough and resigned, leaving behind him when he quit Holland all the priceless Empire period furniture which is still here. His resignation was quite happily accepted by Napoleon, who solved the problem of no ruler by announcing that Holland was, after all, composed of French soil washed down from the Meuse and the Rhine. Since that was the case, he made it a part of France.

Museum Amstelkring or Our Dear Lord in the Attic (40 Oudezijds Voorburgwal)

Even though Calvinism became the religion here in the sixteenth century, the tolerant Amsterdam authorities allowed Catholics to go underground —or, in the case of water-logged Amsterdam, way above ground into attics —to continue their worship in secret. This is only one of some sixty such secret churches that were once here. It is still used for weddings and christenings, and is almost exactly as it was in 1735. One of the many unusual objects here is the small silver box shaped like a coffin. At the time these churches were in use, Catholics could not be buried in consecrated ground, so consecrated earth was kept in the box and scattered, three spoonfuls per person, over the bodies of deceased Catholics before the coffins were closed.

Nieuwe Kerk (New Church) (Mozes en Aaronstraat)

It wasn't with Alexandre Dumas, legend has it, that the idea for his novel of seventeenth-century Dutch history, *The Black Tulip*, originated. It was William III, at his coronation here in 1849 as king of the Netherlands, who gave the novelist the theme (*see* The Hague, Gevangenpoort), suggesting it was about time he gave Holland a little publicity in one of his romances. No sooner proposed than done, in the Dumas fashion.

The Portuguese Synagogue (Jonas Daniel Meijerplein)

The seventeenth-century philosopher Baruch Spinoza worshipped here until his excommunication in 1656 for "proclaiming dreadful heresy," namely asserting that God had to be personified to be understood. The excommunication, coupled with an assassination attempt one night when he was on his way to the theater, led him to quit this city for the little village of Rijnsberg near Leiden. There he ground lenses as a means of making his livelihood and wrote an abridgement of the *Meditations of Descartes*. He liked the solitary life of a lens grinder, for it gave him time to think. But it was an accumulation of lens dust in his lungs that killed him at age forty-five.

Rijksmuseum (Stadhouders Kade)

Forks didn't come into use in Amsterdam until near the end of the sixteenth century, when the fashion for large, stiff, ruffled collars like those in so many of the portraits here made an extension of the fingers necessary for eating.

◆◆◆

The absence of eyebrows and eyelashes on the women in the seventeenth-century portraits here is not poor execution or faulty restoration. It was a common condition of the times, the result of singeing from blowing out candles.

Schreierstoren (Weeping Tower) (Geldersekade and Oudezijdskolk)

From this 1487 tower, Henry Hudson set sail in 1609 on a trip that brought him to Nieuw Amsterdam—New York. The tower is said to take its name from the tears of wives and sweethearts bidding farewell to their men putting out to sea.

Westerkerk (Prinsengracht)

This 1620 church, the happy setting of the marriage of Queen Beatrix to Prince Claus in 1966, was also where the Dutch master painter Rembrandt

Harmensz van Rijn was buried in an unmarked grave in 1669. His body was lowered into the common grave with no one in attendance but the public gravediggers. Such was the final reward to the greatest of Holland's Golden Age artists for never having compromised his talent by painting "popular" pictures for easy money.

Zuiderkerk (South Church) (Nieuwmarkt)

Though the southern part of the Netherlands had been liberated by the winter of 1944–45, Amsterdam and the north had to endure a last winter of Nazi occupation before they would be freed. This winter is remembered as the Hunger Winter, for there was no fuel, gas, electricity, or transport. Reportedly, highly untasty tulip bulbs were dug up to be eaten—mashed and made into soup, mixed with vegetables, or ground and made into biscuits. Twenty thousand died of the cold and hunger in this city that winter, and bodies piled up here at the Zuiderkerk because it was impossible to bury the dead, with no wood for coffins and no gravediggers with the strength to work.

DELFT

Nieuwe Kerk (New Church) (Markt)

The white marble recumbent figure of William the Silent (*see* Delft, Prinsenhof), who was felled by an assassin's bullet in 1584, lies on a black marble base here in the Royal House of Orange burial vault. At his feet is the effigy of the devoted dog who, a dozen years earlier, had barked to rouse the prince as two Spaniards with assassination on their minds crept toward him. Not only that time had the little dog shown his devotion, but when an assassin's bullet finally did find its mark in his master's heart, the mourning dog refused all food, and died soon afterward.

Prinsenhof (Prince's House) (St. Agathesplein, Oude Delftgracht)

It was dinnertime on July 10, 1584, and William the Silent, with his wife, Louise de Coligny, on his arm, was on his way to the dining room when a gaunt, disheveled man appeared in a doorway and demanded a passport. The princess paled seeing him, for he looked so wild and distraught, but the prince, as was his wont, simply smiled agreeably and directed a secretary to provide the passport the man sought. This was not the first time the disheveled stranger had been here. He had come before, and, indeed, had been received by the prince as an emissary from the French court. He'd appeared again in the environs on the preceding Sunday, though not to William himself. Noticed lingering in a courtyard, he had been asked by a guard what his business was. He had replied mournfully that he had no business there—where he really wanted to be was in the church opposite, but he lacked appropriate stockings and shoes. The kind-hearted guard had conveyed his need to the prince, and William, in his usual generous way, had given the guard money for the would-be-worshipper.

But it had not been footgear the stranger had bought with the prince's money. It was pistols and bullets. The gaunt man with the wild eyes was no Protestant emissary from the French court, as he had given himself out to be, but a Catholic fanatic from Burgundy whose lifelong dream was to murder the Protestant prince of Orange.

On that July day, the prince and his party finished their meal and rose from the table. The prince was in the lead as the little group started toward the staircase that led to his chambers. He had only mounted two steps when the erstwhile passport seeker—Balthasar Gérard—fired one of the bullets that the prince's generosity had enabled him to buy—into William the Silent's heart. The fifty-one-year-old prince, the beloved leader of the Dutch people, clutched at the wound and fell, asking God's mercy not only for himself, but, characteristically, for his "poor people" as he died.

Stadhuis (Town Hall) (Markt): THE TOWER

It was in this tower in 1584 that Balthasar Gérard, the Spanish assassin of William the Silent (*see* Delft, Prinsenhof), was imprisoned while awaiting trial and sentencing. His cell required him to remain constantly in a prone position, though the discomfort of this was nothing to compare with the death sentence that awaited him. July 14, four days after the assassination, Gerard was drawn and quartered, then beheaded, and his head placed on a pike in public.

Although a fire in 1618 destroyed most of the original town hall, this tower survived and was incorporated into the present structure in 1620.

GOUDA

Catharina Gasthuis (St. Catherine Hospice) (City Museum)

The Latin words on the plaque here: DESIDERIUS ERASMUS GOUDAE CONCEP-
TUS ROTTERODAMI NATUS ANNO 1457, announce that Erasmus, the celebrated scholar and humanist (who was christened Gerhard Gerhards), was born in

Rotterdam but conceived in Gouda (by a Gouda woman who was having an affair with an unknown priest). By proclaiming this unusual bit of information, Gouda shows that it obviously wants whatever association it can claim to this remarkable man of deep learning, brilliant literary ability, and great tolerance.

HAARLEM

Stedelijk Museum (Frans Hals Museum) (62 Groot Heiligland)

What is now the Frans Hals Museum, a 1608 building of fine architectural design, was originally built as the Old Men's Home of Haarlem. It was here that Frans Hals, at the age of eighty-two, applied for the dole, since he was completely penniless and, though the father of at least eight sons and four daughters, had no one to care for him. The town of Haarlem let him live out his days at the almshouse, and granted him a meager pension of 200 gulden a year only on the condition that he work for it by painting. Hals was commissioned to do a group painting of the governors of the home, and another of the women regents. Painting with what may have been shaking hands at the age of eighty-four, Hals created two of his greatest works; the savage honesty of the portraits they contain may have been his revenge for the ignominy he endured in his final years.

THE HAGUE

Gevangenpoort

It was a gruesome event—the murder here in 1672 of Cornelius and Jan De Witt by a maddened, drunken mob. They broke into this prison to drag the brothers out, finding one lying on his bed, exhausted by torture, and the other gently offering him solace from the Bible. Both De Witts had served their country well, Cornelius as a naval commander fighting the French and English, Jan as grand pensionary of the Dutch Republic, a role that made him virtually regent of the nation. Under his direction, Holland's overseas empire grew. But the brothers' policies became unpopular, and Cornelius was unjustly accused of plotting against young William, prince of Orange (*see* Amsterdam, Nieuwe Kerk), and was imprisoned here. When a message, sent in the name of Cornelius, reached Jan, asking him to come to the prison to see him, the devoted Jan quickly responded. Though his daughter tearfully warned that she feared he was going to his doom, he assured her that could not be so. Friends, too, urged him to remain at home, but he replied that he had a duty to his brother if he were in need. He came here accompanied by no guards, only by serving men and secretaries. Once arrived, his puzzled brother asked why he had come. The message had, indeed, been false.

And while the brothers talked together inside these prison walls, their enemies murmured against them outside and plied the assembled masses with brandy and wine. Cavalry was sent to control the rioters, but when they were informed of an imminent attack on the city itself, the cavalrymen quit the prison to protect the populace. It turned out to be a false alarm, but with the soldiers gone, the storming here began in earnest. With axes and sledge hammers the prison doors were broken down, and the brothers hauled from Cornelius's cell. Touchingly, they bade each other farewell as the mob pushed and shoved them down the stairs to be executed. Cornelius, racked with the pain inflicted by days of torture, could barely stand, but clung to his brother as they descended. They had scarcely begun the descent when Cornelius was struck on the head, yanked away from Jan, and trampled to death in the street below here. Jan lasted a few minutes longer; then a pike was driven into his face, and he was shot in the neck. As he fell to his knees, he managed to raise his eyes and his clasped hands to heaven.

Lange Voorhout

In the first half of the sixteenth century, while he was still ruler of the Low Countries, the emperor Charles V sought to insure the continuation of the beauty of this splendid L-shaped avenue of mansions and park in the center of The Hague. Any man who dared cut down even one tree along the avenue had his right hand cut off as punishment.

Panorama Mesday (65b Zeestraat)

In 1879 the authorities at Scheveningen, the coastal resort area and fishing village adjoining this city, decided to relandscape the great sand dunes to make way for a housing project. Strongly opposed to the proposal, a group of painters, including H. W. Mesdag, one of the key figures of The Hague school of art, got together to *paint* a protest. This painting of the dunes, the North Sea, and the villagers mending their nets was completed in 1881. It is among the largest canvases in the world—45 feet high and 400 feet long.

Scheveningen

Throughout World War II, in order to determine if the person to whom they were speaking was Dutch or German, the Dutch asked for the enunciation of two words that apparently could not be mastered by the Germans. The first was the tongue-twisting Dutch name of this seaside resort of The Hague, Scheveningen; the second was Massachusetts.

LEIDEN

Hooglandsche Kerk (Hooglandse Kerkgracht)

Outside this church, Burgomaster Adrian Van der Werf offered his body as food to the starving citizens of Leiden in 1574.

For more than three months, Leiden had been under siege by the Spanish. Because it was walled, the Spaniards could not get in, but they could —and did—easily cut off all food supplies. All bread and flour were long gone, the maltcake and the dogs and cats and rats and horses had been eaten. Even the cows—kept as long as possible because of the milk that they produced—were being slaughtered one by one and distributed in as small portions as possible. All edible leaves had been stripped from the trees. And then the plague came. Between the shortage of food and the dread disease, more than 6,000 Leideners were dead.

William the Silent begged the Leideners to stand firm against the enemy and not capitulate. He had promised that within three months he would think of some relief for them. And he had. Though walled Leiden was inland, set in pasture and orchard land that had been reclaimed from the sea, that same sea that had been put out by dikes to build the city could be let in again to save the city. And William had done it. He had ordered the dikes broken in sixteen places and the sea was coming in. On that sea, more than 200 Dutch vessels were readied to rout the Spanish.

The flooding waters carried them to within five miles of here. But there the strongest dikes still had to be cut through. They were, but then the wind changed, blowing from the wrong direction, driving the water out, not in, and making it too shallow for the ships.

But then, so the Leideners were later to say, God helped. The wind shifted to the northwest and blew with gale force. The seas churned and rose and the Dutch ships were afloat again.

But there was still another dike to be broken. Again the wind shifted, and the waters ceased to flood. A depth of twenty-eight inches was needed for the passage of the fleet over the flooded fields and streets, and there was a depth of only nine. Meanwhile, every fortification around this city and along the route of the Dutch fleet was in Spanish hands. Villages outside the city walls were being put to the torch. The flames could be seen and the sound of artillery fire heard from this city. Even the valiant people of Leiden feared they could hold out no longer. The pierced dikes and the fleet in the distance notwithstanding, relief was still too far away. Capitulation seemed the only answer. And they had gathered here to tell the burgomaster so.

But Van der Werf would not hear them out. Waving his hat for silence he told them he would die rather than surrender to the enemy. Starvation, he said, was preferable to a dishonorable death. But since, he added, his fellow citizens seemed to feel differently, he was at their disposal.

"Here is my sword," Van der Werf is recorded as having said. "Plunge it into my breast and divide my flesh among you. Take my body to appease your hunger, but expect no surrender so long as I remain alive."

The Leideners listed to their brave burgomaster and took heart. Leaping to the ramparts they shouted to the Spanish that when all other sustenance was gone they would eat their left arms, but keep their right to defend their women and their liberty. "As well can the prince of Orange pluck the stars from the sky as bring the ocean to the walls of Leiden for your relief," the Spaniards taunted back.

But they were mistaken. Again God rescued Leiden, for the wind shifted again and the waters of the North Sea surged and swept through the broken dikes. Within twenty-four hours, water was flooding the fields outside the city, and the Dutch navy sailed to the rescue. They fought a curious sea battle dodging the chimneytops of submerged houses, the topmost branches of submerged trees. Then the Spanish fled and on October 3, 1574, the Dutch vessels filled with foodstuffs reached Leiden. This city, its burgomaster, and its honor were saved.

De Lakenhal Municipal Museum (28–32 Oude Singel)

The stewpot on display here reminds all Leideners of an event near the end of the terrible 131-day seige of this city (*see* Leiden, Hooglandsche Kerk) by the Spanish in 1574. Many a citizen was close to starvation, but a young Leiden lad named Ewout Joppensz squeezed through a breach in the city walls into the Spanish encampment. There he found a copper kettle of simmering stew on a campfire, and carted it back here to this hungry city. The stew, called *hutspot,* is made of beef, onions, carrots, and potatoes, and is still a popular Leiden dish.

Nun's Bridge (opposite Kloksteeg)

It was from the Nun's Bridge on a day near the end of July 1620 that the youngest and strongest members of the English separatist community in Leiden left for the New World. Those who chose to go left Leiden "not out of any newfangledness," in William Bradford's words, "or such like giddy humor—but for sundry weighty and solid reasons." On barges they sailed along the Vliet, through Delft, and on to Delftshaven, whence the *Speedwell* took the Pilgrims to England and the *Mayflower.*

University of Leiden

This prestigious university is a permanent memorial to the heroism of the citizens of Leiden during the seige of their city in 1574. For their brave stand against the Spanish, William the Silent—getting up from his sick bed in Delft to come to congratulate them—offered the people their choice of exemption from taxes or the establishment of a university. It was a university they chose, and it was the first in the Netherlands. Its inauguration took place on February 5, 1575, with an elaborate parade and a floating procession on the river. It quickly became the most important Protestant university in Europe, attracting the finest minds for its faculty.

LISSE

In the sandy soil near here, tulips have thrived ever since their introduction to this country in about 1580. That was when Carolus Clusius, who had been the gardener of Maximilian II of Austria, came home to the Netherlands bringing with him a gift of tulip bulbs from Augier Ghislain de Busbecq, the Austrian ambassador to Turkey. De Busbecq had seen and admired the bright flowers in the gardens of Constantinople and had brought some back to plant in Austria. Their Dutch name—*tulipum*—probably came from a misunderstanding of the Turkish word *tulbend* for the gaily-colored Turkish turbans. Clusius, who became a professor at the University of Leiden, did a great deal of experimenting with the gnarled bulbs, producing tulips in extraordinary hues.

LOEVENSTEIN

It was a daring escape, brilliantly executed. Hugo de Groot—Grotius, the father of international law—was sentenced to life imprisonment here for his endorsement of a religious sect that was out of favor with Maurice of Orange. But there was some leniency in his sentence. In his imprisonment on this island he was allowed visits from his wife and also a regular supply of books. And on them both rested his escape.

The books he requested arrived in large chests, and when they had been read, they were returned in the same chest—along with the prisoner's dirty linen. For a while, the prison guard checked each time the chest left this castle, and examined its contents. But when it seemed that nothing was amiss he grew lax. And so one day, Grotius's wife Maria had her husband conceal himself beneath the dirty linens. Off the chest went to the mainland laundry in Gorcum. There, by prior arrangement, a friend of the great scholar waited for him. Disguising Grotius as a carpenter, he sent him out of the Netherlands.

And what of Maria? There was some talk of keeping her in this prison in her husband's stead. But it never happened. Instead, she became a heroine of her people as well, assuredly, as of her husband.

MAASTRICHT

Ramparts

Situated as it is at a major crossing of the Meuse River, over the centuries this city has endured more than twenty major sieges since its founding in Roman times. One such seige, by the French in 1673, was watched from a nearby hilltop by army commander Louis XIV. It was during that conflict that d'Artagnan, the famous captain of Alexandre Dumas's *Three Musketeers* (and an actual historical personage), was mortally wounded on these medieval ramparts.

St. Pietersberg Caves

Through the centuries, these 200 miles of dark, silent tunnels, where stonecutters cut building stone till 1875, have been a place of refuge. In the eighteenth century they harbored Austrian and Italian mercenaries brought in to help the Dutch combat the French invaders. In World War II they were readied to shelter up to 50,000 people from bombing, but never needed to be put into use. Four monks in the seventeenth century, however, met not salvation but starvation here when the thread they had affixed to the caves' entrance to lead them back broke, and they were never able to find their way out.

◄⊛►

Napoleon Bonaparte, the writers Voltaire and Sir Walter Scott, the philosopher Descartes, and the composer Rossini are among the notable tourists who have visited these galleries cut forty-five feet deep in the soft, chalky marlstone (a kind of sandstone) and have written their names in the soft walls. Here the visitor's signature has never been considered vandalism, just a welcome addition.

Legend has it that Napoleon, visiting these caves, was so enamored of the fossilized head of a Meuse lizard he wished to take home to France that he exchanged it for 500 bottles of fine French wine.

❦

It was in these caves that Rembrandt's *The Night Watch* was hidden from the Nazis during World War II in a specially prepared copper drum. When the war was over and the huge thirteen- by-sixteen-foot painting was being restored before being rehung in Amsterdam's Rijksmuseum, it was discovered that the picture actually showed a daytime scene. The darkening that had led to its being called *The Night Watch* had been largely caused by smoke from peat fires.

MIDDELBURG

Stadhuis (Town Hall) (Markt)

The original of this magnificent gilded and gabled building was built between 1452 and 1520. With its carved oak moldings and high vaulted ceilings, it made an impressive headquarters for the cloth guild, which originally used it. When the Nazis bombed Zeeland in 1940, the Middelburg town hall continued to burn for two weeks, with the ground around it too hot to walk on. Restoration of the marvelous front facade was finally completed in 1967.

OOSTERBEËK

Airborne Museum (232 Utrechtseweg)

On September 17, 1944, 10,000 soldiers of the British First Airborne and Polish brigades parachuted into the countryside here and around Arnhem in an effort to capture and hold the Arnhem Bridge over the Rhine River, thus clearing the way for the advance from the south of British field marshal Bernard Montgomery's army. The campaign, though cleverly conceived and bravely put into action, was bogged down by soggy terrain that slowed the advance of supporting surface troops, leaving the Airborne badly outnumbered and hopelessly positioned. For four days the paratroopers followed the order "Arnhem Bridge—and hold it," but after one of the fiercest and bloodiest battles of the Second World War (only 2,000 of the 10,000 paratroopers escaped), the Germans won the bridge and blew it up. This museum building was dedicated to the Allied courage at the battle. Formerly Doorworth Castle, it served as headquarters for both the Germans and the Allies at various times. There is also a memorial at the rebuilt bridge, the subject of the film *A Bridge Too Far.*

OUDEWATER

Heksenwaag (Witches' Scales): WAAGHUIS (Weigh House) (1 Korte Havenstraat)

Witchcraft was a worrisome business in Europe from the 1480s until the end of the eighteenth century. Those accused who died from torture or burning at the stake in Europe—mostly women—numbered more than a million. One of the primary tests of witchcraft was being weighed, since it was assumed that to fly, witches would have to be lighter in proportion to their height than God-fearing Christians. The weight above which it was certain one wasn't a witch was ninety Dutch pounds (ninety-nine American). The honesty of the weigh-masters at witches' scales throughout Europe was, literally, a matter of life and death. Many were known to be dishonest and open to bribes. In all Europe only the Dutch Oudewater scales were deemed an honest operation. By decree, Charles V proclaimed that anyone found to weigh at least ninety pounds on these scales not only was not guilty of being a witch, but was forever free from further prosecution on that charge. People came from as far away as Sicily, Sweden, and Poland to step on the scales at Oudewater and receive the lifesaving certificate of weight document to take home with them.

ROTTERDAM

Boymans-van Beuningen Museum (18 Mathenesserlaan)

Hans van Meegeren was a splendid painter—so splendid, indeed, that he created six "Vermeers" that even the experts were convinced were long-missing works by the seventeenth-century genre painter. In 1937 this museum paid $286,000 for one of them, and during World War II, German field marshal Hermann Göring—an art collector—acquired another. If he hadn't, van Meegeren might have kept right on painting "undiscovered

Vermeers." But—the war over—van Meegeren was charged with having cooperated with the Nazis by sending a Vermeer to Göring. Which was worse—to be denounced as a collaborator or as a forger? At the end of World War II it seemed safer here to be a forger, so van Meegeren admitted that Göring's Vermeer was a fake. Experts studied the Old Masters van Meegeren said were his and refused to believe that they weren't genuine. Only by actually painting a *new* Old Master under the eyes of a group of judges could he convince the art world he was a forger. When it did believe him, he was put on trial and sentenced to a year in prison. He died of a heart attack before he had completed his sentence.

Monument for a Devastated City (Blaak Straat)

In this statue by Zadkine can be seen the anguish felt by Rotterdammers when, on the morning of May 14, 1940, the Nazis destroyed much of this city with incendiary bombs. Rotterdam was used as an example of what would happen to other Dutch cities if this neutral country did not surrender to the Germans quickly. Nine hundred people were killed; 78,500 were made homeless. The Netherlands surrendered that afternoon. Four years later, the Nazis, though knowing they were defeated, nevertheless leveled the entire harbor area.

Though the sculptured figure in the statue has her heart bombed out, the upraised arms seek the courage to rebuild the city. This the people here did, attending first to their harbor, and then to their homes. Today Rotterdam, even though it is twenty miles from the North Sea, is the biggest and busiest harbor in the world.

SPAARNDAM

In 1950 in this fishing village, Princess Margriet unveiled a statue of Pieter, Mary Mapes Dodge's fictional boy who saved Haarlem from flooding by holding his finger in a hole in the dike. The youth had become known to every schoolchild through the mid-nineteenth-century book, *Hans Brinker, or the Silver Skates.*

THE TULIP TRAIL (Leiden to Haarlem)

They like to tell the story here, where tulips dazzle the eye in April and May, of the English journalist Joseph Addison and this colorful flower. Stopping at an inn here in tulip country one night, Addison could not help listening to a conversation at the next table about Admiral So and So, General This, and Captain That. Finally, he could contain his curiosity about this mysterious military endeavor no longer, and he asked outright who this impressive company of gentlemen being discussed were.

"Gentlemen," he later recalled the puzzled diners replying. "Why sir, these are not gentlemen. They are tulips of the rarest and noblest sort."

In the seventeenth century, when Addison visited here, military titles were in vogue as names for the flower, whereas nowadays, they bear names like the Aga Khan, the Duchess of Kent, the Lady Churchill, the King Gustavus.

ZAANDAM

Czar Peters Huisje (Hut of Peter the Great)

For a little while in 1697, Peter the Great, assuming the name Peter Mikhailov, lived in this little wooden hut to study shipbuilding. But he was soon discovered and left for a larger shipyard in Amsterdam where he was less likely to be recognized.

ZUTPHEN

Warnsveld

On the battlefield here in 1586, England's Sir Philip Sidney died fighting for the Netherlands' cause against the Spanish. As he lay dying, a wounded fellow soldier nearby cried out for water, and summoning virtually his last strength, Sir Philip passed his cup of water to his dying comrade, saying softly, so the story goes, "Thy need is greater than mine."

Norway

ALESUND ✧————————

At the turn of the century, Kaiser William II of Germany, who frequently sailed these fjords, favored this seaport as an anchorage for his yacht *Hohenzollern*. And when, one stormy winter night in 1904, an oil lamp fell over and 800 houses were destroyed by fire, the kaiser provided German architects and supplies to rebuild the town, much in the style of the German Hanseatic city of Lübeck.

ASGÅRDSTRAND

Munch House

In this simple little house the painter Edvard Munch lived and entertained and was the talk of the town. Said to have been the handsomest man in Norway in his day (1863–1944), when he failed to win the pretty girl he courted in this garden, he turned his attention to many women. In this small community he was notable for this endless courting, as well as for his curious habit of hanging his paintings from trees in the garden so his colors would "weather."

BERGEN

When the German merchants of the Hanseatic League controlled the commerce here in the fifteenth century and lived and worked in what today is the Hanseatic Museum on this quay, one imaginative and angry Norwegian teased them ceaselessly. He was the pirate "Little Sir Alf" Erlingsson. Furious at his annoying them, the league once went so far as to send warships after him. But, as always, Alf escaped. In the boldest of the pirate's adventures, he sailed up to this quay one day in disguise, and announced that he knew exactly where Little Sir Alf was hiding and would bring him back to the Germans if they paid him enough. Negotiations went on for several hours. Finally Erlingsson decided he had as much gold as he would get, so waving good-bye to the merchants and promising to come back soon with their pesky pirate, he merrily sailed away.

Bergenhus Fortress

In the Rosencrantz Tower here, the earl of Bothwell, husband of Mary Queen of Scots, was held prisoner when he fled Scotland after having been charged with participation in a plot to murder Mary's previous husband, Lord Darnley. (*See* Denmark, Fåreverjle.)

St. Mary's Church

The thirteenth-century Icelandic chronicler Snorri Sturluson heard his last mass in Norway in this church before going home to his death.

Although he had once been held in high regard by Norway's King Haakon IV Haakonsson, he fell into disfavor when he took an interest in Icelandic politics at a time when Norway sought to take over Iceland. So the king had agents sent after him to Iceland, and they killed him in his cellar in 1241. As one story has it, when the assassins turned the dead man over, they found his masterpiece, *The Saga of the Kings,* in his pocket—and it was addressed to his old friend Haakon Haakonsson.

The National Stage

The violinist Ole Bull was a patriot and a dreamer. He dreamed of a New Norway colony in America and spent two years in Pennsylvania trying to establish it. That dream met with failure. He returned here nearly penniless and gave concerts tirelessly to become richer. But while he was in America, a new dream had developed. This one was of a Norwegian national theater. And in 1850 in Bergen, this dream came true.

A man with great aptitude for discovering creative talent, Bull chose a twenty-five-year-old aspiring playwright named Henrik Ibsen to write and give the prologue at this theater's opening. Impressed by what he saw and heard, the violinist hired Ibsen to work full time for the theater. So it turned out that it was far more than this theater building itself that Ole Bull gave to Norway. His faith helped produce this nation's finest dramatist.

This same sixth sense led Bull to recommend fifteen-year-old Edvard Grieg for the study of music at Leipzig Conservatory. And Grieg came back home to Bergen to live up to Bull's expectations and to become Norway's most famous composer.

Troldhaugen

At this home—Hill of Trolls—just outside Bergen, the composer Edvard Grieg (whose great-grandfather was an immigrant merchant from Scotland) spent the last twenty-two years of his life. The honoring and evoking of nature always played an important part in Grieg's compositions. Indeed, he so respected nature that he would not allow either the trees or the bushes here to be trimmed or cut. They should grow in the way they were intended to, Grieg insisted.

GEIRANGER (STOR FJORD)

At this dramatic spot with its towering mountains, Mark Twain remarked when he visited that surely the children must be tied to the mountainside farms to prevent their tumbling off. By those not acquainted with this region, the remark was assumed to be facetious, but it wasn't. "Ledge children," as they are called, sometimes are tied here.

GRIMSTAD

Fjaere Church: GRAVE OF TERJE VIGER (near Grimstad)

When the British blockaded Norway during the Napoleonic wars, there was a food shortage in this part of the country. Terje Viger, a farmer of Fjaere Church, feared for the lives of his wife and children, for supplies were dwindling, so he set off for Denmark in his rowboat after foodstuffs. He arrived there without incident, piled his little boat high with food for the winter, and started back—only to be apprehended by the British as he neared the Norwegian shore. His entreaties for his loved ones notwithstanding, he was taken to England and kept there for the next five years. When he was released and came home, it was to an empty house. His family had, indeed, died of starvation.

GUDBRANSDAL

Peer Gynt Grave

It was in this valley that the *real* Peer Gynt lived—the eccentric farmer about whose fantastic adventures the dramatist Henrik Ibsen and the composer Edvard Grieg wrote. His burial place is between Harpefoss and Vinstra.

HAMMERFEST

After Thomas Alva Edison displayed his electric generator at the Paris Exposition in 1890, Hammerfest—the most northerly town in the world, and, therefore, the darkest—bought one. A year later, this city became the first community in Norway to have electric light.

KONGSBERG

Christian IV of Denmark and Norway hurried here in the seventeenth century. A boy's cow's horn had rubbed moss off a rock and silver had been revealed. While he was here to see how much silver there was, Christian took charge of the building of this town.

KONGSVINGER

The Fortress

Now a Museum of the Resistance, this seventeenth-century fortress was presented as a gift to the Nazis by collaborator Prime Minister Vidkun Quisling during World War II. In return, Adolf Hitler presented the Norwegian with a cane.

KRISTIANSUND

The fertile soil that covers this rocky land was brought from Spain a century ago by fishermen trading there. Realizing that though their rocks were good for codfish drying they were hardly suitable for the nurturing of flower gardens, the fishermen filled their holds with rich black Spanish soil for the homeward journey. Eventually enough soil was imported in this way to provide Kristiansund not only with flower gardens but with parks.

◄⚬►

In April 1940, thinking Haakon VII was here, the German Luftwaffe bombed this town for four days and four nights (*see* Molde). When the bombing ended, 800 houses—two-thirds of this colorful little codfishing port—had been destroyed. But the indomitable people of Kristiansund straight away began to rebuild with color and charm.

LILLEHAMMER

Seven hundred and fifty years ago Norway was in the throes of civil war. Contending were the Birchlegs and the Baglers. The royal family was in residence at Lillehammer at that time. The enemy was approaching. Two-year-old Prince Haakon Haakonsson was clearly in danger. So the two fastest Birchleg skiers were given a cradle with the child in it and told to hurry as fast as they could across the Gudbrandsdal—the lovely valley where this city is set—to Rena in a neighboring valley. A blizzard notwithstanding, the skiers carried little Haakon thirty-five miles to safety, and he grew to serve as the king of Norway from 1217 to 1263. It is this rescue that is commemorated here each March by the Birkebeiner (Birchlegs) Ski Race between this city and Rena.

Mailhaugen Museum

Dr. Anders Sandvik, a young itinerant dentist of this region at the turn of the century, was very fond of dentistry, but he was equally fond of collecting odds and ends. When a poor patient proposed paying him with an old wooden bowl or an antique ladle or a trundle bed, Sandvik never said he would prefer cash. He gratefully accepted the odds and ends of the Gudbrandsal countryside and brought them here to Lillehammer. Townspeople were a bit taken aback when he arrived one day with a whole building in pieces and set it up in his garden. But that was just the beginning. Soon there were half a dozen antique buildings and their furnishings. After a while the collection became too much for one man so he turned it over to a society for the promotion of the welfare of Lillehammer and they provided this hill for the Sandvik Folk Museum.

LOFOTEN ISLANDS

Moskenesøy

Just beyond this southernmost Lofoten Island snarls the Moskenstraum—site of Edgar Allan Poe's "A Descent into the Maelstrom." Here, in a narrow passageway between this island and Vaeröy, the tide sweeps with such ferocity that a whirlpool is formed. Both man and beast go out of their way to avoid these waters in stormy winter weather (though on calm days the maelstrom can be tranquil, indeed). Hakluyt, writing of them in his *Voyages* in the sixteenth century, remarked that the gurgling and roaring could be heard as far as ten miles away.

But the Moskenstraum is not the wildest of Norway's maelstroms. Twenty miles off is Bodö the Saltstraumen Eddy, the strongest in the world.

Sandøy Island in the Røst Group

A realistic dream awoke a sixteen-year-old youth of the neighboring island of Storfjell on the first of February in 1432. He had dreamed that two calves that were missing would be found here. When morning came, he hurried to tell his father and brother and insisted that the dream was true. Although they scoffed, the father and brother (the name of the family is not recorded) agreed to take a look.

Climbing into their boat, they made their way here. As the boat neared the shore, the astonished trio saw a handful of trembling men on this previously uninhabited island. They were an Italian nobleman and his crew, washed ashore in a lifeboat three weeks before, and barely alive. Indeed, six of the twenty-one who had landed were already dead. The Italians' vessel, bound for Flanders from Portugal laden with wine and spices, had lost her sails in one storm, her rudder in another. Mid-December, the men had abandoned ship, piling into two lifeboats. But only one boat had made it to shore. Though they had managed to find a cattle shelter to stay in, there was virtually nothing to eat, and they were close to starvation when the cowherd's dream brought them help.

LOFTHUS (HARDANGER FJORD)

It was here high in the mountains in a little hut during the nineteenth century that composer Edvard Grieg, listening to the wind in the evergreens and the rush of the waterfalls, came each summer to write music.

MÅSØY

To this North Cape village, Louis Philippe, duke of Orléans and later king of France, came in 1795 when he feared assassination at home. First, he and a companion, dressed as traders, had fled to Denmark, then to Hammerfest, then here where they stayed overnight in a fisherman's shack. It was hard to remain incognito, however. In the morning, the fisherman's wife, opening their door before the pair were up, glimpsed the array of medals on Louis's chest and saw that his companion slept on the floor. Clearly, this was no ordinary guest sharing her house. And on another day here, without thinking, Louis paid an old woman with a gold coin. Immediately, she recognized him as royalty, but soothed his fears by predicting that—his troubles notwithstanding—he one day would be king.

Thinking it safer nevertheless to be in a more remote location, Louis left here for Muoniska, Sweden. While there, he repaid the pastor's hospitality by seducing his sister. A son was born of that union and it is said, to this day, that there is French royal blood here in Norway, for the boy became a Norwegian.

Louis always had warm recollections of this North Cape region that had harbored him in time of trouble. In gratitude, he sent a bronze bust of himself here after he became king. In 1944, it was damaged when this village was bombed and is now in the museum in Tromsø. He also commissioned seventy paintings for Versailles from a Norwegian painter, although they were never done because Louis lost his throne.

MOLDE

There was a report in the spring of 1940 that Haakon VII was staying in a red house here, so with precision, the Luftwaffe bombed every red house in town. Helplessly watching the destruction from a red house among the birches on the outskirts of town were the king and young crown prince Olaf. (*See* Kristiansund.)

NARVIK

On the morning of April 9, 1940, gunfire and explosions awoke the residents of this iron ore port. When they reached their windows, they found the swastika flying where, the day before, the red, white, and blue flag of Norway had snapped in the fjord wind.

Then, a little more than a month later, a combined force of British, French, Norwegians, and Poles drove the Nazis out—inflicting the first defeat that Germany had suffered in World War II. But in June, the Allied offensive here had to be halted and the soldiers sent to the main front. The Germans came back and dug in, and signs of their fortifications may still be seen along the fjord rocks.

OSLO

Ravaged by a fierce fire in 1624, this city was redesigned with fifty-foot-wide streets at right angles to each other in what was then known as "the Dutch manner." The designer was Christian IV, the builder-king of Denmark, who came to supervise and who also renamed the city—then called by the Viking name of Oslo—"Christiania," after himself. It was not till 1925 that it got its old Viking name again.

Akershus

Built about 1300, this fortress-castle has held many a famous inmate through the centuries. Few have been more colorful, though, than nineteenth-century Ole Pedersen Høyland, a clever thief who once managed to escape by stealing the warden's clothes. When he was recaptured, a special cell was built for him, and for several years he occupied it, quietly planning his escape all the while. This time, he cut away the floorboards and fled beneath the fortress walls. Once out, he robbed the Bank of Norway, and was brought back again. Finally, when the could find no other way to escape, Ole Pedersen Høyland hanged himself.

Grand Hotel (31 Karl Johan's Gate)

Down Karl Johan's Gate top-hatted Henrik Ibsen used to walk mornings, when he lived here, to have an aperitif in the hotel café with visiting journalists.

Ladegarden (Hovedøya)

To this bishop's palace James VI of Scotland came in the sixteenth century to fetch his bride, the princess Anne of Denmark. En route to Scotland from Copenhagen, her vessel had been blown off course by a storm and had put in here in Oslo. Here James came to wed her. When not involved in wedding festivities, history recounts, the newlyweds played cards.

Back in Scotland after the ceremony, James charged that witchcraft had been responsible for the storm, and one of Scotland's most sensational witchcraft trials ensued. Some two hundred Scottish witches were accused of having provoked the tempest, and one of them admitted to having tossed a christened cat and bits of a dead man into the sea to rouse it.

Oslo Fjord

It did not, of course, keep the Germans out of Norway in World War II. All it did was delay the takeover of Oslo by half a day. But it showed the Germans the caliber of patriot they would have to face in Norway—his determination to protect his homeland.

On the April morning in 1940 when the German flagship *Blucher,* heralding the invasion, made her way up this fjord, the Crimean War fortress Oscarberg was woefully undermanned. There were twenty-five recruits stationed there, and a lieutenant. A retired commodore-captain had volunteered his services, too. The aged artillery consisted of three Krupp 28-cm cannons dating from 1892.

It was 3:00 A.M. when the lieutenant, August Bonsak, saw a dark shadow on the fortress range finder. Since the recruits were scarcely trained, it was he who leaped to one of the antique guns and fired. The shell hit the vessel's deck. On to the next gun he went and this time hit the *Blucher* at the waterline. Simultaneously, the commodore-commander, Anders Anderssen, fired a torpedo at the *Blucher*. And the 10,000-ton heavy cruiser with 1,500 men aboard, including the admiral in charge of the invasion squadron, sank to the bottom of this fjord. Though the Nazis quickly came with airplanes, that initial fierce resistance from two aging officers at a delapidated fort was a shock the Germans never forgot.

Vigeland Park Rose Garden

To remind King Haakon VII of his homeland when he was in exile in England in World War II, the Norwegian Resistance made sure, each Christmas, that he had a fir tree cut in Norway. The war over and the king home again, he decreed that the custom would not end with his return but that, each Christmas, the tallest fir in Norway should be sent to decorate London's Trafalgar Square. In gratitude for that annual gift, the people of London sent the roses for this garden in 1953.

Vigeland Sculptures in Frogner Park

At the end of the last century, when Adolf Gustav Vigeland was a young woodcarver from the country, making his first drawings, he took them one day to a sculptor here for his criticism. The cold, hungry youth was so exhausted that he fell asleep while his work was being examined.

When he awoke, it was to learn that his work was being roundly praised. That was the start of a monumental career in sculpture that resulted in this sculpture park of hundreds of figures; their centerpiece is a fifty-seven-foot-high granite monolith that weighed 470 tons when it was blasted from its quarry and that took seven months to move here from the quarry.

Enamored of the sculptor, his work, and his plans for more work, townspeople in Oslo joined together over the years to support him. When, in 1921, he asked the city fathers for a house and studio in exchange for all his art, they agreed.

Even in World War II he was allowed by German occupation forces to keep chiseling behind a high fence that shielded his work from public view. When the war ended, and the wall came down, however, the controversy began. His nude symbolic figures—more than 500 of them, all atumble—are still horrifying some who see them, intriguing others, titillating others.

RJUKAN (VEMORK)

It was 1942. Who would have the atomic bomb first—the Allies or the Axis? At the hydroelectric plant here, "heavy water," water with hydrogen atoms in it of double the usual atomic weight, was being produced in sizable quantities When combined with uranium, which the Germans were mining in Czechoslovakia, heavy water could be eminently useful in producing an atomic bomb. It was essential, as Franklin D. Roosevelt and Winston Churchill saw it, that this heavy water production be stopped. Norwegian Resistance was asked to help, and the plant was sabotaged. But enough heavy water remained to still be a danger, and the inside information was that the Germans were planning to get it out of harm's way and into Germany as soon as possible.

The exportation of the heavy water had to be prevented—at all costs. And so the plans were laid to sink the rail-ferry carrying it. It mattered that innocent Norwegian civilians—women and children—took the ferry. But not enough. The sinking would have to be in deep water in Lake Tinn— water deep enough so that the cargo could never be salvaged.

As soon as the Resistance got word that the shipment was, indeed, in prospect, they went to work. Twelve feet of plastic explosive, hidden under a coat, were stowed on the ferry the night before her sailing. At 10:00 the following morning, with fifty-three passengers and several flatcars filled with heavy water aboard, the boat quit her moorings and headed out across the lake that would lead to the North Sea, and thence to Germany. Half an hour later, an explosion shook her; the ferry keeled over; the flatcars broke loose and hurtled into the water. In four minutes the ferry had sunk. To the sorrow of all, twenty-six civilians went to the bottom with her and her cargo of death, although twenty-seven others were rescued.

That was in 1944. On August 5, 1945, the United States dropped the first atomic bomb on Japan.

STOKKSUND

In this treacherous place, the man at the wheel of a vessel must zigzag his way up the fjord. The first time Germany's Kaiser William II, vacationing aboard his yacht *Hohenzollern* at the turn of the century, sailed here, he insisted that he would take the wheel. His stern Norwegian pilot would have none of it, so the story goes. "Being kaiser won't help you here," the pilot told William. "I am the pilot here."

Grudgingly, William had to admit he was right, and presented the pilot with a gold watch with the imperial seal on it in recognition of his wisdom and his efforts.

TAFJORD VILLAGE (TAFJORD)

A rock slide in 1933 sent tons of rubble plunging into the fjord here and the "tidal wave" that followed drowned one hundred villagers.

TELEMARK DISTRICT

Morgedal

As a child here in the nineteenth century, Sondre Nordheim laid planks from the roof of his father's hillside farm to the incline behind, and when the snows came, practiced ski jumping over the farmhouse roof. Next, to facilitate his jumping he developed a new ski binding that attached the heel to the ski so skis no longer tumbled off into the snow. This revolutionized skiing. And in 1868, donning his skis, he took off from here on a 115-mile journey to Oslo to prove to Norwegians that the ancient art of skiing should have a comeback.

Today Nordheim, who emigrated to the United States in 1884, and was largely responsible for introducing skiing to America, is known as the inventor of modern skiing.

TØNSBERG

From this port, the explorer Roald Amundsen left for the South Pole in 1910, sailing his friend Fridtjof Nansen's wooden-hulled polar ship *Fram* (*see* Vadsø). Trying at the same time to be the first man to reach the South Pole was the British explorer Robert Falcon Scott. To prevent Scott's speeding up his expedition, Amundsen kept his own plans secret to the very end, leading all his friends and associates to believe that his destination was to be the Arctic. Using dogs and sledges where Scott traveled ill-equipped with ponies, Amundsen beat the Englishman by five weeks, arriving at the Pole a year after he had left his city.

TORGHATTEN

At this entrance to the Nordland Channel, legend has it, the giants and the trolls of old frequently did battle. One day one of the seven daughters of the king of the giants was bathing naked in the sea when Hestmannen, the son of the troll king, saw her and went in pursuit of her on his horse. But the bather and her sisters caught sight of him in the distance and fled. The giant king, hearing all the commotion, went to see what was happening. Meanwhile, Hestmannen, angry at having lost his prey, shot an arrow after the fleeing maidens. Their giant father was just in time to stop it with his hat. At that very moment the sun came up, turning all of the trolls, and the hat, and the seven fleeing sisters as well, into stone. And that is what they still are to this day. There is no mistaking Torghatten, a rocky island 825 feet high with a hole through it 535 feet long, for anything but the hat of the king of the giants.

TROMSØ

This is a city of sorrowful departures. It was from here in 1928 that the explorer Roald Amundsen, discoverer of the South Pole in 1912, left by airplane to search for the missing Italian explorer, Umberto Nobile. Nobile, it turned out, was safe, but Amundsen never returned. And it was from this quayside that King Haakon and Crown Prince Olaf fled to England on June 7, 1940, aboard the British cruiser *Devonshire* that had managed to slip, undetected by the Germans, into the fjord.

Tromsø Fjord

Crippled by torpedoes fired at her from one-man submarines, Hitler's "unsinkable" battleship the *von Tirpitz* took refuge in the deep waters here in 1944. But her refuge did not last long. The Resistance learned of her whereabouts and passed the word to Emil Lindberg, a radio operator. Lindberg wasted no time in notifying the Allies, and they wasted no time in sending a bomber to dispatch the battleship. On November 12, 1944, the *von Tirpitz* proved not to be so unsinkable as the Nazis had said. Indeed, the automatic bulkheads that were supposed to keep her from sinking served, instead, to trap 1,200 seamen as she sank, keel up, 875 feet down on the bottom of the fjord.

TRONDHEIM

To the court of King Olaf Tryggvesson in the tenth century came a young man from Greenland: Leif Ericson. He told the Norwegian king of the wonders of Greenland and Olaf told the young man of the wonders of his newfound Christianity. Before Ericson left, he had been converted and was charged by Norway's king to convert his fellow Greenlanders when he got home. But it was a long time before he got home. En route, his ship was driven off her course and the first landfall Leif Ericson made was North America.

Statue of King Olaf Tryggvesson (Olaf I)

On a visit to what, today, are Britain's Scilly Isles, the Viking Olaf Tryggvesson met his first Christian and was converted by him. Like most fresh converts, he wanted everyone he met to be converted, too. Since he was a Viking warrior, however, these conversions, as often as not, were by force rather than by peaceful persuasion. All Norway, Olaf decided, should be Christian. He started out by founding this city in 997 and building a church here. An impressive athlete and a handsome man, he was also a courageous and inventive warrior. It was he who, attacking London, tied lines around the piles supporting London Bridge, attached the other ends of the lines to his ships, and had them sail upriver—thereby pulling down the bridge as the old nursery rhyme recounts.

Olaf met his end as the result of an attempted conversion. When he was a young widower, he had sought as a bride Queen Sigrid of Sweden, a widow. Quite properly he had asked her hand, but there was one string attached—that she become a Christian. When the haughty Sigrid refused both Christianity and Olaf's suit, he had slapped her face. The queen never forgot the insult, and in later years joined her forces to those of the king of Denmark in an attack on Olaf's ships. Olaf and his men fought bravely, but when Olaf's favorite ship, the *Long Serpent,* was captured by his enemies, the ignominy was more than he could bear and he hurled himself into the sea.

Stiftsgarden

This rambling wooden structure in which the royal family stays on visits here is one of the largest wooden buildings in Scandinavia. It came to be because of rivalry between the sisters who had it built 200 years ago. Each was trying to outdo the other as construction proceeded: if one built a wing, the other built a wing double the size. The feud finally ended in 1774, when building stopped. The name of the winner in this sibling rivalry is recorded as Geheimeradinde Cecilia Christine Scholer. The loser's name is not remembered.

VADSØ

In his specially constructed heavy-hulled wooden boat, the *Fram*, Fridtjof Nansen (*see* Tønsberg) left here in 1893 en route to the North Pole. On Christmas Day, the ship was caught in the ice. It drifted northward, and when spring came, Nansen and a companion, Frederic Hjalmar Johansen, decided it was time to leave the others aboard ship and strike out on foot to reach the Pole. With dogs pulling sleighs of supplies, the pair set out. They were forced to abandon their efforts, however, and turned south to the island that today is called Fridtjof Nansen Land. There they spent the winter in an igloo they built of stone, living largely on seal meat. And there, unexpectedly, they were discovered by an impeccably attired British researcher, Frederick Jackson, who quickly led the winter-weary men to the yacht that had carried him north. The trio returned here in August 1896, to be greeted with much fanfare.

Amundsen's Mast

It was to this mast that the explorer Roald Amundsen moored the airship *Norge,* with which he flew over the North Pole in 1926. To the same mast the Italian explorer Umberto Nobile moored his airship, *Italia,* two years later before leaving on a similar expedition. Nobile's airship crashed, and Amundsen was lost for good searching for him, though Nobile returned safely. (*See* Trømso.)

VAGNES (SOGNE FJORD)

Germany's Kaiser William II had this enormous bronze statue of the mythical hero Frithjof the Fearless put here in 1912. A noble warrior of Viking days, Frithjof suffered years of trials in his efforts to marry the beautiful princess Ingeborg. The Swedish writer Esaias Tegner retold the old story in verse and Henry Wadsworth Longfellow translated it as *Frithjof's Saga.*

Portugal

ALCOBAÇA ◆⚘◆ ──────

Monastery of Santa Maria

Times change. In 1580, 999 monks lived here and celebrated mass night and day. Two hundred and fifty years later, the monks were expelled and horses stabled in the church nave.

◆⚘◆

Buried here feet to feet are Pedro I and his beloved Inés, for he wished, the king said, to see her before anything else when he awoke on Judgment Day.

Theirs is a macabre fourteenth-century love story. It began when Pedro was a prince and his affianced, the Infanta Constança, came from Spain, bringing with her as a lady-in-waiting the beautiful, golden-haired Inés de Castro. The young prince was smitten; Inés equally so. But the planned wedding took place as scheduled, and for some time, both the prince and Inés resisted temptation out of affection for the infanta. Passion won out, however, and their affair was soon bruited about the court. The prince's father, Alfonso IV, ordered Inés out of the country. She left, but in order not to be too far from her prince, moved just across the border.

A year later, the infanta died in childbirth. Pedro quickly brought Inés back from exile, and she joined him in his palace at Coimbra. There they lived happily and had four children. But disasters began to occur in the land —an earthquake in Lisbon, the plague, a drought. These calamities were all that courtiers opposed to the prince needed. Surely God was frowning on Portugal, they said, for a reason. They suggested that Pedro's illicit love affair was the reason and went to tell the king so.

Alfonso IV listened. He was a righteous man who had never approved of his son's affair. The courtiers further suggested that Inés was plotting with her relatives in Spain to have them usurp the throne eventually. The courtiers urged the king to let them kill Inés.

Moral man that he was, the idea was not especially appealing to him, but he said he would talk with Inés, perhaps he could convince her to leave Pedro of her own accord. In the garden of their palace at Coimbra— subsequently called the *Quinta das Lagrimas,* "the Garden of Tears"—

Alfonso was graciously greeted by Inés and his grandchildren. Her gentleness and loveliness were not what he had expected. Unnerved, he quit the garden soon after he had arrived, and when his courtiers fell upon him is reported to have stammered, "Do as you will."

The prince was hunting that afternoon—the courtiers had made sure of that. And as soon as Alfonso had left, they crept into the garden and within sight of her children, slit Inés's throat. When Pedro returned, it was to a dead Inés and sobbing children.

Servants were able to identify the killers, and Pedro vowed vengeance. For two years, while his father continued to reign, he bided his time. As soon as his father was dead he announced that he would never again marry. No matter what anyone thought, he had been properly married to Inés, and she would remain his wife in death as she had in life.

The courtiers resonsible for the assassination had fled to Spain. Pedro managed to have them returned to Portugal to grisly deaths. Meanwhile, he personally oversaw the carving of the two handsome sarcophagi here, and he had Inés's body secretly exhumed and her bones dressed in coronation robes. Then he ordered a special service in the Church of Santa Clara-a-Velha near the palace in Coimbra, and ordered the court to attend.

When they entered the church they saw two coronation chairs by the altar; the king in one; someone unrecognizable in the other. Before they could get close enough to recognize the bones of Inés sitting beside the king, the church doors had been locked. Pedro crowned his queen and commanded that all his nobles kiss her ring. One after the other, aghast, they paid obeisance to the skeleton. That done, the regally clad bones were carried by night the forty miles here to Alcobaça. Torches held by the spectators along the route made it as if it were "lined with all the stars of heaven," a contemporary chronicler wrote. Finally, Inés was properly entombed. One of the stone supports for her sarcophagus was a monster with the head of one of her assassins—cursed forever to bear the burden of his guilt.

The French dramatist Henri de Montherlant based his tragedy *La Reine Morte* on the star-crossed lovers.

ALGARVE

To remind his Scandinavian princess of her homeland and keep her from homesickness, it is said, a Moorish ruler of this part of southern Portugal planted almond trees because of their snowlike, tumbling petals. In winter, today, almond blossoms still flutter prettily along these roadsides.

BATALHA

Mosteiro de Santa Maria da Vitoria

It seemed unlikely that August day in 1386 that twenty-one-year-old John I could possibly vanquish the forces of the invading king of Castile. The Portuguese were outnumbered five to one, and even though a complement of English archers was assisting, the Aljubarrota battlefield ten miles from here gave every indication that it would be the site of the conquest of Portugal. But young John vowed two vows that day as the asked God's assistance.

Midsummer, the battlefield was blazing hot; the king suffered a great thirst. If he won, he swore, there would always be a pitcher of water for the thirsty by the roadside where the battle was fought. And his second promise was that he would build the most beautiful church man could create in honor of the Virgin. To find its site, he hurled his lance into the air. It was here that it landed, legend says, and God smiled on this site and on the valiant Portuguese. John won the battle, thereby guaranteeing Portuguese independence for the next 200 years.

Gratefully, he set about having this church and monastery built. He hired the most notable architect of the day, Afonso Domingues, to do the design and superintend the construction. Though blind before the job was done, Domingues came each day to "oversee" by listening to the sounds of the workmen. And the workmen were an assorted lot. Because the chapter house on one side of the cloister has a roof that Domingues designed without supporting columns, it fell twice during its construction with resultant injury to many workmen. So the king proposed that prisoners already under sentence of death be used to do the building.

John died before he could complete Batalha, and it is still unfinished. But God and the Virgin seem to have continued to smile, all the same, on John and Queen Philippa who lie buried here, her hand on his on their sarcophagus. Architectural historians say that this Gothic structure is one of Portugal's greatest architectural sights.

As for the pitcher of water, it is still kept filled by the side of the road at Aljubarrota.

BEJA

Regional Museum

A great literary mystery is said to have had its origin here in the days in the seventeenth century when this was the Convent of the Conception. At that time, it numbered among its residents Sister Marianna Alcoforado. In France in 1669 there appeared a series of love letters, allegedly by Sister Marianna to a French army officer. The letters were torrid, entreating, sorrowful, and anxious, and were an instant sensation. So a search began for their Portuguese originals. But they have never been found, and the popular belief is that they actually may never have existed in Portuguese at all, but were the creation of Louis XIV's secretary, Guilleregues, himself a writer.

BUSSACO

Bussaco Forest

It is said that the cypresses here come from seeds brought in the sixteenth century from a Carmelite monastery in Mexico. They grew so beautifully that Pope Urban VIII issued a papal bull in 1643, warning that anyone who damaged the trees would be excommunicated.

Palace Hotel

In 1810, after overnighting in the Carmelite monastery that occupied this site, the duke of Wellington defeated Napoleon's most able marshal, André Massena, at the battle here that historians call the prelude to Waterloo. Twice before, Napoleon's French had tried to invade Portugal, but this was their most resounding defeat. Later, Ferdinand II asked the set designer for the San Carlos Opera House in Lisbon to turn the monastery into a dwelling for him. The result is this extravagant structure, now a hotel.

COIMBRA

Convent of Santa Clara

The gentle queen who became Saint Isabel and fed the poor despite the disapproval of her husband, King Diniz, is buried here. God turned an apronful of bread for the hungry into roses for Isabel, so she could escape her husband's wrath one day when she was asked by His Majesty what her apron contained.

After the king's death in 1325, Isabel retired to this convent—then set much closer to the Mondego River—where she spent the rest of her life. In 1696 the river flooded her tomb, and twenty-four oxen were required to carry her 170-pound, shimmering silver bier to this higher location for reburial.

ÉVORA

One night in 1166, when the Moors were in command of this walled city, Gerald the Fearless sought to recover it for the Portuguese. When he could find no ladder with which to scale the walls, he fashioned one of lances. Once inside, he quickly beguiled the daughter of the Moorish governor and talked her into opening the city gates to his men.

Convent and Church of Calvário

It was unwise in Portugal in the late eighteenth century to cross the powerful marquis de Pombal, the minister of state (*see* Lisbon, Praça do Comércio). There were some who were broken on the wheel for it. But fourteen-year-old Isabel Juliana de Sousa Coutinho defied him, though indirectly, to get her way.

Isabel was an heiress and, as Pombal saw it, a good catch for his second son, so he had the marriage arranged. Isabel wasn't interested. She was already in love with one of her youthful playmates, Alexandre de Sousa Holstein, with whom she had shared an English tutor when she was little.

There was no escaping the marriage, however. Pombal assumed that Isabel would quickly get over her puppy love and settle down peacefully. After the wedding she was indeed "peaceful"—in a way neither Pombal nor his son could have anticipated: the marriage was never consummated, and, for the next three years, Isabel lived in silence. Finally, both her despairing bridegroom and her father-in-law gave up. The marriage was annulled, and Isabel entered this convent. Here she remained as long as Pombal was in power, but when he fell into disgrace, she was released, married her first love, and lived happily ever after.

FARO

From its earliest days, this city was famous for books. Portugal's first books are said to have been printed here by the Jewish community in the fifteenth century. Then, a century later, when Portugal was under Spanish rule,

Queen Elizabeth sent her favorite, the earl of Essex, here. He destroyed Faro—but saved the rich book collection in the library of the bishop of Silvas. That collection—largely of Arab books—became the base for the original Bodleian Library at Oxford Universiy, now one of the world's richest libraries.

FÁTIMA

In the spring of 1916, Portugal, like most of western Europe, was at war. There were a few villagers here who had been called into service, but life continued largely as it had before. Shepherds tended their sheep among the gray rocks, fattened their pigs, and grew a few vegetables. Then three shepherd children playing in a field said they saw a vision, and Fátima was never the same again.

The three youngsters—nine-year-old Lucia de Jesus and her cousins, eight-year-old Francisco and six-year-old Jacinta—were playing among the rocks one afternoon when suddenly there was a white light in the sky, and a young man within the light who declared himself the Angel of Peace. The frightened children did not know what to make of the apparition and said nothing to their parents. They tried to put it out of their minds, and by the following fall they had almost forgotten it. But the angel then appeared again, and once more, they were frightened and uncertain what to do. From being lighthearted, carefree youngsters they turned quiet and solemn and kept to themselves. They made certain that they always tended their sheep together.

On May 13, 1917, just about a year from the time of the first vision, thunder rumbled in a storm-dark sky, as they watched their flocks. Lightning was lashing the clouds. Two flashes of lightning in quick succession made them turn toward a little oak tree where the bolt seemed caught. And above it was a new apparition—a young woman who shone so brightly the youngsters said later that they could scarcely look at her. She asked, as the children recounted it, if they would give themselves to God for the sins of the world. And she promised to return on the thirteenth of each of the following five months. On that last visit, she said, she would tell them who she was.

Trembling this time, the children hurried home and told their parents what they had seen. They were accused of lying and were punished. Their parents decided the children would not do their usual shepherding task on the thirteenth of the following month. But when that day came, they were so distraught that they were allowed to go to the field again.

Again the lovely woman appeared above the oak tree. The children explained that no one believed they had seen a vision and that they were being punished for telling tall tales. The vision promised that she would perform a miracle and make people believe when she made her final appearance on October 13.

The following month, once more, the parents relented and allowed the children to go to the field. This time, it is said, the vision begged for peace and prophesied a second world war greater than the one then in progress. She also warned that the Russians would cease to be Christians. And there was a third prophesy, to this day unrevealed. Lucia is said to have given it to the bishop of this diocese.

After the children returned home with this still more incredible tale, their parents let their visions be known. The curious from all over came in droves to learn more of what they had seen. The mayor had enough of it, though. On the morning of August 13, as the youngsters were readying again to meet the vision, he graciously volunteered to drive them to the field in his carriage.

But instead of going there, he drove to the jail in neighboring Ourem and threatened to boil the youngsters in oil if they did not deny the vision. They refused. In despair he accepted their story and returned them home.

By the time October 13 arrived, hundreds of people had heard the story of the gleaming lady who would perform a miracle and reveal her identity, and they filled the field where the oak tree was. Once more, it was a stormy disagreeable day. Suddenly Lucia cried to them that they should look at the sun, and, as she cried out, the clouds parted and the sun appeared surrounded by strange small lights. It seemed to be hurtling straight toward the assembled crowd but stopped before it reached them. The "vision" was accepted.

In 1918, Francisco and Jacinta died of influenza. Lucia said the vision had predicted it. Not long afterward, Lucia, recognized as somehow holy, was sent to a convent. Seven years later, this basilica was built, and Francisco and Jacinta were buried here. Lucia still lives in a convent in Coimbra.

The Chapel of the Apparitions marks the spot where Our Lady of Fátima (recognized as a genuine holy apparition in 1930) made herself known to the children. An earlier chapel was dynamited by nonbelievers in 1922.

LISBON

Monastery of Jeronimos

Before Prince Henry the Navigator established his settlement at Sagres for the study of navigation and promotion of exploration, he had a small shrine built on this site to the Virgin of Belém, the patroness of seafarers. It was at this shrine that Vasco da Gama prayed the night before he set sail on the voyage that made him the first man to reach India from the West by sea. When he returned, he brought silks and spices, benzoin, and a gold chain as expressions of his gratitude to the Virgin.

By that time, construction was well under way on this enormous structure —monastery, church, and cloister—that Emanuel I had founded in 1496, just before da Gama's departure. Many of the riches brought to the king by his mariners' explorations went into this complex, and here da Gama is buried.

Praça do Comércio (Commerce Square)

It was a sunny All Saints' Day, 1755, and the churches of Lisbon were crowded. Candles flickered at altars. Suddenly, the earth shook—once, twice, three times; buildings shuddered and fell; the candles of the devout tumbled, setting fire to the wooden partitions, wooden crucifixes, wooden saints. Those not trapped in the rubble fled screaming toward this square —then the site of the royal palace—and sought escape from the licking flames in the river Tagus. But the river drew back. Then an hour after the first tremor, it, too, attacked Lisbon. A great tidal wave thundered over this square, sweeping the refugees to a watery death, demolishing the palace. Two more engulfing tidal waves came and went.

When the earthquake ended, 40,000 were dead and 17,000 buildings had crumbled, including 110 churches and 300 palaces. Among the survivors of the catastrophe, however, were both the king, Joseph Emanuel, and his minister of foreign affairs, Sebastio José de Carvalho e Melo, who became the marquis of Pombal. (*See* Évora, Convent and Church of Calvário.)

Brilliant, efficient, energetic, cold-blooded, it was Pombal who saw to the reconstruction of Lisbon. Made homeless by the quake, he lived in his coach for a week, and from there directed the resurrection of the demolished city.

To feed the hungry, he commandeered the cargoes of any vessels not destroyed by the tidal waves. He ordered the demolition of buildings that had not fallen but were cracked and likely to fall. He had the dead buried, the debris cleared away, looters summarily hanged. When the city was clean again, he began planning its rebuilding. Once the Portuguese envoy to

England, Pombal preferred the simplicity of English architecture to the flamboyance of the Portuguese style of his day. On this square, to replace the waterfront royal palace, he built the stately green buildings that still stand here. And Rossio Square was rebuilt. Then, to instill the habit of punctuality in his people, he ordered a shipment of 200 grandfather clocks from England for the public buildings. (That reform, however, never succeeded. Most of those grandfather clocks now grace church sacristies throughout Portugal.)

In instituting reforms, Pombal was ruthless. He became increasingly unpopular and had to take great care to protect himself from attempted assassinations. Also in danger, but unwilling to take heed, was the king, who virtually allowed Pombal to take over the country.

A bit of the playboy, the king continued to have numerous trysts, and one night in 1758, returning from one, he was set upon by his enemies and shot at, but the attackers fled after having only shot him in the arm. For three months, Pombal did nothing. Then he made his wrath felt. Members of two of Portugal's leading families were accused of the attack, tortured, and executed. When, in confessions extracted as their bodies were broken on the wheel, they implicated Jesuits, Pombal had all Jesuits exiled from the country.

Pombal's dictatorship continued until the king's death in 1777. Then he was banished to the country, to the town now known as Pombal, where he died at his home in 1782. It was a remarkably quiet end for so remarkably controversial a figure.

Rossio (Rossio Square)

Here Pedro I is said to have held wild orgies by torchlight with women of the night to try to forget the murder of his beloved, Inés. (*See* Alcobaça.)

♥≼※≽♥

Is this statue, purportedly of King Pedro IV, accurately identified? Some wonder, for, for a long time, only the pedestal stood here. Then Maximilian, newly installed as the emperor of Mexico, died in 1867 at the hands of a firing squad. It wasn't long thereafter that this pedestal had a statue on it. There are those who speculate that the statue is really Maximilian, and was en route to Mexico to grace a square there, when he was killed. When it became available at a good price, Portugal bought it to fill its need and said it was of the dead Pedro.

St. George's Castle

For four months in the twelfth century, Portugal's first king, Alfonso, with the help of English Crusaders, besieged the Moorish stronghold that occupied this site. The Moors were strongly entrenched, and the Portuguese probably never would have entered the fortress had it not been for the bravery of one soldier, Martin Moniz. He galloped to the gate, and threw himself and his horse against it, once it was opened, keeping the Moors from closing it until Alfonso I's men had entered. In the process, Moniz was torn limb from limb.

Tower of Belém

In the heyday of Portuguese exploration, many a vessel, including those of Vasco da Gama, left from the spot on the river Tagus where this Manueline tower now stands. The beach below it came to be called "the beach of tears," for so many families parted company here with sons and fathers and husbands whom they would never see again.

There was always a mass said here before vessels set sail; confessions were heard; wills written. And, if a voyage was a success, it was the sight of this white tower, with a touch of the Moorish to it, that meant that a returning sailor was safely home. For many years, the Tower of Belém stood in the middle of the Tagus, but the shifting of the sands through the centuries has altered the river's course.

MAFRA

Convent and Palace

For years, John V and his wife, Maria Anna of Austria, had longed for a child and had none. Finally, desperately, John promised God that he would build a convent even grander than the Escorial in Spain for the poorest order of monks in Portugal if God would bless him and his queen with a child. In 1713, a son was born, and John proceeded to fulfill his part of the bargain.

He hired a German architect and gave orders that cost was no obstacle —the structure to be built must be glorious to the eyes of God. Fifty thousand men took on the task and were forced to work so hard that a hospital to care only for them was erected. It took 1,000 oxen to haul the stone for this mammoth structure that extends a fifth of a mile in one direction, a sixth of a mile in the other. There are 866 rooms, 4,000 doors, and 5,200 windows in this palace.

It was from this grand edifice in 1910 that twenty-year-old Manuel II and his mother fled Portugal after revolutionaries had shelled the royal palace, and the days of the monarchy were clearly over. (*See* Sintra, Pena Palace.)

ÓBIDOS

Isabel of Aragon, traveling with her young husband Diniz, in the thirteenth century, admired this town of gleaming white houses, and the defensive wall that encircled it—like a golden necklace, she said. Her devoted bridegroom accordingly gave it to her, and for the next seven centuries, until 1833, it was the custom of the kings of Portugal to make a gift of Óbidos to their brides.

OPORTO

Ever since the fifteenth century, residents of this city have been known as "the tripe eaters." As the story goes, it was here in 1415 that the ships were readied to capture Ceuta in North Africa from the Moors. The patriotic citizenry, eager to do all that they could to support their king and his men, slaughtered all the cattle within reasonable distance to provision the ships. All that remained for the city to eat was the tripe—which they happily ate then—and do to this day.

Soares dos Reis Museum (Carrancas Palace)

In 1809, when the English took this city in the Peninsular War, Napoleon's marshal, Nicolas Soult, had to flee quickly without warning. It is said that the conquering Sir Arthur Wellesley (later the duke of Wellington) consumed the dinner in this palace that had been prepared for Soult.

The Sé

A storm in 1147 had driven the ships of French, English, and German Crusaders up the river Douro to take refuge. While they were here, Pedro Piteos, bishop of Braga, took advantage of the situation and, gathering the men together in front of this cathedral, talked to them so eloquently that they agreed to sail to Lisbon to help King Alfonso I take Lisbon from the Moors.

❧

A wily sacristan saved the solid silver in the Blessed Sacrament Chapel here from being carried off to France by Napoleon's soldiers, by coating it with plaster of Paris.

QUELUZ

Royal Palace of Queluz

In this pretty pink palace that has been called a mini-Versailles, Maria I went mad in 1792. She had visions of burning in Hell's fires, and had to be bound to her bed where she screamed endlessly for mercy. Earlier, when she was a happy young bride and before the affairs of state and personal tragedies had driven her to madness, Queluz had been the setting for many a merry party with fireworks and bullfights as entertainment. But once her mind went, this was a gloomy place, indeed. For twenty-four years, until she died in 1816, Maria ruled in madness.

Royal Palace of Queluz: THE GARDEN

Merriment alternated with intrigue here in the early days of the nineteenth century, when red-nosed Queen Carlota plotted against her husband John VI. On hot days, she loved to dabble her feet in the fountain. On cooler days, she ran races with her maids of honor, or played games with her lovers. But there were also more serious times. Demands for a constitutional monarchy were being made, and John was willing to acquiesce to them. Not so his Spanish wife Carlota, nor his son Dom Miguel. Carlota refused to swear fealty to a constitutional monarchy. And she and Dom Miguel, here, and at the Palace of Ramalho near Sintra, continued revolutionary activities until the king's death in 1826.

SAGRES

On this lonesome, barren promontory where, they believed in ancient days, the gods rested after sunset, and the sun could be heard hissing as it hit the sea, Prince Henry the Navigator established a settlement for study of the sky and the winds and the water. Often in the early morning, before the sun had risen, the prince could be found hunched at the cliff top, listening, watching, praying. Prince Henry was a remarkably devout man. In his youth he had taken a vow of celibacy, and when he was not studying, he spent much of the time praying and fasting. When he died, it was found he was wearing a horsehair shirt.

Prince Henry talked the finest of his country's astronomers, cartographers, navigators, and explorers into joining him here to plot expeditions of discovery. He went beyond that and talked fearful sailors into overcoming their fright and sailing into new seas for the glory of Portugal. Perhaps, he would tell them, they might find the rich land of the legendary king, Prester John, whose realm was thought to be somewhere no explorer from the West had yet found.

Cape St. Vincent

On the coat of arms of the city of Lisbon are two ravens said to have guided the boat on which the body of the martyred Saint Vincent was carried to this windswept headland in the fourth century. Even after the body was buried here, the ravens continued their vigil until the saint's coffin had been taken to Lisbon for proper burial. Then they built their nest in the Lisbon cathedral tower, so they could always be nearby.

❧❀☙

Off this most southwesterly point in Europe, England's Captain Horatio Nelson sailed his ship directly into the path of seven Spanish ships in 1797, first exhibiting the great tactical genius that was to make him victorious against the French at the Battle of Trafalgar, eight years later.

SANTAREM

One afternoon in 1491 when John II was swimming in the Tagus here, his son and heir Alfonso and a page were racing on horseback to where he swam. The horse tripped. The young prince tumbled to the ground and was killed. Fishermen carried his body back to his mother, Queen Leonor, in one of their nets. After that, she made the net her symbol, and it was incorporated in stone into royal buildings all over the country.

São João de Alporão Church: TOMB OF DUARTE DE MENESES

Duarte de Meneses, count of Viana, was hacked to pieces by the Moors in Africa in 1454. All that was left to send home to his widow for burial was his ring finger. But his wife had this flamboyant Gothic tomb erected all the same, to hold the finger. Some years later, when it became necessary to open the tomb, the finger was gone, and a single tooth was in its place.

SINTRA

The romantics have it that seventeen-year-old King Sebastian listened, enraptured, to the poet Luiz Vaz de Camões reading his epic the *Lusiads* here on the patio. And Camões promised he would write as eloquently of

Sebastian and the Moroccan invasion the king was contemplating as he had already written of Vasco da Gama in his epic poem. So inspired, the young king set off too soon on the ill-planned onslaught. It cost his own life in 1578, the lives of 8,000 of his soldiers, and the capture and sale into slavery of 15,000 more.

Pena Palace

Many a chatty letter from Queen Victoria of England was carried across the drawbridge here after Maria II married Ferdinand of Saxe-Coburg-Gotha in the nineteenth century, and that romantic German, cousin of Victoria's consort, began construction of this summer palace for his bride. He hired a German architect as romantic as himself to design this structure that combines Arab minarets with Gothic turrets, Renaissance cupolas, and a baroque interior; and it is that architect, Baro de Eschwege, whose statue, in knight's garb of the Middle Ages, can be seen on the rock in the distance.

Also in the distance—nestled in these 300 acres of gardens which Richard Strauss called the most beautiful thing he had ever seen in the world—is the chalet (with cement walls painted to look like cork and pine) that Ferdinand built for his Viennese mistress, opera singer Elissa Hedler. When the chalet was built, there were no tall trees between it and the palace, and Elissa could see the lights from Ferdinand's room. Lighted in a certain way they meant she could expect a night time visit from him.

❦

The last royal resident of this madcap castle was Queen Amélia, the queen who saw her king, Carlos I, and her eldest son, Prince Louis, felled by assassins' bullets in 1908. In this elaborate mid-nineteenth-century folly of parapets and moats and crenellated walls, perched high above Sintra, the mourning queen took refuge. But not for long. Within two years it was clear that the rule of her only surviving son, twenty-year-old Manuel II, was at an end and revolutionary forces were taking over. Selecting her most precious belongings and accompanied by the king's grandmother, Maria Pia, she prepared to join Manuel at the palace at Mafra (*see* Mafra, Convent and Palace). From there they went to the fishing village of Ericeira and set sail on the yacht *Dona Amélia* for Gibraltar, then exile in England.

Royal Palace of Sintra

Deposed, feeble-minded Alfonso VI spent the last nine years of his life in the seventeenth century imprisoned here by his brother Pedro. His only contacts with the world outside were the mass he could hear said through an opening in the chapel wall, and the daily waving of a handkerchief by a loyal friend from the gazebo on the hill opposite his window.

Royal Palace of Sintra: MAGPIE ROOM

When it was whispered to Philippa of Lancaster that her husband, John I, had been kissing one of her ladies-in-waiting here, he reportedly denied that the kiss was any more than casual and friendly. And to chide the rumor-mongering ladies, he had as many chattering magpies painted on this ceiling as the queen had ladies-in-waiting. The Norman motto *Por Bem* —"For Good"—was meant to chide his wife. That one little kiss, it is believed to mean, was all in a good cause.

Royal Palace of Sintra: SWAN ROOM

When the Dutch painter Jan van Eyck came here as an ambassador seeking the hand of John and Philippa's only daughter, Isabel, for Duke Philip of Burgundy, one story recounts that he brought a gift of swans. Isabel married Philip and the swans stayed—to swim not only in the ponds of the royal garden, but also in this painting on the ceiling.

Seteais Palace

The Dutch diamond merchant Guildermeister built Seteais in the eighteenth century and gave grand parties here, at which he determinedly tried to sell diamonds to his guests.

VILA VIÇOSA

Braganza Palace

In 1512, when it was rumored that she had had a love affair with her page, Leonor de Gusmo was stabbed to death here by her husband, Duke James, who then tossed the dagger outside into the little garden.

❧⚜❧

It was here, to the palace where she had been born, that a heartbroken Catherine of Braganza returned during the eighteenth century at the age of fifty-four after the death of her husband, Charles II of England, during the seventeenth century. While she was unable to bear children for her husband, his mistresses supplied him with many. In most regards her life was not a happy one. Not only could she not bear children, but she was accused of a plot to murder Charles. He said it was nonsense, for he knew that she loved him, but he had two of her retinue executed. One of the few pleasures of her sorrowful life was tea drinking, a habit she introduced to the English, and which surely took. Back here—her sorrow at the king's death and her advancing years notwithstanding—she knew some happiness, and when her brother, Pedro II, took ill, served for a time as queen regent.

◆◆◆

What a pleasant evening Carlos I had dining here under the antler chandeliers with his family on January 31, 1908. The antlers were trophies of his hunts. Another hunt for the following day was in prospect with his two sons, Louis and Manuel. Even the unrest of the Republicans seeking to end the monarchy was temporarily forgotten. The next afternoon, the king and his family waved a happy good-bye to their staff, drove across Vila Viçosa's Terreiro do Paço in their carriage and headed for Lisbon. A few hours later, crossing the square of the same name in the capital, Carlos and Louis were assassinated.

Spain

ÁVILA ❧————

Monasterio de la Encarnación (Monastery of the Incarnation)

They were a curious pair to understand each other so completely—Saint Teresa of Ávila and Saint John of the Cross. Teresa de Cepeda y Ahumada was highborn, and there was some question in her mind when, at eighteen, she entered the Convent of the Carmelites during the sixteenth century as to whether she wished to become a nun. Vital and vibrant, she loved the life of her family. When they met, Teresa was twenty-seven years older than John.

Juan de Yepis y Alvarez was shy and quiet. He came from a poor family and he had worked as a male nurse in order to help support them. The misery that he saw among the poor prompted him to become a priest. He had barely begun his priesthood when he met the woman who became Saint Teresa. And here, together, they talked and argued religion; saw visions; dreamed dreams; and reformed the Carmelites, starting the Discalced order (they wore sandals instead of shoes), for both men and women. In it, prayer and strict discipline played a most important part. And both wrote extensively of their religious experiences—she in prose, he in poetry. And both achieved sainthood—she in 1622; he a little more than a century later in 1726. In this century, Pope Paul VI made them both doctors of the church.

BARCELONA

Templo de la Sagrada Familia (The Temple of the Holy Family) (Calle Mallorca)

Begun in 1884, this church was the favorite project of the Catalan architect Antoni Gaudi. Gaudi insisted that the temple should be built only with funds collected from lay sources and rejected the support of both the church and the state. A trolley killed him in 1926 as he was standing in front of his unfinished church—collecting funds.

BURGOS

La Cartuja (Carthusian Monastery of Miraflores) (2½ miles east of town)

Poor bereft Juana the Mad brought the body of her husband, Philip I, here after his death nearby in 1506 (*see* Burgos, Casa del Cordón), and a Carthusian monk, seeking to console her, urged prayer. Indeed, he said, prayer could bring Philip back from the dead. And Juana believed him. For three months she kept his body with her, embracing it, and begging Philip to return to her. When all her supplications failed, she had the coffin closed, and took it with her on a curious mournful journey from Castilian town to Castilian town, hoping that there might be one town alluring enough to rouse Philip from the dead. Now and then, she would ask to have the coffin opened to make sure that her beloved was still inside. It was in September that Philip had died; the following year, his child was borne to the grieving widow. Not until more than three years after his death did she at last consent to have his coffin buried (*see* Tordesillas), and she took up residence nearby. It still seemed possible, though her hopes were fading, that the words of the Carthusian monk would come true and Philip would rise to rule again. When he did, she would be at his side.

Casa del Cordón (House of Cord) (Plaza de Calvo Sotelo)

On a sultry summer's day in 1506, Philip the Handsome (Philip I) played pelota. Hot and exhausted after the game, he gulped cold water and died of a chill, so the story goes. His widow Juana, the daughter of Ferdinand II and Isabella, could not be consoled, and, indeed, she became determined to revive her beloved. (*See* Burgos, La Cartuja.)

Castilla

It was where these hilltop ruins stand that the proud warrior the Cid was married to the niece of the king of Castile in the eleventh century (*see* Burgos, The Cathedral, El Cofre del Cid). Here too the teen-age prince who was to become Edward I of England came to meet Eleanor of Castile, his child-bride and lifelong love, in 1254. (*See* Burgos, Las Huelgas Reales Convent.)

The Cathedral: CAPILLA DEL SANTÍSIMO CRISTO

No one knows how this curious statue of Christ—with skin of buffalo hide but nails and hair that are human—came here, but it has long been venerated. There are those who say that it was created by Nicodemus, who aided

Joseph of Arimathea in burying Christ; that he modeled it after Christ's own figure, and that it floated over the sea here to Spain.

The Cathedral: EL COFRE DEL CID (Coffer of the Cid) (Capilla del Corpus Christi)

When the Cid (*see* Burgos, The Cathedral, Transept), was fiercely fighting the Moors in the eleventh century and in desperate straits for more money to continue his warfare, it is said that he filled this iron coffer with sand and sent it to two moneylenders of Burgos, requesting a loan. He had had the chest sealed, but he assured them that it was filled with riches and should be held as surety. A knight's word was to be honored, after all, so without demanding to examine the contents of the chest, the usurers provided the money requested. Back the Cid went to war against the Moors, and in time, was able to redeem his chest of sand, honorably discharging his debt—or at least, so most accounts have it.

The Cathedral: TRANSEPT

Beneath the pavement here lie the bodies of Burgos's greatest hero, eleventh-century Rodrigo Díaz de Bivar (whom the Moors called el Cid Campeador—the Lord Champion) and his wife Ximena (*see* Burgos, Castilla). An indomitable mercenary, the Cid invaded Moorish territory when the Moors were terrorizing Christian Spain. He and his soldiers laid siege to the rich Moorish city of Valencia for nine months before they were able to conquer it. When, not long after that great victory, the Cid died, his wife —as indomitable as he—succeeded in holding onto Valencia for three more years. But by then, the Moors had become strong enough to regain it. A Christian army sent from Castile to aid in the city's defense was of no avail. Clearly Valencia was lost, and it remained only to help the Christian defenders to make their escape. To divert the Moors' attention, Ximena had the remains of her valiant husband strapped into the saddle of his horse and sent into the enemy lines. Although the Moors knew that the Cid was long dead, they drew back in terror as his horse thundered toward them—and the rest of the retinue returned in safety here to Castile. Some eight centuries later, when Burgos was fighting with the English against the French in the Napoleonic Wars, the heroic Cid's remains were disinterred—and exhibited—to renew their courage.

Las Huelgas Reales Convent (1 mile below the city)

In this convent in 1254, shy ten-year-old Eleanor of Castile became the bride of the fifteen-year-old English prince who would become Edward I. There were days of celebration for the event—a tournament in the city and the knighting of the prince by his prospective half-brother-in-law, Alfonso X. Indeed, it was so colorful and extravagant an occasion—most of it paid for by Henry III, the father of the bridegroom—that complaints were heard in England when the young couple returned. And there were more complaints when it was learned that the little princess lived in far greater elegance in London than the English were accustomed to—with silken hangings on the walls and carpets on the floors, in the fashion the Moors had brought to Spain.

But it all turned out well. Although theirs was a distinctly political marriage, the royal pair really loved each other and when Edward became a Crusader, his devoted wife went with him everywhere. Once, it is said, she saved his life by sucking poison from a wound he had received in an assassination attempt.

Monasterio de San Pedro de Cardeña (6 miles east of Burgos)

When the Cid was exiled by Alfonso VI, he quit Burgos in the dead of night. Townspeople hid behind their doors longing to say farewell to him but afraid of the king's wrath (*see* Burgos, Santa Agueda). It was to this monastery that he came. And many years later, when his remains were returned from Valencia, it was here that they first were interred.

Santa Agueda (Calle de Santa Agueda)

Life would have been kinder to the Cid (Rodrigo Díaz de Bivar), so the epic that bears his name goes, had he not demanded an oath here from his king, Alfonso VI of Castile, in 1072. The Cid had been a loyal supporter of the king's father, Ferdinand the Great, and planned to serve his son, Sancho II, with equal valor, but Sancho was mysteriously murdered and his brother Alfonso, who thereby gained the throne, seemed implicated. The honorable Cid declined to serve the new king until he had sworn in this church that he had not killed his brother. Because the Cid's services as a fighter were so valuable, Alfonso acquiesced, though hardly happily, and retaliated by banishing the Cid from the court. In time, there was a reconciliation, however, and the Cid went off to conquer Valencia for him (*see* Burgos, The Cathedral, Transept.)

CÁCERES

Many powerful noble families lived in this town during the Middle Ages, and the custom developed of constructing ever higher towers on houses to indicate one's superiority over one's neighbors. But in 1477, Queen

Isabella, to gain control over her fractious nobility, ordered all towers lopped off so that no one's house was higher than anyone else's. Only one house, the so-called Stork's House, survived the general leveling.

CÁDIZ

The Phoenicians in 1100 B.C. knew a good port when they saw one, and they founded here the city then known as Gadir. Throughout its history Cádiz has been linked with important naval happenings.

In 1587 Sir Francis Drake inflicted a major blow on Spain's naval power by raiding this port and destroying the seasoned wood stockpiled to build the ships of the Invincible Armada.

In 1805, Admiral Horatio Nelson fought the famous battle of Trafalgar off Cádiz, when in the days of Napoleon, the combined French and Spanish fleets attempted to break his blockade of this harbor. Today the United States naval base at nearby Rota is of strategic importance in controlling both the Mediterranean and the Atlantic.

◆✿◆

It was 1805. The French navy wished to destroy the British, and vice versa. But there were other matters, too, to which Napoleon Bonaparte had to attend. He wanted to be sure that he had a strong hold on Naples, so, on October 19, he ordered his Franco-Spanish fleet of thirty-three ships to quit this harbor for Naples. But the ships never got there. Off the Cape of Gibraltar, Britain's Admiral Lord Horatio Nelson sighted them, and on October 21 the two armadas met. Both sides fought furiously, but the British were the more adept. Clearly, victory was theirs. Then a sniper fired a shot at Nelson's gleaming chest. (Always a proud man, he had refused to tuck his medals away that day.) The admiral fell, mortally wounded. Four hours later Britain's greatest hero of the seas was dead, asking his aide, with his last breath, to care for his beloved Emma Hamilton. (*See* Italy, Naples, Palazzo Real.)

CÓRDOBA

The Mosque

This splendid mosque, begun in 786, prospered and grew and remained beautiful until Córdoba fell to the Christians in 1236. In the beginning the new occupants had the sense to leave the mosque intact, though they converted it into a Christian cathedral. In the sixteenth century, however, it was decided to insert a Gothic church into the center of this building. No one regretted this architectural blunder more than the emperor Charles V. He visited Córdoba in 1526 and when he saw the new church, he observed sadly, "What you have made here can be found in many other places, but what you have destroyed can be found nowhere else in the world."

LA CORUÑA

This waterfront was a busy place indeed on July 20, 1588, when Spain's Invincible Armada of 130 men-of-war carrying 19,000 soldiers and 10,000 sailors set sail to defeat the fleet of England. Their sailing had been years in the planning, and an enthusiastic crowd cheered them as they sailed out of sight, gold prows gleaming. Every detail of the expedition had been carefully worked out by Philip II—every detail but the weather, which battered the Spanish ships and drove them off their course, demolishing 63 of them, drowning 10,000 men, and crippling the Invincible Spanish Armada.

COSTA BRAVA

The rugged beauty of this coastline has been attracting visitors ever since the Greeks built a city called Ampurias here in about 535 B.C. Such hordes of foreign tourists have descended on this area that in the summer of 1973, when the number of visitors to Spain exceeded the indigenous population by one million, signs could be found in the shop windows along the Costa Brava announcing *"Se habla español."*

EL ESCORIAL

In sorrow at his forces having destroyed a church in Flanders dedicated to Saint Lawrence on that saint's name day, and in gratitude for having been victorious all the same, Philip II had this enormous church/monastery/pantheon/dwelling place built. The king himself laid the first cornerstone in 1563, but it was not until twenty-one years later that this enormous edifice —with 120 miles of corridors, 1,100 doors, and 80 staircases—was completed. Built in the shape of a gridiron because Saint Lawrence died on a gridiron, it has had a history that has been gloomy indeed.

Here Philip first learned of the defeat of his Invincible Armada and masked his emotions by saying quietly, "I sent my ships against men, not against the elements." And here he died an agonizing death of gout that had caused such gangrene that the odor drove his courtiers from the room. Ever devout, the king followed the mass from a window in the wall of his room and remarked to those few who attended him at the time of his death, "Look at me and see how all the monarchies of the world end."

GIBRALTAR

The craggy outline of this rock made it in ancient times one of the seven wonders of the world—the Pillar of Hercules.

GRANADA

Federico García Lorca, the poet, dramatist and musician, was born near here and died here under tragic circumstances on August 19, 1936. García Lorca was not a political writer, but to keep him safe in the highly charged civil war climate of 1936, friends with powerful fascist connections urged him to take refuge in their house. And García Lorca did so. But one day when his friends were out and he was home alone, armed men—presumably nationalists—broke into the house and took him to the outskirts of the city, where he was shot.

Alhambra

On the plains outside the walls of this great Moorish citadel—the last stronghold of the Arabs in Spain—forty-year-old Ferdinand II of Spain and forty-one-year-old Isabella camped with their soldiers in 1491 to lay siege. They could wait indefinitely, they agreed, to capture this great palace and citadel. And so, indeed, they built themselves a city that they called Santa Fe, and on and on they stayed.

As it turned out, their city was a great success. Soon merchants with goods from everywhere were coming to it while this once-rich city of Granada that they had surrounded had no traders, no business, no food. Granada's 200,000 residents grew hungrier and hungrier and more and more restive. The time came when they could hold out no longer. So in January 1492, the Moors agreed that they would give up. Out the Puerta de los Siete Suelos the Moorish ruler Boabdil and his weeping wife and children came. Toward him rode the grand cardinal of Spain to accept his surrender. The Moor dismounted. The cardinal dismounted and Boabdil invited the cardinal to take possession of his city in the name of the victors. Immediately, the cardinal raised the flag of the conquerors. Then the king and queen themselves advanced.

Boabdil, again on mount, set forth to greet them, and readied to dismount as he approached the king, but he had been a brave warrior and the king did not require him to leave his horse. The count who was to govern Granada did, however, accept the gold ring of the ruler of this city. Boabdil sadly drew it from his finger and proffered it, wishing the conqueror better fortune than he, the conquered, had had.

◆᯽◆

In the Peninsular War of 1812, Napoleon's armies had mined the Alhambra and had every intention of blowing it to bits, but a Spanish soldier discovered what they had in mind and cut the fuse.

Alhambra: GENERALIFE

Under the cypresses that abound in the garden around this lovely fourteenth-century summer palace, Moorish royalty is said to have had their love trysts.

LA GRANJA (near SEGOVIA)

La Granja Palace

French-born Philip V inherited his love of display and his appreciation of fun from his grandfather, Louis XIV. He always enjoyed being surrounded by what was beautiful. His Italian wife Elizabeth Farnese, presumably to indulge his tastes and to cure him of his homesickness for France and all things French, had this handsome palace and elaborate 158-acre garden built in the eighteenth century, intended to rival her husband's beloved Versailles. Here waters dance in twenty-six fountains. Trees unheard of in other parts of Spain grow and thrive. But despite his wife's desire to please, Philip is said to have remarked pettishly once, when he returned from a long journey and found that she had added still more statues and fountains to the garden, that it had all cost him three million but amused him only three minutes.

GUADALUPE

The Monastery

Because he won the Battle of Salado against the Moors in 1340, Alfonso XI built this enormous monastery in gratitude to the Virgin of Guadalupe to whom he had prayed—a figure found by a cowherd a century earlier. As time went on, this became an increasingly popular monastery. It was here that the papers were signed that sent Christopher Columbus to discover America, and here that the Indians he brought back—the first red men to come to this continent—were baptized.

GUERNICA

This small Basque town achieved tragic notoriety on April 26, 1937, at the start of the Spanish Civil War. A German air squadron bombed here for three hours, killing 2,000 people, an incident which not only provoked international outrage, but prompted Pablo Picasso to paint his huge and stark *Guernica* canvas as an antiwar statement.

IRÚN

Railroad Station

Here Generalissimo Francisco Franco came in October 1940, to meet with a petulant Adolf Hitler in Hendaye, just across the border in France. Franco was late; Hitler was furious. Hitler was seeking the Spanish dictator's permission to have his troops cross Spain to conquer Gibraltar. For nine hours, the talks went on. And when they were over, Hitler did not have the permission he wanted. Seething, he reportedly commented that he would rather have four teeth pulled than go through such an experience again.

LINARES

Plaza de Toros (Bull Ring)

Spain's most revered bullfighter, Manuel Rodríguez y Sánchez—"Manolete"—was killed in this small industrial town on August 28, 1947. For some time, Manolete had been under heavy stress: too many *corridas*, too much all-night travel, too much drinking—and a public who expected too much each time he stepped into the ring. In a radio interview shortly before his death, the matador said wearily, "They ask more of me than I can give. . . . I wish it were October and the season was over."

Islero, the bull that killed him, was the 1,004th bull in Manolete's career. Early in the fight, the matador's helpers noticed the little bull's tendency to hook to the right, and urged Manolete to kill him as quickly as possible. Just as the matador stepped in for the final sword-thrust, Islero jerked his head sharply upward, catching Manolete in the groin. Islero died within minutes, Manolete, whose femoral artery had been severed, toward dawn of the next morning. The stained and torn suit of lights that he wore during this last fight is now displayed in the Bullfight Museum in Madrid.

MADRID

Museo de Carruajes (Carriage Museum) (Campo del Mono)

Among the many beautiful coaches here is the large one of gilt and glass in which King Alfonso XIII and his bride, Victoria Eugenia (the granddaughter of Queen Victoria), escaped assassination on their wedding day, May 31, 1906. The coach was drawn by eight white horses and surrounded by liveried outriders as it passed through the streets of this capital. Suddenly an assassin threw a bomb at the procession, killing several horses and twenty-four soldiers and spectators. Glass shattered, and the bride's dress was spattered with blood, but the royal couple was unhurt. The coach still bears the marks of the attack.

Plaza Mayor

In 1623 two young Englishmen—John Smith and Thomas Smith, they called themselves—came here to Madrid in search of a bride for John. But John was no ordinary Englishman wishing for a Spanish señorita. He was the Prince of Wales destined to become Charles I and ultimately to lose his head; Thomas was the duke of Buckingham. They hoped to arrange a marriage between the Infanta María and the prince. Here in this then-new plaza her brother, eighteen-year-old Philip IV, staged a tournament in the prince's honor.

As it turned out, Charles did not marry María. Some say the Spanish didn't want him; others say he didn't want the Infanta. Those who insist that it was he who ungallantly declined her hand point out Spain got the last laugh. When Charles was beheaded, the Spanish ambassador was able, for very little, to buy much of his fine art collection, and it is in the Prado today.

◆❈◆

Carlos II ("the Bewitched"), feeble of mind and twisted of body, looked forward for days to the auto-de-fé—act of the faith—he decided to have held here in 1680. He had recently learned of the heretics awaiting judgment in prisons. It seemed a capital idea to have them brought before him to learn their punishment. What a colorful spectacle it would make!

And so, on June 30, 1680, for fourteen hours, the procession of more than one hundred prisoners circled the square before the king, his queen, his mother, and the grand inquisitors, and heard sermons about their iniquity and learned their fate. Most were found to be minor offenders, condemned to the galleys or to flogging and bidden to wear a yellow garment with red stripes to inform their fellows of their status and their punishment. But some were doomed to death at the stake and dressed in black garments that bore emblems of demons and flames. Throughout the long proceedings, the simple-minded king smiled his enjoyment at his subjects' terror. The Prado contains a painting of this event by Francisco Rizi.

Plaza da Oriente: EQUESTRIAN STATUE OF PHILIP IV

It was Galileo, it is said, who proposed the way to balance this extraordinary statue of the great rider, Philip, astride his rampant horse. The statue was cast in Florence in 1640, based on a Velázquez equestrian painting.

Prado: GOYA'S MAJA DESNUDA AND MAJA VESTIDA

Were they or weren't they lovers—the beautiful duchess of Alba and the famous court painter? Legend has it that Goya y Lucientes and María del Pilar Teresa Cayetana, the duchess of Alba, met after she had been widowed, and an affair quickly commenced. During the period of the attachment, Goya boldly painted the duchess undressed; and more discreetly, dressed. Both paintings were destined for the lady's apartments, and there they, indeed, went. But they were discovered and brought to public attention three years after their subject's mysterious death.

At the time, it was rumored that she had been poisoned—a rumor that led everyone to examine the paintings more closely. Some authorities said there was not the slightest resemblance between the women in the painting; others nodded sagely and said of course they were one and the same, and it was shameful that the duchess had permitted herself to be depicted undressed. To this day, no one knows if she did or she didn't. It is known now, however (ever since 1945), that the much-maligned duchess was not poisoned. To clarify that matter at last, her descendants had her bones exhumed and examined and it was once and for all determined that the cause of her death was meningioencephalitis.

MAJORCA

Valldemosa: CARTHUSIAN MONASTERY

Two of this island's most famous tourists were the composer Frédéric Chopin and his mistress, the novelist George Sand. Slightly older than Chopin, Sand had a liaison with him that lasted ten years, and she nursed him faithfully as the tuberculosis from which he suffered grew worse. To improve his health, she suggested coming here to this Carthusian monastery, where they spent the winter of 1838. But it was not a happy time. The weather was dreadful and the local inhabitants frowned on the unmarried couple's unorthodox relationship, and especially on George Sand's habits of wearing trousers in public and rolling and smoking her own cigarettes. There were even occasions when she was stoned in public.

MÉRIDA

Originally named Augusta Emerita, this city was founded by the Romans in 25 B.C. as a place for soldiers who had served out their time in the legions —*emeriti.* During Mérida's Roman heyday, its dancing girls were much admired, and many of them were exported to Rome.

MONTSERRAT

The Monastery

Saint Peter himself, it is said, carved the Black Virgin here and brought it from the Holy Land to Barcelona in A.D. 50. When the Moors invaded in 717, it was hidden in a cave in this mountain and not rediscovered until a century had passed. Then shepherds were attracted to the cave by an other-earthly light above it in the sky. They informed the bishop. The bishop came and carried the little figure away. The procession bearing it stopped at this spot mysteriously and would not move on. The Madonna has had hard times since, for the original monastery was largely destroyed by the French in 1811. Through it all, the figure has survived.

NUMANCIA

Although today nothing remains here but the outlines of a few walls on a windswept hill, the name of Numancia has been famous in Spanish history since 134 B.C. The Romans had been attempting to subdue the Iberian Peninsula since 218 B.C., but the guerrilla tactics of the native population had proved too much for the trained legions of Rome. Then Scipio the Younger took over. A crack commander, the man who was to burn Carthage to the ground eight years later, Scipio decided to toughen up his troops for the siege of the city. He confiscated such luxuries as the depilatory tweezers then in fashion, banned all hot baths, and made the soldiers breakfast standing up—not to mention imposing forced marches and constant drills.

The Romans besieged Numancia for eight months, during which most of the population of 10,000 perished. Legend has it that all the people committed suicide before the Romans took the city—except for one small boy, trapped in a high tower. Scipio pleaded with him to come down, for he wanted a captive to display for his triumph in Rome. But the last of the Numancinos refused and leaped to his death.

OVIEDO

The Cathedral

After surviving for six centuries, this fourteenth-century flamboyant Gothic cathedral almost met with destruction on the eve of the Civil War. Striking miners from the surrounding coalfields took over Oveido in 1934, set fire to the university, bombed banks and museums, and fiercely attacked this cathedral, knocking down its tower, blowing up the *Camara Santa*—the coffer that contained, it is said, thorns from the Crown of Thorns. But the government troops held out against the insurgents, refusing to be dislodged, and thereby preserved this ancient edifice.

PALOS DE LA FRONTERA

On August 3, 1492, Christopher Columbus, newly created admiral of the ocean by Queen Isabella, set sail from this little town—then a port—with the *Niña*, the *Pinta* and the *Santa María.* It was a fearsome voyage in prospect—finding a new, quicker route to India based on his assumption that the world was round—and the night before, to assure that all 120 crewmen would be aboard in the morning, Columbus insisted that all men sleep on their ships. Then, at dawn they filed into mass at the Iglesia de San Jorge and immediately afterward were en route to the discovery of the New World.

Also departing from and returning to this little port then on the river Odiel was Hernando Cortés, conqueror of Mexico, who in May 1528 unloaded a magnificent train of Indian princes he had captured, strange birds and animals that Europe had never before seen, chests of gold and jewels, cloaks of brilliant feathers. How they whetted the appetite of Francisco Pizarro, who was here at the time, beginning himself to think of his life of exploration that would end with the brutal conquest of Peru.

Convent of Santa María la Rábida

One day in 1484, a tall, handsome man with hair that was prematurely white knocked at the door of this convent, in ruins today. A widower, he held by his hand his five-year-old son Diego. The man, Christopher Columbus, introduced himself and asked the prior, Juan Perez de Marchena, if he would keep his son for him while he traveled. It was one of the most serendipitous meetings in history. Perez was fascinated as the tall foreigner told him of his wish to find a short route across the Atlantic to India rather than following the traditional route around the Cape of Good Hope. For hours and days and weeks, it is said, the two men talked in the prior's cell and studied maps and charts. Then, encouraged by the prior's enthusiasm, and with a letter from him to Queen Isabella's confessor in hand praising the project, Columbus set off for the court at Seville.

But the time of his arrival was less opportune. Ferdinand and Isabella were readying for the conquest of Granada and they had no time to consider farfetched plans for shorter routes to India. So, for the next six years Columbus waited to put his proposal before the royal pair. Waiting, he eked out a living making maps, and fell in love with a woman of good family named Beatriz Enríquez who bore him a second son. Finally he got consideration of his project, and waited longer as a royal commission weighed his request for monies. Then the commission rejected it. It was a despondent Christopher Columbus, indeed, who returned here after his son. He would go on to France to see if he could talk the French court into being his sponsor.

But Prior Juan Perez would not hear of such a scheme. Down he sat and this time wrote a letter directly to the king and queen. No one knows what that letter said, but it resulted in the prior's being ordered, himself, to visit Isabella.

Somehow, some way, his magical pen and tongue convinced Isabella of the merits of Columbus's dream, and when the prior returned here it was

with the welcome news that the queen herself would see Columbus. Seven
months later, the discoverer of America was on his way. (*See* Palos de la
Frontera.)

PAMPLONA

Warfare has made this city notable in history and it was, indeed, a general
—the Roman Pompey—for whom it is named.

But it was in the days of the emperor Charlemagne that it achieved its
greatest fame. In 778, an angry Charlemagne, called here because of conflict between those citizens who favored union with Castile and those who
favored union with the French House of Navarre, assailed this city, causing
much destruction. In retaliation, as Charlemagne's army headed back toward France through the nearby Pass of Roncesvalles, a complement of
Pamplona Basques fell upon the emperor's rear guard. Its valiant commander was the emperor's nephew, Roland—too proud to blow his horn and
summon aid. Only when clearly there was no hope, did he, with his last
breath, blow his horn. The heroic battle is the theme of the French epic,
the *Chanson de Roland.* In the poem, however, the Basques become Sarac-
ens.

❧

Ernest Hemingway made friends, caroused and wrote *The Sun Also Rises*
in this city that is especially famous for its gaiety each July during the
Festival of Saint Ferminius, when bullfights are a nightly occurrence.

Basílica of San Ignacio (Avenida de San Ignacio)

In 1521, when the French were attempting to seize this city, a young Basque
captain, Íñigo Lopez de Recalde, was wounded in the knee in the street
opposite this church. His recovery was long, for a stone splinter had
crushed one leg. While convalescing he read the Bible indefatigably and
studied the lives of the saints. Determining to devote his life to God, the
young captain became a priest and a missionary and, ultimately, a saint—
Saint Ignatius of Loyola, founder of the Society of Jesus, the Jesuit Order.

PASTRANA

Palacio de Pastrana

This castle will always be linked with the memory of the one-eyed princess of Eboli, the aristocratic Doña Ana de Mendoza. She and her husband were among the favorites at the court of Philip II in the sixteenth century and wielded considerable political power in their heyday. Small, dark, and intriguing—especially with the dark patch she habitually wore over one eye —Doña Ana was ambitious, strong-willed and unscrupulous in her drive for personal power. Although the historical rumor mills link her name romantically with that of her sovereign, the scheming princess of Eboli fell resoundingly from royal favor. She was banished from the court and locked up here. Confined to one room, which she was never permitted to leave, she lived in this state for thirteen years until her death. There are a variety of explanations for her famous black patch: a hunting accident, an injury sustained by fencing—or merely an unbecoming squint.

SALAMANCA

When Hannibal finally put an end to a long siege here, he gave his troops leave to pillage this city. He first ordered its inhabitants to leave—the men without their jackets or cloaks or, of course, their swords. But the wily women of Salamanca hid their husbands' swords under their own clothes and took them outside the city to arm their men.

SANTIAGO DE COMPOSTELA

With sandals on their feet, gourds around their waists, and scallop shells attached to their hats, thousands of pilgrims of the Middle Ages trekked across Europe to visit the burial place of Saint James, a missionary to Spain who was beheaded by the order of Herod when he made a return trip to Judea in A.D. 44.

Although his disciples fled back here with his body and buried it, their influence was not great enough to keep this province of Galicia Christian and, as pagan year followed pagan year, the missionary's burial place was forgotten—until one starry night in the ninth century.

Then shepherds followed a bright gleam in the heavens and found his grave in this spot. Some years later, when the Spaniards were engaged in a fearsome battle with the Moors and their cause seemed to be failing, a knight with a white standard emblazoned with a red cross appeared in their midst and spurred them on to victory. When he was identified as Saint James, Saint James became the patron saint of Spain. And soon he was urging on the soldiers not only in campaigns against the Moors, but against the Indians in the Americas as well. Whenever he was seen on his white charger in the clouds, victory seemed to follow.

So it is no wonder that soon the trains of pilgrims were coming here to pray to him for their own private victories. Indeed, so many came that a French priest wrote one of the world's first travel guides in 1130 describing the routes that could be followed to reach Saint James's burial place, and where the travelers could find good drinking water and friendly people en route.

As for those scallop shells the pilgrims wore, they gave their name to the famous dish of scallops served in a scallop shell—*Coquilles St. Jacques* (scallops à la St. James).

SARAGOSSA

Some 50,000 residents of Saragossa—more than half—died of plague, wounds, or starvation in 1808 and 1809 when Napoleon's troops twice besieged this city. But few episodes in Spanish history have been so valorous.

Their patriotism fired by Jorge Ibort, a peasant leader affectionately known as *Tío Jorge*—"Uncle George"—by a priest who invoked the aid of the Virgin of Pilar; and by a handsome general, José de Palafox y Melzi, the people refused to surrender. Indeed, when the surrender request was made, the general is said to have replied, "When you have killed me, then we will talk." As he was a hero, so Byron's Maid of Saragossa in *Childe Harold's Pilgrimage* was a heroine, taking her lover's place at his gun when he was shot. And in that first siege in the summer of 1808 the stalwart citizens of Saragossa were successful, and the French went away.

But the respite was only temporary. Six months later, the French were back, and for the next two months, they never gave up their attack. Even so, it was only when, house by house, they mined this city, that they forced it to give in. The Spanish defense elicited the grudging remark from the French general that "the brutes certainly know how to fight."

SEVILLE

Hospital de la Caridad (Hospital of Charity) (Callo Temprano)

For years, it was only wine, women, and song that interested the seventeenth-century Seville nobleman, Miguel de Manara—the prototype for the Don Juan of music and story. But then, one day, staggering home from a drinking party, he met a funeral procession—and his life changed, for the body he saw being carried was his own.

Gasping with horror, Miguel, then and there, decided to change his ways. He gave his wealth for the founding of this Hospital of Charity and joined the Caridad, a brotherhood dedicated to burying the bodies of executed criminals. And here he died, a saintly and pious man.

But that was not the end of Miguel de Manara; it was barely the beginning. An imaginative friar named Gabriel Téllez, who was a contemporary, wrote in play form the first version of the legend of the great seducer under the pen name Tirso de Molina. As in the later versions, the reprobate Don Juan has done so much damage that a brotherhood of Franciscan monks invite him to their monastery and murder him. When people ask where he is, they sadly say that he was carried off to hell by a statue on the monastery grounds. The Tirso play was produced, but was received without particular acclaim. Then José Zorrilla y Moral, a popular nineteenth-century playwright, turned the story into the romantic drama *Don Juan Tenorio*. It was an overwhelming success. The French playwrights Corneille and Molière next wrote about him. Mozart made him his hero in the opera *Don Giovanni*. He inspired Byron's sixteen-canto poem *Don Juan*. More recently, George Bernard Shaw used the Don Juan story in *Man and Superman*.

Far from being a forgotten corpse buried before his time, Miguel de Manera inspired some of the world's finest creative works.

Isabel II Bridge

Near here is the site of the Carcel Real (Royal Prison) in which Miguel de Cervantes Saavedra was imprisoned around 1597 to 1602. It is probable that he began to write the first part of *Don Quixote* while in this jail. Several years before, there had been arrears when Cervantes was a minor bureaucrat in charge of collecting taxes. According to the practices of the time, any bureaucrat in arrears with his financial accounts was jailed. No particular stigma went along with this type of confinement. A bank now stands on the site, with a plaque identifying it as the site of the jail.

Old Tobacco Factory

In this eighteenth-century tobacco factory made famous by Bizet's opera *Carmen,* courses in the humanities of the University of Seville are now given.

SIGÜENZA

The Cathedral

Don Martin Vasquez de Arce was a page to Queen Isabella of Castile; he was only twenty-five when he died at the gates of Granada in the last campaign to defeat the Moslems. The queen commissioned a funerary statue of the young knight to be placed over his tomb here. Don Martin's effigy (1495) is one of the finest in the history of Spanish sculpture. He is dressed in chain mail, but his attitude is peaceful, as he is absorbed in the pages of a book. The statue shows to perfection how the medieval knight was about to change into the Renaissance courtier.

TARIFA

Castillo de Guzmán el Bueno (Castle of Gusman the Good)

On behalf of the king of Castile, Alonso Pérez de Guzmán was valiantly defending from the Moors this fortress that is now a barracks. Under no circumstances did he intend to give in. But the enemy had his nine-year-old son. That, the Moors were sure, would put a different complexion on the matter.

They dragged the child to the foot of the battlements where his father stood. Unless Alonso surrendered the fortress, they said, they would cut the boy's throat. The father blanched, but stood firm. Throwing his own dagger to the enemy he cried out, "If you have no weapon to commit such an iniquity, here is mine!" The son was executed in full view of the father, but Alonso did not surrender. The king, likening Alonso to Abraham who was willing to sacrifice his son Isaac to God, therefore dubbed him Guzmán el Bueno, and that is the way all Spanish history remembers him.

TOLEDO

The Alcázar

In the summer of 1936, Loyalist Republican troops laid siege to this massive fortress for more than ten weeks, attempting to force the surrender of the Fascist commander, José Moscardo e Iriarte. Not only Moscardo's troops, but 600 civilians found themselves besieged here. One afternoon the phone rang in Moscardo's office. It was the Loyalist commander. Luis Moscardo, the sixteen-year-old son of the commander, was his hostage, he announced, and he threatened to shoot him unless the Alcazar surrendered. Luis was then given an opportunity to talk to his father. "They will shoot me unless you surrender," the son said. The father's reply: "Then commend your soul to God and die like a hero!"

The boy was executed, and the Alcazar never surrendered. It is possible that Moscardo, in making his decision, remembered the similar plight of the medieval soldier Guzmán el Bueno. (*See* Tarifa.)

Santo Tomé

The count of Orgaz, who died in 1323, was always most generous to the church, especially to the Augustinian monks. He also gave money for a convent named in honor of Saint Stephen. So it was only fitting that when the count was to be buried, the saints to whom he had been generous—Augustine and Stephen—appeared and laid his body to rest. El Greco painted the miracle in 1586 for this little church, where it remains to this day. The painting is said to contain the self-portrait of the artist and the likeness of his young son, Jorge Manuel, both as bystanders.

TORDESILLAS

In 1494 the Spanish Borgia pope, Alexander VI, divided the New World that was being discovered in those days into two parts by means of a treaty here between Spain and Portugal. But his Spanishness showed. By the treaty's terms, Spain acquired everything in Latin America except Brazil.

Santa Clara Convent

The exhausted, nearly hopeless twenty-eight-year-old Juana the Mad (*see* Burgos, La Caruajas) finally stopped her journey in search of a place where her dead husband, Philip the Handsome (Philip I), might choose to come to life, at this convent. She, at last, agreed to let his body be buried here in Tordesillas, and then she locked herself away in this convent where she remained until her death forty-four years later. Once, after her son Charles V had attained the throne, he paid her a visit to judge her sanity. He quickly (but undoubtedly opportunely, too) pronounced her quite mad, for were she sane, she would have been the queen. There are those who have always insisted that she regained her sanity, but nevertheless she was kept imprisoned.

As for Philip, in time she seemed to have quite forgotten him, and his body was taken away and reburied in the royal pantheon in Granada.

VALENCIA

The Cathedral: CHAPEL OF THE HOLY GRAIL

Joseph of Arimathea, it is said, saved the Holy Grail—the agate chalice from which Christ drank at the Last Supper—after that final feast, and after many adventures it reached Spain in the fourth century, this cathedral in the fifteenth. Among those in story and song who have searched for it have been Lancelot, Galahad, Parsifal, and Lohengrin.

Plaza Mayor

One of the less honorable acts performed by the epic hero, the Cid, following his siege of this city in 1094, was the tossing of the defeated Moorish leader into a fiery pit because the Moor courageously refused to reveal where the royal treasury was.

Once in control of the city, the Cid, who had been exiled from Burgos (*see* Burgos, Santa Agueda) without his wife and family, begged the king of Castile to let them join him here, and when they did, he proudly took them to the highest hill to show spread out below the great city he had captured.

VALLADOLID

House of Cervantes (Calle de Miguel Iscar)

Under abysmal conditions in an apartment here, Miguel de Cervantes Saavedra is believed to have written a good part of *Don Quixote*—and to have received the news that the book was to be published.

VALLE DE LOS CAÍDOS (Valley of the Fallen)

To honor the 80,000 dead of both sides in the Spanish Civil War that left this country devastated in 1939, Generalissimo Francisco Franco commissioned this 138-foot-high monument that is built into the hills. And he himself, as the leader of the rebel Nationalist army in that conflict, is buried here.

YUSTE

Monastery of Yuste

Within the peaceful walls of this monastery, Europe's mightiest ruler of his day retired in 1555. Charles V, Holy Roman Emperor, king of Spain and sovereign of the Americas, was racked by gout and disillusioned with the world when he voluntarily abdicated to his son, Philip II. In this modest series of rooms where the emperor spent his last days is the wooden litter in which he made the painful journey from the northern coast here to Yuste. He who had fought on so many major battlefields of Europe could only sit then on a small balcony and fish for trout in a pool especially constructed for this purpose. Bedridden in the last months, he had a window installed in his bedroom wall, which gave onto the altar of the monastery church, so that he could follow the mass.

When he died he was buried in a simple wooden coffin. But he had asked his son to build him a worthy tomb. Philip complied, ordering the construction of the great Pantheon of the Kings in the Escorial (*see* El Escorial), with huge sarcophagi of dark marble. The outspoken Spanish writer Unamuno, however, thought it a sacrilege to transfer the emperor's remains to what he termed "those great soup tureens" of the Escorial.

Sweden

FALUN ❧ ────────

Falu Grava

One Midsummer Day in 1687, holidaymakers danced and sang at this annual June event, when suddenly the hill on which they danced gave way, and into this copper mine they fell—happily, with no injuries. It was surprising that it had taken the hill that long to collapse, for it had been riddled with mines for more than four centuries. In the 1200s a goatherd had noticed odd red lines on the skin of his goats; he had talked to his neighbors about this, and as a result the copper deposits here—once the richest in the world—were discovered. (Some say this copper was found so long ago, indeed, that King Solomon ordered Falun copper to decorate the temple at Jerusalem.)

Whatever the date that the mining began, in one of those earlier centuries, one man who fell into the pit was not so fortunate as the Midsummer Day merrymakers. Mats, the miner, simply disappeared from sight. Then, fifty years later, miners unearthed a body that was perfectly preserved—petrified, apparently, by the copper in the mine water. The workmen hurried back to the village to report their find. There, some remembered Mats who had never come home. At the time of his disappearance, Mats had been betrothed. In the interests of science, the latter-day miners carried his body to the eighty-year-old crone who had been his fiancée. White-haired and wrinkled, the old woman bent over the rosy-cheeked, blond young man and slowly nodded her recognition of him.

KALMAR

Kalmar Castle

Some attribute Eric XIV's insanity in his later years to a party here when, as he was being tossed in a blanket, he hit his head on a ceiling boss.

MARIEFRED

Gripsholm Castle

For six years, Mad King Eric—Eric XIV—paced a tower room here, imprisoned by his brother, John III. Then he was moved to Örbyhus Castle in 1574 and poisoned with pea soup.

Eric had inherited the throne from his father, Gustavus Vasa. He was handsome, intelligent, musical, artistic, and a good sportsman. He should have been a perfect king, but his attributes were marred by a volatile temper and a suspicious nature. For a time, his shortcomings notwithstanding, he ruled reasonably. He was a romantic, and proposed marriage twice to Queen Elizabeth of England, sending her a portrait he had had painted of himself in his grandest attire. When she rejected him, he asked Mary Queen of Scots for her hand. When he did not win her either, he approached—and was turned down by—two ladies of the German nobility. Some say it was these disappointments that destroyed his equanimity.

In fits of rage, Eric began having nobles of whom he was suspicious murdered, and he is said to have put one noble to the sword himself. Scarcely had he pulled his sword from the body when he regretted his impetuous act. Taking Eric's unbalance as an excuse, his younger brother John seized the throne, sending Eric and his nut-seller mistress-made-queen, Karin Mansdotter (wooed and won when the grander ladies had refused him), off to confinement in this castle. (*See* Finland, Turku, The Castle.)

Eric might simply have stayed in prison here with the blond Karin for life, but his mental state showed signs of improving, so John arranged for his brother's murder. As for Karin, she stayed in Finland, where she became renowned for her good works. August Strindberg wrote a play about Eric.

MORA

Statue of Gustavus Vasa

This hillside statue of Gustavus Vasa marks the spot where in 1521 the man later known as "the father of the Swedish nation" begged the people of this town to unite their neighbors in the province of Dalecarlia against the oppressive Christian II, king of Denmark and Norway, who had recently proclaimed himself king of Sweden as well. At Christian's coronation in Stockholm, he had ordered the massacre of many anti-Denmark Swedish nobles, including Vasa's father and brother-in-law. (*See* Stockholm, Stortorget.)

But the people of Mora were not certain they wanted to fight against the Danes then overseeing their lives. Although the Danes were growing more oppressive, and the murder that Gustavus described of eighty-two of Sweden's noblemen in Stockholm was surely appalling, how many of their own sons and husbands would die in full-scale combat? So, they listened on that snowy Christmas morning here and sighed at Gustavus Vasa's fatigue—he had just escaped from imprisonment in Denmark himself—but turned down his suggestion that they talk their fellow Dalecarlians into war.

Furious and disappointed, Gustavus put on his skis and started toward the Norwegian border fifty-three miles away. From there, the chances were good of his escaping to a Hanseatic League city, where he could make further plans for a rebellion. And it was important that he not dally. The Danes had a price on his head, pursuers on his trail. He hurried, limiting the stops he made for food and rest. But as he neared the border town of Salen, he saw skiers in the distance behind him. He sped toward the woods, trying to lose them. Then he heard his name called—in Dalecarlian, not Danish accents.

After Gustavus had quit this little town in disgust, people had remained in the churchyard discussing his warning. When they went home, they had continued discussing. All the rest of the day the town fathers had deliberated, periodically interrupted by messengers from Stockholm bearing further details of the Stockholm bloodbath. No one was safe from Christian, the messengers said. He had given orders that all peasants must surrender their arms.

Clearly, townspeople decided, they must heed Gustavus's warning and prepare for revolt. So they had sent their two fastest skiers after him. Back to Mora Gustavus skiied with them, and was acclaimed their chieftain. Two years later, after successfully ousting the Danes, Gustavus Vasa, at twenty-seven, was declared the first king of Sweden. To commemorate his flight toward Norway, an annual international ski race follows his route from Salen and ends here.

ÖVERGRAN

Skokloster Castle

Although, for reasons of state, he never married her, there was only one true love in the life of the seventeenth-century king Gustavus Adolphus, it is said. She was Ebba Brahe, a childhood friend. They did, indeed, become betrothed, and Gustavus Adolphus gave his fiancée the ruby set with diamonds that is displayed here in the Brahe family castle. But his mother insisted that the engagement be broken, deeming it unwise for a prince to marry one of his subjects. Instead, Gustavus Adolphus was forced into a singularly unhappy marriage with a German princess; its sole joy was the birth of his daughter Christina. Then he went off to the Thirty Years' War to fight the Hapsburgs. The nearsighted Gustavus Adolphus was killed at Lützen in Germany when, in a fog, he galloped head-on into the enemy cavalry.

STOCKHOLM

The Blue Tower

When he was sixty, the playwright August Strindberg had his last love affair here—with Fanny Falkner, his landlord's daughter, who was twenty years old. Three times married and divorced, Strindberg occupied the top floor of this house alone and was served his meals by pretty Fanny. Never able to withstand the attraction of a pretty face and figure, the elderly playwright soon was wooing the young woman. Totally bedazzled, he proposed, quite forgetting the difference in their years, and bought Fanny a fur coat, hoping to cement the bargain. That was the end of the romance. Her straitlaced, God-fearing parents would not have their daughter treated as a kept woman, even if a marriage *was* in prospect. The engagement was broken, and Strindberg died a few years later, in 1912.

Drottningholm Court Theatre

This theater on the grounds of the royal summer palace lay idle for more than one hundred years. On the night of March 16, 1792, King Gustavus III, himself a playwright and an actor and a great patron of the arts, was killed by an assassin's bullet at a masquerade ball at the Royal Opera House here in Stockholm. (Verdi based his opera *A Masked Ball* on the assassination.) With the king's death, the curtain was virtually rung down on this court theater. There were occasional attempts over the next few years to give performances here, but this pretty little theater had meant so much to Gustavus that entertainments in it without him had lost their sauce, and by 1800 there were no more presentations here at all.

The intricately designed stage machinery from Italy soon was covered with cobwebs. The cut-glass chandeliers grew dusty. Court servants made the theater their sleeping quarters. Captains of the guard used one room as their mess. Horses were stabled here. The entrance hall became a granary, and vegetables, potatoes, and fruits for the court were stored backstage. Flagpoles and bric-a-brac from the palace filled up the auditorium where Gustavus had so happily watched the best performers of his time.

Then one day in 1921, Agne Beijer, an official of the Royal Library, needed a particular painting to illustrate a book he was writing. He remembered the "storehouse" in the court theater and thought he might find there what he was after. He went backstage. What he found as he rummaged was mind-boggling. There were thunder machines and surf machines, as well as thirty stage sets from Gustavus's day, exactly as they had been left 129 years earlier. Here were sets for Racine and Voltaire, perfect in every respect but for the dust.

Beijer quickly had them dusted off. He told the court and the city of his discovery and within a year had raised enough money to have the curtain rise again. It has risen every summer since.

Lake Mälaren

On an arklike boat on this extensive lake, the young inventor Alfred Nobel was "exiled" in 1864 after an experiment on land in which his youngest brother and four associates were killed. It was such experiments, and his eventual development of dynamite, that led him to establish the international peace prize to end all wars. He had vividly seen what destruction explosives could do.

Alfred Nobel, his father Immanuel, also an inventor, and his brother Emil, home from college on a holiday, were working with nitroglycerin in the laboratory wing of the Nobel house here, when suddenly the house and the neighborhood were rocked by an explosion, and Emil was dead. Although it was said that the accident probably occurred because Emil was not well acquainted with the properties of nitroglycerin (though Alfred and his father were), the police took no chances. Any further experimentation, they said, would have to be out of town. So Alfred constructed a laboratory boat, which he anchored just beyond the city limits on this lake.

Riddarhustorget

On June 10, 1810, Count Hans Axel von Fersen, who had fought with Lafayette in the American Revolution and risked his life for France's Marie Antoinette, was dragged from his carriage here and stoned to death by an angry Stockholm mob.

When the count and the future queen were both young, they had met in Paris, and he had fallen in love with her. The attachment was strong enough that when the American Revolution broke out, Fersen quickly sought a place in Lafayette's army, because, he said, too many people were noticing the way he looked at the queen and she at him.

The American Revolution over, Fersen returned to France, presumably enough cured of his love to accept a command post in the French army. But in that post, he continued to see both the queen and the king. He was with them at Versailles in 1789 when a mob angered by the bread shortage in Paris marched on the royal palace. Though the marchers retreated, Fersen was sure that was not the end of the matter. In ensuing weeks, as the revolution did, indeed, progress, he devoted himself entirely to trying to save the queen. Disguised as a taxi driver, he helped her escape from the Tuileries Palace when it was under attack. It was he who was the engineer of a plan to get her to America. But all his efforts failed and when, in 1791, she and Louis were beheaded (*see* France, Paris, Place de la Concorde), brokenheartedly, Fersen came home to Sweden. Sad and weary, but angry, too, he determined to avenge the royal couple's deaths.

Though he had not determined on a way and was involved in no plotting, the Swedish people feared that he would go to any lengths to wreak vengeance. So when the prince who was to succeed to the Swedish throne dropped dead unexpectedly, the mob was sure there had been foul play and Fersen's hand was in it. And that was why, on that June afternoon, they hauled Count Fersen into the street and pummeled and stoned him to death as he went to meet the prince's funeral procession.

Stockholm Castle

The winter of 1650 was a particularly cold one here in Stockholm. Icy winds swept in from the Baltic Sea and across Lake Mälaren. Despite them, the French philosopher-mathematician René Descartes, invited to the Swedish court by the newly crowned queen Christina, dutifully crossed the wind-swept bridge that led from the French embassy, where he was staying, to the castle early each morning. Christina had asked him to Sweden to instruct her in philosophy and, being an energetic young woman, had set the lesson hour at five. Descartes, not accustomed to either northern cold nor draughty castles, caught pneumonia and, at fifty-five, was dead. The castle where he died burned down in 1697, and construction was immediately begun on the present one.

Royal Flagship Wasa

The Royal Flagship *Wasa,* sails full, cannon ports open for a farewell salute, set off from here on her maiden voyage on August 10, 1628. Armed with sixty-four bronze cannons, built to carry 133 sailors and 300 soldiers, she was the showpiece of King Gustavus II's navy. Her destination for that day was the naval base across the harbor, where she was to take on ballast and join the squadron waiting there.

But suddenly the wind came up. Sweeping off the cliffs here, it filled the sails of the *Wasa*. With no ballast aboard, she heeled, and with her cannonports open for the farewell salute, the water poured in. Here, in one hundred feet of water, before a thunderstruck crowd of wellwishers, the *Wasa* foundered. To the bottom she went, with all sails set and all flags flying, and some thirty seamen, their wives and children aboard.

Immediately, there were efforts at salvaging her, but they, like the *Wasa*, foundered. In the next half century, with the aid of a diving bell, fifty-four of the sixty-four cannon were recovered. But for the next 273 years further salvaging attempts were abandoned. The *Wasa* lay largely forgotten—except by an amateur treasure hunter of this century, Anders Franzen, who read old stories of her. Feeling after a time that he knew where she lay, he went diving himself for her. His efforts were rewarded when one day he returned to the surface with an old oak plank. Delighted, he notified authorities of his find.

For the next five years, the Royal Navy and the Neptune Salvage Company worked on raising the ancient vessel. To do it without damaging the *Wasa*, five salvage ships had to be used at once. In 1959, the ship was stirred from her centuries-old berth for the first time. In seventeen more moves, she was painstakingly lifted from one hundred feet below the surface to fifty-five feet below, and in April 1961, 333 years after her maiden voyage to the harbor bottom, the Royal Flagship *Wasa* surfaced again. Because, for those three centuries, she had been encased in mud, and because the waters of the harbor here are brackish and distasteful to sea worms, she was almost totally intact. Only her forged iron parts had rusted away. Indeed, butter, of sorts, still remained in containers in her hold. The *Wasa* is now kept in a humidified pontoon building that is open to the public.

Stortorget

Neither Swedes nor Danes have ever forgotten the infamous day in 1520 when King Christian II of Denmark celebrated his coronation as king of Sweden by having eighty-two Swedish noblemen and clergy beheaded (*see* Mora).

Following the coronation, which was in the days when Denmark, Norway, and Sweden were united under a single ruler, Christian invited the notables of the capital to a banquet at the castle. At it, he danced gracefully with the Swedish ladies and chatted amiably with the Swedish gentlemen. The following day, he invited the nobles back.

But this time the door was locked behind them, and the archbishop of Sweden charged them with heresy. Three years earlier, parliament had ousted him from office for malfeasance, and his castle had been taken and destroyed. The angry ex-archbishop, warning the new king that the same nobles who had turned him out might turn against the king, had demanded retribution. Christian had acquiesced.

Down to the dungeon, up to the tower, into the chapel—wherever there was room for them to be held—the accused nobles and town officials and ecclesiastics went. The next day, the executioner arrived; the troupe was led to this market place, and one after the other, for three hours, the men who had dined and danced so merrily two days before to honor their new liege lost their heads in the Stockholm bloodbath. And the heads were piled in a pyramid here.

Town Hall

When the First World War ended, Ragnar Östberg, the architect for this building that has been called the most exciting architectural accomplishment of its kind in Europe since the Renaissance, was just completing work on it. The prewar plan was that it would have a gleaming copper roof. But the war had made the price of copper prohibitive, and, sadly, Östberg informed the public he would have to substitute a lesser metal. Stockholmers were aghast. They had been promised copper. They would have copper. A collection was taken up. Anyone who bought a copper plate for the roof could have his name engraved on it, so future generations would remember him. It took a while, but Stockholmers got the roof they wanted. And on its pinnacle are the three crowns that are the symbol of the realm. Stockholmers are wont to pun that these are three crowns (coins) left over from their collection.

UPPSALA

Linneanum

One sunny afternoon in 1729, a professor of theology from the university here, strolling in these gardens, noticed an earnest young man kneeling in a flower patch studying the blossoms. The theologian, also an admirer of flowers, struck up a conversation. The two talked botany for a while, and the theologian noticed that the youth was thin, his clothing poor. He invited him home for dinner and more conversation and a look at his library. The youth, twenty-one-year-old Carolus Linneaus, responded to the hospitality of his new friend by giving him a study that he had written on the sexual nature of plants.

The impressed theologian promptly spoke to the university's chief scientist about the youth, and soon Linneaus and Olof Rudbeck, the scientist, were fast friends, planning a field trip to Lapland for Linnaeus so he could study flowers in the northern wilderness.

Linnaeus went on to study medicine in Holland and to establish a practice there. Then in 1739, he was invited back here to Uppsala to a professorship in botany and medicine. His classes were soon among the most popular in the university. His field trips, it is said, were heralded with the playing of French horns and kettledrums. To this garden, the royalty of Europe sent their favorite seeds to this great botanist, who is responsible for today's classification of plants.

The Slott

In 1654, the whole nation wept, it is said, when their young queen, twenty-eight-year-old Christina, renounced the throne in the Rikssal here. When she was only four years old, her father Gustavus Adolphus had held her in his arms and asked his parliament to look after her as he went off to the Thirty Years' War, from which he never returned.

Extremely intelligent, intensely curious, at odds in her teens with her regent, she declined to marry the man he wished her to. She fell in love with her cousin, Charles Gustavus, instead but decided against marriage altogether as, discoursing with foreign emissaries at the court, she became secretly interested in Catholicism. Secrecy was essential, for it was a criminal offense to convert in Sweden at that time.

Once, Christina was talked out of abdicating. The second time, she could not be. She demanded assurances before she quit the throne, however, that her successor would be the cousin she had loved. Then she quit Sweden altogether, heading for Rome so she could be close to the center of the Catholic faith she had embraced. Never shy or retiring, schooled, after all, to be a queen, she somewhat startled church authorities there with her imperious manners and her dabbling in affairs of both church and state.

VADSTENA

Abbey Church

God Himself, it is said, was the architect for this fifteenth-century convent founded by Scandinavia's only woman saint, Saint Bridget. In her busy lifetime, first as wife and mother, next as mistress of the king's household, then as a nun here at Vadstena, and finally as a nun in Rome, Bridget received and had written down more than 700 revelations from God, among them the design—down to its smallest detail—for this convent. In its reliquary, both she and one of her daughters, Catherine, lie buried.

They tell proudly here of Saint Bridget's forceful personality and fearlessness, even in the face of the devil. He and the saint met, so the story goes, when both were visiting a Stockholm brothel, he to steal a soul, she to save one. The devil had a young woman pinned to the floor, his claws in her shoulder, when Bridget arrived and tore him off his prey. Unaccustomed to having souls pulled—literally—out from under him, the astounded devil jumped out the brothel window, either in terror or in rage.

Palace of Gustavus Vasa

From the ramparts of this sixteenth-century Swedish Renaissance castle, Gustavus Vasa's oldest son, Magnus, is said to have thrown himself into the lake when he thought he saw a mermaid lure him.

VISBY

Town Walls

In the Maiden Tower in the northwest corner of this 10,000-foot-long wall, a pretty maiden was immured in the fourteenth century, after she had opened the city gates to the king of Denmark.

In those days, this city was the richest member of the Hanseatic League, and these high walls, topped with 50- to 65-foot-high turrets, were built to ward off looters. But Waldemar IV Atterdag, king of Denmark, was not stopped by high walls. Disguised as a commoner, he visited this city in 1360, met and wooed the goldsmith's daughter, and learned from her the whereabouts and the quantity of treasure here. Then he left, promising to return.

A year later, he was back, this time with ships and warriors. His love of the year before let him and his men inside the walls. The invaders demanded three giant beer kegs and ordered that they be filled with silver and gold or the city would be burned to the ground. Townspeople, having no choice in the matter, complied. And, simultaneously, the looters went looking for other valuables. From the rose window of the Church of St. Nicholas two giant garnets had always gleamed. Lighted by candles at night, they served as a beacon for ships. These were pried from their window and carried down to the Danish ships along with the kegs of silver and gold.

But Waldemar's ship filled with riches fared little better than the goldsmith's daugher he had left behind. A storm blew up, and the vessel foundered. The king himself barely escaped. The two stolen garnets, seamen swear, still bear witness to that fourteenth-century invasion, for when the sun goes down in a certain way, they can be seen to this day shimmering red in the sea.

Switzerland

ALTDORF ✦────────

The William Tell Monument

In the fifteenth century, the counts of Hapsburg cast covetous eyes on their neighbors—today the Swiss forest cantons of Schwyz, Uri, and Unterwalden. Indeed, since the Hapsburg strength was considerably greater than that of the Swiss mountain men, they sent bailiffs to carry out their orders in the Swiss villages. The bailiff of this village on the shores of the Lake of Uri was a man named Gessler, legend has it. (History, too, has him existing, but gives his name as Conrad von Tillenburg.) More despotic than most, Gessler hung not the Hapsburg flag but his own hat on a stick above the main street here and ordered all who passed by to salute it. The chamois hunter William Tell, one of Altdorf's eminent citizens, refused. The bailiff was furious.

Noticing that Tell had his young son by his side, Gessler ordered the boy to stand by the marketplace tower and had an apple balanced on his head. Then Gessler ordered the father to split the apple in two with one of his arrows.

Carefully, Tell reached into his quiver and pulled out two arrows. Carefully, he put one in his belt, the other to his bow, and pulled. The apple fell in two halves. Even Gessler offered his congratulations. But his eye lit on the second arrow, and he asked what it was for. "Had I struck my son instead of the apple," the story has Tell replying, "that arrow was for you."

The angry bailiff ordered Tell bound and announced he was personally taking him to the prison at Küssnacht across the lake. Captors and prisoner boarded the boat for Küssnacht. But halfway across, a storm blew up, and Tell, the only native of the region, was freed from his bonds to steer the boat away from the rocks and shoals. He avoided most of them but headed directly toward one from which he knew he could leap to shore.

As the boat neared the rock, Tell leaped off and shoved the boatful of captors away with all his strength. Then, his second arrow ready, he clambered across the rock to the shore and took a shortcut to Kussnacht to ambush Gessler. When his captors' boat reached its destination, Tell's arrow found its destination, too—in Gessler's heart. The German romantic poet Schiller turned this story of love of country into the drama *Wilhelm Tell*, and the composer Rossini transformed it into the opera of the same name.

BASEL

Town Hall

This cheerful red sandstone town hall, gaily decorated with the coat of arms of this city, had been standing not even a quarter of a century when it was threatened with destruction by rioting Protestants in 1529. Basel was a hotbed of Reformation activity. The town councilors were gently urging tolerance, proposing that both Catholics and Lutherans should be free to worship as they chose. But the fervent new adherents of Protestantism would not listen. A crowd of 1,000 hauled cannon to the front of the Rathaus and warned the council to heed them and dismiss the twelve councilors who were Catholics—or else. That done, the Protestants spent the next week raiding churches and destroying images.

On and off for many years until then, the Dutch humanist Desiderius Erasmus, the author of *Praise of Folly,* had happily called Basel his home. He had taught at the university, written tracts and treatises, and had his portrait painted by Hans Holbein the Younger, who, though German-born, had also come to live in Basel. But Erasmus was a Catholic. He was eager for reform within the church but not for a complete break with it. As a result, he had both Catholic and Protestant enemies. It seemed wise to quit the city before more turmoil erupted. Word got out that he was planning to leave. He was called before the magistrates who wanted to know why, on a certain occasion, when meeting with Basel's leading reformer of the day, Erasmus had insultingly covered his face with his cloak. Erasmus explained that he had had a toothache. The interrogation further convinced him it was time to move elsewhere. Again, he planned a secret flight. But he thought better of it and openly quit the city, seen off, without incident, by a coterie of devoted friends. Touched by his send-off, as the boat was about to depart, Erasmus recited a poem of thanks to this city for its hospitality and generosity.

Later, when the tumult had died down, Erasmus returned. He is buried in the cathedral.

BERN

The Bear Pit

For more than 500 years, there has been a tradition of keeping live bears here in Bern.

It is said that the bear became the symbol of this city when its founder, Duke Berchtold V of Zähringen, was hunting with his men in the neighboring forest back in the twelfth century. He announced in a peremptory, ducal way that he would name the city he was planning to found after whatever animal was killed first in the hunt. The first animal was a bear *(Bar)*, and although the keeping of bears did not begin immediately, by 1441 town monies were being appropriated for the catching and feeding of bears.

When the French under Napoleon invaded in 1798 and stole the Bernese bears, it was a sad day indeed. The bears were not all that Napoleon's forces stole, and his memory is hardly honored here today. Along with the animals, the troops took millions of dollars worth of gold, which Napoleon wanted in order to finance his invasion of Egypt. But the boat—and all its Bernese wealth—sank off the Egyptian coast.

COLOGNY

The summer of 1816 was cold and rainy here. It was weather conducive to sitting around a blazing fire. That was exactly what the poet Percy Bysshe Shelley, his wife Mary, and their neighbors, the poet Lord Byron, and his doctor companion Polidori, chose to do.

The Shelleys had rented the Villa Montalegre here, and in the evenings they read ghost stories around the fire. One evening, Byron proposed that they all write ghost stories of their own. Shelley, Byron, and Polidori began writing, but Mary had no success. Then one night the men talked of Darwin and experiments he had reputedly done, bringing *vermicello* (little worms) to life. When Mary went to bed, she could not sleep. She was haunted by a vision of a pale student kneeling beside a hideous creature he had made, and into which he had breathed the spark of life.

Mary shuddered and got out of bed, seeking reality, she later wrote, in the cold parquet floor and the moonlight struggling through the openings in the shutters. But her vision would not leave her. Indeed, it was intensified, as she imagined the black lake outside her window and the white Alps looming beyond. When the sun came up, she sat down to write. And her ghost story was *Frankenstein,* the tale of the monster made from corpses dug up from graveyards and collected in dissection rooms, the archtypical science-fiction story.

EINSIEDELN

The Monastery

To this wooded place, now a major pilgrimage destination, the hermit Meinrad came in the ninth century seeking a quiet place to worship God in peace. With him he brought a black Madonna that was a gift from the abbess of neighboring Zurich. Meinrad was not to have peace, however. It soon was rumored that he had many riches in his forest hideaway, and robbers from Zurich murdered him for his supposed wealth.

In his happy, brief time communing with God and nature far from the conflicts of man, Meinrad had tamed two ravens to forage for him. They had witnessed their master's murder and they followed his killers back to Zurich. There, their croaking over the men's heads led to the murderers' apprehension, an investigation, and ultimately, their execution. The story of the murdered hermit and his ravens attracted attention, and before long, a Benedictine abbey was built here where Meinrad's cell had been. But this story of miracles does not end there.

Soon it came time to consecrate the abbey church, and the bishop of Constance was called on. As he readied himself on the night preceding the ceremony, a voice told him there would be no need for a consecration, for Christ himself had consecrated the church. Pope Leo XIII, notified of the strange event, declared it a miracle and offered indulgences to any who came here on pilgrimage. They came in droves, the rich and the poor—and enough of the rich to make this, next to the abbey in St. Gallen, the wealthiest monastery in this country.

GENEVA

Brunswick Monument

Duke Charles II of Brunswick lived a pitiful life. English-born, he was called away from his native land when he was twenty to rule the German duchy of Brunswick, which was his inheritance. He was neither a skillful nor likable ruler, and it was not long before his people sent him packing back to London. There, he was so often involved in scandals and lawsuits and was so in fear for his life that he slept in an iron cage. Finally he was involved in a perjury suit and became something of an international figure when he escaped from England to France in 1861 in a hot-air balloon.

For the next twenty years, Paris was his home, and he cut a swashbuckling figure, dashing about in a sunny yellow coach. But when the Franco-Prussian War loomed on the horizon, he quit Paris for Geneva, where he apparently lived the happiest years of his life. At least, in his will he left this city $5,000,000, on condition that it would erect a monument to him, designed after a tomb he admired in Verona. Further, he wished his head so set that it would lie in the direction of Lake Leman and the mountains.

Grateful for the gift, the town fathers commissioned the work this duke had requested. But by mistake, it is his feet, not his head, that point to the mountains and the lake.

Café Landolt

Lenin and Trotsky plotted the Russian Revolution here over cups of coffee and tea, and glasses of wine, legend has it. Historians tend to question whether Trotsky participated in the discussions, but Lenin did indeed frequent the Landolt, when he was a refugee here in the early years of the First World War. (*See* Zurich, Hauptbahnhof.)

Corraterie

Back in 1602, a kettle of vegetable soup hurled from a window here is said to have helped save Geneva from invaders.

In those days, the neighboring duke of Savoy sought to take over Geneva. He sent soldiers to scale the city walls one night when the city slept.

Stealthily, the Savoyards put up their ladders, and stealthily, the first of them climbed over the wall. Only then did the Swiss guards detect them. A skirmish ensued. A drummer escaped to sound the alarm. But already, old Mere Royaume, an engraver's wife, was awake and at her windows. Below, she saw the heads of the soldiers. On the fire, a cauldron of vegetable soup was simmering. Quickly, she hauled it to the window and threw it out onto the invaders' heads.

By then, the drummer had awakened the city, and more citizens poured from their houses to knock down the ladders. But it is always Mere Royaume who is cited as the heroine that night, and on December 11 each year, the anniversary of the Escalade, every confectioner's shop in Geneva sells miniature cauldrons made of chocolate and overflowing with marzipan vegetables.

Statue of Jean Jacques Rousseau

It took a lot of doing to get this statue erected, even in the 1850s, more than half a century after the death of this Geneva-born philosopher. He had been an embarrassing figure in this strict Calvinist community, writing as he had about man's being innately good when churchmen were preaching of original sin. Indeed, the city government had Rousseau's *Émile* and the *Social Contract* burned by the public executioner in 1762.

Fifty years later, the world recognized the contributions of Rousseau to philosophy, but Geneva still had a hard time accepting him. A group of progressive citizens, however, urged the town fathers to erect a statue to his memory. Grudgingly, they agreed. But what would be the site? One of them came up with a perfect one—the far end of this little Ile des Bergues facing the empty lake—a place where no one ever came.

As it turned out, however, Rousseau had the last laugh. By 1862, Geneva was such a bustling, traveled city that a new bridge—the Pont du Mont Blanc—had to be built. Passersby on it today could not ask for a better view of the statue of this controversial native son.

Town Hall

Had it not been for a Swiss investment banker seeking permission from Napoleon III to invest money in Algeria, there might be no International Red Cross. But, thanks to his journey in search of the French emperor, an agreement establishing that humanitarian body was signed here in 1864.

Jean Henri Dunant was the son of a prosperous Geneva family. He early had humanitarian and theological instincts but was advised by his relations that business was a much more profitable way of life. Finally agreeing with his elders, he set off for Algeria, a territory newly acquired by France, to investigate making money in grain mills there.

He bought land and erected several mills, only to realize he then needed more land to grow more grain to feed the mills. He returned to Switzerland and was successful in finding shareholders for his project, including his family, who invested much of their money in it.

With funding obtained, he approached the French government for permission to buy additional land. The government stalled interminably, and Dunant decided to go to the top—to Napoleon III himself. But gaining access to him, Dunant reasoned, was likely to be a problem, so, to catch his attention, he wrote a little laudatory book about the emperor and had it handsomely printed. With the book in hand, he set off to find Napoleon III, who was at war with the Austrians in Italy.

Dunant arrived a day late at Solferino, where the emperor had been fighting. The battle was over, and Napoleon was gone. The bodies of 40,000 dead and wounded littered the fields, however. Dunant could hardly believe the bloodiness of the scene. Napoleon III and Algeria were forgotten. His energies went instead into corraling the local women and getting them to tend the wounded.

Dunant returned to Geneva a different man. Thenceforth *all* of his interests were humanitarian. He suspended all his business projects to write a book about the horrors of Solferino and set out across Europe to enlist the interest of all the governments he could in establishing a neutral body to care for the injured in war. And his efforts were crowned with success when the First Geneva Convention was signed here in the Hôtel de Ville. At last Dunant could get back to business again.

But that was not to be. Napoleon turned down his request for Algerian land, and Dunant went bankrupt, his creditors hounding him. Leaving Switzerland, he lived for a while in London, then Paris, then Germany. He was so poor that his family had to provide for him. Mournful and disgraced, he returned to his homeland and settled in the village of Heiden in Appenzell. There he remained, forgotten, till a Swiss newspaperman happened upon him and wrote a story about his great achievement and his subsequent sorrows. His deeds were then so warmly remembered that he was chosen in 1901 to share the first Nobel prize for Peace.

Voltaire Institute

Geneva has always prided itself on the way it has welcomed foreigners, but one foreigner it drove out was the French philosopher-dramatist Voltaire, who lived here on the Rue des Delices for eight years.

Being a playwright, it stood to reason that he would want to see the plays he wrote on the stage. Geneva's strict Calvinist laws forbade such entertainments. That being the case, Voltaire moved four-and-a-half miles across the border to France, where he built a château and a church, and virtually constructed his own town, Ferney, inviting watchmakers to set up shop to annoy the watchmakers of Geneva. And there he happily put on his own plays on his own estate and sometimes acted in them. His audience? The pious people of Geneva, of course, who came in large numbers.

Voltaire's enthusiasm for Geneva was hardly warm. He once said disdainfully of this then city-state, "When I powder my wig, I powder the whole republic."

His house still stands and can be visited at Ferney-Voltaire.

LAUSANNE-OUCHY

Hôtel d'Angleterre

It was here in June 1816, when it was called the Anchor Inn, that the poet Lord Byron wrote the *Prisoner of Chillon* after a storm-tossed day of sailing on Lake Leman. Some stories have it that Percy Bysshe Shelley, whom he introduced to sailing, was his boating companion that day. Six years later Shelley was drowned in Italy sailing on another stormy day. (*See* Italy, Lerici.)

LUCERNE

The Lion Monument

At the height of the French Revolution, bloodthirsty republicans stormed the Palace of the Tuileries in Paris, where Louis XVI and his family were sequestered. The royal family's red-coated Swiss Guard valiantly defended them. But when it looked to the king as if there were no escaping, he ordered the guard to lay down their arms. Dutifully, the Swiss obeyed the royal order, and all 786 of them were murdered at their posts by the crazed throng. To commemorate their loyalty and heroism, this statue of the courageous lion was erected here early in the nineteenth century.

Mount Pilatus

The spirit of Pontius Pilate, it is said, haunts this 7,000-foot peak that looms, often shrouded in mists, to the south of this city.

Recalled to Rome after his condemnation of Christ, Pilate committed suicide. His body was thrown into the Tiber. The waters tossed and churned, and Pilate was blamed. So, the body was removed and carried to the Danube. Similarly, the Danube was beset by storms. Next, Pilate was deposited in the Rhône. The Rhône's waters grew roiled. Finally, the body was brought to the Alpnacher See that in those days was here at this mountain top. But Pilate's spirit rested no better here.

An exorcist was called, and he and the unquiet spirit finally arrived at an agreement: except on Good Friday, or if stones were thrown at him in the water, Pilate promised not to trouble the waters. But on Good Friday, his tortured soul could not be kept from rising, he said, and on that day, he would sit in his scarlet robes on his judge's seat above the lake, and woe betide those who saw him then, for they would die within a year.

The agreement, surely, was better than the turbulent waters in all seasons, but Lucerne town fathers were still so concerned for the welfare of their citizens that they forbade climbing to the top of the mountain and punished those who tried. Not till the end of the sixteenth century did they alter the law, allowing travelers to ascend to this spectacular peak.

Schweizerhof Hotel

At this handsome and fashionable hotel overlooking the lake, charitable Leo Tolstoy made a spectacle of himself by inviting a begging street singer to join him for a drink—to the great dismay of the other guests and the help who soundly took him to task for his action. Tolstoy responded in kind.

Tribschen (Richard Wagner Museum)

In this lovely villa above Lake Lucerne, Richard Wagner wrote *Die Meistersinger von Nürnberg, Siegfried,* and *Götterdämmerung,* and soothed King Louis II of Bavaria, his patron, in times of trouble. Louis appeared here frantically one midnight threatening to abdicate over an impending war with Prussia. Wagner, who hardly wanted to lose his patron, talked him out of it.

And it was here that Cosima von Bülow, the daughter of Liszt and wife of one of Wagner's closest friends, the conductor Hans von Bülow, set up housekeeping with Wagner when her husband was away conducting in Basel. Eventually divorced by von Bülow, Cosima married Wagner after his first wife, Minna, died. It was here at Tribschen, to celebrate Cosima's birthday—Christmas Day—that the *Siegfried Idyll* was first played in 1870.

MEIRINGEN

Reichenbach Falls

Here, Arthur Conan Doyle, wearying of his great detective creation Sherlock Holmes, tried, unsuccessfully, to lay him to rest. On the edge of this 2,780-foot-high waterfall, Conan Doyle had Holmes grapple for his life with his archenemy, Professor Moriarty. Moriarty hurtled to his doom, and the author hoped Holmes's fans would assume that their hero had too. But they didn't. They clamored for more of the pipe-smoking detective's adventures. So Sherlock Holmes came back.

His "disappearance," he told his friend Dr. Watson in "The Return of Sherlock Holmes," was designed to convince Moriarty's accomplices (as Conan Doyle had wanted to convince his readers) that Holmes, too, was on the rocks at the foot of these spectacular falls.

MONTREUX

The Château of Chillon

In one of the darkest subterranean dungeons here, François de Bonivard, Lord Byron's *Prisoner of Chillon,* spent six years in the sixteenth century and wore a path in the cold stone floor. The true story of Bonivard's imprisonment had a somewhat happier ending than Byron's tale, which told of three brothers languishing in the dungeon, one dying, a second about to die, and the third managing to break his fetters to aid his moaning brother, only to find he had reached him too late.

The real François de Bonivard was born to a well-to-do family in the duchy of Savoy near Geneva in 1493. Among his family's properties was a Benedictine abbey not far from Geneva, and young Bonivard, though a layman, became its prior, a job primarily concerned with the abbey's finances.

These were the days when the Savoyards were attempting to take control of the independent city-state of Geneva, and tensions were always high. Although he was a Savoyard, Bonivard was an independent-spirited young man and sided with the independent-spirited Genevans. This infuriated the duke of Savoy, who had him captured and imprisoned for two years. At the end of that time, the duke thought he had been sufficiently subdued and restored him to his abbey post.

But the duke was mistaken. Bonivard continued to speak his mind when he chose. Once again, he was waylaid by the duke's men and this time imprisoned here at Chillon. At first, his quarters were pleasant enough. Then the duke's treatment grew harsh, and Bonivard was thrown into the dungeon here where the lake water laps incessantly at the walls. He could only tell if it was morning if the water outside the wall slits was blue. Afternoons, the lapping waves took on a gray-green hue.

For six years Bonivard walked and walked, wearing a groove into the dungeon floor. Finally, in 1536, the army of the city-state of Bern came to the aid of beleaguered Geneva, and while there, they rescued Bonivard.

Life outside had changed considerably during his imprisonment. The reformer, Jean Calvin, had taken over Geneva. Bonivard's abbey had been secularized. Because of his patriotism and his suffering, he was recompensed for its loss, however, and other quarters were found for him. He was commissioned to write a history of the Reformation in Geneva and was given a living stipend as well. Apparently, it was a reasonably good one, for he proceeded to marry three times and to cut a rather dashing figure in the somber Calvinist city to which he had returned. There was considerable clicking of tongues over his behavior.

After his third wife's death, when he was quite elderly, he took in a young nun who had quit her convent, and for whom he felt sorry. The authorities frowned on his kindliness and said he must marry the young woman. Bonivard pleaded that he was too old. The church authorities insisted, and the two were wed. But the union was even more ill-fated than Bonivard had imagined it would be. His wife was accused by neighbors of adulterous acts with an ex-priest. Although Bonivard testified eloquently in her behalf, apparently all patina of the imprisoned hero had worn off. The authorities scoffed at him, beheaded his wife's presumed lover, and drowned her in a sack.

STEIN-AM-RHEIN

Monastery of St. George

It was a sixteenth-century thief, found out by an abbot, who was responsible for some of the handsomest frescoes that adorn these walls.

David von Winkelsheim was one of the first, and most revered, of the abbots of this Benedictine monastery. As such, he was frequently called on to preach in neighboring communities.

Nearby Zurzach was the site each year of Europe's largest linen and leather fair, and when it occurred, the abbot invariably went there to say mass. On one such occasion, he was exploring the fairgrounds after mass when he heard a minstrel singing of the theft of 100 gulden from St. George's church. He stopped to listen. Suddenly, the song was interrupted by a gaunt, angry young man shouting that the minstrel was wrong, that there had been only 1 gulden and 13 smaller coins in the pilfered offering box. The abbot listened with interest. Then he approached the outraged youth and inquired how he knew the sum so precisely. Face to face with the abbot, the thief admitted his guilt. He tearfully explained that he was a penniless painter and had stolen the money for brushes and paints. But then, he said, he was so hungry he had spent it on food instead.

Rather than turning him over to the authorities (such action, in those times, might even have led to his execution), the abbot asked the thief if he would like to make amends by doing 1 gulden 13 batzens' worth of painting at the monastery. To this day his frescoes of Zurzach, Hannibal, and Scipio, the conqueror of Hannibal, are among those decorating these walls.

ZERMATT

The Matterhorn

It was hardly a happy victory, the 1865 conquest of this 14,780-foot-high peak, for it sent four plunging to their deaths. Until 1857, no mountain climber, no matter how intrepid, had dared approach the awesome four-sided pyramid. Geologists came here to look at it. Botanists, including Louis Agassiz, visited this little village of Zermatt to study the Alpine flora. The grandeur of the Matterhorn evoked wonder, but no climber dared to scale any of its faces—so smooth and precipitous that even the snow does not cling to them.

But in 1860, Edward Whymper, a twenty-year-old English artist, was sent here to illustrate a book, *Peaks, Passes and Glaciers*. Whymper was dazzled by the majesty of the mountains. Drawing them was nowhere near enough. They had to be climbed.

In 1861, he made his first attempt to scale the Matterhorn but did not get far. For the next four years he kept trying, each time getting a little higher, but never high enough. Then, in 1865, a complement of people appeared on the scene unexpectedly who made his successful climb possible. There was Lord Francis Douglas; an eighteen-year-old enthusiast for mountain climbing, Michel Croz; a guide, who had accompanied Whymper on earlier climbs; the Reverend Charles Hudson, a twenty-seven-year-old clergyman, generally considered the finest mountain climber of his day; his nineteen-year-old companion, Douglas Hadow; Old and Young Peter Taugwalder and Joseph Taugwalder, Zermatt guides. Every one of these men longed to conquer the mountain. Together, they were sure they could. They would try the northeast approach, they decided, for it was less precipitous than it looked. And so at dawn on July 13, they set out. At 1:40 on July 14 they reached the summit no man had ever reached before. They had no flag with which to claim their victory, but Croz took off his blue Savoyard smock and tied it to a tent pole that he thrust into the snow.

The climbers stayed several hours at the scene of their conquest. Then they began their descent.

First in line for the journey down was Croz. Next was Hadow, and behind him came Hudson, so he could assist the younger, less experienced Hadow if an emergency arose. Then came Lord Douglas and Old Peter, Whymper, and Young Peter. Joseph Taugwalder had returned earlier, before the climb to the top began.

They moved slowly, silently, carefully, with Croz occasionally stopping to help Hadow fit his feet into foot holes. Suddenly, Croz and Hadow lost their footing, hauling Hudson and Lord Douglas after them. The rest would have followed, the weight of the first two pulling all, had the rope not broken between Douglas and Old Peter. Whymper never forgot its resounding snap in the still mountain air. Below him, he saw his companions sliding, their arms outstretched, their hands opening and closing, desperately trying to grab at the rock as they fell. But there was no hope for them. "They passed from our sight uninjured, disappeared, one by one." Whymper later wrote.

It took a while before the three remaining had the courage to continue the descent. While they waited, Whymper examined the broken end of the rope and found to his horror that it was the oldest, weakest rope they had carried that had mistakenly been used to tie them all together.

The remainder of the descent went without incident. The trio reached the base the following day, and a search party went to look for the fallen. All bodies but Lord Douglas's were recovered. The Mattherhorn had been conquered. "None will ever know the feelings of those who first gazed upon its marvellous panorama," Whymper wrote. "It was defeated at last with an ease that none could have anticipated, but like a relentless enemy—conquered but not crushed—it took terrible vengeance."

ZURICH

Casa-Bar

They had some rollicking good times here in 1916–17 when this was the Café Voltaire and the Rumanian poet with the monocle, Tristan Tzara, started the art movement known as "dadaism." Founded to protest against the destruction of life and reason that seemed to be taking place during the First World War, dadaism mocked the established rules of writing and music, painting and philosophy, and substituted a calculated madness. The new mad movement needed a name, so one afternoon a group of its proponents opened a French dictionary here, slipped a knife into it and, eyes closed, pointed to a word on the page. The word was *dada*. Its definition? "Hobbyhorse."

The Cathedral

More than 200 miles away the emperor Charlemagne was stag hunting one day in the eighth century, when the stag he was chasing bolted away, and the emperor's horse, with Charlemagne astride him, bolted too. Neither stag nor horse stopped, so the story goes, till they got here to the river Limmat, when the stag fell to its knees, and so did the horse.

Charlemagne learned that three martyrs were buried at this place, a Roman legionnaire named Felix, his sister Regula, and their servant Exuperantius. In the days when Zurich was a pagan city, these three had preached the gospel and been summarily beheaded. But they miraculously picked up their heads, put them under their arms, and carried them to the spot where fellow converts buried them. Charlemagne decided they should be honored with a church at their burial site. That church burned to the ground in the eleventh century, and was replaced by this Romanesque structure. The two Gothic towers were added later and a statue of Charlemagne the Founder was set in one. It is said that this city and church always remained especially dear to him, and he visited frequently.

In the sixteenth century, however, this city's churches and convents suffered gross indignity when the fiery Protestant reformer Ulrich Zwingli was appointed to the cathedral's pulpit. He ushered the Reformation into Zurich by tossing many of the cathedral statues into the river. In true Swiss banker fashion, though, he first had them stripped of all their gold and precious gems so these valuables could go into the city coffers.

Hauptbahnhof

In March 1917, with crowds shouting "Death to Lenin" and "Long Live Lenin," Nikolai Lenin left for Petrograd (now Leningrad) with thirty fellow Bolsheviks on the famous "sealed train" that did not let passengers on or off until it reached its destination. He had spent three years in Switzerland (*see* Geneva, Café Landolt), the last of them here in Zurich.

The departure of Lenin and his comrades had been arranged by the Germans—to get them abroad to their fellow Bolsheviks in Russia so they would take over the government and pull Russia out of World War I.

Among those with Lenin on that fateful day, when he set off in his derby hat and winter coat and thick-soled hobnailed boots, was his wife Nadezhda Krupskaya, who had shared the crowded room here with him at 14 Spiegelgasse. They remembered it, above all else, for the vile smell from a nearby sausage factory that filtered in whenever a window was opened. Lenin spent as little time there as he could, preferring to study and write in the library. Or on Thursdays, when the library was closed, he would eat chocolate bars and read on the green grass of the Zurichberg overlooking the Lake of Zurich.

Villa Wesendonck

Enraptured with the city of Zurich and this spot above the lake, Otto Wesendonck, a German silk merchant, built this villa in the 1850s and frequently invited his great friend, the composer Richard Wagner, to come to visit. Wagner and his wife Minna were equally taken with the location, and when land beside the Wesendonck Villa became available, Wesendonck bought it and built a little house for the Wagners. It was a generous act but not exactly repaid with generosity, for Wagner and Mathilde Wesendonck soon found they had much in common—she wrote poetry, and he set it to music—and they fell in love. Historians remain uncertain as to whether theirs was a genuine love affair or a deep platonic relationship, but Minna Wagner was certain it was the former. When she intercepted a letter from Wagner to their neighbor, she was furious about it, and this marked the end of her marriage to Wagner.

But in the Mathilde Wesendonck period of his life here, Wagner wrote *Tristan and Isolde,* and there is no question but that Mathilde was its inspiration.

Index of Names and Places